"LET'S SEE

Alison deposited the balls inside the rack. Brandon leaned over. Broke. In fewer than five minutes, he'd run the table.

"Wow," Alison said. "You really are good."

"And a dollar richer."

"Too bad we weren't betting when you let me win."

"If we'd been betting, I wouldn't have let you win."

"If we're going to play again, you need some kind of handicap that'll give me a chance."

"Sweetheart, I could tie one hand behind my back and I'd still beat you."

"Well, then," she said, taking a step closer to him, "maybe you should teach me how to play better."

He smiled. "Maybe I should."

They looked at each other a long time. Gradually the moment shifted, and Brandon's vision grew a little blurry around the edges until the only thing in sharp focus was Alison's face. She blinked, and it seemed as if those golden lashes stroked her cheeks in slow motion before rising again to reveal those beautiful brown eyes. A strand of hair fell along her cheek, then curved beneath the junction of her jaw and throat. Then his thoughts went completely off the rails. He started to imagine pushing that strand of hair aside and touching his lips to the place it had been...

BUCKLE UP FOR SEXY FUN WITH

HOT WHEELS AND HIGH HEELS

Heartstrings
and
Diamond Rings

JANE GRAVES

FOREVER

NEW YORK BOSTON

Copyright © 2011 Jane Graves
Excerpt from *Black Ties and Lullabies* copyright © 2011 by Jane Graves
All rights reserved. Except as permitted under the U.S. Copyright Act of 1976, no part of this publication may be reproduced, distributed, or transmitted in any form or by any means, or stored in a database or retrieval system, without the prior written permission of the publisher.

Forever
Hachette Book Group
237 Park Avenue
New York, NY 10017

www.HachetteBookGroup.com

Printed in the United States of America

First Edition: October 2011
10 9 8 7 6 5 4 3 2 1

Forever is an imprint of Grand Central Publishing.
The Forever name and logo are trademarks of Hachette Book Group, Inc.

The publisher is not responsible for websites (or their content) that are not owned by the publisher.

For Charlotte and Ryan,
the best daughter and son-in-law
I could ever have hoped for.
Thanks for all the wonderful holidays,
Saturday night dinners,
and family celebrations.
The fun is just beginning!

Heartstrings
and
Diamond Rings

Chapter 1

Relationships, Alison Carter thought, *are all about modest expectations*. As she watched Randy inhale the last of his honey-glazed pork chops and drain his wineglass, then swivel his head to watch their waitress's ass as she passed by, Alison added, *And that soul mate thing is a crock*.

The more she repeated those mantras to herself, the better she felt. After all, there was nothing really wrong with Randy. They'd met at a party where he'd gotten too drunk to drive and she'd taken him home, and then they'd started to date. A sales rep with a big paper company, he had a townhome in Plano, not large, but bordering a somewhat prestigious area only a block from a golf course. He wore suits you couldn't tell from designer originals, and shoes that looked like real leather. He did drive an actual Mercedes, a few years old with a great big payment, but a Mercedes nonetheless.

"You look great tonight," Randy said, now that the waitress with the perfect ass had disappeared into the kitchen.

"Thank you," Alison said. "So do you."

She wasn't lying. He wore a pair of slacks, a sharply

starched dress shirt, and a sports coat, looking as nice as she'd ever seen him, which really wasn't bad at all. In the candlelit ambience of the restaurant, he actually looked handsome.

As for her looking great, she wasn't so sure. Yesterday she'd spent ten minutes in front of an evil three-way mirror at Saks as Heather convinced her that the dress she wore really didn't make her butt look big. Since junior high, Heather had always been one of those rare friends who never told her she looked good in something when she really didn't. Sometimes the truth was hard to swallow, but in the end it meant there was at least one person on earth she could trust. And if Randy truly loved her for her, did the size of her butt really matter, anyway?

They'd been seeing each other for nearly eight months now, and it had been a decent eight months. No, she didn't have hot flashes of pure sexual hunger whenever he kissed her. She didn't sit around at work all day doodling his name on a sticky note pad. She didn't always leap up to answer the phone when she knew it was probably him. But after she turned thirty, she decided there were trade-offs she was willing to accept. She could wait for burning sexual attraction to strike her out of nowhere, or she could knock off the lottery mentality and go for the sure thing if it meant she might actually get to have the home, husband, and family she'd always wanted. It might not be great, but if they worked at it, it could certainly be good.

Modest expectations.

One day last week on her lunch hour, she'd seen Randy in a jewelry store at the mall. Then there was the phone conversation she'd overheard him having with somebody named Reverend McCormick. And then she'd spotted a

Hawaii travel brochure on his desk at home. She brushed all those things aside, telling herself they didn't mean ring-wedding-honeymoon, only to have Randy tell her he had something very important to talk to her about and make dinner reservations at Five Sixty, the hottest new restaurant in the Dallas metroplex. Oddly, the only emotion she seemed to be able to summon was relief. But that was okay. Relief beat the hell out of desperation.

The waiter poured them more wine, then took their plates. Alison cuddled up next to Randy and stared out the window. Five Sixty sat at the top of Reunion Tower, fifty stories in the sky, offering sweeping views of the Dallas metroplex. Dusk was becoming night, and with every second that passed, the city lights grew brighter and more mesmerizing. In that moment, Alison truly believed there wasn't a more romantic place on earth. When Randy turned and kissed her, she was surprised to feel a little of that first-date flutter she thought was long gone.

"Alison," he said finally, fixing his gaze on hers, "I think we've grown very close over the past few months."

Her heart bumped against her chest. This was it. After all these years, after all the wrong men, after all the blind dates, after all her waiting and wishing and hoping, she was finally making the leap toward matrimony.

Thank God.

"Yes," she said. "We have."

He brushed a strand of hair away from her cheek and stared soulfully into her eyes. "And I wouldn't even be asking you this if I didn't think our relationship was very, very strong."

Alison nodded. "Of course."

"Like a rock."

"Yes," she agreed.

"You're so beautiful. Have I told you that lately?"

She gave him a smile that said, *Yes, but don't hesitate to tell me again.*

"And you're open-minded." He pondered that a moment. "Very open-minded, I'd say."

Actually, she'd never thought of herself as particularly open-minded. But it was okay if he thought so, because that was a good thing...right?

He shifted a little, suddenly looking uncomfortable, and Alison smiled to herself. It was so cutely traditional for him to have a hard time with this. In fact, she was sure she saw him blush.

"I think Bonnie is open-minded, too," Randy said.

Alison blinked. "Bonnie?"

"Yeah. And you seem to get along well with her."

Bonnie was a friend of Alison's, but Randy didn't really know her all that well. Like all men, he was far more acquainted with Bonnie's breasts than her face. God bless Bonnie—she could sprout two heads and the men of the world would never know it. But why was Randy bringing her up now?

"Uh...yeah," Alison said. "I guess we get along okay."

"I assume you think she's, you know...attractive."

Yes. Bonnie was attractive. In a wide-eyed, short-skirted, body-flaunting way. "I...suppose so." *What is he talking about?*

"Anyway, I was wondering..." He inched closer and stared directly into her eyes, and her heart practically stopped. She stared up at him adoringly.

"Yes?"

"You. Me. Bonnie. What do you think?"

Alison just stared at him. "What do I think about what?"

He laughed a little. "You know. The three of us. Together." He leaned in and kissed along her neck. "Seeing you with another woman would be such a turn-on."

For the next several seconds, it was as if Alison's entire circulatory system contracted, stopping the blood flow to her brain. Surely he must have said, *Will you marry me?* but somehow it had come out sounding like *Wanna have perverted sex?*

"What did you say?"

"A threesome. You, me, and Bonnie.

Don't just repeat it, damn it! Change it!

"When we were at that party at John's house last month," Randy said, "Bonnie seemed to be as open-minded as you are." Then his voice slipped from soothingly sexual to blatantly carnal. "I think she'd go for it, don't you?"

Alison yanked herself away from him. "Are you completely out of your mind?"

He stared at her dumbly. "What's the matter?"

"What's the matter? *What's the matter?*" Alison sputtered aimlessly for a moment, words escaping her. Then she leaned in and spoke in an angry whisper. "That's what you wanted to talk to me about?"

He shrugged. "Well... yeah."

"You brought me here to ask me that?"

He looked befuddled. "Well, it is kind of a big step, so I—"

"What were you doing in that jewelry store three days ago at lunch?"

"Jewelry store? How'd you know I was at a jewelry store?"

"Just answer me. What were you doing?"

"Getting a battery for my watch. Why?"

Alison felt a wave of nausea. "You had a Hawaii vacation brochure on your desk at home."

"I did?"

"Yes. You did. Where did it come from?"

He shrugged. "I don't know. It was probably junk mail."

The nausea continued to roll in, like surf crashing over a rocky beach. "Okay, then. You haven't been to church since you were twelve. So who the hell is Reverend McCormick?"

"Who?"

"Randy," she snapped, "I overheard you talking to somebody named Reverend McCormick last week."

Randy blinked. "Oh. I donated some of my old clothes to a church charity. Tax deduction. How did you—"

"Never mind."

Alison dropped her head to her hands, feeling dumber and more deluded than she ever had in her life. How had this happened? What could she have seen in those bland brown eyes of Randy's that made the concept of together forever seem like an actual possibility, particularly since he was still staring at her with a look that said, *Now don't be too hasty—have you ever actually considered the advantages of lesbian sex?*

"Randy, listen to me carefully. Are you listening?"

He nodded, a hopeful look on his face. Hopeful. What did he think she was going to do? Suggest a plan to catch Bonnie off guard in the shower?

"My answer is no," she told him, her voice quivering with anger. "Now, that's not just any old no. It's no, not in a million years, not if we're the only three people left on earth and I'm the odd woman out and it's the only chance I have to participate in sex again for the rest of eternity. It's that kind of no. Are you getting my drift?"

His face fell into a disappointed frown, as if he were a spoiled six-year-old who couldn't understand why a spotted pony with a silver-trimmed saddle or a month-long tour of Disney World was out of the question.

"Maybe you just need a chance to think about it," he said.

"Randy," she said with a growl in her voice, "you're going to get up from this table right now. You're going to leave. And if you so much as glance back over your shoulder, I'm shoving you through the window. It's fifty stories to the ground, and I don't give a damn. Do you hear me?"

Randy drew back with a startled expression. "But why? Just because I had one little idea to spice up our sex life you didn't like?"

Alison's mouth dropped open. "One little idea? *One little—*"

"So forget I mentioned it," he said with an offhand shrug. "No big deal. We can still have regular sex. Just you and me—"

She grabbed him by his lapels and dragged him forward. "Get. The hell. *Out.*"

"Come on, Alison," he said, a nervous laugh in his voice. "You really don't want me to—"

She leaned away and whacked him on the arm with her doubled-up fist. "I said *out!*"

When she reared back to smack him again, he threw up his arms to ward off the blow. He scooted out of the booth so quickly he banged the edge of the table with his hip, knocking over his glass of pinot noir. The wine spread like a gigantic Rorschach blob on the white linen table-cloth. He stared down at it dumbly.

"Out!" Alison shouted.

He took two shaky steps backward, his shocked expression shifting to a vindictive glare. "Yeah, well, you know what?"

"What?"

"That dress makes your butt look *huge*!"

A pure, unadulterated, I-hate-you kind of anger welled up inside Alison that she'd never felt before. As he spun around and stalked off, she closed her hands into fists and banged them on the table. The last wineglass standing shimmied a little, but she managed to grab it before it fell over. In three seconds she'd drained its contents and smacked the glass back down on the table, feeling the wine burn all the way down her throat. It hit her nauseated stomach like cold rainwater on hot lava, and she swore she could actually feel the sizzle.

She closed her eyes to try to gain back a modicum of control, and when she opened them again, she realized the restaurant had fallen silent, the waiters had frozen in place, and everybody was looking at her as if she were a rabid dog foaming at the mouth. She sat up straight and put her hands in her lap, trying to look calm, sane, and sensible. Judging from the fact that everyone was still staring, she wasn't succeeding.

The waiter walked tentatively back to the table, staying slightly more than arm's length away. "Uh…Madam? Will there be anything else?"

Yes. A gun so she could chase Randy down and blow him away. A big, fat box of Kleenex so she could cry her eyes out. A trench coat so everybody in this restaurant wouldn't be looking at her ass as she walked out the door, wondering if Randy had been right.

"No. Nothing."

In the time it took for her to decide that the wine-red Rorschach blob on the tablecloth looked like a pissed-off woman castrating a depraved man, the waiter returned with the check.

The check. Well, crap. Not only had this been one of the worst nights of her life, now she had to pay through the nose for the privilege of participating in it.

She winced, paid the check, and left the restaurant. And sure enough, she felt the collective gazes of every patron in the place focused squarely on her backside. The moment she got home, she was burning this dress.

She went into the elevator and leaned against the wall, feeling a little woozy as she shot down fifty stories. But it wasn't until she stepped into the hotel lobby that it dawned on her that Randy had driven her there, and she had no way home.

No car, no fiancé, no hope, no nothing.

Alison trudged through the underground passage to Union Station, where she went to the surface again and sat down on a bench to wait for the northbound train. Anger had carried her this far, but now, in the silence of the aftermath of her future going right down the tubes, she couldn't stop the tears from coming. God, she hated this. Sitting alone at a train station by an overflowing trash can beneath garish lights wearing a dress she now despised, crying her eyes out. Could it get any worse than that?

Then she felt something that made her realize that the

answer was *Yes, of course it can get worse. What were you thinking?*

Rain.

First came a few drops. Then a few more. *No, no, please, no...*

All at once she heard a huge thunderclap and the heavens opened up. She hurried to one of the pitifully small overhanging shelters, but suddenly the wind was blowing in mighty gusts, swirling the rain and drenching her. She stood there in dumb disbelief as the rain trickled down her face and soaked through her dress, turning her into a soggy, pitiful mess.

Unbelievable.

She remembered movies where everything on earth went wrong for the heroine, and then to seal the experience, she'd get rained on. *Overkill*, Alison had always thought. *That never really happens.*

Yeah. Right.

When the train came several minutes later, she sniffed a little, dried her eyes with her fingertips, boarded a car, and plopped down on a seat. Evidently she looked really pitiful, because even the insane homeless people shied away from her.

Under normal circumstances, she'd walk home the few blocks from the 15th Street station, but she didn't relish the thought of doing it in the rain. She grabbed her phone, called Heather, and asked her to pick her up. Since Alison wasn't exactly radiating the excitement of a newly engaged woman, Heather started to worry, but Alison told her she'd fill her in when she got there. Just last week, Heather and her husband, Tony, had returned from celebrating their second anniversary in Las Vegas. Alison tried not to be pea green with envy about that, but it was a hard-won battle.

You got the last good one, Heather. Hang on to him.

Alison thunked her head against the window, her thoughts a jumbled mess. This couldn't have happened. It just couldn't have. How had all her marriage dreams morphed into a scenario only a pornographer could love?

Easy answer. Because she was a fool.

Randy had never given her any indication that he was Mr. Wonderful. She'd just chosen to hope that maybe he was. He was merely a clueless degenerate who'd taken a wrong turn and wandered into her life. She, on the other hand, should have pulled off those damned rose-colored glasses the moment she'd met him and smashed them into a million pieces.

As the train went underground and picked up speed, whizzing through the tunnel toward Cityplace, Alison thought about how other women were getting married and having families right and left. What was wrong with her?

Okay, so she hadn't exactly been a genius when it came to picking the right men. First there had been Tim Chapman. A few months in, she'd woken up one night to find him licking her toes. That she might have been able to overlook, but when he wanted her to wear six-inch heels in the bedroom and carry a whip, she decided enough was enough. Then there were the two years she'd wasted on Richard Bodecker, who turned out to be gay. Alison might have realized it sooner, but since he owned a Harley dealership and spit a lot, she'd stayed in denial even longer than Richard himself.

And then there was Michael Pagliano, who scratched

his balls in public. Just stood there in a movie line or wherever and scratched away, as if nobody were watching. But since Alison had been three months away from her thirtieth birthday and feeling a little desperate, she'd decided to overlook it. Then he took her to a five-star restaurant, which was good, and blew his nose on a cloth napkin, which wasn't. It was then Alison decided she couldn't close her eyes to his downside any longer.

Then came Randy.

So there they were. The men she'd been able to attract over the years. A clueless degenerate, a foot fetishist, a gay biker, and a ball-scratching nose blower. She wasn't dumb enough to think all men were rotten, but she was beginning to believe she was a magnet for the ones who were.

Thirty minutes later at the 15th Street station, the pouring rain had lightened into a steady drizzle. Heather was there to meet her, umbrella in hand. She wore a pair of faded jeans and a white tank top, and the damp evening made her curly brown hair even curlier than usual.

"Uh-oh," Heather said as Alison ducked under her umbrella with her. "It's bad, isn't it?"

"If eight months of my life going down the tubes is bad, then yes. It's bad."

"Tell me what happened."

"Let's see. The *Reader's Digest* version. Randy's an asshole, and I'm an idiot."

Heather winced. "Get in the car. Then I want to hear everything."

Once they were inside the car, Alison told Heather the whole story, and Heather's eyes grew wide.

"He wanted a threesome? With Bonnie?" She paused.

"Well, okay. If a guy's a big enough jerk to want a three-some, of course it would be with Bonnie."

Tears welled in Alison's eyes, and she hated it. Randy was *not* worth it.

"Oh, hon," Heather said. "I know you had such high hopes. I'm so sorry this happened."

"No. Don't be sorry. What he did tonight saved me from wasting even more time on him."

"That's true. But it doesn't stop it from hurting."

And of course that made Alison cry even more, and Heather gave her a hug. "Randy's an idiot," she murmured, patting Alison on the back. "He didn't deserve you."

Alison nodded, even though she really didn't feel like such a great catch right about now.

"You want me to go beat him up for you?" Heather said. "He's bigger than I am, but I'm *way* more pissed."

"Would you? That would be *wonderful*." Then she sighed. "Nice thought, but maybe you'd better not. This night is bad enough already. I don't want to have to bail you out of jail." She eased away from Heather and dropped her head back against the headrest, feeling miserable. "I'm a dating disaster. I'm done with men."

"No, you're not."

"Yeah, I am. I'm going to become a nun."

"You're not Catholic."

She rolled her head around to look at Heather. "I could adapt. I'm not too fond of kneeling, but I do like wine. Trade-offs, you know?"

"What about confession? That won't exactly be a walk in the park for you."

"Yeah, maybe the first one will be a little lengthy. But

once I purge the past ten years or so, the next ones will be a breeze. I mean, come on. After I'm a nun, what could I possibly have to own up to?"

"Oh, right. Like the moment a cute priest walks by, you won't be lusting in your heart?"

Alison sighed. "That's my problem, isn't it?"

"What?"

"Doesn't matter if he's Mr. Right or not. I'll find a way to cram that square peg into that round hole or die trying. God, Heather. What's *wrong* with me?"

"Nothing's wrong with you. Randy's the one with the problem."

"But what if I end up with somebody even worse than Randy because I'm so desperate to get married that I'll settle for anyone?"

"You would have figured Randy out sooner or later, even if he hadn't...you know. Gone all pervert on you. Just be glad you're rid of him."

"And who am I supposed to put in his place?"

"Do you have to figure that out now?"

"Sometime before I'm eighty would be nice."

"You have fifty years before you're eighty."

And Alison knew what those fifty years were going to be like. A few years would pass. Then a few decades. And before she knew it, she'd be staring at some hairy-eared octogenarian over their morning oatmeal at the home and wondering how long it might take to get him to pop the question.

"It's not like you've exhausted every possibility out there," Heather said. "You just haven't met the right guy yet. Give it some more time."

"But I've already tried everything! Singles bars. Speed

dating. Video dating. Match dot com. E-Harmony. I've even considered setting fire to my own condo to try to meet a cute firefighter."

"Now there's an approach I wouldn't have thought of."

"Yeah, but it'd be just my luck that he'd be a firefighter who wore women's underwear or had a wife he wasn't telling me about." She sighed. "Do you understand how much I suck at picking out men?"

"Have you thought about letting somebody else pick one out for you?"

"No," Alison said with a wave of her hand. "No way. I've had enough bad blind dates to last me a lifetime."

"I'm not talking about letting your Aunt Brenda fix you up. That was a disaster."

Alison cringed at the memory. She'd never met a man before who grew marijuana in the backseat of his car.

"I'm talking about a professional," Heather said.

"Huh?"

"A matchmaker."

"Matchmaker? You mean, like one person who decides who you're supposed to spend the rest of your life with?" Alison screwed up her face. "Sorry. That's just weird."

"No, really. I work with a woman who went to this matchmaker in downtown Plano, and she set her up with a really great guy. She was engaged four months later and married within the year."

Just the words "engaged" and "married" in the same sentence made Alison's heart go pitty-pat. But she knew the truth. Nothing was ever that simple.

"Pardon my skepticism, but what's this friend of yours like? Tall? Skinny? Blonde? Ex-cheerleader? Trust fund?"

"Short, a little overweight, brown hair, ex-debate team, good job."

Now Alison was listening. Minus the debate team thing, Heather could be describing her.

Alison pulled out her phone. "What's this matchmaker's name?"

"Uh...I can't remember. Rosie...Roxanne...something like that."

Alison Googled "matchmaker" and "Plano."

"Oh, my God," she said. "Did you know there's a matchmaking service dedicated to finding you somebody to cheat with?"

"You're kidding."

"I guess that one's for later. Before I can cheat on a man, first I have to find a man." She flipped to another site. "And here's one called Sugar Daddies. They match rich old men with hot young women."

"How young?"

"Judging from these photos, barely legal." Alison poked the screen. "I'm still not seeing...wait. Rochelle Scott? Matchmaking by Rochelle?"

"Yeah. I think that's it."

"Hmm. Says she's been in business for thirty-five years. Nobody stays in business that long if they're not successful, right?"

"Oh, she's successful, if you judge by what she charges."

"How much are we talking?"

"That's the downside. She charges fifteen hundred dollars for five introductions."

Alison winced. Three hundred dollars per man?

Then she thought about the thousand dollars she'd

once paid to spend a week at a singles resort in Florida. Instead of coming back with a man, she'd returned with a horrible sunburn and so many mosquito bites she looked like flesh-colored bubble wrap. She wasn't one to throw money around indiscriminately, but if the woman could actually deliver, it might be worth it.

She looked back at her phone and clicked through the website. "Listen to this," she said, reading from the woman's bio. "Rochelle Scott has a degree in psychology. She's been matchmaking for thirty-five years. Out of more than three hundred marriages, there have been only sixteen divorces." She looked at Heather. "That blows the national average out of the water. I'm going over there Monday."

Heather's eyebrows shot up. "Now, wait a minute. I just threw that out there as something to think about. You need to let the sting of tonight wear off a little before you hop right back out there."

"Nope. I'm thirty and alone, and it's bad. I imagine forty and alone is even worse."

"Doing anything on the rebound is usually a mistake. Forget about it for tonight. Come up to my place. Tony's working late at the bar, so we can trash talk men all we want to."

"Right. You have nothing to gripe about where Tony's concerned."

"Yeah? That's what you think. He still hasn't grasped the concept that dirty underwear goes in the hamper and that onion rings aren't health food. And don't get me started on his collection of *Sports Illustrated* swimsuit editions. You'd think they were the Dead Sea Scrolls the way he—"

"Heather," Alison said, "right about now, I'd kill for a messy guy eating onion rings while he's staring at hot women in bikinis. Particularly if he looked like Tony." Her eyes teared up again, and she hated it. "You know, when we were both single, it wasn't so bad. But now...now you have Tony, and..." She sniffed a little. "I'm happy for you, Heather. I really am. But I'm really starting to feel like the odd woman out." She let out a painful sigh. "It sucks to be me."

"Don't you say that," Heather told her. "Don't you *dare* say that. You already have a good life. You have a great job. A nice place to live. Good friends. Money in the bank. And you're a good person who does nice things for other people. So it does *not* suck to be you."

Alison sighed again. "Is it really so wrong to want the last piece of the puzzle?"

"No. Of course not. I know how much you want to get married. I'm just saying that maybe you need to give the husband hunt a rest for a while."

"I would, except for that damned clock ticking inside my head."

Heather smiled. "He's out there, you know."

"Who?"

"Mr. Right. Your knight in shining armor. Your forever guy. You just have to be patient. One day, when you least expect it—"

"Don't try to cheer me up. I'd rather wallow in my misery."

"No problem there. I have a really nice bottle of vodka I've been saving for an occasion like this."

"Will you keep me from doing something dumb if I drink too much? And yes, I'm referring to the state fair incident."

"Of course. And did I mention I also have a gallon of Blue Bell Cookies 'n Cream?"

"Perfect. That's why I can't find a man, you know. My hips aren't big enough."

Heather started the car and drove the few blocks to the condo complex where they both lived. Alison ran up the stairs to her place to get out of the big-butt dress. As she stepped inside, Lucy, Ethel, and Ricky galloped into the living room, leaped onto her Queen Anne chair, and started in with a whiny chorus of meows as if she'd been lost at sea for thirty years and had finally been rescued.

She turned her back to them and looked over her shoulder. "So what do you guys think? Does this dress make my butt look big?"

More meows. In her state of mind right then, Alison took that as a unanimous *yes*.

She grabbed cat food from the pantry. The cats did their usual serpentine around her ankles, then played musical bowls as she was dumping food into them. Lucy had always been the troublemaker, clawing her way straight up the drapes, then pouncing on Ricky's head as he strolled by. He'd spit at her, she'd whack him with her paw, and then five minutes later they'd be curled up on the sofa in a wad of tabby cat nirvana. Ethel stayed out of the fray most of the time by plunking her hefty self on top of the bookcase in the living room, refusing to get involved in her brother's and sister's love-hate relationship.

It was impossible to state just how much of a pain in the ass the three of them could be, and Alison loved them right down to their claws of destruction and their six a.m. drag races up and down the hall. She hadn't intended to adopt them, but maybe it was a good thing she had.

The way her luck was going, they might be all she'd *ever* have.

She put on sweatpants, a T-shirt, and a pair of flip-flops and felt marginally better. She decided she was going to eat enough ice cream to get brain freeze, then warm her head back up with half a dozen vodka shots. And through it all, she intended to obliterate everything Randy from her phone, her Facebook, and her e-mail. If she got inebriated enough, when she got home, she'd head over to the forums at the Knot and spam them with *love sucks* messages, then grab a couple of issues of *Modern Bride* from her magazine rack and shred them.

Now, *that* was wallowing in misery.

Then Monday on her lunch hour, she'd head over to see Rochelle and pray the woman could work miracles.

Chapter 2

At noon on Monday, Alison brought her car to a halt in front of a dreamy little two-story prairie-style house on the outskirts of downtown Plano. It was painted a soft, mossy green with burgundy trim, and its front porch spanned the width of the house. Ivy twined around the porch rails. The landscaping was a little scraggly and overgrown, but an hour or two with pruning shears and a weed eater would do a world of good. In spite of the fact that she lived in a contemporary condo, whenever Alison closed her eyes and dreamed of marriage and family, she was living in a house like this.

A lot of the houses in this area had been converted to office spaces—a lawyer here, a therapist there, a dentist, a yoga studio. A lot of those people worked downstairs, lived upstairs. If not for the small sign beside the house at 614 State Street that read "Matchmaking by Rochelle" with an arrow pointing around to the rear of the house, Alison wouldn't have had a clue she was in the right place. She'd called ahead that morning to ask for an appointment. A man had answered who she assumed was Rochelle's husband. He told her noon was fine, so here she was.

Circling around to the back of the house, she found a French door with a sign that said Please Come In. She opened the door into a large room that probably hadn't been redecorated since the house was new. That could have been a bad thing, but it was all so charming that Alison couldn't help smiling. A flowered sofa with curvy Victorian lines and brocade pillows filled one wall. Beside it, a slender, elegant lamp with gold scrollwork sat on a Queen Ann end table. The midday sun filtered through a big stained-glass window, casting a multicolored glow on the polished hardwoods. A lot of people might have thought the house was a little old, a little dusty, a little dreary, and definitely in need of repairs. But to Alison, a house like this was a home.

Then she glanced to the other side of the room where a man sat behind a desk. He looked up as she closed the door and rose to greet her. The moment their eyes met, she stopped short, feeling as if her feet were fused to the floor.

Oh, my God.

Alison knew she was a walking cliché—a woman who adored men who were tall, dark, and handsome—but she just couldn't help it. She just accepted the fact that it was imprinted on her DNA and lived with it.

And, boy, was she living with it now.

He was at least six one or six two, with thick, dark hair and deep brown eyes. A hint of a five o'clock shadow darkened his face, giving him a rugged sensuality that made her think of winters in Wyoming in front of big, roaring fires. He wore jeans and a blue cotton shirt with the sleeves rolled to his elbows, revealing strong, tanned forearms. With a practiced sweep of her eyes she'd acquired through years of careful practice, she automatically took note of his left hand.

No ring.

There was only one explanation for this man's presence here today. Not only was Rochelle a master matchmaker, she was also psychic. She'd read Alison's mind, found her this incredibly gorgeous man, and had him waiting for her. Fifteen hundred bucks and he was hers.

Now *that* was service.

"You must be Alison," he said, coming around the desk and holding out his hand, flashing her a friendly smile. "I'm Brandon. Brandon Scott."

She shook his hand, and it was perfect—warm and smooth, his handshake firm but gentle. *I could get used to hands like these*, she thought, even as she knew fate would never allow her the chance to. This was the kind of genetically blessed man who never gave a woman like her a second glance.

He motioned to a guest chair in front of the desk. "Have a seat."

She sat down tentatively, then looked over her shoulder. "Uh . . . I'm looking for Rochelle?"

He sat back down at the desk, his smile dimming. "I'm afraid she's not here. Rochelle died of a heart attack two weeks ago."

Alison blinked. "Died? But the person I talked to this morning—"

"That was me."

"But I don't understand. If Rochelle isn't here—"

"Rochelle may be gone, but her business is alive and well."

"So there's a new matchmaker?"

"Yes." A smile spread slowly across his face. "You're talking to him."

Alison couldn't have been more stunned if he'd slapped her. Matchmakers were supposed to be little old ladies who offered you a cup of tea, then paged through a dusty book and magically located your soul mate. They weren't supposed to look like a man who'd stepped right out of her daydreams.

"You?" she said. "*You're* a matchmaker?"

"I'm Rochelle's grandson."

Alison felt a stab of sympathy. "Then she was your grandmother? Oh...I'm so sorry. Her death must have been such a shock."

"Thank you," Brandon said, his face darkening. "It was rather sudden. But my grandmother loved this business, and she wanted it to go on. I'll be maintaining the clients she was working with at the time of her death as well as soliciting new business."

Alison felt the strangest push-pull she'd ever experienced in her life. Under normal circumstances, she'd pay fifteen hundred bucks just to look at this guy for an hour or so. But allow a strange man to pick out a man for her? How incredibly weird was that?

"I'm sorry Mr....uh..."

"Brandon."

"Brandon. I don't think this is going to work out."

"Oh? Why not?"

"I was expecting a woman, so—"

"Ah, so you think only a woman can be a matchmaker?"

Wasn't that obvious? "Well, you have to admit that a matchmaking man is a little...weird."

"What makes you think a man wouldn't be capable of choosing the perfect partner for you?"

"Well, no reason, really," Alison said, suddenly feeling very uncomfortable. "Except that men don't usually understand women very well. So finding them the right man—"

"You're absolutely right. Most men don't understand women. But I'm not the kind of man you're used to dealing with. Trust me when I tell you," he said with a sly smile, "I know women."

If he meant "know" in the biblical sense, she had no doubt hundreds of women would like very much to be known by him. But when it came to a woman's psyche, she doubted his understanding was much different from the average man's. In other words, no matter what he professed, he was clueless about women.

He sat back in his chair. "You think I'm clueless about women, don't you?"

When her thought came out of his mouth, Alison blinked with surprise. "I-I didn't say that."

"You didn't have to. I'm also pretty good at reading body language."

Oh, hell. Now he was looking at her body, which she'd never been terribly proud of, which made her want to slither out the door and never come back.

"I guess I'm going to have to prove it to you," he said.

Her heart thumped. "Prove it to me?"

He narrowed his eyes and stared at her thoughtfully for a few moments. "I'd say you're about..." He tilted his head. "Twenty-eight, twenty-nine, but no older than thirty one. You've been in a couple of pretty serious relationships over the years, but they all ended badly. You want to meet new men, but you've gotten so cynical that you believe the worst about them before they even open their mouths. Lately you've started to believe it's actually possible you're going to spend the rest of your life alone."

Alison swallowed hard, feeling as transparent as a plate-glass window. "You just described half the women in the Dallas metroplex."

His eyes never leaving hers, he tapped his fingertips together thoughtfully. "You think about men all the time. I wouldn't say it's an obsession, but you're definitely focused. For instance, when you shop for a dress, you don't buy one based on what you like. You buy one based on what you think your man of the moment will like."

She thought about evil three-way mirror at Saks and Randy's big-butt proclamation. This guy was getting too close for comfort.

"When I say the word 'bridesmaid,'" he went on, "you don't think about a beautiful wedding. You think about the three or four ugly bridesmaid dresses cluttering your closet."

Wrong. Two. That was all she had. Just two. And to be fair, the one she wore in Heather's wedding really wasn't ugly at all.

"And since you're looking all the time," he said, "it's hard for you even to have a conversation with a single man without evaluating him as husband material."

Alison's heart jolted. "That's not true."

"Yeah? When you came into this office and saw a man sitting behind this desk, what was your first thought? Did you think, 'What's a man doing running a matchmaking service?' Or did you scope out my left hand for a ring?"

Alison's mouth fell open. "I did not—"

He held up his palm. "Hey, when you're focused on finding the right guy, everybody's a candidate. I get that. But now you've gotten to the point where you don't trust your own judgment anymore, so you're willing to pay somebody else to do your judging for you."

"Somebody else, maybe," she said, feeling as flustered as she ever had in her life. "But I thought that somebody was going to be Rochelle. I still think a woman would be best."

"Because you still think a woman knows more about women than a man ever could?"

"No offense."

"None taken. It's a common misconception." He leaned forward, resting his forearms on the desk, his gaze fixed on hers. "Tell me, Alison. Why is it that you're not engaged, but you have a subscription to *Modern Bride* magazine?"

Alison's face heated up with embarrassment. "That's it. This isn't going to work. A man who's a matchmaker is just *wrong*."

He smiled at her.

"No. It really is. Particularly since you haven't been at this very long. Like, hardly at all. How am I supposed to trust you when you have no track record?"

He pointed to the mahogany staircase along the far wall that led to the second floor. "See those stairs over there?"

Alison turned around. "Yeah?"

"When I was a kid," he said, "I used to sit on those stairs, listening to my grandmother talk to her clients. Most of the women were a lot like you. They'd been out there trying so hard to make the kind of love connection they'd always dreamed about, but they always came up empty. But my grandmother..." A smile passed over his lips. "She had a knack. An intuition. Almost a sixth sense about who belonged with whom. And no matter how skeptical they were when they walked through the door, six months later, when they were wearing a ring, suddenly they weren't skeptical anymore. Was she a hundred percent right all the time? No. But she sure increased the odds for a lot of women to find good men."

The sincerity he radiated seemed to waft over to Alison and wrap itself around her like a warm blanket. But the very reason she was here—because she didn't trust herself when it came to making decisions about men— was precisely what kept her from feeling comfortable trusting this one.

"But that was your grandmother. I don't mean to be negative, but are you sure you can do this?"

"My grandmother took tremendous pride in her business. If she didn't think I was competent to run it, why else would she have willed it to me?"

Okay. So that was a pretty good point.

"What kind of guarantee do you have?" she asked him.

"No guarantee. I offer five quality introductions. If I made my services unlimited, would my clients make an effort to really get to know the people I match them with? Or would they give it a half-hearted effort, always assuming somebody better was just around the corner?"

"So I could give you fifteen hundred dollars and end up with no one?"

"That," he said with a smile of supreme confidence, "is not going to happen."

Everything about this man seemed positive and sincere. Even if she wasn't quite sure he was up to snuff as a matchmaker, she didn't doubt *he* believed he was. And because she was a little short on self-confidence herself, she really admired it when she saw it in somebody else.

"Excuse me," he said suddenly, reaching into his jeans pocket. "Sorry. I need to take this call."

Call? She hadn't heard a ring. Then she realized he must have had his phone on vibrate.

He hit the talk button. He turned away a little, as if to make his conversation more private, but she heard him loud and clear.

"Brandon Scott," he said, and then a big smile crossed his face. "Hi, Susan!" he said in a cheery voice. "So you and Jeff had lunch together. How did it go?"

Alison's eyes may have been on a Victorian print on the wall to her right, but her ears were tuned to every word that came out of Brandon's mouth.

"Wow," Brandon said. "That's great news! I'm so glad you hit it off." A pause, and then he laughed. "Now you know that's not true. I'm not better at this than my grandmother was. I'm just glad I was able to pick up on the work she'd already done with you and go from there."

They chatted for a few minutes more, with Brandon admonishing Susan that no matter how much fun she and Jeff were having, next time she needed to watch the clock so she wasn't an hour late getting back to work.

Alison felt a shot of envy. She wanted to be the woman on the other end of that phone who'd had such a great first date that she'd forgotten all about the time. Not once in her life had Alison done anything but muddle through a first date and pray there was more to the guy than bad table manners and a driving need to talk endlessly about his divorce.

Finally Brandon hung up and turned back to Alison. "I'm sorry. Now...where were we?"

Alison was still thinking about that phone conversation. Could he do for her what he'd done for Susan? Introduce her to a man who made time stand still?

"We were talking about your fee," she said hesitantly. "It's a little...high. I mean, compared to Internet dating..."

He nodded thoughtfully. "Think of it this way, Alison. Internet dating is like a ten-dollar buffet. You pick out several things that look good, put them on your plate, and hope you can stomach at least a few of them. Matchmaking is like eating at the chef's table at a gourmet restaurant. You put yourself in his hands and trust that you're in for a five-star experience."

She had to admit that analogy really hit home. After all, hadn't Randy very nearly made her barf?

"Still, it's a lot of money," Alison said. "I'm going to have to think about it."

"I understand completely. But I'm also sure you understand that matchmaking is a very personalized service, which means I can take only so many clients at a time. My schedule is booking up fast."

"How fast?"

"I have room for only two more clients this month."

"But it's only the fifth."

"Exactly." He rose from his chair, came around his desk, and held out his hand. "It was nice to meet you, Alison. If you decide you'd like my help, give me a call. We'll talk more about what you're looking for in a man.

If not this month, then maybe we'll see each other next month, okay?"

She rose and shook his hand. "Uh...yeah. Thank you for seeing me."

"Of course. You have my number. Just let me know when you'd like me to introduce you to your future husband."

With that, he sat back down, pulled out a file, and laid it open on his desk, moving ahead with business as usual. Alison walked to the door, each step a little slower than the last. *Future husband.* She loved the sound of that.

It wasn't as if she didn't have the money. But was it a smart use of her money?

She admitted to being a little impulsive, but it was usually limited to things like ordering octopus at a sushi bar, or dyeing her hair red. The fact that she'd even considered using a matchmaker was crazy enough. Could she actually spend fifteen hundred dollars to let a man find her a man? This could turn into a bigger disaster than her Florida trip, where she'd ended up as mosquito bait.

Or she could find the man of her dreams.

No. That was crazy. *This* was crazy.

She started to open the door, only to stop short, her hand on the doorknob. But if not this, then what? Was she just going to wait around, doing nothing, hoping for a man to stop her on the street and tell her he was the one?

Just take some time to think about it. A day, or an hour, or at least a few minutes...

Then she had a terrible thought. What if she waited until next month, and Brandon gave away her perfect match to another woman who hadn't hesitated to seize the opportunity?

Feeling a surge of conviction, she spun back around. "Brandon?"

He looked up. "Yes?"

"If I write you a check today, when can we get started?"

He pulled out his phone and hit a few buttons, then looked back up at her with those dark, sexy eyes, a smile of satisfaction playing over his lips.

"How does Thursday look for you?"

Chapter 3

The moment Alison left the house, Brandon slipped the check she'd written him into his shirt pocket. He slapped shut the file on his desk, stuffed it randomly into a file drawer, and trotted up the stairs to the second floor. He stepped into the first room on the right, where Tom was leaning across the pool table, his cue in place, taking aim.

"That was fast," Tom said. "I'm guessing she told you to forget it. But hey. Nothing ventured, nothing gained." A flick of his cue sent the four ball into a side pocket.

Brandon pulled Alison's check from his shirt pocket. "Think again."

Tom's eyes grew wide. He dropped his cue, came around the table, and jerked the check out of Brandon's hand. He looked at it with disbelief. "No. No way. You did *not* just convince that woman to give you fifteen hundred dollars to find her a husband."

"Did you think I couldn't do it?"

"Hell, yes, I thought you couldn't do it!"

Brandon plucked the check out of Tom's hand and stuck it back into his pocket. "I thought you had faith in me all these years."

"Of course I have faith in you, as long as it involves a real business. But conning a woman into believing you're a matchmaker? Who the hell would have ever thought you'd ever be able to do that?"

"Con?" Brandon said. "There's no con involved here. I fully intend to deliver the services I promised."

"Right. You don't know crap about matchmaking."

"What's to know? I'll look through my grandmother's files. Find a guy who looks decent. Set her up with him. What's so hard about that? I have five shots at it, for God's sake. The odds are with me."

"Okay," Tom said, racking up the balls. "So you managed to get fifteen hundred bucks out of one client. That's a far cry from the thirty thousand you need. Where's the next client coming from?"

"I placed an ad on the *Dallas After Dark* website. When it comes out next week, I'll have more business than I know what to do with."

Tom lifted the rack, and Brandon grabbed a cue to break.

"Our option to buy the warehouse is good for only six months," Tom said as Brandon's break drove the six ball into a corner pocket. "If you don't get the money by then, I'll have to bring in another partner. But you're the guy I want. Are you sure you can pull off this gig?"

Yes. He was sure. Because there wasn't anything he wouldn't do to make it happen.

For years, Brandon had crisscrossed the country, making real estate deals and making money. He stayed in no-tell motels, played a little pool in the evenings, had a few drinks, and then got up the next day to guide a crew in renovating his latest project. It had been an incredible high—finding distressed properties in cities across the country, then racing the clock to turn hovels into showplaces and get them sold before his construction loans came due. Once in Vegas he had four projects going at once, and the money piled up until his bank account was so stuffed he couldn't imagine ever being broke again.

Then the bottom had fallen out of the real estate market.

He still remembered that horrible feeling when he had loan payments due and not a dime left to pay them. The projects had gone into foreclosure, leaving him with big losses, bad credit, and nowhere to turn.

Brandon and Tom had partnered on several projects in the past, so when Tom contacted him about the Houston deal, he sat up and paid attention. The owner was so motivated to sell that he'd have taken just about any offer, but it took a guy with vision to be able to see the possibilities for the old warehouse.

Brandon was that guy.

Turning that dilapidated warehouse into loft apartments was going to take some work, but even in a depressed market that area was so hot it practically sizzled. They couldn't miss. And if the company that owned the adjoining property succeeded in getting the zoning changed from residential to mixed use and put in the urban living center they wanted to, Brandon and Tom's investment would go through the roof. That part was a long shot, but even without it, they could easily walk away with a substantial profit, and Brandon would be off to the races again.

The seller had agreed to finance the deal as long as they came up with the down payment cash he was desperate for, so their creditworthiness had never been called into question. The only thing that stood between Brandon and that project was a lousy thirty thousand dollars, his half of the down payment. Three years ago, he'd have never been concerned about a pitiful amount of money like that, but he sure was now.

Then he'd found out his grandmother had died and he was her sole heir.

"I'll have the money," Brandon said as he dropped the three ball. "Don't worry about that."

"Didn't she leave any cash at all?"

"About eight thousand. So all I really need is twenty-two."

"Are you sure there's not some loophole in the will that will let you sell this house? Getting the money that way would be a whole lot easier than by playing matchmaker."

"Nope. I can live here as long as I want to. But if I move out, the house goes to my grandmother's church."

"I can't believe she willed her house to a church. That's so weird."

"Not for my grandmother. She practically had a pew with her name on it at the First Baptist Church for the past thirty years." Brandon aimed carefully, taking out the one and the five in a single shot.

Tom nodded down at the pool table. "You might want to consider selling this monstrosity. It's bound to be worth something."

"Not without restoration, and that costs a bundle. But I wouldn't sell it, anyway. This is a nineteenth-century Brunswick Monarch. I'm putting it in storage when I go."

"It's ugly as hell."

"Beauty is in the eye of the beholder. And if I ever see

you set a beer on it, I'm chopping off your arm at the elbow."

"What's the problem? It'd just blend in with the other rings."

"You heard me."

Tom was right. This pool table had seen better days, though it must have been amazing when it was new. Built of burled elm, it was inlaid with a mosaic of walnut, rosewood, and ebony in diamond patterns. The legs were four cast-iron lions stretching from beneath the table out to the corners, each one finished in fourteen-carat gold. Built at the end of the nineteenth century, it was still in the house when Brandon's grandmother and grandfather bought it in the 1950s. By then its condition was already compromised. The felt was scuffed and faded, the wood scratched and stained.

He remembered the long hours he'd spent playing on this table when he was a teenager. When he'd been forced to live with a grandmother he barely knew, it had been something to escape to when the awkwardness got to be too much. After everything that had happened, he spent the first few months gritting his teeth and smacking balls so hard they sometimes ended up on the floor. But gradually his finesse returned, the soft clack of the balls calming his angry, bitter thoughts and letting him breathe a little.

Looking back, he realized now that his grandmother had known what was going on in his head. She'd known just how much he had to work out, and not once had she ever interrupted him when he was in this room. She'd been the only stable influence he'd ever known, the one person who'd given him half a chance to be a normal kid.

"I'm keeping the table," he said, hitting the two ball into a side pocket. "But for the rest of the stuff, I called out a company that specializes in estate sales. They told me I could get only a few thousand for the furniture because of its condition, but that won't get me where I need to go."

"Did you check under the mattresses?"

"Give it up, Tom."

"But did you *check*?"

"No, and I also didn't rip up the floorboards or look for hidden closets. Trust me. There's nothing here."

"So you're going to be a matchmaker." Tom shook his head slowly. "Words I thought I'd never say."

Brandon couldn't have imagined it, either. But he'd also never been one to ignore opportunity when it was staring him right in the face. Once he dug through his grandmother's records and saw the high price she charged her clients, he realized all he had to do was play matchmaker himself, increase the number of clients, and in six months he'd have all the money he needed. And because he had this house to stay in, he'd have no living expenses to speak of. He knew people would question a man as a matchmaker, but he'd hustled enough real estate deals to know how to shoot from the hip and pour on the charm. He had no doubt he could convince just about anyone— man or woman—that he could introduce them to their perfect match.

And where his grandmother was concerned, he couldn't imagine that she'd intended him to become a professional matchmaker when she willed him her business. She merely expected him to liquidate it, pocket the money, and move on. So if he could make a little bit more from the business before he left town, was there anything wrong with that?

"When you close up shop in six months," Tom said, "what do you intend to do with the clients you have on the hook?"

"Give them prorated refunds. If I haven't given them five introductions yet, I'll refund for those they haven't received. It's all figured into the operational budget."

"Looks like you have this all worked out," Tom said.

"I never step foot into any situation without a plan."

"What about the clients your grandmother was already working with?"

"Two asked for refunds. I think the others figured they might as well stay on and see how I did."

"So how'd you convince this woman?" Tom asked. "Reading those women's magazines must have helped."

"Oh, yeah. You want to get inside the head of a woman, read a couple of those. That'll do it."

Especially the article on women who were obsessed with men, most of whom were also obsessed with getting married. It had given him some pretty good talking points about that particular state of mind. The *Modern Bride* thing had been an educated guess, but judging from the look on Alison's face when he mentioned it, he'd hit pay dirt.

"I also took a call from another client I'd successfully matched up. That helped convince her."

"But you haven't worked with any other clients yet."

"She doesn't know that."

Tom blinked. "You faked a phone call?"

"Just because it hasn't happened yet doesn't mean it's not going to. Think of it as a dramatization of a future conversation I'm sure to have."

Tom looked at him dumbly. "You make my eyes cross sometimes, you know that?"

"Yeah. I know. That's why you've never been able to beat me at pool."

"Hey, don't get cocky. I've beaten you a time or two."

"Once in Miami when I'd had eight beers and no sleep, and once in Phoenix when that bartender's breasts fell out of her tube top."

"See, you get distracted, too."

"That woman must have been a thirty-eight F. A man would have to be dead and buried not to get distracted."

"So what's the woman like who just hired you?" Tom asked. "Maybe you should put her aside for yourself." He raised an eyebrow. "Or maybe for a trusted friend such as myself?"

"Conflict of interest," Brandon said.

"Oh. Pardon me. I didn't know there were matchmaker ethics."

"I'm making them up as I go along." Brandon swung his cue, sending the six ball to hover for a moment in the jaws of the corner pocket before finally dropping in. "As for the woman, she had 'nice girl' written all over her."

"Then never mind what I said about keeping her for yourself. You don't like nice girls."

True enough. He preferred women who liked to drink hard, play pool, and have the kind of sex that made continents collide, then hop on their Harleys and head on down the road.

"She just hasn't met the right guy yet," Brandon said, "and she's gotten cynical. It shows. Toss in a little desperation, and pretty soon she's man repellent. Guys can smell it. Didn't start out that way, but now she can't break the cycle."

"So you're going to break it for her?"

"I'll give it a shot. Set her up with a guy who seems decent and see what happens. No guarantees, but I'm betting I can make her happy. After all, my intuition is as good as anyone else's, isn't it?" Brandon called the corner pocket and dropped the eight ball into it, then stood up and leaned on his cue. "Sorry, buddy. That's one more in the win column for me."

Tom sighed. "Where's a bartender's boobs when you really need them?"

"Feel free to stick around here until we can get the Houston deal off the ground. Big house. Plenty of room."

"I may take you up on that." Tom frowned. "It sucks these days that every penny counts, and God knows I don't have any other deals in the works."

Brandon felt equally frustrated, but he hadn't worked his ass off all these years to give up now. He'd started on a construction crew right out of high school when real estate was booming, because it was the one industry where jobs were plentiful. But, God, how he'd hated it. Baking in the Texas sun, sweating like crazy, going home every night with every muscle aching. It hadn't taken him long to see that the guy who owned the deal and made the big bucks was the guy who didn't sweat. That was the guy Brandon wanted to be.

He'd read everything he could get his hands on about investing in real estate, and when he approached a seller to make his first offer, he'd been shaking in his boots. But he managed to make a decent deal, and by the time he renovated the property and sold it, he'd made an eleven-thousand-dollar profit. He was hooked.

And, God, he wanted to get back in the game.

But he was willing to wait it out, bide his time, work his plan. He'd never put much stock in the notion of true love, but he knew there were plenty of starry-eyed people out there like Alison Carter who did. All he had to do was match them up, collect the cash, and eventually he'd be back on top again.

Chapter 4

That afternoon, Alison sat at the bar at McCaffrey's with Heather, feeling dumber with every moment that passed. The more she tried to explain Brandon's taking over his grandmother's matchmaking business, the more skeptical Heather's expression became.

"Let me get this straight," Heather said. "You actually hired a *man* to find you a man?"

"This is the twenty-first century. Gender roles are blurred. A person can be anything he wants to be. It's only narrow-minded people who don't accept that."

"Yeah? How do you feel about buying tampons when the clerk is a man?"

She hated it. In fact, she'd wait in a line twice as long just to get a woman to ring her up. "Come on, Heather. Do you really think that bothers me?"

"Would you buy a bra from a man?"

Alison's face crinkled. "Well..."

"So I guess you're narrow-minded, huh?"

"No, I'm not," Alison said, regaining her composure. "If he were a trained professional...uh...bra-fitter-seller person, I wouldn't mind at all."

"Yeah? Picture him staring at your boobs. 'No, honey. That fit is *all* wrong. I think you need a 34B.'"

"Hey! My gynecologist is a man."

"Only because he was your mother's gynecologist, he's approximately a hundred and twelve years old, and you've been going to him since you were eighteen."

"Brandon is a matchmaker. He won't be getting anywhere near my boobs and my . . . whatever. It's like hiring a lawyer or a plumber or something. I'm paying him for a service, and that's that."

"He just got started. That means he has no experience."

"He said when he was younger he used to listen when his grandmother was talking to clients. He was inspired by her."

"Which is not the same as doing the job himself. So what has he been doing up to now?"

Alison paused. "I'm not sure."

"Yet you gave him fifteen hundred dollars? Just like that?"

I couldn't help it. He was gorgeous and charming and I have the backbone of an amoeba. "I had a good feeling about him."

"You also had a good feeling about Randy. Look what happened there."

"Oh, all right!" Alison said, resisting the urge to pound her forehead against the bar. "Look. It isn't as if I haven't second-guessed this a dozen times already. But I have to do something or I'll be alone forever."

"You're better off never getting married than being married to the wrong man."

Alison sighed. "Yeah, I know. But it doesn't stop me from wishing the right man would wander by sometime before I'm on Social Security."

"You'll find him soon enough. I'm just not sure this guy can make that happen."

"Well, he'd have to really be into matchmaking to take over his dead grandmother's business, wouldn't he?"

Heather thought about that for a moment. "Yeah. I guess so. But it still seems kinda strange. What has he done for you so far?"

"He gave me a questionnaire to fill out. I'm going to drop it by his office tomorrow on my lunch hour."

"You filled out a questionnaire? This is supposed to be personalized service. That's why you're paying him an arm and a leg."

"He needs to have the basics. Then I'm sure we'll discuss what I'm looking for in a man."

"Assuming he hasn't already left town with your fifteen hundred bucks."

"Will you stop being so cynical? Maybe he just believes in true love and wants to help people find it."

"Come on, Alison. Does that sound like your average man?"

No, but Alison had already determined that Brandon had a few qualities that were definitely above average. If his intuition was as finely developed as his body, his business was going to be a screaming success. She just wished she had a handle on the way he made his matches. The questionnaire hadn't asked her much more than online dating sites did, so how was he supposed to know the specifics of what she was looking for? And whether she was the right match for the men he set her up with?

But of course they would talk. Personalized service, right? That was what she was paying for.

Please, God, let this go well so I don't look like a fool about men.

Again.

"So what does he look like?" Heather asked. "I'm picturing a little guy with horn-rimmed glasses and a receding hairline."

"Uh...no. That's not exactly the right description. He's more like—"

In that moment, she happened to glance out the window, and she couldn't believe whom she saw.

"Oh, my God," she murmured. "There he is."

"Where?"

"Coming up the sidewalk outside."

Heather whipped around to watch as Brandon made his way toward the door, and her eyes grew so wide Alison thought they were going to pop out of her skull.

"Him?" Heather said.

"Yeah."

Heather sucked in a breath, then let it out slowly. "Oh, my."

Alison felt the tiniest bit of vindication that he had that effect on Heather, too. And judging from the way the waitresses' jaws practically hit the floor as he walked through the door, that lack of immunity probably spanned most of the female population.

"What's he doing here?" Heather asked.

"He lives nearby. Guess he's coming in for...I don't know. A beer?"

Unfortunately, Heather's surprise turned back to skepticism with the speed of light. "I guess now we know why you had such a good feeling about him."

"Now, hold on," Alison said. "I know what you're thinking, but his looks had nothing to do with it."

"Oh, come *on*! You're a sucker for guys like him. Did you or did you not buy a one-year gym membership from a guy just because he looked like George Clooney?"

Alison frowned. "His looks had nothing to do with that, either. It was January second. Buying a gym membership on January second is practically an American tradition."

"You can't think straight around guys like him," Heather said. "You lose your head. It falls right off your shoulders and goes rolling down the street."

"We have a business arrangement," Alison snapped. "I hired him to do a job, and that's that. His looks have nothing to do with—"

"He's coming over here," Heather said.

Alison went still, gripping her martini with glass-shattering pressure. "He is?"

"Calm down," Heather said with more than a tiny bit of sarcasm. "It's a business arrangement, right?"

Right. That was exactly what it was. *Business, business, business . . .*

Alison hoped maybe Brandon would just walk past them and grab a booth, or head across the room to play a little pool, saving Heather the effort of going all judgmental on him up close. Unfortunately, he caught Alison's eye, recognized her, and slid onto the stool beside her. He leaned one forearm casually against the bar and gave her a lazy smile, already melting into the place as if he'd been coming there all his life.

"Hey, Alison," he said. "I didn't expect to see you here."

"I didn't expect to see you, either."

"It's one of the first things I do whenever I'm new in town. I find a good neighborhood bar. A man has to have his priorities." He turned to Heather. "You must be a friend of Alison's. I'm Brandon Scott."

"The matchmaker?"

He gave her a warm smile of affirmation. "That's right."

"I'm Heather McCaffrey."

"McCaffrey? You own the place?"

"My husband and I do."

"I like it," he said, circling his gaze around the room. "Comfortable. Friendly. Big screens. Pool tables. And the boar's head above the bar is a nice touch. I assume there's a story behind the wedding veil it's wearing?"

"Yeah. There's a story." And the look on her face said *But I'm not going to tell you.*

Alison wondered if Heather knew she was scowling at him. Probably. If there was somebody she didn't like, she generally let the world know it. But there was no reason not to like Brandon. None at all. Being almost unbearably handsome was something he'd been born with and couldn't help, and it certainly didn't mean he couldn't be a competent matchmaker. Horn-rimmed glasses and a receding hairline did seem more in line with that profession, but really, who was she to judge?

Just then, Tracy caught sight of Brandon and sauntered down the length of the bar to take his order. She was one of those women who had perfect legs, a tiny waist, and artificial boobs the size of twin Hindenburgs, who radiated an aura of leg-spreading availability with all the subtlety of an Amsterdam whore. In other words, men couldn't pry their eyes away with a crowbar.

"Hey, there," Tracy said, giving Brandon a luminous smile. "What can I get for you?"

"Blue Moon," Brandon said, returning her smile with a megawatt one of his own, which didn't surprise Alison in the least. Pretty people always responded to pretty people. It was a law of nature. And in the meantime, average people had the misfortune of having to watch the kind of mating ritual they were genetically barred from taking part in.

"I don't think I've seen you around here before," she said in that super sexy voice designed to waft right into a man's ears and turn him to mush.

"I'm new in town," Brandon replied.

"Why, that is just about the best news I've had all day. Am I going to see you around here a lot?"

"You kidding? Look around. What's there to keep me away?"

"Not me," Tracy purred. "That's for sure."

The moment a woman like Tracy entered the picture, it was as if a cloak of invisibility fell over Alison. She came *this* close to asking Tracy how she could flirt so shamelessly with Brandon when it was possible that, because he'd sat down next to her as soon as he arrived, they were a couple.

Oh, get over yourself. The woman isn't blind.

Tracy walked away to grab Brandon a beer, her tiny little ass swishing back and forth. Right on cue, Brandon swiveled his head to watch.

Alison let out a silent sigh. She'd come to the conclusion a long time ago that an ass like Tracy's had a built-in tractor beam, and men were helpless to resist it.

"So, Brandon," Heather said. "Alison tells me your grandmother died and you're taking over her matchmaking business."

He turned back. "That's right."

"Isn't that kind of a weird profession for a man?"

Alison cringed at the question, but Brandon seemed unfazed. "Yeah, I guess it is," he said. "But my grandmother did a lot of good for a lot of people. I'd like to pick up where she left off."

"What profession did you leave to become a matchmaker?"

"Real estate investment."

"Hmm. I bet you're one of those guys who flips houses."

"Actually, yeah. Houses, commercial space, apartment buildings—whatever netted the most money at the time. Unfortunately, that industry isn't looking so good these days."

Heather flicked her gaze to Alison, and she read it loud and clear. *See? This guy is a wheeler-dealer from way back. Stay on your toes.*

"So you were close to your grandmother?" Heather asked.

"Yeah. So were a lot of people. You should have seen her funeral. There must have been two hundred people there."

"That's nice."

He nodded. "A lot of the people there were ones she'd matched up. They were married. Happy. And grateful to her. That's when I made the decision to follow in her footsteps."

"So you're going to be finding people their soul mates?"

"That's right."

"Happily ever after? Till death us do part?"

"That's the goal."

"Ever been married yourself?"

"Nope," Brandon said. "Never have."

"Committed relationship?"

"Heather, *stop*," Alison said.

"I've been traveling all over the country for a long time now," Brandon said. "Hard to commit when you're here today, gone tomorrow. How fair would that be to a woman?"

Good answer, Alison thought, but Heather still looked skeptical.

"So you've never even had a committed relationship," Heather said. "Isn't your being a matchmaker kind of like a person who's never been in a kitchen trying to teach somebody how to cook?"

"Heather!" Alison said. "Will you *hush*?" Then she turned to Brandon. "Ignore her. She's always like this when she's off her meds."

"Yeah, I do crazy things when I'm not popping pills," Heather said. "Like hire a man to find me a man."

"Heather is just a skeptic," Alison said. "A great big *intrusive* skeptic. She doesn't even believe men landed on the moon."

"And I don't believe little green men have landed here, either," Heather said.

"Hmm," Brandon said. "I've always heard they were gray, not green."

"Their color is irrelevant," Heather said, "since they *don't exist*."

"I don't know. There's some pretty compelling evidence out there."

"Depends on how gullible you are."

"So how do you account for alien abductions?"

"Vivid dreams."

"Area Fifty-four?"

"Mass hysteria."

"Crop circles?"

"Teenage pranks."

"UFOs?"

"Weather balloons."

"Bigfoot?"

Heather drew back. "What does Bigfoot have to do with aliens?"

"He came from somewhere, didn't he?"

"Yeah. And I can't decide which is more rare. Bigfoot, or a matchmaking man."

"That's easy," Brandon said with a smile. "Bigfoot videos are a dime a dozen. But have you ever seen footage of a matchmaking man?"

"Exactly," Heather said, smiling too. "It's looking more and more like something you just made up."

Alison wanted to hide her face in her hands, but Brandon didn't miss a beat. "I admit it's a little unusual, but make no mistake. I *am* going to find Alison her perfect match."

A little shiver ran up Alison's spine. *God, I hope so. And I hope you do it before Heather puts out a contract on you.*

Tracy set a beer in front of Brandon, then looked disappointed when he grabbed it and stood up. "Think I'll play a little pool. It was nice to meet you, Heather." He turned to Alison. "And I'll see you tomorrow. Noon, isn't it?"

"Yeah. Noon."

As he walked toward the pool tables, Alison's head turned to watch as if it had assumed a life of its own. The man had the most perfect ass, showcased inside a pair of jeans that looked as if they were made to fit him and him alone. And she wasn't the only one staring. Tracy moved back down the bar to maintain a better line of sight, like a snake slithering after its prey. Alison had no doubt she would eat Brandon alive if he gave her half a chance.

"Tracy's such a slut," Alison muttered. "Why do you keep her around?"

"This is a bar," Heather said. "Most of our customers are men. Do you really have to ask?" Then she looked over at Brandon, her face falling into a frown. "He's too smooth. Something's up."

"Did you have to be so rude to him?"

"I wasn't rude. Just...inquisitive."

"*Inquisitive?* That's what you call that?"

"Come on, Alison! He's thirty-something years old, he's never been in a committed relationship, yet he's going to find a man for you?"

"He told you why. He traveled a lot."

"Doesn't matter why. He's never had what he says he can find for you. Am I wrong to think that's a little odd?"

"Well, no, but—"

"Look. I know how important this is to you. I just don't want that guy taking you for a ride. Keep your eyes open, okay? And not just to look at his pretty face."

Chapter 5

J ust before noon the next day, Alison parked by the curb in front of Brandon's house and stepped out of her car, astonished at the heat that already permeated every molecule of air she breathed. As she circled the house, that heat seemed to rise up off the sidewalk like an invisible apparition from hell. Even the sun-loving petunias that lined the flower beds looked sad and droopy, as if they'd like to fold up their petals and sink back into the ground for good.

Alison decided she'd add a summer cabin in Colorado to the wish list she'd been compiling in her mind since she was twenty years old, filled with those things she'd probably never have but were nice to think about. Already on the list were a yacht in the Mediterranean, an all-you-can-eat spree at an ice cream factory, and a private Bon Jovi concert.

Oh, yeah. And a husband.

She opened the back door and stepped inside the house, surprised to feel sultry air that was nearly as hot as the air outside. And Brandon was nowhere in sight.

She called out to him, but she was greeted with silence. She went to the foot of the stairs and called out again.

Still nothing. She thought about just sitting down to wait because surely he'd be along in a minute, but it was like a sauna in the house. Much more of this, and her makeup would melt right off her face.

She grabbed her phone. Dialed Brandon's number. She heard six rings before he finally picked it up.

"Alison," he said, a little breathlessly. "Oh, boy. Is it noon already?"

"Yeah. And it's my lunch hour, so I'm a little tight on time."

"Come around to the side of the house."

"What?"

"Not the driveway side. The other side."

And then he hung up.

Alison stared at her phone for several seconds. What was going on?

She left the house, circled back around to the front, and then crossed the lawn. As she came around the corner of the house, she finally saw Brandon. He was kneeling in front of an air-conditioning unit that looked to be about a hundred years old, a look of frustration on his face. The lid was off the unit, and tools were scattered all over the grass.

It had been oppressively hot for June in Texas, but for the first time, Alison couldn't have cared less. The heat made Brandon sweat. The sweat soaked his T-shirt. Which caused his T-shirt to cling to his torso. And that clingy shirt revealed the planes of his chest, the contour of his abs, and the slope of his shoulders as he worked. She knew her attraction to a sweaty man with tools was positively prehistoric, but once again she was a walking, talking cliché of womanhood. Vaguely she wondered if he noticed her dazed, transfixed reaction. Not that she could have done much about it, but it would have been nice to know if she was coming across as dumbstruck as she felt.

Sweat beaded on his forehead. He swiped the shoulder of his shirt across it, then turned and gave Alison a smile. "Sorry. Air conditioner problems. Guess it's a miracle this old thing has made it this far."

His face. Quit looking at his body and focus on his face. "Can you fix it?"

"Not sure. It's the fan motor. I've got the new part, but it's not going on like it's supposed to. Hear that vibration?" He sighed. "It's just hard to get the new blade balanced on the shaft. Fortunately, it only has to stay running until—" He stopped short. "Until fall. Prices will be cheaper then, and I can have a new unit installed."

"Uh...we have a meeting?"

"Can't go back into the house. It's too hot in there, and I'm a mess."

Yes. He was a mess. And if only every man on earth did messy the way Brandon did, the world would be a far, far better place.

"I guess we should reschedule," she said.

"Did you fill out the questionnaire?"

"Yes. But you really need to put the form online. It'd be easier to fill out."

"My grandmother wasn't exactly operating in the twenty-first century. Photo?"

"I e-mailed you one before I left the office."

"Let me see the questionnaire."

She pulled it from her purse and handed it to him. He began to read it, his brows drawing together thoughtfully.

Alison tried not to look at his long, strong fingers and the way his forearm muscles flexed as they flipped the pages. This was serious business, and she wasn't going to get distracted. She was going to stand firm and ensure she got the quality service she'd paid for. Before she left there, she wanted to be absolutely certain he knew enough about her and the man she was looking for that he could match them up with his eyes closed.

"So you're in marketing?" he said.

"I work in the marketing department of Spangler Sweets."

"Oh. So you're a creative type?"

"Mostly I deal with consumer statistics and focus groups."

He nodded, still looking at the questionnaire.

"I'm not sure that questionnaire is as comprehensive as it needs to be," Alison said. "All it asks is—"

Suddenly the air conditioner made a horrendous squeaking noise. Brandon tossed the questionnaire aside and stuck his hand inside the unit. He flipped something, and it fell silent.

"Damn it," Brandon muttered. "Sorry, Alison. Hold that thought for a minute." He looked around helplessly, holding his hand on the part inside the unit. "Would you hand me that wrench?"

She leaned over to grab it from the grass and handed it to him. He stuck it inside the unit and gave it a twist, his forearm straining and his bicep flexing. It was a sight so hypnotic that Alison couldn't have dragged her eyes away if a storm had struck. Thank God it wasn't tornado season.

Suddenly she heard high-pitched screams, then laughter. She glanced over the chain-link fence into the back-yard next door, where a couple of kids were splashing around in a wading pool.

"Those kids have the right idea," Alison said. "That's the way to cool off in this heat. Assuming you can't fix your air conditioner."

"Don't even think that."

"A wading pool is cheap."

"But a new zoned air unit isn't."

"They sure are having a good time over there," she said with a smile. "I remember playing in a blow-up pool just like that one with my brother when we were little."

"Do you mind helping me out again?" he asked.

"Sure."

"Hold this ruler for me." He set it on top of the motor next to the thingy that went up into the fan blade. "Right there. And don't move it."

She took hold of the ruler and held it where he asked her to. "What are you measuring?" she asked.

"The distance from the fan blade to the motor along the shaft."

"You act as if you've done this before."

"Not nearly enough to really know what I'm doing."

She came closer to Brandon so she could hold it steady, and she could actually feel the heat emanating from his body.

"You know, my dad's pretty handy," she told him. "He fixes everything around his house, including his air conditioner. I could get him to come over and take a look at it if you want me to."

"If I can't get this thing moving, I just might take you up on—*shit!*" He yanked his hand away from the unit.

"What's wrong?"

"Sliced my finger on the fan blade."

"How bad is it?"

"Never mind. Don't worry about it."

"It's bleeding."

"Not much."

"Brandon. It's *dripping*." She grabbed his hand and turned it over to get a good look at the wound. "That's pretty deep. Doesn't look as if it needs stitches, but it needs to be washed off."

"I'll run it under the garden hose in a minute."

"No. You need soap."

"After I finish here."

"When's the last time you had a tetanus shot?"

"Haven't got a clue. Just let me finish this, and—"

"What is with men, anyway?" she said. "What? They can sever a limb and swear it's a paper cut. Get in the house and clean that cut before you get a horrible infection." She reached into her purse and pulled out a few tissues. "Here. Wrap this around it so you don't bleed all over the house."

With a heavy sigh, Brandon came to his feet and grabbed the tissues. He wrapped them around his finger and headed inside the house. Alison followed him into the kitchen, where he went to the sink and washed out the wound. Then she handed him a couple more tissues to hold against it until the bleeding stopped.

"If it soaks through those," she said, "I have more. Press hard so the bleeding will stop."

Brandon rolled his eyes, but he did as she asked. As they waited, Alison looked around the kitchen. It was as inviting as his office was, with that turn-of-the-century charm she loved so much. Somewhere along the line somebody had added a few cabinets to bring the house into more modern times, along with a dishwasher and an updated range and oven, but that was about it. On one wall sat a huge fireplace with an arched hearth with what looked like the original andirons. The floors were original brick, and the kitchen staircase that led to the second floor had the original curved newels and elaborate balusters. Amazingly, all the owners over the years had pretty much left the place alone to be what it was meant to be.

"This is such a great house," she said with a smile. "It's unusual to see one this old that hasn't been screwed with linoleum or track lighting or—" She shuddered. "Paneling."

"It's a money pit. Not only does it need a new air unit, it needs new wiring throughout. The foundation needs work. The basement leaks."

"But it'll be worth every penny you put into it. This is a really hot area for renovation."

"Can't think about that now," he said. "Right now I need to concentrate on getting that air unit fixed."

Alison breathed deeply, then let her eyes drop closed. "I love houses like this one. You can almost smell the history."

"That's mold from the leaky basement."

"But it's so comfy and cozy," she said. "Look at how the afternoon sun streams into the breakfast room. Isn't it pretty?"

"All I see is my electric bill going through the roof."

"And here I thought you had a romantic soul. I mean, you're a matchmaker, aren't you?"

He turned away. "I guess it's all those houses I've

bought and sold over the years. I've always had to look at the bottom line."

Just then Alison heard a noise almost as horrendous as the squeaking of the air-conditioning unit. She turned, surprised to see a slender Siamese cat saunter into the kitchen. She leaped onto the windowsill in the breakfast room, then turned to look at Alison with her brilliant blue eyes.

"I didn't know you had a cat," Alison said.

"She was my grandmother's. One of the neighbors was keeping her until I moved in. I guess she's mine now."

"What's her name?"

"Jasmine."

Then she meowed again, a noise somewhere between a screech and a yowl. Alison wasn't sure, but she thought she saw the walls vibrate and the wallpaper come loose.

She laughed. "Big voice for such a little cat."

"The first time I heard her I thought somebody was strangling her."

Alison walked over to the window where the cat sat. Closer now, she could see a few gray hairs in the black mask on her face, and when she ran her hand down her back, she felt the prominent backbone of an older cat.

"How old is she?"

"Let's see ... my grandmother got her as a kitten when I was seventeen, I think. That makes her almost fifteen, so she's getting up there."

"Yeah, but I've heard of cats living to be twenty, so she's got plenty of life in her yet." Alison stroked all the way down to the crooked tip of her tail. "They say the crook in a Siamese's tail developed so she could hold her mistress's rings while she bathed."

"So that's a breed thing?" Brandon said. "I thought she mashed it in a door."

"She's such a sweet girl," Alison said, scratching behind her ears. The cat leaned into her, twisting her head around to get the full advantage of Alison's fingernails. When Alison finally pulled her hand away, the cat turned and patted her leg with her paw, begging for more attention.

"One of my cats does that," Alison said with a smile.

"One of your cats?" Brandon said. "How many do you have?"

"Three." She held up her palm. "Wait. I know what you're thinking. Don't even go there. Three is absolutely normal. *Four* means you're a crazy cat lady." She squeezed her eyes closed. "Please, God, don't send me one more stray kitten."

"So all yours are adopted?"

"I found them in the bushes outside my condo. They were only a few weeks old. Their mother had gotten hit by a car, so I took them in, telling myself I'd find homes for them. I bottle-fed them until they were old enough to be adopted."

"Then you decided to keep them instead?"

"*One*," she said. "That was all. But then, I thought 'Which one?' And I kept thinking 'Which one?' until they were about six months old. By then they were shredding my furniture and knocking things off my shelves and waking me up at six in the morning to be fed. At that point I'd have had to pay somebody to take them. So I thought, oh, what the hell. And I'm not even a cat person."

Brandon smiled. "You are now."

She nodded at Jasmine. "So are you. How's that working out for you?"

"How would you like to adopt her? You already have three. You wouldn't even notice another one."

"But then I'd be a crazy cat lady, remember?"

"Would that really be so terrible?"

"Yes! The only thing people poke more fun at than an unmarried man who still lives in his mother's basement is an unmarried woman with four cats."

"Sorry, Jasmine," Brandon said to the cat. "I tried, but it looks like you're stuck with me."

She meowed back at him. If you could call it a meow. It sounded more like the hinges squeaking on a thousand-year-old drawbridge.

Brandon pulled the tissues away from his wound. "I think the bleeding has stopped."

"Good. Put a Band-Aid on it."

"Uh…"

"I'm guessing you don't have a Band-Aid."

"Afraid not."

"Just a minute…" Alison dug through her purse and came up with a small red plastic Band-Aid dispenser.

Brandon looked stunned. "I didn't know they made Band-Aid dispensers."

"I have a breath mint dispenser, too," she said. "And one for stamps. Not that I send that many letters anymore, but—" She stopped, but too late. She'd already made herself sound like the biggest geek alive.

"So what else do you have in there?" Brandon asked.

She shrugged, looking away. "Just the usual stuff."

"The usual stuff is money and credit cards and makeup."

"Yeah. I have those."

Brandon tilted his head. "How about nail clippers?"

"Uh...yeah."

"A flashlight?"

She paused, feeling dumb again. *Geek, geek, geek.* "Yes."

"An umbrella?"

"Hey! That's *not* a weird thing to carry around. Who likes to get rained on?"

He looked at her carefully, his eyes narrowing. "Dental floss?"

Her heart skipped. "Dental floss? That's ridiculous. Please. I do *not* have dental floss."

He grinned. "Yes, you do."

"No, I *don't*."

"Liar."

Alison slumped with dismay. "Are you psychic? Is that the deal? Because if you are, this whole deal is *off*."

"Come on, Alison. It's not like I'd tell you what color panties you're wearing."

"Thank God for that."

"I mean, I *know* what color they are, but—"

"No, you do *not*!"

"Blue."

Alison tried not to react, but she felt her face heating up. Okay, so she was definitely a blue kind of girl. Pink was too prissy, white too virginal, red too slutty, beige too blah. After that there wasn't much left. Still...how did he *know*?

Brandon smiled. "Alison? Are you blushing?"

"Of course not," she snapped. "Will you just hold out your hand?" She pulled the backing off the Band-Aid and wrapped it around his finger. "There. Done. Now, go fix that air conditioner. And this time don't slice your finger halfway off."

She tossed her purse back over her shoulder and walked to the front door. They stepped out to the porch, where she pulled out her phone and brought up her calendar. "We need to reschedule our meeting. What day and time are good for you?"

"We don't need to reschedule."

"Come on, Brandon. My answers on that questionnaire don't tell you much."

"I know. You just copied over a lot of the stuff from your match dot com profile."

Alison froze. "How did you know that?"

"I read it."

"You're on match dot com?"

"Professional research."

"So what's wrong with my match dot com answers?"

"Have you found a husband on match dot com?"

Alison paused. "No."

"Well, there you go."

"But if that information isn't enough," she said, "how do you expect to help me unless we talk more?"

"Your questionnaire gives me the basics. But that isn't all I know about you."

"So what else did you do? Hack into my e-mail and look at my Facebook account?"

He laughed. "No. I try to keep it legal."

"Then what?" she said warily.

"I know you're a very trusting person. After all, you gave me fifteen hundred dollars to find you a husband under circumstances that were a little unusual."

True. But that hadn't been trust. That had been desperation.

"You're a good salesman," she said. "And frankly, the jury's still out on whether you can deliver."

"And I know you're a sympathetic person, or you wouldn't have taken in three homeless cats."

"I'm a sucker. Big difference."

"And you're not a status seeker."

"What makes you say that?"

"The cats again. Three pedigreed Persians says one thing. Three scruffy strays says something else."

"Hey, they found *me*, not the other way around."

"And you don't mind helping people."

"How do you know that?"

"You helped me when I was working on the air unit."

"What was I supposed to say? 'No, I won't hand you a wrench?'"

"And when I cut my finger."

"I don't like watching people bleed."

"And you're prepared for damned near anything. With what you have in that purse, you could land on a desert island and survive for six months."

She started to object to that, but could she really?

"But the number one thing I know about you is that you're family oriented."

"My answers on the questionnaire told you that."

"No. You're *really* family oriented. That's your number one trait in the man you're looking for. He has to want a family as much as you do."

"Why do you say that?"

He nodded next door. "You liked watching those kids playing in the wading pool."

"It's hot. Who wouldn't be eyeing a swimming pool?"

"They were making a lot of noise."

"They were just having fun."

"Right. That's how you see it. Some people would be annoyed by it, but you actually enjoyed it. And just watching them was nostalgic for you, because you remembered how you and your brother used to play in a pool just like it. I'm betting you had a close family growing up, with lots of nice memories, and that's what you want for yourself now. A close family. Happy kids." Brandon smiled. "How am I doing?"

How was he doing? He was right on the nose. *That* was how he was doing. And it was pretty damned unnerving. But hadn't he done the same thing to her the first time they'd met, with all that stuff about bridesmaid dresses and a subscription to *Modern Bride*?

"Yes," she said. "You're right. I want kids."

"Lots of them."

She frowned. "Who do you think I am? Octomom?"

"Eight at one time might not be on your agenda, but you definitely want to be a mother, and more than once. One who always has tissues and Band-Aids. Oh, yeah. And you're very close to your father."

Her heart gave a little jolt. "I give up. How do you know that?"

"Because you didn't think twice about offering his services as a handyman to a near stranger. And I'm betting he wouldn't hesitate to help whomever you wanted him to."

"Oh, he'd hesitate. He'd ask me all kinds of questions. 'Who needs help? What's the project? What tools do I need to bring? Where do I need to go? What time do I need to be there? Do I need to stop by the Home Depot? So what's wrong with this guy that he can't fix his own air unit?'"

Brandon winced. "He'd say that last thing?"

Alison smiled. "Oh, yeah. I'm afraid he's a little opinionated."

"And he'd do anything for his daughter."

He would. And Alison would do anything for him. She knew she should feel happy that Brandon seemed to have a handle on the truth—family was number one to her. But stating it all so clearly the way he had made her ache in a way she hadn't in a long time, and she felt even more desperate to fill the gaping holes in her life that seemed to widen with every day that passed. And as she looked at Brandon now, she had the most hopeless feeling that if he couldn't find her a husband, it was never going to happen.

"It's getting late," she said. "I need to get back to the office."

Brandon nodded. "Your friend Heather didn't seem to like me too much when we met yesterday. Any particular reason?"

She'd hoped he would overlook that. "She just thinks it's weird that my matchmaker is a man."

"I think it's a little more than that."

"She doesn't want me to get my hopes up."

"You mean she doesn't want me taking your money and giving you nothing in return."

"No, it's not that. Really. It—" She paused, then let out a sigh of resignation. "Okay. It's that."

"Why the skepticism?"

"We've known each other forever, and I love her to death. She's just kind of overprotective. Like a sister.

A pushy, intrusive, opinionated sister who doesn't know when to shut up sometimes."

"Sounds like the way you described your father."

"Yeah. I'm surrounded by them. People I love but want to kill sometimes. It's my cross-eyed bear."

"What?"

"Sorry. Make that 'cross to bear.'" She smiled. "When my brother and I were little, my mother used to say my father was her cross to bear. My brother thought she said cross-eyed bear. So now, every once in a while, I still— oh, hell. It'd dumb. Never mind. I have to go."

Brandon smiled. "Okay. I'll be in touch."

As she walked to her car, she thought, *Okay, what has Brandon learned today?* That she was a borderline crazy cat lady who kept an entire drugstore in her purse, mispronounced simple phrases, ran a homeless shelter for cats, and thought screaming children in wading pools were charming. Even if he were the best matchmaker ever born, what chance did he have to find a man who'd be compatible with all that?

And what if Heather was right? What if he really didn't know what he was doing? Then she really didn't have a prayer.

She got into her car and started the engine, telling herself that as long as he didn't put two men's photos next to each other and flip a coin on her behalf, everything was going to be just fine.

Chapter 6

Later that evening, Brandon sat on the sofa in his office with Alison's questionnaire on the coffee table in front of him. He'd grabbed a pile of files, intending to go through a few until he found a man to set her up with. But now, an hour later, he'd already returned to the file cabinets twice to retrieve more candidates, which he was sorting into three piles: *maybe, no*, and *hell no*. Actually, *hell no* had only one file in it. What had his grandmother been thinking when she'd taken on a client who thought his perfect match was a woman who loved taxidermy as much as he did?

He tossed one more file into the *no* pile, then looked up to see Tom come into the room. He stopped short, his gaze fanning over the sea of files Brandon had surrounded himself with. "What are you doing?"

"Matchmaking," Brandon muttered. "I'm glad you're home. You can help me."

"Me? What do I know about matchmaking?"

"About as much as I do."

"Hey, this was your insane idea, not mine."

"Do you want me as a partner on the Houston project or not?"

With a sigh of resignation, Tom sat down on the sofa with Brandon. Brandon scooped up a pile of files and slapped them onto his lap. "Here. Go through these."

"Whose dream man are you looking for?"

Brandon grabbed Alison's questionnaire with her photo attached and handed it to Tom. "Alison Carter. Here. Look at this."

"Hmm," he said, tilting his head as he looked at her photo. "She's kinda cute."

"Want to go out with her? She's looking for a man who wants to get married, have kids, buy a minivan, and take summer vacations at Disney World."

Tom dropped the questionnaire as if it were laced with botulism. "Not my type," he said, visibly shuddering.

"Don't sweat it. If I set a woman up with you, my business would be over." Brandon picked up another file and opened it. "Basically we're looking for the marrying kind. Family man. For her, that's a deal breaker."

"What is it with women who are obsessed with getting married?"

"Works both ways," Brandon said. "What is it with men who let themselves get hooked?"

"Good point."

Brandon couldn't understand Alison's undying need to be thrust into painfully boring domesticity for the rest of her life with a man who was probably equally boring, but who was he to judge?

"Looks aren't all that important to her, but he shouldn't be butt ugly. She has cats, so no pet allergies. Nonsmoker. Preferably a professional man. Solid income, at least."

Tom thumbed through one of the men's files. "I can't

believe your grandmother had all these clients. Why wasn't she a gazillionaire?"

"They're not all paying clients. She did a lot of networking at charity events, church functions, just about anywhere she went. She talked to friends of friends, got referrals here and there. Whenever she met people she thought would be a nice match for somebody in the future, she interviewed them and then built a file. Then if they fit one of her paying clients, she made the match."

"So only a small percentage of these people were actually paying her?"

"Yes. But it was only the paying customers who were guaranteed the matches."

"How did your grandmother ever make any sense of all these files?"

"She knew all her clients because she interviewed them in the beginning. I'm just going to have to wing it with the ones already here."

"If all these files were in a computer database, you could search them."

"Yeah, wouldn't that be nice? But it would take me forever to transfer everything myself. If I hired someone to do it, it would cost me a fortune. Can't spend every dime I make keeping a business alive that's going to be dead in six months." He sighed. "This is what I'm stuck with."

As Tom opened one of the files, Brandon pointed out the *maybe, no,* and *hell no* stacks. Unfortunately, the *no* stack continued to grow.

"Here's one," Tom said finally. "He's a dermatologist. Owns his own home. He'd like to start a family."

"Sounds perfect. Let me see."

Tom handed him the file, and Brandon slumped with dismay. "He's fifty-two years old. What kind of man wants to *start* a family at age fifty-two?"

"I know. Kinda scary. Does this client of yours have an upper age limit?"

"Forty."

"That narrows the field a lot."

"Yeah, I know. Keep looking."

"Aren't these files arranged by something? Age, height, underwear preference? *Something?*"

"Red for girls, blue for boys. After that, they're alphabetical. That's it."

After a few more minutes, Brandon found a nice-looking guy who owned a string of dry cleaners and had a great income, but he was divorced with kids and didn't want any more. Tom found a guy who was thirty-one and family oriented, but he wanted to raise that family in Costa Rica, and Alison specifically said she didn't want to leave the Dallas metroplex.

"How are you doing finding new clients?" Tom asked.

"Signed a guy this afternoon. Jack Warren. He's forty-eight, well off, and so busy with his computer consulting business that he says he doesn't have time to do a lot of dating in order to find a woman. He's divorced and looking for wife number two."

"How'd he feel about another man finding him a woman?"

"Actually, once he was over the shock of it, I convinced him that a guy knows best what another guy wants."

"One new client a week isn't going to cut it."

"My ad at *Dallas After Dark* comes out in two days. That should generate quite a bit of business."

Brandon hoped so, anyway. If it didn't, he was going to have to rethink his marketing strategy in a major way.

"Holy shit," Tom said suddenly.

"What?"

"I didn't know your grandmother visited prisons looking for clients."

"What are you talking about?"

"Check out this guy."

Tom handed Brandon the file he'd been looking at. The guy had the craggy face of a street fighter who'd been in a brawl or two, and dark, fathomless eyes that made Brandon wonder exactly what was behind them. His mouth was turned up in something like a smile, but it did little to take away the hardened criminal look.

Then he read his grandmother's handwritten note. *Very sweet man. Remind him to smile a lot.*

Sorry, Grandma, Brandon thought. *The smile's not helping.*

Brandon thumbed through the file. "Says here he owns a landscaping company. That's pretty normal."

"Except it also means he owns a whole bunch of razor-sharp gardening tools. Not much of a leap to serial killer, is there?"

Actually, it was a big leap, but Brandon couldn't blame Tom for the fact that it had crossed his mind. But judging from his grandmother's notes, the guy probably used his gardening tools strictly for gardening. Also judging from her notes, she'd never made a successful match for him. Fortunately, he was one of the few who hadn't returned Brandon's call when he was letting his grandmother's clients know he was taking over her business, so maybe Brandon wouldn't have to pick up where his grandmother left off.

"I don't believe it," Tom said, reading from another file. "Here's a guy whose favorite movie is *Steel Magnolias*."

"So he's sensitive. Women say they like that."

"They say they do, but they really don't. What they really want is a man who'll drag them back to their caves and ravish them, not sit around the campfire and cry. It's in their DNA."

"What tells you that?"

"An article in *Psychology Today*. There was a copy in my doctor's office. It also said that people who resemble each other physically make the most successful couples. Ones who are at the same level of attractiveness."

"So looking alike means a couple will be happy?"

"That's the theory."

"If that were true, every man on earth would marry his sister."

"No. Think about it. People naturally gravitate toward people who look like them. You never see a really hot guy with an ugly woman. And you never see a beautiful woman with an ugly guy unless he's loaded."

True.

Brandon opened the next file. The guy was thirty-four and never been married. Worked in pharmaceutical sales. The answers on his questionnaire mirrored Alison's pretty closely. And he was definitely looking for a wife. He wasn't champing at the bit for children, but it was an issue he was willing to discuss.

"I think I have one," Brandon said. He handed the file to Tom. "What do you think?"

Tom thumbed through the file. "Not bad. The family thing is there, and where kids are concerned, she could probably talk him into—" Tom's face suddenly crinkled. "Uh-oh. He's a vegan."

"Yeah, I saw that. What is that, exactly?"

"They don't eat animal products. Or wear them, either. And no dairy or eggs. I had a girlfriend once who was a vegan. Try taking her out to dinner."

Brandon couldn't see a guy like that being compatible with Alison. Maybe it was the fact that she was so family focused. Family automatically brought to mind an image of people gathered around a table at Thanksgiving, and they weren't getting ready to slice the tofu.

"Okay," Brandon said. "He's not perfect. But he's the best we've found yet. Put him over there and keep looking."

"I've been through my stack," Tom said. "Got any more?"

Brandon went to where the files were stored, dismayed that he'd been all the way through cabinet number one and was starting in on number two. He grabbed an armful of files, handing half of them to Tom and going through the other half himself. Three files later, he had another candidate.

"Okay," Brandon said. "Here's one who's close. He works as a software engineer for a big tech company. He's interested in having a family, and...well, crap. He has three dogs, and Alison has cats. Think that's a problem?"

"Nope. Cats and dogs aren't natural enemies. They can get along just fine, assuming the adjustment phase is slow and thorough."

Brandon looked at him dumbly. "Is there any dumb little factoid you don't know?"

Tom shrugged. "There was a copy of *Dog Fancy* on the table in the waiting room when I was getting my tires rotated."

"He has another downside," Brandon said. "He's only five seven. She's five six."

"Is height a deal breaker for her?"

"Her questionnaire says it isn't. But it seems shallow to say it, so I'm betting most women won't admit that it is."

Brandon laid both men's photos on the table in front of him, then put Alison's in between them. "Okay. Which one does she look more like?"

"The guy on the left."

"The short one. Think she'll overlook that?"

"Hard to say. I think she'd have more of an issue with that than the vegan thing, but I don't know." Tom reached into his pocket, pulled out a quarter, and tossed it to Brandon. "Love's a crapshoot, remember? Or should I say a coin toss?"

Brandon didn't like the idea of leaving it totally to chance. He liked Alison, and he really did want to set her up with the right guy. But he didn't see a clear winner here, so what the hell?

He poised the coin to toss it. "Okay, heads I set her up with Vegan Guy, tails Mr. Vertically Challenged." He flipped the coin, caught it in his hand, and slapped it onto the back of his other hand.

"Heads," Brandon said. "Vegan Guy it is. Let's go have a beer."

Chapter 7

The next afternoon at five o'clock, Alison sat at a table in the basement meeting room with five other board members of the East Plano Preservation League, listening to Judith Rittenaur drone endlessly about their mission statement. Judith was an uptight, sour-faced woman who thought things like mission statements were as critically important as Middle East peace accords. Alison thought they fell somewhere between the list of pool rules at her condo complex and a sticky note reminding her to take out the trash.

She shot Heather a subtle *shoot me now* look, and Heather returned the sentiment with a barely-stifled yawn. Alison returned to doodling around the edge of her agenda with a black Sharpie. If only that Sharpie had been an ice pick, she could have stabbed it into her brain and put herself out of her misery.

"Read it again with those changes," Bea Bennett said, sounding weary in her role as president of the board. Bea was a sixty-five-year-old retired nurse. Age and experience had given her both the capacity to know what was important and the ability to wade through the crap that wasn't. Unfortunately, protocol prohibited her from leaping over the table and ripping that piece of paper right out of Judith's hands.

Judith cleared her throat, as if she was about to deliver a State of the Union address. "To preserve, promote and serve as an advocate for the irreplaceable historic buildings of East Plano for the economic and cultural benefit of all citizens, as well as foster an appreciation of their historic significance and encourage neighborhood revitalization through preservation, planning, and re-adaptation of the existing cityscape."

All Alison heard was *blah, blah, blah*. Judging from the looks on the faces of the other board members, serial *blahs* were all they'd heard, too. Judith had taught eighth grade English in a private Christian school for the past thirty years, which she thought gave her the moral duty to litter their mission statement with indecipherable crap only a linguist could understand.

"Re-adaption of the existing cityscape?" Heather said. "Don't you just mean 'renovation'?"

"Well...yes."

"Then why not just say that?"

"Because dull language is the plague of our civilization, that's why."

"It's already too long even without all that exciting language," Heather said. "A single short, concise sentence should be plenty."

Across the table, Judge Jimmy shifted his considerable bulk until his chair groaned and squeaked, shaking his head with disgust. "She's right. Damned thing's longer than *War and Peace*."

"Am I the only board member who takes this seriously?" Judith said.

"We're not the freakin' United Nations," Judge Jimmy said. "Whittle it down."

Judge Jimmy Todd had spent thirty years on the bench as a civil court judge, and his claim to fame was cutting to the chase. His hearings and trials were shorter than other judges' by half. *Now, get the hell out of my courtroom*, he'd say once things were over, and people generally did. Quickly.

Now that Jimmy was retired, his wife had suggested he volunteer for something to get him out of the house. Most people liked it better when Jimmy stayed home and irritated his wife instead. Not Alison. Anybody who kept these board meetings short and to the point was her best buddy.

"But it needs to be long to get our mission across," Judith said. "Mission statements guide an organization on its mission. You don't shortchange your mission statement. If you shortchange your mission statement, then, well...you don't know..."

"What your mission is?" Heather said.

Judith's lips tightened, looking like two slices of salami that had been left out in the sun.

"The way I see it," Heather said sweetly, "it's a mission just to write the mission statement."

Judith was totally humorless, but she did recognize sarcasm when she heard it, particularly when it came from Heather. Last year, Judith had proposed a really dumb change to the bylaws, then tried to strong-arm a couple of the more wimpy board members at the time into voting for it. That had been Heather's first board meeting, and it was her input that swayed everyone back to the side of reason. That had been more than enough to earn her

Judith's eternal wrath. Heather left that meeting swearing she'd never come back, and it had taken two martinis at McCaffrey's and a lot of begging before Alison convinced her to stay.

Finally they worked on some of the verbiage until most people seemed to agree on it, only to have Karen the Clueless ask what the difference was between a vision statement and a mission statement, launching another pointless discussion. Karen was a homely little woman in her late thirties, whom Judith had thought would be a perfect board member because she was an interior designer. As it turned out, she'd gotten that interior design degree from an Internet site that specialized in getting gullible people to spend hundreds of dollars to get a piece of paper worth absolutely nothing. She was very sweet, but to date, her chief contribution to the board had consisted of keeping the plants in the room healthy by exhaling carbon dioxide. Alison fingered her Sharpie again, wondering if it was pointed enough to penetrate her skull if only she swung it hard enough.

"Judith," Bea said, "why don't you finalize the new statement, e-mail it to everybody on the board for their review, and we'll vote on it at our next meeting?"

"Why can't we vote on it now?"

"Because if we vote on it now," Bea said, "we can't vote on it next time, and since I already said we're voting on it next time, voting on it now would be pointless."

While Judith's brain was busy trying to sort all that out, Bea glanced at her agenda. "Okay. Committee reports. Alison, do you have all the houses for this year?"

"Yes. We have all four." Alison reached into her notebook. "Here are some photos, along with the owners and addresses."

Alison passed out the info sheets on each house, and she felt a little thrill when Bea's eyes widened with surprise.

"You did it?" Bea said. "You got Edith Strayhorn to let us use her house?"

"I took her to tea last Saturday and told her it would be a shame if the residents of Plano never got to see the inside of such a perfect example of late nineteenth century Queen Anne architecture. She still wasn't thrilled at the prospect, but she finally said yes."

"We've been trying to get her house for years," Bea said. "Good job."

Alison was still glowing over that achievement. Edith's house was a landmark in East Plano, rising in stately elegance on 15th Street. The other houses on the block were merely pale imitators.

"So what do you guys think of the other houses?" she said.

"I like the one-story bungalow," Karen said.

In spite of the fact that the Strayhorn house was a wet dream for anyone who liked historical architecture, the bungalow was Alison's favorite. It looked like a storybook house, with ivy climbing up trellises, beds overflowing with flowers, and the kind of front porch where people sank into wicker chairs, drank lemonade, and stayed a while. Also on the list were an early twentieth century home with fish scale and diamond shingles on the gables, and an elaborate Victorian-era cottage with a sunburst pattern above the front door.

"I've seen this Victorian cottage," Judith said, pointing

at one of the sheets and crinkling her nose as if she'd smelled rotten eggs sitting in a pile of dog poop. "It's at the end of the street next door to a gas station."

"That's what older areas of town tend to be like," Alison said. "If we excluded houses next to gas stations and convenience stores, we'd never be able to get houses for the tour."

"Convenience store?" Judith said, drawing back with horror. "Are you telling me one of them is next to a *convenience store*?"

Alison sighed. Had she *said* that? "Judith. That was just an example."

"But what a great idea," Heather said. "If we run out of refreshments, we can hop next door for a couple of bottles of Gatorade and a box of Ding Dongs."

Judge Jimmy and Bea snickered a little at that. Karen got a quizzical look on her face that said she thought Heather might actually be serious. And Judith looked at Heather as if she were the most shameless human being ever to draw breath.

"We need to get another house," Judith said.

"Nah," Heather said. "One next to a gas station is no big deal. Beats the one last year that was next to a whore-house."

Every bit of color drained away from Judith's face, making her look even pastier than she already was. "*What* did you say?"

"Nothing," Alison said. "She didn't say anything."

"It was that little cottage on Sixteenth Street," Heather went on. "Those two women who lived next door did a booming business."

Alison's eyes drifted closed. *Ah, God. Heather,*

why must you always say what everybody else is thinking?

"We never knew for sure what those girls did for a living," Bea said quickly. "Now, next on the agenda—"

"Yeah, we did," Judge Jimmy said with a knowing nod. "I know hookers when I see 'em. They were definitely hookers."

"But Judith doesn't want to *hear that*," Bea said, "so maybe we shouldn't *talk about it*."

Judith glared at Bea. "You told me they were actresses and that was stage makeup."

"Well," Heather said, "sometimes there *is* a lot of acting involved in—"

Alison kicked Heather under the table. Bea cleared her throat and looked at her agenda again. "Okay. Photographs of the houses for the program. Alison, can you do that again this year?"

"No problem."

"Okay. On to food and beverage. Karen?"

"Maggie's Café is donating appetizers, as always," Karen said. "And Brennan's Beer and Wine has agreed to donate the wine. As always."

And, as always, Karen had poured her heart and soul into the project, always searching for new and exciting ways to improve the event. *Atta girl, Karen. Keep breathing.*

And, as always, Judith's mouth scrunched up with irritation the moment Karen spoke the word "wine." She wasn't above preaching that the path to hell was littered with empty alcohol bottles. Alison pitied the poor kids who had her for a teacher. If they listened to Judith, prom night was going to be a real bore.

"I just want it to be known that I'm against serving alcohol at this event," Judith said.

"I believe we're all aware of that," Bea said.

"The bottom line," Heather said, "is that alcohol loosens people up. Mimosas in the morning, wine and beer in the afternoon. They'll buy more raffle tickets. We'll make more money."

"You're a CPA," Judith said. "Of course all you think about is the bottom line. But this isn't just about the money."

"So it's not about the money?" Heather said. "Hmm. Then somebody needs to define 'fund-raising' for me."

Judith's face got all red and crinkly at that, and by the time the meeting was over, she still looked like a dried-up cranberry. She gathered her belongings and marched from the room with a snotty dismissiveness that made Alison wish she'd trip over a trash can and fall flat on her face.

"Sorry about the whorehouse thing," Heather said as she and Alison walked up the stairs with Bea. "When Judith is around, my mouth starts moving and I can't stop it."

"Don't worry about it," Bea said. "If not for the comic relief, I'd probably haul out my gun and blow her brains out."

"You carry a gun?" Heather said.

"Hell, yes." She looked back and forth between Alison and Heather. "Don't you?"

"Uh...no," Alison said.

"What kind of Texans are you?"

"Ones who don't want to shoot ourselves in the foot," Heather said.

"Yeah, I used to be uptight about guns, too. Then about ten years ago I got mugged in the parking garage coming off the night shift at Med City. I've been packing ever since." She patted her purse and gave them a smile. "And even if the law doesn't allow it, it makes me happy just to know I could take Judith out."

Alison knew there was a reason she liked Bea. They had the same homicidal fantasies.

"We're going for a drink at McCaffrey's," Alison said. "Want to come along?"

"Can't. My book group's tonight. We're reading an autobiography of a one-legged woman who climbed Mt. Everest. Only one leg, but plenty of balls. I like that."

Well. What an interesting woman that would be. Anatomically speaking.

"Next time then," Alison said.

Bea nodded and climbed into her ancient Jeep, and Alison and Heather headed down the street toward McCaffrey's.

"Thank God," Heather said. "If Judith ends up with a hole in her head, Bea's an even better suspect than I am."

"I swear next year I'm booking a tour home next to a crack house."

"Judith would have a heart attack," Heather said. "Oh, wait. That's not a bad thing. Bea would save a bullet." They turned on 15th Street to head west. "I don't like old buildings. I hate meetings. I want to rip the head off anybody who even speaks the words 'mission statement.' And people like Judith Rittenaur make me insane. So tell me again why I'm on that board?"

"Because you're a CPA, our last treasurer embezzled

two thousand dollars, and we needed somebody honest."
She paused. "And I begged."

"Oh, yeah," Heather said with a weary frown.

"So you don't want to help with the home tour this
year?"

"If somebody else collects the money, I'll put it in the
bank. Does that count?"

"Old houses are nice," Alison said. "Stable. Comfortable. Permanent."

"Drafty. Musty. Creaky. With spiders and rats in the basement. I like my brand-new condo just fine, thank you."

Just then Alison's phone rang. She looked at the caller
ID, and her heart did a tight little somersault.

"It's him," Alison said.

"Who?"

"Brandon."

"So answer it."

She stopped and punched the talk button. "Hello?"

"Hey, Alison. Brandon Scott. I just wanted to let you
know I have your first match."

Alison's heart was suddenly beating double time. "You
do?"

"Yep. And you're going to love him."

Brandon sounded so confident that he might has well
have said, *I found you a husband. Put on a wedding dress
and be at the church at four*, which made the tiny hairs on
Alison's arms stand up with excitement.

"Good," Alison said, trying to play it cool. "That's
good. Tell me about him."

"I'll e-mail you his photo and his information," Brandon said. "Then you can get back to me and tell me if it's
a go."

"But what if he doesn't want to go out with me?"

"I already talked to him. He's looking forward to meeting you."

So he'd seen her profile. And her photo. And he wanted to meet her anyway?

No. She had to stop this. The worst thing she could do was act like a loser no matter how many times she'd lost.

"Just a minute..." Brandon said, and Alison heard the clacking of a keyboard in the background. "There. I sent it to you. Can you give me a call back once you decide?"

"Yeah. Sure."

"I already know what your answer's going to be," Brandon said, that self-assurance coming through loud and clear once again. "But I'll wait patiently, anyway."

She could actually hear the smile in his voice, which made a smile pop out on her own lips. His positive attitude was as contagious as the flu.

"So he has a match for you?" Heather said after she hung up.

"Yes," Alison said, trying not to sound smug. "He e-mailed me some information about him."

Heather grabbed Alison by the arm and pulled her over to a nearby bench. "Let's have a look."

Alison swiped through a few screens on her phone and pulled up Brandon's e-mail. "Okay," she said. "His name is Greg Faraday."

"Alison Faraday..." Heather said, trying the name out. "Okay. That'll work."

For a long time now, Heather had been insistent about first and last names sounding good together, an obsession that began about the time she'd dated a guy whose last name was Feather.

"He's a pharmaceutical salesman," Alison said. "Lives near the West Village."

"Hmm. High-rent district." Heather leaned in for a look, then raised an eyebrow. "Six-figure income, huh? Yeah, right. That's what they all say."

"This isn't match dot com. These men are thoroughly screened."

"How old is he?"

"Thirty-four. His profile says he wants to get married, and he's open to the idea of having children."

"Open to the idea? Does that mean he really doesn't want kids, but he doesn't want to say so?"

Alison rolled her eyes. "It probably means that he's open to the idea of having children. Will you stop reading everything under the sun into this?" She scrolled down, pleased to see he actually admitted to liking action-adventure movies and sports cars, and there wasn't a word about walks in the park and heart-to-heart talks while sitting in front of a roaring fire with a glass of fine wine. Finally. A man who didn't pander to a woman just to get a date, then plop himself in front of Sylvester Stallone movies and NASCAR and holler at his woman to make him a sandwich.

"Oh, my," Alison said, trying not to swoon. "He's six feet tall."

"Yeah? Subtract four inches for exaggeration, and he's only five eight."

"Once again," Alison said impatiently, "these candidates are thoroughly screened by my matchmaker. He makes sure they're telling the truth."

She was surprised at how good it felt to say that. She finally had somebody on her side in the battle of the sexes, somebody who was looking out for her best interests. Somebody with a smart, discerning mind pre-screening the men who wanted to date her. Never again would she meet a guy online and then find out later that he was tall, dark, and handsome only in a roomful of ugly albino dwarfs.

Then she scrolled down to the man's photo, and the slow burn of excitement she'd felt for the past few minutes turned into a full-fledged bonfire.

"Wow," Heather said. "Not bad."

No. Not just "not bad." He looked good. *Really* good. He had sandy brown hair, green eyes, and a nice smile. He looked pleasant and responsible and friendly, the kind of man she might actually be able to have a future with.

No. Stop. Don't jump the gun. Last time you thought any old guy would do, you ended up with Randy.

"So are you going to go out with him?" Heather asked.

Alison swallowed the *hell, yes* that almost shot out of her mouth. "He looks like a decent candidate," she said instead. "Why shouldn't I give him a try?"

"Just watch yourself," Heather said. "And remember First Date Protocol."

"Always." *Wherever you're going, meet him there. If he rambles on about his mother, run. And no matter how hot he is, no sex on the first date.*

Alison looked back at Greg's photo and couldn't resist feeling a little vindicated. "It looks as if my matchmaker may have come through for me, huh?"

"We'll see," Heather said. "Come on. Let's go have that drink."

A few minutes later, they came through the door of McCaffrey's. The early evening crowd was light, with soft country music playing. Tony leaned over the bar as they approached and gave Heather a quick kiss.

"How was the meeting?" he asked them.

"Your wife is a smart ass," Alison said.

"Ah. Judith Rittenaur must have been there." He smiled at Heather. "You just can't keep quiet, can you?"

"I need something to entertain me during those damned meetings." She rolled her eyes. "Now I know why the last treasurer embezzled two grand and disappeared."

Alison started to pull out a stool to sit down, only to see a familiar face at the other end of the bar. She came to attention.

"My father's here again," she said, her eyes narrowing. "What's my father doing here?"

"Uh...having dinner?" Tony said.

Alison looked at her father's plate, and even at this distance, she could tell what was on it. And she was *not* happy about it.

"Has he been coming in a lot lately?" she asked Tony.

"Well...yeah."

"And you didn't tell me?"

"He kinda...swore me to silence."

"Tony!"

"Hey! Haven't you ever heard of bartender-customer confidentiality?"

"Oh, for God's sake," Alison muttered. "Who do you think you are? A priest?"

Tony looked at Heather, and Alison read his expression loud and clear. *Poor Charlie is so screwed.*

"There's bound to be something for me to do in the kitchen," Heather said, already walking away. "Call me when the bleeding stops."

Chapter 8

As Heather hurried away, Alison walked down the length of the bar. "Dad? What are you doing here?"

He froze, his fork halfway to his mouth. "Oh. Hey, there, sweetie."

"What are you eating?"

His fork continued its journey into his mouth, and he talked as he chewed. "What does it look like I'm eating?"

"Chicken fried steak and onion rings. My God. Do you have any *idea* how much fat is in those things?"

"Yep. That's what makes them so damned good." He grabbed an onion ring, swirled it in ketchup, and stuffed it into his mouth.

Tony looked over his shoulder as he poured a beer. "Hey, I tried to sell him on the turkey burger, but he wasn't buying."

"Only pussies eat turkey burgers," Charlie said to Alison. "You want your old man to look like a pussy?"

"I want my old man to live to *be* an old man," Alison said. "What good does it do for me to clean out your kitchen and fill it with decent food if you just come here and eat this stuff?"

"You're a broken record, just like your mother was.

Back then it was Dr. Whatever's protein diet. If you ate carbs, you were going to die. I ate carbs. I didn't die."

"Cholesterol is different." Alison slid onto a barstool next to him. "If your cholesterol is too high, your arteries will get all clogged, and then you'll have a heart attack. Do you want to have a heart attack?"

"How about I eat some green stuff once in a while? Will that make you happy?"

"As long as the green stuff isn't guacamole dip and a margarita."

"Oops," Tony said to Charlie. "Looks like she's on to you."

Charlie glared at him. "Hey, kid. Don't you have some other customers to bother?"

Tony just smiled and moved on down the bar to set beers in front of a couple of the regulars.

"How was your doctor's appointment this morning?" Alison asked.

"Like every other doctor's appointment. They poke around on you, stick you for blood, tell you to pee in a cup, and send you home."

"When do you get the results of your lab tests?"

"When they call me."

"Which is going to be—?"

"When the phone rings."

Alison sighed. "Are you taking your medication?"

"It gives me the runs."

"But are you *taking* it?"

"Yes, I'm taking it." He slid his plate toward her. "Here. Why don't you eat some of these onion rings if you don't want me to?"

"I can't," Alison said on a sigh. "They go straight to my hips."

"Suit yourself," he said.

But as he was pulling the plate back, she grabbed it. "Well, maybe just one."

She doused an onion ring with ketchup and took a bite, feeling as if she'd just been transported to heaven. Good Lord—was there anything better than a big ol' greasy fried onion ring? *Anything?*

"So what's new with you?" Charlie asked.

Alison started to tell him she was going on a date with a new man, but he'd only ask her where she'd met him. She couldn't lie—her father had the eyes and ears of a human lie detector. And then the rant would begin. If he thought a guy who ate turkey burgers was a pussy, he'd definitely go off on a matchmaking man.

"Job okay?" Charlie asked.

"Yeah. Focus groups out the wazoo. Turns out people love chocolate-covered pretzels, but they hate pretzels with chocolate in the middle. Go figure."

Her father stopped eating and looked at her. "Pretzels with chocolate in the middle? How do they do that?"

"I don't really know," Alison said. "Maybe the same way they get that cream in the middle of a Twinkie."

Her father shrugged and kept on eating.

"Heather and I just got back from a board meeting of the Preservation League," Alison told him. "The home tour is going to be great this year."

"I don't get it," Charlie said. "People pay good money to see inside other people's houses. What's with that?"

"It's because they're historic homes."

"So's mine, but nobody's beating down my door wanting to see it."

"Dad, your house was built in 1972. Not exactly a banner year for interesting architecture."

"Good thing. I don't like strangers in my house."

"That's because you're a grumpy old man. Next you'll be yelling at kids to get off your lawn."

"Nah. I like kids. It's adults I can't stand."

Her father's crabbiness was nothing new. He'd been that way since Alison could remember, but underneath that gruff exterior was a surprisingly big heart and a giving nature. Not that there weren't strings attached. He'd give a person the shirt right off his own back, but not before he told him exactly how to wash it, hang it, and wear it. Men didn't come any more opinionated than Charlie Carter, and Alison was still in awe that he'd managed to find and marry the one woman on earth he couldn't intimidate. The way the two of them had gone at it sometimes would have convinced a casual observer that divorce court was just around the corner.

Charlie, do I look like the maid to you? Pick up your damned newspapers off the bathroom floor.

Listen to me, Lorena. I don't care if I end up weighing four hundred pounds. I want Bud. Not Bud Light. They made that Bud Light crap just to get girls to drink beer.

PMS? You're damned right I have PMS! It stands for Pass My Shotgun, which means you'd better sleep with one eye open, buster.

Hey, Lorena! What the hell is with that new laundry soap? It makes my clothes smell like a freakin' flower garden. Another man smells that, I'm gonna get my ass kicked.

But no matter how sharp the words were that they threw at each other, they seemed to bounce right off. As a child, Alison had never sensed animosity. The older she got, the more she understood the underlying fondness they shared, and by the time she was a teenager, she saw it as a dance of pure love. They'd hurl their half-hearted insults, and then five minutes later Alison would glance into the kitchen to see her father goose her mother in the ribs as she washed her hands at the sink. She'd spin around and he'd pull her into a kiss, then slap her on the fanny as he headed back out the door.

And so it went for thirty-four years, right up to her mother's last hours. *Find another woman, Charlie*, she'd said. *You're not happy unless you have somebody to torment.* But Alison still remembered the tears in her mother's eyes as she spoke, and the way her father had held her hand in a desperate grip, silently begging her not to go.

That seemed like a thousand years ago. Another lifetime. And her father had never even looked at another woman since then, no matter how often Alison encouraged him to. He said he and Blondie got along just fine by themselves, but the company of a golden retriever went only so far when it came to filling the void in his life. And as much as Alison loved her three cats, they couldn't do the job for her, either.

"Gotta go, sweetie," Charlie said. "Need to let Blondie out before she pees on the rug."

"I'll see you on Thursday for movie night."

"Fine. But we're not watching another one of those girly things. I'm still getting over *Titanic*."

Alison frowned. "A ship sank. I thought you'd like that."

"Yeah, and if that DiCaprio kid and Whatserface

hadn't gotten in the way, I might have been able to enjoy it."

"Don't worry, Dad. We'll make sure there are cops and guns and car chases. And maybe some kung fu."

"Now you're talking." Charlie slid off the stool and tossed a few bills on the bar.

"Promise me you'll at least try the turkey burger next time," Alison said. "With a side of coleslaw, or maybe a green salad."

He made a face. "That sounds like crap."

Sounded like crap to Alison, too, but she didn't have clogged arteries. "You'll thank me at your ninetieth birthday party."

"No thanks. I don't want to live to be ninety."

"That's because you're not eighty-nine."

"You need to stop worrying about me," he said as he walked away. "I'm healthy as a horse, unless you count the damned hemorrhoids. I'll see you on Thursday."

"Hey, Dad."

He turned back.

"What do you know about air conditioners?"

Charlie shrugged. "Enough to make sure they stay running. Why do you ask? Somebody need some help?"

"Not sure yet. Stay tuned."

"You just give me a call, okay? I'll hop right over."

When Alison hadn't heard from Greg by midafternoon the next day, she was starting to think maybe he didn't exist after all and Brandon really had skipped town with her fifteen hundred bucks. She was up to her eyeballs in a report comparing consumer opinions about the crispness of their new peanut butter sandwich cookies. They had to be tough enough to stand up to milk dunking, but not so tough they cracked molars. Judging from the feedback on the prototype, something needed to change or Spangler Sweets was going to be paying a lot of dental bills.

She eyed the Mallorific bar on the corner of her desk. She'd put it there that morning as today's test to see how long she could go without ripping it open and snarfing it in three heavenly bites. She checked her watch. Two forty-five. If she went until three o'clock, she'd set a new record. Eventually—say, by the time she retired—she'd be able to go an entire day without succumbing to her sweet tooth in spite of the fact that she worked at Willy Wonka's chocolate factory.

The truth was that just about everyone who worked for Spangler Sweets was addicted to some product it produced, and most of those people were just a little bit overweight. Okay, most were downright hefty. A good percentage of her co-workers would probably accept regular home shipments of Choco-Pretzels or Coconutty Drops in lieu of health insurance and a decent pension. It was a daily struggle for Alison to keep her hands off the merchandise, which was spread far and wide throughout the building. On the other hand, it was nice to work in a place where she could stand next to her co-workers and feel thin by comparison.

She'd held this job for just over a year and loved it, particularly when she compared it to her last job. When she graduated from college, marketing jobs had been few and far between, so to pay the bills, she'd applied for the loan officer training program at Southwestern Savings Bank. After several years doing the most boring job imaginable, for which she was entirely unsuited, she'd gotten this job at Spangler Sweets and had been thankful ever since.

When her phone rang a few minutes later, she had to dig under mounds of paper and a Subway sack before she found it. When she saw Greg's name on the caller ID, her heart kicked up a notch. Before she picked it up, she took a deep, calming breath through her nose and let it out through her mouth, which was the only thing of value that had stuck with her from the yoga class from hell.

As it turned out, Greg sounded nice. Normal. As if he'd never had even a passing thought about having two women in his bed at once, blowing his nose on a cloth napkin, or coming out of the closet. A few minutes later, they'd made a date for seven on Saturday night at Sonoma Bistro, a trendy wine bar in the West Village. He offered to pick her up. A nice gesture, but a violation of First Date Protocol would have doomed the date from the start. By the time she hung up, her faith in Brandon had risen. Just a little. No sense in getting all girly excited when so much could still go wrong.

"Hey, Alison."

The voice was so close behind her that Alison nearly jumped out of her chair. She turned to see Lois Wasserman hanging over her like a vulture. Lois was approximately as wide as she was tall, a dead ringer for Rosie O'Donnell. Assuming, of course, that Rosie gained fifty pounds, bleached her hair, and then teased it into a fright wig.

Lois nodded down at the Mallorific bar on the corner of Alison's desk. "You gonna eat that?"

"Yeah. I'm gonna eat it."

"You are?"

"Yeah."

"You sure?"

"Yeah. I'm sure."

Alison turned back to her spreadsheets again, which should have been a signal to any member of the civilized world to turn around and walk away. Not Lois. She was clearly raised by those vultures she loved to imitate—a flock of overbearing, overeating creatures that had taught her how to circle unobtrusively, then go in for the kill. Several seconds later when Lois was still standing there, Alison turned back with a frustrated sigh.

"Lois. There are plenty more in the kitchen."

"Plumbers are in the kitchen. The sink backed up all over the floor."

"I thought you kept a stash at your desk."

"I'm on a diet."

"You're on a diet, but you want my Mallorific bar?"

"I didn't say it was a good diet."

Lois shifted her considerable bulk from one foot to the other, still focused on that Mallorific bar, annoying Alison to no end. In fact, she annoyed just about everybody who worked there. Probably the only reason she still had a job was that, by some freak of nature, she just happened to be an amazing graphic artist. She could wear a wrinkled pea green blouse, a multicolored broomstick skirt, and flip-flops to the office, only to turn around and produce work so beautiful it made the bigwigs weep with joy. It was a mystery nobody had ever been able to figure out.

But right now, Alison had the most unsettling feeling that if she kept saying no about the Mallorific bar, Lois would peck her eyeballs out.

"Take it," she said finally.

"What?"

"Take the candy bar."

"Are you sure?"

"I'm sure."

"Is it your last one? I don't want to take your last one."

"Yes, it's my last one. On second thought—"

Before Alison even knew what was happening, Lois was on that candy bar like a vulture on a hyena carcass, ripping open the wrapper with a flick of her wrist and then digging her beak—uh, *teeth*—right into it.

"Sounded like you were making a date earlier," Lois said as she gnawed through the gooey lump of marshmallow, cashews, and chocolate. "Were you making a date?"

"Yeah. I was making a date. Thanks for eavesdropping. How else would I know you care?"

"Must be nice to have a date. I haven't had a date in forever. That customer service guy Jonathan asked me out last week, but he stinks."

"Stinks?"

"Yeah. He stopped wearing deodorant. Said it was killing the planet."

Alison had news for Lois. If Jonathan thought it was a good idea to ask her out, body odor was the least of his problems.

"So don't breathe when you're around him," Alison said.

"Right," Lois said, rolling her eyes. "Like I can do that for a whole date?" *Chomp, chomp, chomp.* "So where'd you meet this guy you're going out with?"

"He's a friend of a friend."

"Blind date?"

"Not exactly."

Chomp. "Then what exactly?"

"None of your business."

"Fine. Don't tell me." *Chomp, chomp.* "But I know you got a date because you're skinny. Guys always like skinny women. What chance do the rest of us have?"

She walked off, stuffing the last bite of the Mallorific bar in her mouth, and Alison felt a surge of contentment. God, she loved working there. Nowhere else on the planet was she seen as the skinny girl who scooped up every man in sight, cherry-picked the good ones, and tossed out the rest for the more undesirable women to fight over.

She looked at her watch. Two forty-nine. If she waited eleven more minutes before checking to see if the plumbers were finished, it counted toward her record. Then again, if she laid off the Mallorific bars and all other sweets between now and this weekend, she might be able to squeeze into that cute little skirt she'd bought at the spring clearance sale at Ann Taylor. But the closer the clock crept to three, the more she got to thinking maybe her little black dress that showed off her cleavage, didn't cling to her hips, and had room for a sack of Mallorific bars from the inside out was a way better choice for a first date, anyway.

A minute after three, she congratulated herself on her new personal best, then tiptoed across the just-mopped kitchen floor behind a guy who was putting away his tools and hiking up his Wranglers to cover his butt crack. She snagged a Mallorific bar, then couldn't resist grabbing a bag of Butterscotch Bits from a box on the counter to round out her afternoon snack.

Yep. The little black dress it was.

*   *   *

The next morning, Brandon sat at his desk, going through files, wondering for the umpteenth time if he had a chance of making this business work. His only successful match so far was for Jack Warren, the guy he'd signed as a client a few days ago. He'd introduced him to a thirty-eight-year-old attorney named Melanie Davis. Neither one had ever been married except to their jobs, and both were allergic to children. She liked his wine expertise and his West Plano McMansion. He liked her biting wit and her cosmetically enhanced breasts. They made plans to see each other again before the first date was even over. With luck, Alison's first date with Greg would be equally successful.

Now, if only he could generate more new business that brought in new money.

Just then his grandmother's land line rang. He looked at the caller ID. Unknown caller. Could it be the new business he was looking for?

With a surge of hope, he picked up the phone. "Matchmaking by Rochelle."

A long pause. "Brandon? Is that you?"

At the sound of that voice, Brandon's blood turned to ice. "Yeah. It's me."

"Hey, Brandon! How's it going, kid?"

Tension instantly filled him, decades of anger and resentment swirling around inside his head. "What do you want, Darryl?"

"Wow. That's a pretty frosty way to greet your old man, isn't it?

A dozen different emotions washed over Brandon, and

not one of them was welcome. After what had happened all those years ago, the word "Dad" no longer crossed his lips, and frosty was a really good way to describe the way he felt every time he heard his father's voice.

"I didn't know if I'd find you there or not," Darryl said. "I don't have your cell number anymore."

Damned right you don't. "You missed the funeral."

"Oh. Yeah. About that. I was tied up. Couldn't make it."

Brandon knew what that meant. Either he was up to no good and lying low, or running from some guy he'd hustled and shouldn't have.

"You couldn't make it to your own mother's funeral?" Brandon said.

"I told you," he said, anger creeping into his voice. "I was tied up."

You're a damned liar. "Why are you calling?"

"Because I thought maybe I'd like to see you."

No. No way. If he saw his father, it would be just like the last time in New Orleans when they'd barely gotten through one drink before the fight started all over again. Darryl had stalked out of the bar, leaving Brandon with the tab and the sick feeling that nothing had changed. That nothing would ever change.

"I don't think that's a good idea," Brandon said.

"You know, you might think about letting go of that grudge one of these days. Family's family after all, isn't it?"

That made Brandon's blood boil. *Family.* The man didn't know the meaning of the word. And when it came to holding a grudge, no one on this earth was better at it than his father.

No one.

"Just tell me what you want," Brandon said.

"Okay. Fine. It appears my mother made a small mistake in her will. Seems she left everything to you."

"That's right."

"Do you think that's fair?"

"Wasn't my decision to make."

"It is now. The house—"

"She left it to her church."

"Her church? You've got to be kidding me."

"Are you really surprised about that?"

Darryl let out a humorless, derisive laugh. "Now that you mention it, no. In fact, I'm surprised she didn't leave every dime to some Bible-beating televangelist."

Brandon bristled at that. As a teenager, he'd hated like hell when his grandmother had dragged him to church. As an adult, he hated like hell to hear his father mock it.

"So if she left her house to the church," Darryl said, "why are you there?"

"It's mine as long as I want to stay here. But I won't be staying long."

"What's still in the house?"

"Nothing that's worth much."

"Maybe I should come take a look."

Brandon imagined what that would be like. His father wanted to sift through the house to see if there was anything worth pawning. He'd open cabinets, pick through closets, and turn over sofa cushions. And when he was satisfied there was nothing to add to his bottom line, he'd be gone. But suddenly the last thing Brandon wanted was his father touching a single thing in this house. And he sure as hell didn't want him in the middle of the business he was trying to get off the ground.

"I told you there's nothing here you'd want," Brandon said.

"The Brunswick. That's bound to be worth something."

"No. It's in bad condition. Maybe I'll restore it someday, but for now it's pretty worthless."

"There has to be something else. China? Jewelry?"

"She was buried with her wedding rings, so don't even go there."

"Hey, it's only fair, don't you think?" Darryl said, his voice escalating. "What kind of mother cuts her own son out of her will?"

"One who made a decision that was hers alone to make."

There was a long silence. Brandon's heart was beating like mad, the way it always did whenever he was forced to confront his father. But no matter how it made him feel, he wasn't giving in.

"Okay, I hear you," Darryl said finally, and Brandon heard that edge to his voice, the one that said he was trying to get his temper under control. How many times had he heard that as a kid?

"But those are just material things, right?" Darryl went on. "What about the important stuff? Photo albums. My mother's recipes. The family Bible. You'd actually deny me those things? This is my mother we're talking about."

As if he expected Brandon to believe that? "I told you there's nothing here you'd be interested in."

"Maybe I'd like to see that for myself. And maybe you'd like to see your old man."

No, no, no! "I already told you. I'm leaving soon. I have...I have a deal brewing in Houston."

"Real estate?"

"Yes."

"Thought that industry was in the toilet right now."

"Not when you know what you're doing."

"So you're still making money?"

Hell, no, he wasn't. But the last thing he wanted was for the old man to know just how down and out he really was.

"Yeah, Darryl. I'm still making money."

"Then cutting your old man in for a little bit of your grandmother's estate really shouldn't hurt much, should it? Surely she had at least a little cash. Or maybe—"

"I told you there's *nothing*."

"Hey! I'm your father! Doesn't that mean anything to you?"

"Look, Darryl. I can't help it if you're broke. But if you think you're coming to me for money—"

"Is that what you think? That I *need* the money? For your information, I've got some action myself here in Atlanta. Tournament in two days. I should be able to walk away with the whole thing. So I really don't need a damned thing from my mother's estate, now do I?"

Knowing what he knew about his father, that was unlikely. He was a stellar pool player, assuming he kept his head down and his emotions under control. But that never happened.

Never.

"No," Brandon said. "I guess you don't."

"That's right. I don't. So you just keep that pittance your grandmother left you. Apparently you need it way more than I do."

And then he heard a click, and the line went dead.

Brandon hung up the phone and sat back in his chair, anger eating away at him. He hated this. He hated the way his stomach churned and his brain grew foggy after just one lousy five-minute conversation. It reminded him of how he'd felt as a kid, when his father had jerked him from one town to another, working just long enough to put food in their mouths before moving on again. Or worse, he'd piss somebody off and be forced to leave town. Every time they moved, it meant Brandon had to start at a new school. When he was nine or ten, he'd been the quiet kid nobody even knew was in the room. What was the point of getting to know anybody when he wasn't going to be there for long? But by the time he was a teenager, he was entering every classroom with the kind of screw-you attitude that made most teachers want to give up the profession just from looking at his scowling face.

It's the nine to five that keeps a man down, Brandon. Remember that. You let yourself get caught up in that, and you'll die a slow death.

When he was a kid, he'd hung on his father's every word. It wasn't until he was older that he began to realize there was nothing to back up the old man's words. The truth was that he didn't move around to avoid the nine to five. He just didn't want to work, so he'd screw off, or show up drunk, or do something else that got him fired. Then the hustling would start again. And by the time Brandon was fifteen, his father had taught him to follow in his footsteps. Once the man realized just how good his son was and that he had a gold mine on his hands, he stepped up the hustling like a man possessed.

That had been the beginning of the end.

Sometimes, when he hadn't been around his father for a while, Brandon got to thinking maybe it could happen. They really could bury the hatchet, forget the past, let bygones be bygones. Then he'd talk to him again, and all that wishful thinking would go straight to hell.

The truth was that if he never saw his father again in this lifetime, it would be too soon.

Chapter 9

Alison detested first dates, so by the time Saturday night came, she'd already worked herself into a wad of tangled nerves. First dates were like minefields. No matter which direction you stepped, something could blow up right in your face.

She drove to the West Village and managed to wedge her car into a parking space in a tiny lot three blocks away from the restaurant. As she got out, she tugged on the hem of her dress to make sure it was hanging straight so she wouldn't look half drunk before the night even began.

She took a yoga breath and walked toward the restaurant. Whenever she'd gone on dates with men she met on match.com or Yahoo! Personals, they always turned out to be shorter than their profile said they were, ten years older than the photos they put online, and "physically fit" meant they had a highly developed right bicep from opening and closing their refrigerator door.

And every one of them had issues of some kind. In her early twenties, it had been a lack of focus. Okay, so that was generous. What she really meant to say was that they still lived with two other guys in a one-bedroom apartment decorated with pizza boxes and dirty laundry and spent all day playing World of Warcraft. Her mid-twenties led her to guys who lied a lot about their jobs and the four other women they were seeing besides her. Now that she was thirty, suddenly every guy she met had already been through divorce court.

Supposedly Greg was none of those things. But Alison had been burned so many times that a better outfit for the evening might have been a little black asbestos jumpsuit.

She strode up the crowded sidewalk, sidestepping two hand-holding men and their Yorkshire terrier, then a couple of granola heads wearing tie-dyed T-shirts and looking for a tree to hug. An eclectic crowd hung out in the West Village, but the indigenous population was mostly young, upscale, and rich, and judging from the reviews online, they *loved* Sonoma Bistro.

She reached the restaurant and went inside, not the least bit surprised to see dark wood, wine casks, and brick walls. How original. She'd never been to a wine bar decorated like a wine cellar. What would they think of next?

"Excuse me. Are you Alison Carter?"

She turned quickly to see a man standing behind her. Greg? No. It couldn't be. He looked just like his photo. Didn't that violate dating law?

If so, this guy had committed a third-degree felony.

He had the same boyish smile and the same sandy brown hair as he did in his photo, both of which coordinated perfectly with his sparkling green eyes. Just looking at him made little zings of pure pleasure shoot down her spine.

"Yes, I'm Alison."

"Oh, good," he said on a sigh of relief. "You know how it is sometimes when you meet somebody for the first time. They never look like their photo. But in your case...well, let's just say I'm pleasantly surprised."

A slow grin spread across his lips, lips that looked so kissable that Alison was already imagining what they'd feel like against hers.

Easy there, Sparky. Sexy lips do not a soul mate make. And he's a vegan, remember? Can you really fill your fridge with tofu and beans for the rest of your life?

The hostess led them to the best table in the restaurant. The vegan thing came up right away, and Greg asked if she minded him ordering for both of them. The prospect of eating so scantily made Alison a little wary, not to mention the fact that a man ordering for her usually offended her feminist sensibilities. But he asked so kindly with a sparkle in those beautiful green eyes that she just couldn't hold it against him.

He ordered a bottle of Shiraz that was to die for, and she wasn't all that crazy about wine. Then an appetizer, which consisted of a flat bread with roasted red peppers, garlic, and sweet basil that Alison couldn't get enough of. But it wasn't until they were halfway through their entrees—whole grain pasta with grilled vegetables, fresh spinach, and an array of spices that gave her a culinary orgasm—that Alison finally came to the conclusion that she might indeed be able to eat like this for the rest of her life.

They talked about anything and everything—the news of the day, the movies they'd seen, where they lived. He dropped his gaze to her cleavage only a couple of times—enough to show he liked what he saw but not so much that getting laid might be number one on his hit parade. He listened intently when she told him about her job, tilting his head with what looked like interest and laughing at the stories that were supposed to be funny. After two glasses of wine, she let herself think that maybe she really was as fascinating as he appeared to think she was.

"So you're in pharmaceutical sales," she said. "That sounds interesting."

"Actually, it is," he said. "The hours are long, and the clients can be really difficult sometimes, but..." That cute grin again. "I can't argue with the compensation." Then he leaned in and spoke with what looked like utter sincerity. "I admit it, Alison. I'm pretty traditional. I think it's important for a man to be able to support his wife and family in the manner they deserve. Not that I'm against a working woman. I'd just like her to do it because she wants to, not because she has to."

And just like that, the heavens opened and angels began to sing.

She couldn't believe it. Brandon had done it. He'd actually done it. He'd found her a wonderful man. The money she'd spent to find him felt like pocket change compared to the reality of the man who was sitting in front of her now. She felt the weirdest rumbling sensation just beneath her solar plexus. Under any other circumstances, she might have brushed it off as indigestion, but when she was in the presence of a man who just might be *The One*, it was more like a swirl of hope, telling her from the inside out that this—*this*—was the man who would make her life complete.

The rest of the evening felt fuzzy and unreal in a delightfully dreamlike way. Later, when they left the restaurant, Greg told Alison he'd walk her to her car. It turned out they'd parked in the same lot, and they passed his car on the way to hers. When he pointed it out to her, she quite simply couldn't believe it.

He drove a Jaguar convertible?

"Beautiful car," Alison said, congratulating herself on shutting her mouth before the second part of that comment popped out: *May I have your baby?*

"Want to go for a spin?" Greg asked.

She came very close to hopping right over the door and plopping herself in the passenger seat, only to remember First Date Protocol. But it wasn't as if she was meeting a guy for the first time from an Internet dating site. Brandon had vetted this guy from top to bottom and deemed him to be a quality match, so who was she to worry?

"Sure," she said with a smile. "I'd love to."

Greg opened her door for her—extra points—then circled the car to hop into the driver's seat. He was just so sweet and warm and attentive that he couldn't possibly be real. This had to be a dream. A wonderful, lyrical dream filled with fluffy clouds and castles and ocean waves and magical forests, and...oh, my. Over there. Wasn't that a *unicorn*?

Alison didn't giggle out loud—that would have been weird—but inside her head she was tittering like a schoolgirl.

Greg swung the Jag onto McKinney Avenue and hit the gas. People on the sidewalk turned to stare as they drove by. She only wished she could ask him to slow down in case somebody didn't get the opportunity to see her riding in this gorgeous car with this wonderful man.

In minutes they'd reached Woodall Rodgers. Greg eased the Jag onto the entrance ramp, then gunned it onto the freeway. They buzzed along, weaving in and out of traffic as they drove past the West End. As they circled around the west side of the American Airlines Center, Alison leaned her head back against the headrest and closed her eyes, enjoying the whine of the engine and the feel of the wind as it whipped her hair into a frenzy.

Then all at once, she heard the pulse of a siren. She sat up suddenly and turned to look behind her.

A police car?

"Uh-oh," Alison said. "Were you speeding?"

Greg gave her a sly grin. "Sorry. I just couldn't help it. All these horses under the hood are hard to rein in sometimes."

Alison gave him a forgiving smile. Could she really be angry? After all, if she'd been driving this car, she probably would have been speeding, too.

Greg slowed down, then turned onto the shoulder and brought the Jag to a halt. The police car came to a stop behind them. Several minutes passed, but for some reason, the officer wasn't getting out of his car.

"What do you suppose is taking him so long?" she asked.

Greg's sunny expression grew a little cloudy. "He's probably just running my plates. But don't worry. We'll be out of here in a minute."

But then another police car pulled up behind the first one.

"Two of them?" Alison said. "Isn't that kind of weird for just a routine traffic stop?"

Greg's Adam's apple bobbed with a heavy swallow. "Uh...yeah."

Just the way he said that made Alison's heart suddenly start whacking her chest. "So what's going on?"

Greg was silent, his gaze glued to his rearview mirror. When a third police car drove past him, then swung to the shoulder to park right in front of his car, he squeezed his eyes closed and pounded his fists on the steering wheel. "Shit!"

Alison jumped as if he'd slapped her. "What's the matter?"

"They must have found out. Shit, shit *shit*!"

"Found out what?"

Greg groaned. "Damn it! The money was just so *good*! How was I supposed to turn it down?"

"Money? What money?"

"How else was I *ever* supposed to drive a car like this? Not working as a fucking night manager at Wendy's, I'll tell you that!"

"Wendy's? What does Wendy's have to do with—"

"Sure, I'm a good-looking guy," he said, talking with his hands now, like a crazy man who'd just broken free from a strait jacket. "Some chicks think I'm really hot. But it's funny how hot goes away when I'm staring at them through a fucking drive-through window!"

Alison leaned away, plastering herself against the passenger door, wondering who this madman was and what he'd done with her mild-mannered vegan. Her nerves—the ones that had had been doing dainty little pirouettes all evening—were suddenly stomping around as if they were running from Godzilla.

Oh—could that be what was happening here? A gigantic Japanese monster was on the outskirts of Dallas, and the police were warning all the residents? *Please, God, let it be that and not one more date gone to hell.*

"And once I had more money than God," Greg said,

"I figured, hey, why screw with finding my own women? Why not pay somebody else to do it? It's like ordering room service. I told that dude what kind of woman I wanted, and she showed up. I sure as hell couldn't have done *that* on a fucking night manager's salary at Wendy's!"

"I'm going out on a limb here," Alison said, "but were you once a night manager at Wendy's?"

"Yeah, and if I'd asked you out, you would have told me to go fuck myself, wouldn't you?"

"Well—"

"See? *See?*" He spat out a breath. "I really liked you, you know? I think we could actually have had something together. But we can't now, because I'm fucked. Totally *fucked!*"

What is this man talking about?

No. Better question. Why were all those officers getting out of their cars now? Why were they drawing their guns? Why did this look like every arrest on every episode of *Cops* she'd ever seen, except Greg had all his teeth, no tattoos, and was wearing a shirt?

Then she found out. And through it all, one furious thought filled her mind, practically burning a hole through her skull.

Brandon Scott was a dead man.

Chapter 10

"This movie sucks," Tom said, as he took another swig of his Bud. "I didn't know there were people left on the planet who didn't have cable TV."

"My grandmother didn't need it," Brandon said as he sat sprawled out in his grandmother's favorite floral chair, his feet up on the matching ottoman. "All she watched were soap operas and televangelists. That weird converter box allowed her to get those on her analog TV, so she didn't bother with cable."

"Find something better before I die of boredom."

"There isn't something better."

"There was that *Dragnet* marathon on channel twenty-two."

"Like I said. There isn't something better."

The thought of being subjected to this kind of programming for the next several months just about killed Brandon, but his only alternative was to shell out a bundle for a new HDTV and a big monthly charge for cable. When that option came due on the Houston property, he didn't want a couple thousand bucks standing between him and being able to make the deal happen.

He'd just switched from the movie and was running the dial, when he heard a knock on his front door.

"Expecting somebody?" Tom asked.

"Nope."

Then more knocks. More very insistent knocks. What the hell?

He tossed the remote aside and went to the door, where he peered through the peephole.

Alison Carter?

Truth be told, he barely recognized her. Her brown eyes were bugged out, her nostrils flared, and her lips were all crunched up with fury. He didn't get it. She'd seemed so sweet before. But clearly she was a force to be reckoned with, kind of like a category-five hurricane.

More knocking. "Brandon! I know you're in there! Open the door!"

"Oh, God," Tom said, looking around the doorway into the entry hall. "That's not the scary Hooters waitress from Denver, is it? Brittany Whatsername? I thought you got a restraining order against her."

"Nope. It's one of my clients."

"Your clients scream at you?"

"Not so far."

He opened the door. Alison swept past him like a tidal wave crashing through the house. Then she spun around to face him, her fists rising to her hips and her brows drawing together in a tight furrow. In spite of the impending storm, he was having a hard time keeping his eyes off the cute little black dress she wore. It dipped down at her cleavage, and with every angry breath she took, her breasts shifted provocatively. Unfortunately, angry women didn't usually like it when a man's attention was on anything besides what they were hollering about, so as quickly as his gaze fell, he jerked it back up again.

"Alison?" he asked. "What are you doing here?"

"We need to talk."

"Didn't you have a date with Greg tonight?"

"Yes," she said, her voice quivering with restraint. "And it was the worst date of my *life*!"

"The worst?" Brandon said skeptically. "Really?"

"I once went out with a man who brought his mother with him. *That's* what I'm comparing it to!"

"Wow," Tom said. "And this one was worse than that?"

"Hold on," Brandon said, raising his palm. "What happened that was so bad?"

"You set me up with a *drug dealer*!"

Brandon leaned away, truly shocked. Drug dealer? The man was a vegan. How many drug dealers were vegans?

"How do you know he deals drugs?" Brandon asked.

Alison's eyes narrowed into angry slits. "We were driving on the freeway. He got stopped for speeding. They ran his plates and saw the felony drug warrant. Greg had no clue the cops were onto him until they surrounded his car."

"Oh," Brandon said. "I'm guessing that's what he meant by pharmaceutical sales?"

"Yeah? You think?"

"Wait a minute. You were driving with him? Don't you know you should never get into a car with a guy you don't know on the first date?"

Alison's eyes flew open wide. "You set me up with a felon, and you're lecturing me on *dating safety*?"

Okay, so that was a little weak. "I'm sorry, Alison. I had no idea. Really."

"You're supposed to vet the guys I go out with. That's part of the reason I'm paying you a freakin' fortune to find me a husband!"

"Vet?"

"Are you telling me you don't do background checks?"

Brandon froze. Background checks?

Thinking back, he realized now his grandmother had done those, but it had completely slipped his mind that maybe he should be doing them himself. If his grandmother had indeed checked Greg out, maybe it was before there was a warrant out for his arrest. Brandon didn't know exactly what had happened, only that he couldn't afford for it to happen again.

"You can't imagine how humiliating it was," Alison said hotly. "I had to stand on the side of the road while the cops handcuffed my date and stuffed him inside a police car. They were going to drag me in, too. Guilt by association. It was all I could do to convince them that I'd never even met him before tonight and the strongest drug I'd ever touched was Tylenol PM."

"So where were you when this happened?"

"On I 35 just outside downtown Dallas."

"That's at least fifteen miles from here. How did you get home?"

"Oh, no problem there. One of the cops gave me a ride back to my car at the restaurant. Everybody in the whole neighborhood thought it was positively *riveting* to watch me get out of a police car."

"I've always wondered what the inside of a police car was like," Tom said, his eyes alight with interest. "I hear the backseat is plastic so when somebody's arrested for DUI and they barf, they can just wash it out with a hose."

"Where the hell did you read *that*?" Brandon said.

"On Ask dot com. You can learn all kinds of things there. For instance, do you know what the loudest animal on earth is?"

Alison looked at him with disbelief, then turned slowly back to Brandon. "Who's this?"

"A friend. Alison, this is Tom. Tom, this is Alison. She's one of my clients."

"No. Past tense. I *was* one of your clients. I want my money back. Every penny. And I want it *now*."

"Uh-oh," Tom said. He pulled Brandon aside and whispered, "I read in *Entrepreneur* magazine that whenever a customer asks for a refund, eight out of ten times you can talk him out of it as long as you—"

"Go away," Brandon snapped.

"But—"

"Now."

Tom turned to Alison. "I'm going away now. But in case you were wondering, it's the blue whale. A hundred and eighty-eight decibels. They can be heard from—"

"Go!" Brandon said.

As Tom disappeared into the den, Brandon turned to Alison. "I can explain."

"Yeah?" she said, folding her arms and looking at him expectantly, that scowl still stuck to her face. "Let's hear it."

"Well, I'm just now learning my grandmother's procedures," he said, willing his brain to come up with something. "It appears there was a... glitch."

"A glitch?"

"Greg came to my grandmother a few months ago. I'm thinking the warrant must have happened after she ran his background check. I know now that I should update them at a certain point, but I guess this one just got past me."

He gave her an *I'm sorry please don't hate me* look that he sincerely hoped would appeal to her forgiving side. He wasn't sure it was working.

He took a step closer to her, running a hand through his hair, then blowing out a breath. "I'm going to level with you, Alison. This business is important to me. Really important. I have to make it a success. If you could possibly see your way clear to overlook this one tiny error—"

"Tiny error? Really, Brandon? *Tiny?*"

"Okay. It was a big mistake. But it's one that'll never happen again. But the question is, did you like Greg?"

She looked aghast. "*Like* him? The man is a drug dealer!"

"I mean before you found that out. Were you having a good time?"

"Oh, yeah. Our date was a real barrel of laughs."

"Alison. *Before* you found out what he was."

She paused. "Well, yeah. I guess. But—"

"Did you have things in common?"

"Yes, but—"

"Did you find him physically attractive?"

"Well, yeah. But—"

Brandon held up his palm. "Now, see there? I set you up with a guy you really liked, didn't I? I mean, if you overlook the fact that he ended up in jail."

She shook her head dumbly. "Did you just *hear* yourself?"

"I know. Strange conversation. But if you think about it, otherwise he was a solid match. I can do it again, only this time, I'll make sure the guy is squeaky clean."

"So you're telling me your plan is to give me Greg minus the felony warrant?"

"Well, yeah," he said. "More or less. If you'll give me another chance, I know I can set you up with the right guy."

He gave her the most sincere look of contrition he could muster. A few seconds passed, and even though she still had her arms crossed and her eyes narrowed, he could tell her anger was losing steam.

"It was horrible to get stopped by the police," she said.

He nodded sympathetically. "I know."

"I felt like a criminal."

"I understand."

"I'll probably have nightmares."

"I'm really sorry about that."

"It was *traumatic*."

"Trust me, Alison. This was a random glitch. It will never happen again."

"I'd have to be out of my mind to let you set me up again."

"Look. I really want this business to be a success. I *need* it to be a success. But if one of my first clients is dissatisfied, what chance do I have?"

Alison opened her mouth to say something else, only to close it again. "Don't do that."

"Do what?"

"Make me feel sorry for you."

He just stared at her.

"Because I don't. Not even a little bit."

"I was just hoping you'd let me make good on my mistake."

Alison rolled her eyes and looked away.

"I know you're an understanding person. I could tell that from the first moment we met."

She pursed her lips with irritation.

"A sympathetic person."

Her eyes shifted to him, and then she looked away again.

"A kindhearted person who doesn't hesitate to give people second chances."

"Brandon—"

"Come on, Alison. I'm just asking you to give me another chance. Just one more chance so I can—"

"Oh, all right!" she said, throwing her hands in the air. "I'll let you find me another match!"

He smiled. "You won't be sorry."

She pointed a finger at him. "But if you think I'm paying for this mess tonight, think again. That one didn't count. I still get five matches if that's what it takes."

"Of course. I wouldn't even think of taking your money for this one."

"And you *will* do background checks from now on."

"Of course."

"You're getting only one more chance, you know. If the cops show up again, this whole deal is *off*."

"Not gonna happen."

"Then we understand each other?"

"Yes, ma'am."

"Fine." Then she put her hand to her forehead and closed her eyes. "God. I am *such* a pushover."

"No, you're not. You're just the kind of person who gives other people the benefit of the doubt."

"Right," she muttered. "God only knows who you'll set me up with next. An escaped convict? A terrorist? Or maybe a serial killer? You know. His neighbors think he's nice and quiet, but he has body parts in his basement. Think how much fun *that* date's going to be."

"No way. I promise you if the next guy has so much as a traffic ticket, he doesn't make the cut."

"Small problem there. *I* have traffic tickets."

Brandon smiled. "Don't worry. I'll warn the guy ahead of time that he's dating a criminal."

Alison bowed her head, shaking it sadly. "I'm going to regret this. I just know it." She walked to the door. "I have to go home now and take a shower. I smell like the inside of a police car."

"Yeah?" Brandon said, following her. "What does a police car smell like?"

"Gunpowder and sweat."

"Are the backseats really plastic?"

"I didn't have the nerve to look around. Believe me, the less I saw, the better."

"I'm sorry you had such a rotten evening. But I promise I'm going to make it up to you."

"Okay," she said wearily. "Fine. Give it a shot. After all, things can only go uphill from here, right?"

"Give me a little time. I want to get this one right."

"Fine."

"I'll be in touch."

"Good night, Brandon."

"Good night, Alison."

She opened the door and left the house, and Brandon watched as she walked down the porch steps and got into her car parked at the curb. It was a late-model Toyota. Attractive but sensible. Exactly the kind of car he would have expected her to drive, because she was a nice girl. And he'd set her up with a bad, bad man.

Damn.

He went back inside and into the den, where Tom was sprawled on the sofa with a bowl of popcorn on his stomach.

"She's kinda cute when she's infuriated," Tom said. "What's she like when she's not?"

"Never mind," Brandon said. "I have to rethink this thing."

"Did she fire you?"

"No. I talked her into giving me another chance."

"I can't believe the guy was a drug dealer. Maybe getting a handle on background checks would be a really good idea."

"Yeah? You think?" Brandon flopped in the flowered chair. "I can't imagine why a guy like him would even go to a matchmaker. Got some factoid that explains that?"

Tom shrugged. "Drug dealers need love, too?"

Brandon closed his eyes. "Damn. Now I have to deliver for sure, or Alison definitely will want her money back."

When Alison got home from Brandon's house, she was happy to see that Heather and Tony's condo was dark, which meant they were both working late at the bar. Thank God. The last thing Alison wanted to do tonight was spill her guts about her evening with the handsome drug dealer and her brush with Dallas's finest. She had to figure out how she was going to say *He set me up with a felon and I'm going to let him do it again* without sounding certifiably insane.

Another wasted evening, she thought, crossing yet one more day of her life off her mental calendar. The older she got, the faster those pages flipped.

She curled up on her sofa and switched on HGTV, where she watched *House Hunters* and imagined that the newlyweds searching for their first home were her and her new husband. *The couple is looking for an early twentieth-century property*, the announcer would say. *They want four bedrooms and a big yard to accommodate the large family they plan to have. They have a budget of one million dollars...*

Okay, so the budget part was over the top. But if she was going to daydream, why not daydream big?

Halfway through the first episode, Lucy draped herself over Alison's lap as if she didn't have bone in her whole feline body. Ricky lay upside down on the carpet by the sofa, his four white paws in the air, looking like road kill. Ethel lay upright on the sofa at Alison's feet, her paws and tail tucked so tightly she could have fit neatly inside a meat loaf pan. If another stray kitten did eventually make its way into her life, she only hoped it was a boy. A girl cat named Fred would be really weird.

An hour later, as *House Hunters* came to a close, the blissful TV couple found the historic Chicago townhome with the view of the river they were looking for. Alison wondered if she'd ever have more than her two-bedroom contemporary condo on the commuter rail line in Plano, Texas, which came complete with about three too many cats and one too few husbands. Later she fell asleep on the sofa and dreamed she spent the next five years having conjugal visits with Greg while he did his sentence, only to have him dump her for another woman the day he was finally released.

By midafternoon the next day, Heather had texted her approximately half a dozen times, and for every time she failed to text back, Alison knew her suspicion about the quality of her date grew exponentially. But she couldn't hide forever, so finally she texted back, *McCaffrey's at six.*

At six o'clock, they were sitting in a booth at McCaffrey's, and Alison was telling the story. At two minutes after six, Heather drew back with horror.

"Brandon set you up with a *felon*?" she screeched so loudly she rattled the martini glass in front of her.

"Will you keep your voice down?" Alison said.

"Sorry," Heather said. "I tend to scream when I'm appalled."

"I was a little appalled too. You know. At first."

"At *first*?"

"I mean, I'm still appalled that the guy was a drug dealer. But like I said, where Brandon's concerned, it was just a glitch."

"Glitch? *Glitch?* I thought you were going to tell me the guy dressed in drag or he was a chain smoker, or something. *Drug dealer* never popped into my mind."

"Come on, Heather. Even you agreed the guy looked good on paper. And Brandon isn't going to charge me for that match."

"Well, I should hope to hell not!"

"He'll do better next time."

"Next time? You're letting him have a *next time*?"

Alison frowned. "Yes. I am."

"God, Alison, don't you see what you're doing? This guy doesn't have a clue how to be a matchmaker, and you're letting him use you as a guinea pig."

"I'm just giving him another chance. What do I have to lose?"

"A little bit of time and a whole lot of money."

Intellectually, Alison knew that. But emotionally, there was something about Brandon she just couldn't stop coming back to. He exuded the kind of confidence she wished she felt herself. Told her in no uncertain terms that he could find her the man of her dreams when she had a hard time believing it on her own anymore. In spite of what had happened last night, he gave her the one thing she desperately needed.

Hope.

Chapter 11

A few days later, Tom and Brandon sat at the bar at McCaffrey's, having a beer and watching the Rangers game they couldn't get on his grandmother's TV. It was late afternoon, and the crowd was light—just he and Tom, plus two other guys Brandon had never met before. Together they chatted about batting averages and trades and the pitching staff. But Brandon was having a hard time concentrating on the game. He was too preoccupied with the fact that his ad on *Dallas After Dark* had come out yesterday, and so far he hadn't had a single call.

"Unless a satellite fell out of the sky," Tom said, "your phone is working. Will you stop staring at it and watch the game?"

Brandon folded his arms in frustration and tried to concentrate on the game, but it was a hard-won battle. Realistically, he couldn't expect his phone to start ringing off the hook right away. People would have to see the ad for a little while. Think about it. Consider the benefits of using a matchmaker. Go to the website to get more information. And then they'd give him a call and set up an appointment.

Or the ad was going to generate nothing, and he'd be screwed.

And then there was Alison. He'd been through a bunch of his files again with no luck, finding something not to like about every one of the men, even the other guy in the coin flip. He knew that was probably because he was gun-shy after setting her up with Greg the Vegan Drug Dealer. But if he couldn't find Mr. Right for her, sooner or later he'd have to settle for Mr. Close to Right and hope for the best.

"Still think you're going to be able to do the match-making thing?" Tom asked between innings.

"I still have time to get it moving," Brandon said, but for the first time, his confidence was wavering. If he didn't get some more new business coming in soon, he wouldn't be able to do the deal in Houston. That would mean he'd have to go back to being a lackey on somebody else's construction crew, and he'd always said he shoot himself before he let that happen.

He remembered when he and Tom had pulled off one of the Vegas deals at a time when things were so hot there the contracts practically singed their hands. They'd left the title company, headed for the gaming tables, and before the night was over, Brandon had turned a ten thousand dollar stake into fifty, making him feel as if he couldn't lose. Before the night was over, he and Tom picked up a couple of party girls, grabbed a limo, and made a night of it, throwing money around as if their pockets were bottomless. Brandon had woken up the next morning with the hangover of the century and a woman next to him whose name he didn't even remember. And still he'd felt as if he was on top of the world.

He wanted that feeling back again.

Tracy was tending bar, seemingly watching the game right along with them. But she never missed an opportunity to lean this way or twist that way when she was getting a beer or adjusting the sound on the TV or washing out a glass, giving everybody present a nearly unobstructed view of her most cherished assets. But it was Brandon she focused most of her attention on. When a commercial came on, she leaned her forearms on the bar and gave him a smoldering stare.

"I heard the most outrageous rumor about you," she said.

"Yeah? What's that?"

"Heather said you're a matchmaker. You set people up. Find them their soul mates."

"Listen to Heather. She knows what she's talking about."

"Then it's true?"

"Every word."

"A man who makes love matches." She sighed. "That is *so* hot."

When Brandon responded by turning his attention back to the television, Tracy ran her fingertip along his hand. "I have an idea. Why don't you tell me what kind of woman you're looking for, and I'll see if I can do a little matchmaking for *you*."

"Actually, I'm not looking right now."

"Now, I don't believe that for one minute. A man like you is always looking." She leaned in and spoke softly. "And trust me—I'm the one you're looking for."

Since the first day he'd come in here, Tracy had been turning herself inside out for his attention. Under any other circumstances, he'd have returned her interest, but these days he didn't have the option of hopping in the sack with any woman who happened to catch his eye.

"I think you have some new customers," Brandon said.

Tracy turned around to look at the man and woman having a seat at the other end of the bar. With a frown of frustration, she walked down to take their order.

The man sitting next to Brandon shook his head with disgust. "I *hate* women like her."

Brandon was shocked to hear him say that. So far he hadn't noticed any of the other male customers having a problem with Tracy's...uh, *direct* behavior.

"What do you mean?"

"I'm surprised she doesn't have a mattress strapped to her back. I divorced a woman like her. Cheated on me right and left."

Ah. Now it made sense.

"That's too bad," Brandon said.

"I'm just glad to be rid of her. She had a roving eye from the day we got married. I'm not sure, but I think she screwed my best man in the back of his SUV two hours before we walked down the aisle."

Brandon wanted to ask the guy why, if he had a suspicion like that, he married her anyway. But he was probably just one of those too trusting guys who didn't stand a chance against an evil, manipulating woman.

The guy took a sip of his beer and sighed. "Where are all the good women? Seriously. Where *are* they?"

All at once, the matchmaking sector of Brandon's brain lit up like Christmas. "So you don't like pushy women?"

"Pushy, calculating, slutty. Can't stand them. I just

want a nice woman without all the drama. Is that too much to ask?"

"Do you want to get married again?"

"Absolutely. I loved being married. I just didn't love being married to a woman like *her*."

A man who loved marriage, but hated infidelity?

Brandon thought about the networking his grandmother had done, finding quality singles in all kinds of places to match up with her paying clients.

Maybe he needed to do the same.

A few minutes later, he'd found out the guy's name was David Pence. It was his first time at McCaffrey's. He had time to kill before meeting a salesman to sign the papers on a new car he was buying, so he'd dropped in. When Brandon told him what he did for a living and that he'd like to introduce him to that good woman he was looking for, he seemed excited.

A few questions later, and Brandon learned that David was an electrical engineer, thirty-eight years old, had a good income, didn't smoke, and he wanted kids. And the fact that he was repelled by women like Tracy told Brandon that the perfect woman for him just might be Alison.

By the time the guy left the bar, Brandon had made an appointment with him to come by the office the next day, bring a photo, and fill out a questionnaire. And authorize a background check, because he wasn't making *that* mistake again. Since Brandon was soliciting him with a particular woman in mind, he couldn't charge him for this match, but if things didn't work out between him and Alison, he might be able to convert him to a paying customer later.

All in all, it had been a productive afternoon.

"Can't believe he said that about Tracy," Tom said as David was walking out the door. "I'd do her in a heart-beat."

"I think that was David's problem with her," Brandon said. "She'd do any guy in a heartbeat."

Tom perked up. "*Any* guy?"

"Just wait until closing time. If she hasn't already hooked up, you'll look way better to her then."

"Gee, thanks. I can always count on you to give my ego a real boost. But I think it's you she's after."

"Not interested."

"In fact, there are a lot of women around here who are clearly out to get you. Any reason you're not taking advantage of that?"

"Because a bed-hopping matchmaker isn't exactly the image I need to be conveying. Word will get around."

"So you actually intend to go months without getting laid? That would be a first."

Brandon didn't much like the thought of that, either, but he wasn't going to allow anything to get in the way of getting the money he needed. It was the only shot he had right now, so even if he had to maintain the sexual habits of a priest, he wasn't about to let it go.

When Brandon told Alison about David and then sent his information to her, she felt that tiny stirring of hope she always did whenever a new man was on the horizon. Still, she tried her best not to get her hopes up. Brandon had yet to prove himself, so this date could turn out even worse than the last one.

The next Friday night, she met David at the restaurant he'd suggested, which turned out to be one of those see-

and-be-seen places she generally hated. Everyone was crammed butt-to-butt in the bar, swaying to the music and spilling martinis down each other's backs but looking fabulous while they were doing it. Alison only had so much fabulousness in her, and she wasn't sure this was a place where she wanted to waste any of it.

David himself, though, seemed as good as he'd sounded on paper. Dark hair, dark eyes, nice build, nicely dressed. He was thirty-eight, but if not for the touch of gray at his temples, she would have thought he wasn't much older than she was. When he turned and saw her for the first time, he smiled in a way that didn't *seem* phony, though some guys were really good at faking that first impression. She herself had mastered it. Fortunately, this time she could let her face relax into a genuine reflection of the way she felt, which was *So far, so good.*

The hostess escorted them to a table away from the bar where it was quieter, which was nice, even though they were still within sight of the beautiful people. David picked up the wine list. "How about a bottle of wine?"

"That'd be good," she said. Actually, great. First date nervousness sucked, and a little alcohol always made her brain settle down. A few minutes later they were sipping cabernet, and Alison began to relax.

"So you're an electrical engineer," she said. "That's interesting."

"Usually, yeah. But right now I'm stuck working on an optical emission spectrometer for metal analysis." He rolled his eyes. "Boring."

She nodded with sympathy, even though she didn't have a clue what he was talking about.

"And you're in marketing?" he asked.

"Yeah. I work for Spangler Sweets. I'm basically a candy pusher. Our products are as addictive as meth, but we don't get thrown in jail for selling them."

It was her go-to opening line about her job that she used to determine if a guy had any sense of humor at all. A smile was all she was looking for. David actually laughed, which meant she could relax a little more.

The waitress brought their appetizer—chicken satay with a sweet cucumber sauce. But just as Alison was getting ready to dig in, David sat up straight, his eyes going wide as he looked at something over her right shoulder. She turned to look. No celebrity had walked in. Nothing was on fire. So what was he staring at?

"Is something wrong?" she asked.

He turned his eyes back to Alison, looking a little flustered. "No. Nothing's wrong. Nothing at all."

Then his gaze shifted back to the something that was nothing. Alison looked over her shoulder again. Three women had just sat down at a table in the bar.

"Are you looking at those women?" she asked.

"Nope. Don't see anybody. Doesn't the chicken satay look good?"

"Yeah," Alison said warily, because David's eyes kept shifting from the good-looking chicken to the women at the bar and back again.

"Are you sure you don't know those women?" she asked.

"Okay," he admitted. "I do. One of them is my ex-wife, Janet."

Alison's heart seized up. Well, *crap*. An ex-wife showing up was never good. Never.

Never.

"But don't worry," David said, putting an appetizer on his plate. "I have no feelings for her anymore. None at all."

"Are you sure about that?"

"Absolutely. I just know she's talking about me. That's all."

"How do you know that?"

"That woman to her left is Stacy Rankowsky. She's the reason we broke up in the first place. Filled my wife's head with all kinds of crap about how I was controlling and manipulative. She once called me a Neanderthal. Me! I'm telling you, Alison, I'm the most easygoing guy you'll ever meet." He took a bite of the chicken satay. "Oh. This is so good. You have to try it."

Alison picked up one of the appetizers and dipped it into the sauce. One bite told her he was right. These were heaven on a wooden skewer.

"So tell me, Alison. Have you lived in Plano long?"

"I grew up in Dallas and then moved here after college. I have a condo near the rail line, which is nice because—"

And then he was looking over her shoulder again.

"What's wrong?" Alison asked.

"This is no accident," he said, frowning. "She must have found out I was going to be here."

"How would she have found out?"

"My friend Derek must have told her."

"Why would he do that?"

"She probably wheedled it out of him."

"Uh...she's your ex. Why would she care?"

"You sure ask a lot of questions, Alison. Wouldn't you rather concentrate on what's going on between us?"

Well, yeah. Except she wasn't the one who had digressed in the first place.

For the next ten minutes, David made what looked like a concerted effort to put all his attention on Alison, but even when he wasn't looking at Janet, he was tapping his fingertips on the table as if he was nervous or pissed or both, his jaw looking as if it was set in granite. But that was only during the times when he wasn't smiling insincerely at Alison and swearing his ex meant nothing to him.

"Don't take this wrong, David," she said as he glanced over her shoulder for the sixty-fourth time. "But I think it's possible you still have feelings for Janet."

"Feelings? For her? *No*." He made a scoffing noise. "Not just no, but *hell* no." He smiled at Alison. "You're the one I'm interested in right now. Now, where were we?"

"We were talking about our jobs," Alison said. "I was telling you about this boss I used to have who—"

"Now they're laughing," David said. "Stacy looked over here, and then she said something to the rest of them, and they're laughing. And Janet is laughing more than the other two put together."

"But you're over her, remember? So does it really matter?"

He laughed nervously. "No. Of course not. Old habits, huh? So...tell me about your boss. I could tell that was going to be an interesting story."

He put his elbow on the table and rested his chin in his hand, giving her his undivided attention. So Alison launched into the story, which was another one of her staples on a first date because it really was funny and most guys laughed. But as she got to the most amusing part of all, she saw David's gaze drift over to the table full of women. He jerked it back, but then it drifted again.

"David? Would you like to meet up another night? You know—sometime when your ex-wife isn't sitting across the room?"

"Of course not! I told you. Past history. Water under the bridge."

"I'm not so sure about that."

"Well, I am."

"How long has your divorce been final?"

"Five weeks."

Alison nearly choked. "Five *weeks*? And already you want to date other women?"

"Yes," he said, frowning. "Like I said, I am *so* over her. So why waste another minute of life? And life was hell with Janet, let me tell you. One time I stayed out all night drinking with my buddies, and when I got home, do you know what she'd done? She'd piled my *Playboy* collection on the patio and set fire to it!"

Stayed out all night? *Playboy* collection? Maybe she was on Janet's side on this one. "What nerve. Gee, maybe you were right to divorce her."

"That's what I've been trying to tell you! Divorce is too good for her!" He took a heavy gulp of wine. "I got her back, though," he said, revenge lighting his eyes. "I flushed her tropical fish down the toilet."

Okay. This was getting weird. Particularly since the fish flusher still couldn't seem to keep his eyes off the pyromaniac.

"Look at that," he said, coming to attention. "They're laughing again."

"I'm sure somebody just told a joke, or something."

"It's time I gave her a piece of my mind." He pushed his chair away from the table.

"Uh...David? I don't think that's a good idea."

"Why not?"

Should she really have to explain why not? *Really?*

"Because you're on a date with me, but you're fixating on your ex-wife. Sorry, but that's a little weird."

"How many times do I have to tell you? *I'm over her.*" He rose from his chair. "I'll be back in a minute. Then we'll go back to having a nice date. Okay?"

She had news for him. That ship had sailed.

He strode toward Janet's table, only now Janet was getting up, looking really pissed, and walking away from him. She strode toward the front of the restaurant and disappeared around a corner with David storming after her.

Alison was stunned. World War III was on the horizon. Thank God they were taking it outside.

She sat there for a moment or two more, wondering what to do. No, wait. There was no wondering here. It was time to go, preferably before David returned and this charade began all over again. Somewhere in the back of her mind, she was regretting that one more date hadn't worked out, but she was so fixated on putting as much distance between her and the fish flusher that, at least for now, she just didn't care.

She grabbed her purse and headed for the front door of the restaurant, stopping off at the ladies' room before the long drive home. She went inside, turned the corner from the dressing area to the bathroom stalls, and heard voices.

"I hate you," a man's breathy voice said, "You know I hate you."

"I hate you, too," a woman's voice said. "Why do you think I divorced you?"

"You didn't divorce me. I divorced you!"

"It takes two to split, you bastard!"

David? And his lovely ex-wife, Janet? Cussing each other out in a bathroom stall?

But then there was more heavy breathing. A grunt or two. A little moan here and there.

What the hell?

"But you know I can't live without you," Janet said. "I hate you, but I can't live without—oh, God, yes. *Yes!* Like that!"

Alison looked under the door to see only one set of feet. Male feet. So what had happened to Janet's feet? Alison tried to visualize the exact configuration of body parts, but that particular X-rated puzzle was still in pieces.

"You like that? Of course you do. You're a bad girl. You've always been such a bad girl. You like it dirty, don't you?"

"Yes. Dirty." *Gasp.* "Make it *dirty.*"

And it didn't get much dirtier than doing it in a bathroom stall.

"I saw you with that woman," Janet said. "Do you want her, David? Do you? Or do you want me?"

"You. I've always wanted you." *Gasp, gasp, gasp.* "Even when I hate you, I want you. Christ, it's a curse!"

"Yes, David. Do it to me. Do it hard. Oh, God, that's good...so good...so...*aaaghhh...*"

More gasps. More groans. More screams.

Just then the ladies' room door opened and a woman walked in. As if it were just any old day in a restaurant bathroom, she walked toward the stall next to where the action was. Just then, Janet let out an orgasmic moan that rattled the walls, mingling with David's grunts of satisfaction.

The woman leaned away quizzically, her brow scrunching up. She turned to Alison. "Is there a *man* in there?"

Alison leaned over and spoke in a confidential whisper. "Yes. I think she's sick and he's helping her."

"Yeah? Sounds to me like she's horny and he's screwing her." Then she proceeded into the adjacent stall and closed the door behind her.

Okay. That woman might be able to pee with a live sex show going on next door, but that was a line Alison just couldn't cross. Instead, she left the restaurant, drove down the street, and used the bathroom at a McDonald's. Then she washed her hands, looked in the mirror, and wondered: *This is a first date. How did I end up here?*

She got in her car to drive to Brandon's house, where he was going to give her an answer to that question, or else.

Chapter 12

Brandon had just about fallen asleep in front of the TV when he heard somebody banging on his front door. Tom got up and looked out the peephole. "Uh-oh."

Brandon came to attention. "What?"

"It's Alison."

Brandon grabbed his phone and looked at the time. *Crap.* Too early. She clearly wasn't dropping by to tell him what a screaming success her date with David had been. He jumped out of his chair and went to the door.

"Go back to the den," he told Tom.

"You sure? If she starts swinging that purse, you might need some backup."

"Will you just *go*?"

As Tom left the room, Brandon opened the door to find Alison standing on the porch, her arms folded and her mouth set in a grim, angry line.

"We need to talk," she snapped.

"Uh...okay."

"Is Tom home?"

"Yes."

"Then come out here. I don't need to hear anything more about whale noises."

She turned around and sat down on the porch swing, her arms folded, glaring at him. The night was hot, and cicadas were screeching madly in the trees. Brandon had a feeling that in a moment Alison was going to be doing some screeching of her own. He closed the door and walked over to sit down beside her, bracing himself for the onslaught.

"I assume this is about your date with David," he said.

"You think?"

"Okay. Tell me what happened."

"Well, let's see. David had sex on our first date. It just wasn't with me."

"What?"

"He saw his ex-wife at the restaurant. He followed her into the ladies' room. Turns out it's not just something they made up for porn movies. You really can do it in a bathroom stall."

Brandon sat back in disbelief. "He did his ex-wife in a bathroom stall while he was on a date with *you*?"

"Wow," she said with a touch of sarcasm. "Sounds even worse when you say it."

"He told me he hated women like her. That she was cheap and slutty and she cheated on him."

"Which quite obviously turns him on."

"He told me he was over her."

"He told me he was over her, too. About sixty-seven times. Then he met her in stall number two. Judging from the pillow talk, he hates her but he can't live without her. It appears the feeling is mutual."

"So you listened to the whole thing?"

"At first I was in denial. Then I was in shock. Then I had to pee, but I sure as hell wasn't going to do it there, so I went to a McDonald's. What a way to end an evening."

Brandon started to tell her that sarcasm really didn't suit her, only to realize that right about then, it kinda did.

"Maybe he was trying to prove to himself that he was over her," Brandon said.

"Well, if that's the case, he blew it big time, didn't he?"

Okay. He was in trouble now. It wasn't going to take three strikes. Alison was going to call him out at two. He tried to think of any excuse for his failure that he could possibly think of, but he couldn't come up with a damned thing.

"I'm sorry, Alison," he said, shaking his head. "I checked out that guy from top to bottom. His questionnaire was great. Didn't have so much as a parking ticket. He sounded like the perfect match for you."

"The guy has been divorced only five weeks," Alison said. "You didn't think *that* was a big red flag?"

Brandon drew back. "Five weeks? That's *all*?"

"So he didn't tell you?"

"God, no, or I never would have set you up with him!"

"Don't you think that would have been a really smart question to ask?"

Yes. It would have. So why hadn't he thought of it?

"Do you know this is a man who flushed his wife's tropical fish down the toilet?"

"*What?*"

"But only in retaliation for her piling up his *Playboy* magazines and burning them."

Brandon shook his head in disbelief. This didn't sound like the guy he'd talked to at McCaffrey's the other day. That guy had seemed reasonable and levelheaded, even if he was down on his ex-wife. After all, she'd cheated on him, hadn't she? It was reasonable to Brandon that he'd be at least a little bitter. But the guy Alison was describing was just this side of pathologic.

"I guess it's a love-hate thing," she said. "Can't live with her, can't live without her. But at least they have a little passion going. That's more than I can say."

"What do you mean?"

"Do you know that the weirdest place I've ever done it was in a bed? What does that say about me?"

"You like to be comfortable?"

"Nope. I lead a really boring life."

"So you want me to set you up with a guy who drags you into a bathroom stall and has sex with you?"

Alison thought about that. "No. I don't think I can have both. If I want a family man, I have to settle for a little bit of ordinary. If I want passion, I'll end up with a guy who runs back to his ex-wife at the drop of a hat. But that's what love is all about. Modest expectations. That way you can't be disappointed."

"That's bullshit."

She whipped around. "What?"

"Don't settle for a life like that."

"An ordinary life? What's wrong with that?"

"Forget ordinary. You should be looking for something extraordinary."

"Nope. I just want a nice, normal life with a nice, normal man. If a little bit of *blah* comes with that, so be it."

Blah. She hadn't put that on her questionnaire. Maybe he needed to keep that in mind for the future.

"I don't know why I didn't see what kind of guy he was," Brandon said. "I mean, I had no trouble reading you, right? So why couldn't I read him? Or Greg, for that matter?"

"I don't know," Alison said. "All I know is...this isn't working."

That hit Brandon right between the eyes. She was right, of course. And it probably never would work. Not just his attempts to match Alison up, but the business in general. Yeah, he'd finally had a couple of successful matches, but his ad had flopped, he wasn't finding any more new clients, and he didn't see any way on earth to make this business the short-term success he desperately needed. At the very least, he needed to stop trying to set Alison up before he humiliated her one more time.

Brandon sighed. "Maybe it's time I gave you your money back after all."

Alison glanced at him, then looked away again. "Yeah. Maybe that would be best."

Brandon was surprised at just how rotten that made him feel. Yeah, he'd just been using this business as a means to an end, but he hated failure in any form. To have to throw in the towel when he'd barely gotten started ate away at him like nothing else. He'd hit rock bottom in real estate, and now he was failing at the one thing that was supposed to help him bring that back. Where was he supposed to go from here?

"If you'll give me a minute," he said, "I'll go inside and write you a check."

When Alison nodded, he rose from the swing and went inside. He walked to his office at the back of the house and flipped on a single dim lamp. He sat down at his desk and pulled out his checkbook, only to stop and look around the room. And suddenly he was overcome with that same feeling he'd had as a teenager, that gut-level feeling that he couldn't do a damned thing right—a feeling that had been hammered into him by his father from the time he was five years old.

Then his thoughts took a different turn, this time to his grandmother. He remembered watching her at this very desk, her bifocals low on her nose as she pored over the file in front of her. He wondered if she'd ever screwed things up with a client as badly as he'd screwed things up with Alison. Probably not. He couldn't imagine a guy like David getting past her.

Just write the damned check. And then tomorrow you need to shut the whole thing down and move on to plan B.

Unfortunately, he didn't have a plan B.

When he came back outside, Alison was still sitting on the porch swing, rocking it aimlessly back and forth with her toe. His grandmother had rocked that swing the very same way as she'd spent long, leisurely summer evenings drinking sweet tea and chatting with her neighbors. "*Come sit with us, Brandon,*" she'd say whenever he came home, "*and I'll get you some tea.*" But he'd been sixteen years old, all swagger and attitude, with a chip on his shoulder the size of a redwood tree. He'd always just mumbled something indecipherable and disappeared into the house, where he went upstairs and whacked a few pool balls around as he plotted what he was going to do when he was out of this hokey place.

But now, as he looked at this hokey place through the eyes of an adult, he saw something else. For all the trouble he gave his grandmother during the two years he'd lived there, she was the only person on earth who'd ever cared enough to give him something resembling a normal life.

He held out the check. Alison stared at it a long time before finally taking it. He waited for her to put it in her purse and walk away, and in that moment he knew just how much he was going to miss her and how much he hoped she'd eventually find the man she was looking for.

Instead, she tore it up.

"What are you doing?" he asked.

"Never mind what I said before. I want you to try again."

Brandon's mind spun with disbelief. His first thought was that she was giving him a shot at redemption, which meant his matchmaking business might not be dead after all. His second thought was, *Are you out of your mind?*

"I don't understand. I sent you on two terrible dates, and now you want a third one?"

"I know that doesn't make much sense, but…" She shrugged. "I just got to thinking about it, and if David really didn't tell you how short a time he'd been divorced, you couldn't have known what a flake he was."

"But it's like you said. I should have asked."

"But didn't just the fact that he wanted to go out on a date say, 'Hey, I'm over my ex-wife'?"

Brandon sat down beside her. "You actually want me to set you up again?"

"I know how much you want to make this work. It was your grandmother's business and you want to do right by her. You just need to get the hang of it. I wouldn't feel right not giving you another chance."

Brandon couldn't believe this. She needed to take that check to the bank first thing Monday morning and never look back. Couldn't she see she'd been right in the first place? Couldn't she see that every date he set her up on was going to end in disaster?

Couldn't she see he was a big, fat *fraud*?

"Alison," he said, "you're being way too nice."

"You know, people tell me that a lot." She shrugged. "It's not like I don't *try* to be nasty, but I just can't get it to come out right."

"You need to stop trying. It's hopeless."

"Hey! I told you off pretty good the other night after my date with the drug dealer, didn't I?"

"Yeah, but then you gave me another chance. And here you are doing it again."

"See? *See?* No matter how hard I try, I just can't hold on to nasty." She sighed with resignation. "It's my tragic flaw."

"Stop trying. I've known a lot of nasty people. Nice is better."

"But that's the problem," she said. "I'm nice. Men don't like nice. They want hot and sexy. They want bad girls. *Blonde* bad girls. I tried blonde once. I looked like Lady Gaga. After she'd eaten a truckload of Twinkies."

"Are you always this down on yourself?"

She shrugged. "Truthfully? These days, yeah. Sometimes I am. I mean, look at what happened tonight. David left me to go into a bathroom stall to bang his slutty ex-wife. Men say they want nice girls, but most of the time they're lying. What they want is a lady in the living room and a whore in the—well, in David's case, the bathroom."

Brandon thought about the women he'd been with in his life. He wouldn't have classified any of them as "nice girls." Most of them were shrewd and savvy and a little rough around the edges. They knew the score because they were playing the same game he was. Nothing lasting, nothing permanent, nothing connecting them in any meaningful way.

And then there was Alison.

He'd never spent time with a woman like her, a woman whose only goal was to have a normal life with a nice guy, a couple of kids, and his and hers minivans. There had to be plenty of men on this planet with the same goal, so it was unbelievable to him that some guy hadn't already grabbed her.

"The right guy is out there for you," Brandon said. "Trust me on that."

"I know. And you'll find him for me, won't you?"

She looked up at him with plaintive eyes, her lashes so long they brushed her cheeks, which were flushed pink from the warm, sultry evening. For the first time he noticed how the moonlight cast a pale golden glow on her ivory skin, making it look so warm and touchable that he imagined pressing his hand to her upper arm and dragging it all the way down to her wrist just to see what it felt like. Most men wouldn't say she was beautiful. Not in the conventional sense. But there was something about her that appealed to him in a girl-next-door kind of way, and that had never been his type before.

"I'm going to try," he said.

She gave him a smile of encouragement. "You'll get the hang of this business. Practice makes perfect."

"Yeah? Well, first I have to have somebody to practice on."

Alison blinked with surprise. "But you have lots of

clients, don't you? You told me you had room for only two new ones this month."

Shit. He'd roped Alison in by telling her his schedule was filling up fast, and now he was telling her he didn't have enough clients?

Time for some fast thinking.

"I have so many of my grandmother's clients who were already in place to deal with that I thought I wouldn't have time for many more. But if I'm going to get this business off the ground, I have to find some new clients."

"Oh. So how did your grandmother solicit business?"

"She didn't. She was strictly word of mouth."

"Then you need to build a reputation as good as the one she had."

Nope. That wouldn't work. He didn't have the time to build this business with the glacial speed his grandmother had, if he could even build it at all.

"I did run an ad on *Dallas After Dark*," he said, "but I'm not getting much response."

"Well, at least you're advertising in the right place," Alison said. "*Dallas After Dark* definitely targets singles."

"Then why aren't those singles calling me?"

"Some of your ad elements may be wrong. Or it could be placed wrong. Any number of reasons."

"Oh, yeah. You're in marketing, aren't you?"

"Show me the ad. Maybe I can give you some advice."

Brandon grabbed his phone and pulled up the website, his phone glowing softly in the faint porch light. "There. In the right column."

She took his phone and looked at the ad. "Oh. No wonder."

"What?"

"This is blah. Ordinary. Lost in the middle of ads for stripper bars and psychics. And why are you still calling it Matchmaking by Rochelle?"

"I was afraid people wouldn't call if they knew a man was running things now."

"Wrong. The best thing you have going for your business is you."

"Me?"

"Yes. You have no competition."

"What do you mean?"

"Do you know of any other male matchmakers?"

"I've always thought of that as something I needed to overcome, not something in my favor."

"Nope. You should always be looking for that one thing that sets you apart from the competition. You already have a niche because you offer the same personalized service your grandmother did. Toss in the fact that you're a man, and you'll get attention. Add the fact that you're a young, *attractive* man, and you're definitely one of a kind."

"Wait a minute. You came to me only because you thought I was a woman. Then you freaked out when you found out I was a man."

"Freaked out? I didn't freak out."

Brandon smiled. "Yeah, you did."

"I was just a little surprised."

"Nope. It was a bona fide freak-out."

"Oh, come on! You're acting as if I ran screaming from your office."

"No. But you should have seen the look on your face."

Alison slumped with resignation. "You know what?

Just once I'd like to put something past you. That would make me really, really happy."

"Well, you've got me where marketing is concerned. I still don't see how being a man is going to give me an edge."

"When I came to your office the first time, the shock of it just about made me turn around and leave. I wasn't prepared for what I got. But if you present yourself properly, people are going to know in advance exactly who you are and what you can do for them."

"And just how do I go about presenting myself properly?"

"I can take care of that."

"You can? How?"

"I'll show you. But first..." She raised an eyebrow. "What's in it for me?"

"Uh..."

"How about we barter? Your services for mine. You comp your matchmaking fee for me, and I'll bring you all the clients you can handle."

No cash on the table? That got his attention. Of course, it meant he'd have to take cash back out of his pocket. But if she could do what she said she could, it would be like trading one client for several clients. Mathematically speaking, unless it netted him absolutely nothing, he couldn't lose.

"Hold on," he said. "If you're talking about placing more ads, I can't afford that."

"No problem. You never should have paid for advertising in the first place."

"How else am I supposed to get potential clients through the door?"

"With PR. You don't pay for that. I'll write you a press release. Send it to several media outlets. Once they read it, I guarantee the local press will run stories about you."

"Because I'm a man who's a matchmaker?"

"Exactly. Journalists need content, and they're always looking for an angle. A slant. A great hook that'll get people's attention. We'll provide them with one. I'll e-mail it to a bunch of magazines, bloggers, radio stations, all that. With exposure like that, I guarantee you'll have all the clients you could possibly hope for."

Brandon felt a little thrill of anticipation. He'd lost hope. Now, with Alison's help, he felt as if he could actually pull this off.

"Now, the question is, are you ready to be interviewed?" she asked.

"Interviewed?"

"That's what's coming."

"Uh...yeah. I guess."

"Just talk to people the way you talked to me the first time I came to your office, and you'll have the singles in this town wrapped around your little finger."

Brandon liked the sound of that, too.

"Another thing," Alison said. "You need a new name for your business."

"Like what?"

"I don't know. I'll have to think about it."

He gave her a sly smile. "I could be the Love Doctor."

She screwed up her face. "Get serious. You know that's been used about a thousand times before in a thousand different ways. Radio shrinks...advice columnists..."

"Porn sites."

She raised her eyebrows. "Porn sites?"

"Oh. Didn't I tell you about my doctor-nurse fetish?"

She looked at him dumbly. "You have a hard time focusing, don't you?"

"Not at all. What you're telling me is that I need a name that's uniquely mine."

"Exactly."

"Any suggestions?"

"It's all about emotion," she said. "Your name needs to reflect that. Put yourself in the position of somebody who's looking for their soul mate."

Well, there was something he had no idea how to relate to. "I'm drawing a blank."

"Think about how relationships feel in the beginning. There's that whisper of love in the air. That sense of hope. That tiny little tug on the heartstrings. That feeling that this person just might be *the one*."

Now he really felt like a fraud. How was he supposed to sell the prospect of love everlasting when the longest relationship he'd ever had consisted of a three-day weekend in Vegas?

Suddenly Alison smiled and snapped her fingers. "That's it."

"What?"

"That's your new name. Heartstrings."

"Huh?"

"It has all kinds of positive connotations. You'll need a good tagline, but it's something you can work with."

"Wrapping people in strings? Sounds like you're trapping them."

"People come to you because they want to be trapped. They want to be wrapped up in soft, fuzzy little strings from their heart to their soul mate's heart. That name could be good. It could be *great*."

But Brandon wasn't convinced. "Sounds kind of...I don't know. Weak?"

"Well, I suppose you could call it Brandon's Great Big House of Burning Love. How's that work for you?"

He grinned. "Now you're talking."

"Men. *God*." She shifted around on the swing to face him, talking with her hands now. "Listen to me. It's not weak. It's gentle. Big difference. You have to think how people who want to fall in love think. They want to feel the warmth and safety of a relationship. They want to feel the soft, comforting touch of a partner, that one person on earth who will always be there for them. And not just women, though they're the only ones who'll admit it. Guys, too. *That's* what they're looking for."

She spoke with such passion that he knew the words came straight from her heart. She wasn't only telling him what women in general wanted. She was also telling him what *she* wanted.

"So are we going with Heartstrings?" she asked.

He appreciated her help. Hell, he was dying for it. But what was she going to say in a few months when he bagged up all the profits from this business and hit the road for Houston?

It didn't matter. He needed new clients, and Alison was a pro who was willing to help him get them. He'd be out no cash because he was comping her fee, and she swore to him that a free press release would be far more effective than expensive advertising. So what else was there to think about?

Maybe the fact that he was being just a little bit dishonest.

Then again, so what if he closed his business in a few months? He'd traded her even up, hadn't he? His services for hers? This was business. Nothing more.

"Heartstrings it is," he told her. "So tell me what this press release is going to say."

"You leave that to me. I'll run it past you before it goes out. And I'll need a photo of you to send along with it. I'm pretty good with a camera, so I can handle that. But you're also going to need a new logo to go with your new name so you look professional."

"But that'll cost me. I already told you I don't have money for that."

"All it will cost you is a box of Godiva chocolates. Can you handle that?"

"I don't get it."

"You don't have to. I'll take care of the rest. You're going to have all the business you could ask for."

"You'd do all this for me?" he asked.

"Hey, I'm not doing it for you. I'm doing it for me. If I can get you more people to practice on, maybe you'll get the hang of it before you match me up again."

He smiled. "No. You're doing it because you're a nice person who likes to help other people."

"So we're back to the nice girl thing again? I told you before. *Men don't want that.*"

"The man you're looking for does."

"Then find him for me, will you? I'm not getting any younger." She sighed. "Let's just hope the next guy really is over his last love. I don't know if I can take another bout of hot sex in the ladies' room that I'm not participating in."

Just then, Jasmine strolled across the front porch and jumped up onto the swing. She put one paw on Alison's leg, then looked up at her.

"Oh, look at her!" Alison said. "She's such a sweet kitty. She actually *asks* if she can get into my lap." Alison scratched her behind her ears, and Jasmine plopped down. "She could teach my cats a thing or two about manners."

"Now, see?" Brandon said, smiling. "You *need* her."

"Oh, come on," Alison said. "You know you want this precious kitty."

Sooner or later he'd have to find her a new home. But how? She was his grandmother's cat after all. He couldn't just take her to a shelter.

He decided he'd worry about that when the time came.

"I'll need to write you a new check since you tore that one up," Brandon said.

"We'll settle up when I see you next. Give me two days, and I'll have everything ready to go." She smiled. "Don't worry. Things are going to work out just fine."

He believed that. He believed her when she said she knew what she was doing and could get him the clients he needed. The question was, could he hold up his end of the bargain and find her a husband?

After Alison left, Brandon grabbed a beer and came back out to the front porch, flipping off the light so he wouldn't draw bugs. He sat there a long time in the dark, sipping the beer, thinking about how he'd entered into this business with little more than the bare bones of a plan and a whole lot of audacity, thinking he'd get in, toss the dice on enough matches to get him the money he needed, and get out. But now for the first time, he was beginning to realize that the business he'd intended to bleed dry and then toss away just might be more important to people than he realized.

And there was something about Alison that made him want to give her the happily ever after she was dreaming of.

On Monday morning, Alison sidled up next to Lois's cubicle. As soon as Lois saw her, she poked her computer keyboard and closed the website she was looking at, as if everybody in the entire office didn't know she spent at least an hour a day on a *Twilight* fan forum.

"What do you want?" Lois said, pretending to concentrate on the Photoshop image that was now on her screen.

"I need a favor."

"I don't do favors."

"I need a logo."

"So hire a graphic artist."

"You're a graphic artist. The best graphic artist I know."

"Don't kiss my ass. You know how I feel about ass kissing."

"How about if we barter a little?"

Lois turned slowly back to face her. "What did you have in mind?"

Alison pulled out the unmarked sack and gave Lois a peek inside.

"Godivas?" Lois said in a panicked whisper. "You can't bring Godivas in here! That's like cheating on the company!"

"Oh, yeah?"

"Yeah! Somebody in accounting brought a sack of

those mini Snickers bars to the office once and got an official reprimand, and you're flashing *Godivas*?"

"That never happened. Somebody started that rumor as a joke."

"It was no joke. Management doesn't like to see competitor's products anywhere in the office. I don't mess with management."

"Lois," Alison said, whispering enticingly. "It's *Godiva*."

Lois scowled at her. "You're a horrible person, Alison. I know everybody thinks you're really nice and everything, but you're not."

"There are only two people in on this. You and me. And I'm not telling."

Lois looked back into the sack at the gold box and actually licked her lips. Any moment Alison expected her to flap her arms, take off, and buzz around the box of chocolates like a vulture over a dying rat.

"Candy first," Lois said. "Then the logo."

She reached for the sack, but Alison pulled it away. "I need it by tomorrow afternoon."

"Anything in particular you want?"

"I'll e-mail you some info on the company. You can take it from there."

"I'll have a mock-up for you in the morning."

"Deal."

Alison handed her the sack, which she quickly stuffed into her lower desk drawer. But not five minutes later, Alison saw her grab the sack out of the drawer again. She flicked her head back and forth, checking for witnesses, then disappeared into the ladies' room. Good God. What kind of person ate a box of Godiva chocolates while sitting in a bathroom stall?

A really, *really* compulsive one.

On her lunch hour, Alison wrote the press release. By the next afternoon, Lois had the final logo for her. It was a pair of hearts connected with strings, just as Alison had expected, but it was stylized just enough that it didn't look dumb. The tagline Alison had decided on, *Tying Two Hearts Together Forever*, was in a serpentine pattern beneath it in a casual font. It looked enticing and interesting but highly professional at the same time. How Lois could be Lois and still come up with good stuff like this, she didn't know. Brandon had traded a box of Godiva for pure gold.

True to her word, Alison showed up at Brandon's house two days later with the press release in hand. They sat down on the porch swing, and Alison handed it to him.

"Tell me what you think."

He scanned the headline. *Matchmaking Man Helps Singles Find Their Soul Mates.*

"So that'll get attention?" he asked.

"Oh, yeah."

"I like the logo."

"Isn't it great?"

It was. But as Brandon read the rest of the press release, he started to get a really funny feeling inside. Alison had written about how he'd inherited the business from his grandmother, who had been a matchmaker in Plano for thirty years. How he used to sit on the stairs in her turn-of-the-century home listening to her talk to her clients and help them make the love connection they'd always dreamed about. How matching people with their soul mates was in his blood, so he was driven to make his own clients' dreams come true.

It was everything he'd told Alison as if it were the truth, and there was barely any truth in it at all. Yeah, he'd heard his grandmother talking to her clients. But it was more like he heard a snippet or two as he was blowing through on the way to the kitchen, or coming through the back door and heading upstairs. But telling Alison he'd spent only two years living with his grandmother before turning eighteen and hightailing it out of town wouldn't have been quite as effective a sales pitch.

The press release went on to talk about the personalized service he offered, just as his grandmother had, but from a twenty-first-century perspective. Then Alison had added a few bullet points containing statistics on the success people have using personal matchmakers versus Internet dating. And she finished with, *Oddly enough, Brandon Scott hasn't yet found that one special person for himself, but he's convinced that'll be his reward for helping other people find true love.*

"I took a few liberties with that last line," Alison said. "Hope you don't mind."

Hey, what the hell. Let's both lie. "It's fine."

"Do I have the contact information correct?"

He glanced at the bottom of the sheet. "Yeah."

"Now it's photo time. Let's see... over there."

She pointed toward the porch railing and got out her camera.

"Okay," she said when he was in place. "Smile."

He did. She snapped a few photos and looked at the screen. "Nope. That's a phony smile."

"It didn't feel phony."

"It never does. But it sure looks it. Try again."

He smiled again. Same story.

"Relax a little," Alison said.

He did. Or tried to. And it still looked fake.

"Okay," Alison said. "I want you to be serious for a moment. No smiling."

"Uh...okay." He gave her a deadpan look.

"Now. I want you to imagine David and his ex doing it in a bathroom stall."

He smiled.

Click.

"Sorry," Brandon said. "That shouldn't make me laugh."

"We have to laugh about it, or we'll cry." Alison looked at the screen and smiled herself. "There. Perfect." She grabbed her purse. "Gotta go. I'll send the press release and your photo out first thing tomorrow. Be ready. You're liable to get some action pretty quickly."

"Do you really think so?"

"I really think so."

A little voice was egging him to tell her the truth, but he knew how she'd feel about that. Maybe this press release would net nothing, and he wouldn't have to feel bad about it.

Then again, if it didn't net something, he was finished.

At ten-thirty the next morning, Brandon was at his desk, sipping a cup of coffee, when the phone rang. He picked it up from his desktop and answered it.

"Hello?"

"Is this Brandon Scott?"

He sat up. "Yes?"

"This is Kelsey Dunn from *Dallas After Dark*. We just received your press release. I was wondering if you'd be available for an interview sometime today or tomorrow?"

"Uh . . . yeah. Sure."

"We'd like to run a story on your matchmaking service. I think our readers will be very interested in getting to know you better."

Brandon's heart was suddenly beating double time. "I'll have to check my calendar, but I think I'll have some free time this afternoon."

Feeling a surge of hope, he made an appointment with her for four o'clock. And before the day was out, he was contacted by the *Dallas Morning News*, a radio station, and a local blogger who offered advice to the lovelorn and asked him if he ever did any guest blogging.

And just like that, he was in business.

Chapter 13

The next week was a blur for Brandon.

After doing two print interviews, a blog interview, and a radio interview with a popular morning show, his phone had started to ring. Within a couple of days, he'd signed three new clients and had introductory appointments with two more.

By the time Friday came, he was ready for a beer and a game of pool, so he grabbed Tom and they headed to McCaffrey's.

"So it's actually working?" Tom said as he racked up the balls. "I was beginning to think you were going to have to throw in the towel."

"Nope. And I did the math. If everything continues at this rate, I'll have all the money I need to close the deal."

"Then keep making those matches," Tom said.

Brandon smacked the last ball into the side pocket to end the game. When he looked up again, he saw Alison come through the door. She waved, her face lighting up with a sunny smile. He smiled and waved back at her, and when she started walking toward him, for some reason, his heart started to beat a little faster.

They'd talked several times this week about the interviews he was doing and the clients he was signing. Her excitement over his success was so contagious that every time the phone rang, he hoped it was her. Seeing her in person was even better.

Especially tonight.

She wore a casual halter dress with a snug skirt that stopped midthigh. Up to now, he'd seen her in longer skirts or pants, and he was stopped cold by the sight of her legs, which were clearly one of her better features. What added to the fantasy was a pair of hot pink pumps with heels just this side of stratospheric. Her hair was pulled up to the crown of her head in some kind of shiny barrette thing with pieces of hair falling out of it and grazing her cheeks.

She came up beside them at the pool table. "Hey, guys."

"Hi, Alison," Tom said. "You look great tonight."

"Thanks. The shoes are a little slutty, I'm afraid. Not really my style, but Heather convinced me I needed to branch out."

"So where are you heading tonight?" Brandon asked. "This isn't your usual McCaffrey's look."

"It's girls' night out. As soon as Heather's finished here, we're meeting some friends for a wine tasting."

"So you're a wine enthusiast?" Brandon asked.

"Not exactly. You know that guy you see sitting on a curb downtown drinking from a bottle of Ripple in a brown paper sack?"

"Yeah?"

"He knows more about wine than I do. But at least I drink it out of a glass."

"So where's Heather?" Brandon asked. "I don't feel comfortable here unless she's giving me the evil eye."

"In her office in the back, I imagine. I'm a little early."

"Do you think there's hope that she'll ever stop hating me?"

Alison smiled. "There's always hope. Hey! I heard you on the drive time radio interview this morning. You were *great*."

"Yeah? I wasn't sure about that. Did you hear the host ask me if I cherry-picked my hottest women clients for myself?"

"Don't worry. You said exactly the right thing. 'No, Steve, I don't, but if you'd like to hire me as your match-maker, I'd be happy to cherry-pick one for you.' That was a *great* answer."

"So how about I cherry-pick you for Steve?"

Alison pursed her lips with mock irritation. "Are you *trying* for a third strike?"

Brandon grinned. "Okay. Bad idea. But I do need to find you a new match."

"Take your time," she said. "It's more important right now that you get new clients signed up."

"Nope. You're my number one client. I'll have some-body for you soon."

"I know," she said with a soft smile. "I have faith in you."

He knew she did. And that was why he felt like a total fraud. *Just make damned sure you get it right this time.*

And then he heard a little throat clearing. He turned to see Heather standing behind him.

"Hi, Heather," Brandon said with a smile.

"Hello," she said with all the warmth of a cadaver. "Alison? Are you ready to go?"

"Yep," she said, grabbing her purse from the bar. "See you guys later."

As she walked away, Tom said, "Wow. Heather's a little cold, isn't she?"

"Yeah. She thinks I'm out to con Alison."

"Intuitive, isn't she?"

"I'm not conning anybody. Alison has helped me, and I intend to help her."

"Well, then. Better luck with her next match. Then again, anything will be better than the first two, won't it?"

Then Brandon realized Tom was talking to him but watching Alison through the window as they walked to Heather's car, clearly enjoying the view as much as he was. And for some reason, that pissed him off.

"Will you stop staring at her like that?" he said.

"Like what?"

"She's not that kind of girl."

"Maybe not, but those shoes say she is. You know what I said about her not being my kind of woman? Maybe I'm reconsidering."

"Right. You'll turn into a family man about the time hell freezes over."

"I didn't say my kind of woman for a lifetime. But a night or two is a definite possibility. How about making me her next match?"

"Knock it off. That's not what she's looking for, and you know it."

"Fine," Tom said. "I can't touch. I can't even look. So what can I do?"

"Go after Tracy."

Tom glanced to the bar, where Tracy was leaning over to wash glasses, her top so low cut she was in danger of her breasts falling out. Something told Brandon that if it happened, it wouldn't be the first time.

"Good advice," Tom said. "I'm on it."

As Tom walked away, Brandon turned back to the window and watched Alison in precisely the way he'd told Tom not to. As she got into the car, he noticed her legs again. They were amazing—smooth, tanned, and curvy. Someday he wanted to run his hand from her thigh to her ankle and back up again, and watch as tiny little goose bumps rose in its wake. Of course, if he did, he'd be overstepping his bounds in ways he'd promised himself he wouldn't. In the end, she wasn't his kind of woman any more than she was Tom's. But still there was something about her...

He probably needed to take his own advice. *Don't touch. Don't even look.* But he figured as long as he didn't actually *act* on any of his errant thoughts about Alison, he was in the clear.

When Brandon and Tom got home that evening, the sun had just slipped beyond the horizon. A spectacular red gold sunset warmed the entire neighborhood, set to music by a mass of crickets that took their jobs *very* seriously. Tom went inside to watch a baseball game, but after the flurry of activity that week, Brandon was content just to grab another beer, sit on the porch swing, and rock for a little while.

He'd taken to doing that more and more, just sitting out there in the evenings, rocking back and forth and watching the neighbors do what neighbors did. On one side of him lived a young, dark-haired woman. He'd seen her in her yard a few times piddling around with her flowers, but otherwise she seemed to keep to herself. The young couple next door on the other side went for a stroll almost every evening with the wading pool kids in tow. The old woman across the street, the one who'd taken Jasmine in when his grandmother had died, came out most evenings and hand-watered her periwinkles. Then she scoured her lawn for any weeds that dared show their ugly little faces and attacked them with a weed popper. Across the street and a few doors down lived a meticulous, thirty-something guy who always wore a pressed T-shirt and shorts and walked his perfectly groomed Lhasa apso at precisely eight o'clock every evening. Fortunately, he never hit the road without a poop scooper and a plastic bag, for which Brandon thanked him. Various kids bicycled or skateboarded up and down the block.

Sometimes people stopped to chat a little, particularly in the beginning so they could express condolences about his grandmother's death. But these days they mostly just waved, and Brandon waved back.

The night wind *shusshed* through the leaves of the live oak tree in his front yard, lulling his brain into a pleasant state of relaxation. He took another sip of beer, closed his eyes, and concentrated on how the ice-cold liquid felt as it slid down his throat. Up to now his life had been so busy. Frantic sometimes. He'd hopped from one town to the next like a man possessed, always under the gun to get a project finished before moving on to the next one. But now...

Now there was something about just sitting there, holding the bottle against his knee, his eyes closed, and rocking back and forth that soothed him right down to his soul.

A minute or so later, he heard a soft tap, tap, tap. His eyes sprang open, and he looked around to see a young woman standing at the bottom of the porch stairs.

Strangely, it was almost dark outside, but she wore a pair of sunglasses. In one hand she held a small pot of purple flowers. And in the other...*oh.*

A white cane.

He came to attention. "Uh...hi, there."

She stopped short. "Mr. Scott?"

"Yes."

"Oh!" she said, laughing a little. "I didn't know you were on the porch." She pointed to her sunglasses. "Sorry. I have this blindness thing going on. Keeps me from realizing all kinds of things."

Brandon stood up and came down the steps.

"I'm Delilah James," she said, tucking her cane beneath her arm and holding out her hand. "Your next-door neighbor."

Now he recognized her. And he also realized why he'd waved at her a few times when he saw her in her yard and she'd never waved back.

"It's nice to meet you," he said, shaking her hand. Closer now, he could see she was probably in her late twenties. She wasn't beautiful, exactly, but there was an ethereal quality about her that would command just about anybody's attention. She had sleek, dark hair, porcelain skin, and a body so delicate that a puff of wind just might send her floating away like dandelion fuzz.

"I brought you these," she said, holding out the flowers. "A belated 'welcome to the neighborhood' gift. I should have gotten over here sooner, but I'm afraid I've been a lousy neighbor. Better late than never?"

He took the flowers. "Thanks. That's nice."

"I'm sorry about your grandmother. She was a nice lady. And it was a nice funeral."

So she'd been there. But since about two hundred other people had been too, he didn't remember seeing her. "Thanks. I appreciate that."

"Mr. Scott? Could we talk for just a minute?"

"Uh...sure. As long as you call me Brandon."

"Okay. Brandon."

They went up the porch steps, and Brandon directed her to the swing. He set the plant beside the front door and sat down beside her.

"I heard you on the radio a few days ago," she said. "I didn't know you'd taken over your grandmother's business."

"Yep. I'm the new matchmaker on the block."

"The guy who interviewed you was a real ass."

Brandon laughed. "What is it they say? All publicity is good publicity?"

"Well, I hope for my sake you're not too busy now. I'd like to hire you."

Brandon froze. "You need a matchmaker?"

"I know what you're thinking," she said with an off-hand wave. "You're thinking 'Boy, she's a real catch. I mean, with her stunning beauty and scintillating personality, why in the world would a girl like her need to hire somebody to find her a man?'"

Okay, so her blindness probably put her in a bit of a compromised position where dating was concerned, but surely she had other qualities to offset the apprehension some men were likely to have.

"Actually," Brandon said, "that's exactly what I was thinking. You don't seem like the kind of woman who would have any problem meeting men."

"Uh...I did mention the blindness thing, didn't I?"

"So that's been a problem for you?"

"Yeah," she said, her smile fading. "Just so you'll know, though, I haven't always been a loser at love. I was even engaged once. Before my accident. But after... well, he decided having a blind wife wasn't the direction he expected his life to go."

Bastard. Brandon didn't even know the guy, but that didn't stop him from hating him. "Not all men are like that."

"I know. I'm just having a hell of a time finding the ones who aren't. For some reason, blind girls seem to scare men away. Go figure."

"That's not fair."

"But that's reality. And if you saw what was behind these sunglasses, you'd know why."

For the first time, around the edges of her sunglasses, he saw the remnants of damaged skin that even grafts couldn't completely erase.

"Lab accident," she went on. "I was a biochem major at the University of Texas. Acid and glass can be really ugly things."

Every bit of the elation Brandon had felt all week because of the new clients he'd signed up seemed to fizzle away. Those were ordinary people with ordinary dating problems. But this...

"Why don't you tell me a little bit about yourself?" he said, mostly because he didn't know what else to say.

"Hmm. Let's see... I like gardening. Can't see the flowers, but I can still smell them, which is why my house is overrun with roses. And I like the feel of the dirt in my hands. Weird, huh? I have a good job, not exactly as a research chemist, but I won't be a financial drain on

a guy. I own the house I live in. I like movies, but—"
She held up her palm. "Okay, I have to admit I'm not
too crazy about action-adventure films. It's not that I have
anything against stuff exploding. I just have a hard time
these days trying to figure out what it is that's blowing
up." She smiled. "I know, I know. Deal breaker for some
guys. But there you go."

Brandon liked this woman. He liked her a lot. But how was
he going to get the average guy to see past the obvious? The
answer was that it was going to have to be an above-average
guy, and there weren't too many of those out there.

"If you want me to fill out a questionnaire or something, I'd be happy to," Delilah said. "I have a friend
who'll help me with it."

"Uh . . . that'd be great."

"If you have hard copies, I can pick one up tomorrow
when I bring you a check. What's your fee?"

He didn't even want to say it. The moment he took her
money, he was obligated to help, even if he was in over
his head. *Way* over.

"I charge fifteen hundred dollars for five introductions."

He actually hoped maybe that would scare her away
and he wouldn't have to deal with this. Instead she made
a scoffing noise and said, "That's all? Hell, the way my
love life is going, I'd pay fifteen hundred bucks for *one*
introduction."

No. Don't tell me that. I'm not worth it!

"So," she said, taking a deep breath and letting it out
slowly. "What do you think, Mr. Matchmaker? Is there
hope?"

Brandon opened his mouth to say something, only to

close it again. Hope? Hell, there was always hope. But considering that he wasn't really a matchmaker, what were the odds that he'd be able to pull this off?

"Hmm," she said thoughtfully. "You're not answering me. It's times like these I really hate not being able to see people's faces."

"I'm sorry," he said. "I was just...I was just mentally going through my files. I'm sure there's somebody in there who'll be perfect for you."

The moment the words were out of his mouth, he wanted to yank them back. He had no idea if he'd be able to make a match for this woman. None at all.

"You're a little uptight about this, aren't you?" Delilah said.

His heart skipped. "No. Of course not."

"Don't worry, Brandon. I'm a realist. I know I'm a tough sell. If this works out, okay. If not, that's okay, too." She stood up and gave him a cheery smile. "So...if you happen to come across a guy who doesn't mind dating a poor blind girl, let me know, okay?"

She grabbed her cane and started down the stairs, only to turn back. She paused for a long time, and he noticed her hand tightening on the porch railing.

"When you were on the radio," she said, her voice softer now, "you said that you think there's somebody out there for everybody. Do you really believe that?"

Brandon closed his eyes. *Please don't ask me that.* "Of course I do."

She seemed to think about that for a moment, and then she gave him a smile.

"I just decided I'm going to take your word for that. After all, you're the professional, right?"

"Yeah," he said, even as he thought *fraud, fraud, fraud*. "I'm the professional."

She turned and continued down the stairs. Brandon watched as she walked back to her house, trying to imagine what it must have been like for her to have her life change so profoundly from one second to the next. He admired the hell out of her just for having the guts to get up and get on with her life.

And here she was putting her trust in him.

He didn't like people depending on him. That implied a sense of responsibility he'd never believed himself to have, and now he had to take it whether he wanted it or not.

He imagined leaving Plano in a few months and handing her money back to her. *Sorry, sweetheart. Guess Mr. Right isn't going to be so easy to find after all. Good luck with the rest of your life.*

He'd lied to her before. He had no idea if there was somebody out there for everybody. Surely there had to be some people in this world who were destined to go through it alone. And he'd always believed he was one of them.

He sincerely hoped Delilah wasn't.

The next afternoon, Alison and Heather were once again sitting around the table with the other members of the board of the Preservation League. It was their second meeting that month, with more to come. It was always like that in the weeks leading up to the home tour. So many details, so little time. There were the sponsors to think about. Volunteers. The program. Press releases. Raffle baskets. Ticket sales. Tour guides. More meetings. More details. More things she had to remember.

More Judith.

Bea hadn't even arrived to kick off the meeting yet, and already Judith was arguing with Karen about the hors d'oeuvres Maggie's Café was donating. Thirty seconds into the conversation, Alison wanted to toss her Sharpie aside and send a letter opener straight through her own skull.

"Those mini quiches were dry as a bone last year," Judith said. "The egg was like rubber. I could barely eat one. You need to tell them that. No mini quiches unless they can keep them moist."

"You want me to actually *say* that to them?" Karen said.

"Why not?"

"Because it's a *donation*, Judith," Heather said. "You don't solicit a donation and then bitch about the details."

"It's more than just details. It's a health hazard."

"Health hazard?"

"Somebody could choke on it."

Then by all means, Judith, eat up.

Just then Bea came through the door and tossed her notebook down on the conference room table. "Bad news, boys and girls. I just got off the phone with Mrs. Strayhorn. She's backing out of the tour."

Alison's heart seized up. "What? No. She can't back out. The tour is less than two months away!"

"She says she's afraid people will steal things."

"But I told her that wouldn't happen," Alison said. "I told her we'd have plenty of people staffing her house."

"She's not so sure *they* won't steal from her."

"I'll talk to her again," Alison said. "Try to change her mind."

"Nope. What if she backs out again only a few days before the tour and leaves us with no chance of getting another house?"

Good point.

"I wonder why Mrs. Strayhorn called you instead of me?" Alison said.

"She said you were such a nice girl that she didn't want to tell you she'd changed her mind." Bea paused, raising an eyebrow. "Gee, I wonder what that says about me?"

"What about the stuff about the Strayhorn house up on the website?" Karen said.

"And the programs are getting ready to go to press," Judith said.

"Don't worry about the website so much," Bea said. "But we do have to stop the programs. If those have to be reprinted, it'll break the bank."

Judith turned to Alison. "So what are you going to do now?"

"I'm not sure," Alison said. "But I'll get another house. I just don't know where."

"There's that house on State Street," Karen said. "On the corner of 16th. Painted beige and burgundy. Two-story Victorian with a wraparound porch—"

"I tried that one. It's vacant now. The old man who lived there died, and the house is tied up in his estate." She turned to Bea. "Are there any women in your book group who might have a house that'll work? Or know somebody who might?"

"I've hit them up in the past. But I'll hit again."

This was a disaster. Finding four people with the right

homes who didn't mind opening them up to hundreds of people traipsing through them was a staggering feat every year. If they left it at three homes, they'd feel obligated to drop the admission charge, which would really cut into their profits.

And then it dawned on her. She did know of another house. Why hadn't she thought of it before? She turned the thought over in her mind. Yes . . . *yes*. It would be perfect.

"Wait a minute," she said. "I know just the house."

Bea perked up. "You do?"

"It's a pretty little prairie-style bungalow. Nearly original. It's on a beautiful block. The house is in good condition, and a lot of the furniture is vintage."

"Sounds perfect," Karen said. "Where is it?"

"I'll tell you all about it once it's in the bag."

"Hold on," Judge Jimmy said. "Before we get all excited here, are you sure you can get this house?"

"I'll get it," Alison said. "One way or another."

Half an hour later, the meeting broke up. Bea, Heather, and Alison went up the stairs together.

"Uh . . . there's a small problem with the house that I didn't bother to mention to the whole board," Alison said.

"Problem?" Bea said.

"It's going to need a little work to get it up to par for the tour. The owner just inherited the property, so he hasn't had a chance to do much to it. Since I'll be asking him to use it on short notice, I thought it'd be a sign of goodwill if we offered to help."

"Uh . . . Alison?" Heather said. "Whose house are we talking about?"

Yoga breath. "Brandon Scott's."

"Yeah, that's what I thought. Do you really think that's a good idea?"

"What are you girls talking about?" Bea asked.

"Nothing," Alison said, and Heather rolled her eyes. "It's the perfect house. It just needs a little work."

"How much work are we talking about?" Bea asked.

"Mostly spring cleaning kind of stuff. Minor repairs. Maybe a little painting. Can you guys help?"

"I painted my whole house by myself once," Bea said. "Just give me a roller."

"And I'll ask my father to help, too," Alison said, then turned to Heather. "Can you and Tony help?"

"Yeah, sure," Heather said in a deadpan tone. "Sign us up."

They reached Bea's car. "Just let me know when we're getting together for a work day."

"Will do," Alison said.

As Bea drove away, Heather turned to Alison, her fist on her hip. "Brandon's house? Really?"

"Don't worry. You'll be there the whole time to protect me from his evil ways."

Heather twisted her mouth with irritation.

"Look. If we don't get another house, and fast, we're screwed."

Finally Heather sighed. "Well, I guess we are under the gun. Do you think he'll agree to let us use it?"

"I guess we won't know until I ask, will we?"

Chapter 14

As Brandon listened to Alison's proposal, he decided he needed to stop answering his door if she was on the other side. Every time he let her in, she told him things he didn't want to hear.

"So you want me to open up my house to a bunch of strangers?" he said.

She smiled. "More or less."

"Hell, no."

She drew back. "What do you mean, *hell no*? You haven't even thought about it."

"I don't need to think about it. Strangers traipsing through my house? No, thanks."

"Just pretend you're selling it, and they're prospective buyers. You used to do that all the time, didn't you?"

"Yeah, but I didn't live in those houses."

"It's not that big a deal. One day. That's it."

"I thought tour homes were supposed to be all pretty and perfect. Mine isn't."

"It could be. I know it's a little rough around the edges, but the architecture is wonderful, and a lot of the furniture is from the same period. I have a few people who have volunteered to do whatever we need to do to make it presentable."

"Let me get this straight," Brandon said. "Not only will I have people wandering through here for hours on tour day, I'll also have a bunch of people in my house banging around getting it ready?"

"But think what that's worth. Cleaning, minor repairs, maybe a little painting—what would you have to pay for that?"

Brandon didn't really care about the condition of the house. Let the First Baptist Church worry about that when he left town and it took possession.

"There's too much work that needs to be done," he told her. "It'll take more effort than you and your friends want to put in."

"We just need it to look good on the surface. It won't be all that hard."

"No, Alison. I just really rather not."

"But it would be good PR for your business. Feel free to hand out your business cards. The more you integrate yourself into the community, the stronger your business will be."

If only she knew that was the last thing he wanted to do for the long haul. "I haven't had business cards designed yet."

"That'll cost you . . . hmm. Say, a box of Godiva?"

"I still don't get that."

"Trust me—you don't want to know."

"Truthfully, I have about all the business I can handle already."

"Uh . . . thanks to *whom*? Is her name . . . Alison Carter?"

"Hey, I comped your matchmaking fee, so we're even on that."

"You still owe me."

"Yeah? How do I still owe you?"

"You set me up with a felon, remember?"

He rolled his eyes. "I thought we put that to rest."

"But I suffered psychological damage."

"Oh, you did not."

"No. I did. It's just a delayed reaction. One of these days I'm going to be standing in the grocery store or something and suddenly start crying uncontrollably, and it'll be your fault."

"You are *so* full of crap."

"Oh—did I mention this is for a good cause? The East Plano Preservation League. We do all kinds of good things for the preservation of history in East Plano."

"Such as?"

"I'll get you a copy of our mission statement. It spells it all out. Trust me—it's a doozy."

Brandon shook his head. "I really don't think it's a good idea."

"But—"

"No."

The smile melted away from Alison's face, and she let out a disappointed sigh. "Oh. Okay. I understand." She dropped her eyes, studying her shoes for a moment, then brought them back up to stare at him, looking like a homeless kitten in the rain. There was something about those big brown eyes staring up at him that made him lose his train of thought. Then that train hopped to another track, and he started wondering what such a sweet, innocent woman would look like in a tangle of sheets with morning sun streaming through the window.

And then it struck him.

She wasn't nearly as innocent as those eyes made her seem. In fact, she was downright calculating.

Hey, stupid. Wake up. She's playing you!

"Will you stop that?" Brandon said.

"Stop what?"

"Begging."

"I didn't say a word."

"You didn't have to. Your eyes are doing all the talking."

She tilted her head, adding a layer of lost little girl to the homeless kitten thing.

"Will you stop that? *God*, you're relentless."

And still she stared at him.

Brandon closed his eyes with a heavy sigh. "You're not going to get off this, are you?"

"Nope."

"And you're going to make me feel like crap if I say no, aren't you?"

"Oh, yeah."

Say no, say no, say no. But still she was looking at him. He was going to regret this. He just knew it.

"Fine," he said glumly. "You can use my house."

"Yes!" Alison said, clasping her hands together. "You're the best! *Thank* you!"

Brandon couldn't believe how the silliest things made Alison so happy. Yeah, he didn't much like the idea of opening up his house to strangers, but he didn't hate the expression of pure joy she wore right now.

"Wait a minute. When is the tour?"

"It's not until the second week of October, but that'll be here before we know it. I'd like to get the big stuff done around here in the next couple of weeks. Then we can come back a day or two before to do a final sprucing up. Will that be all right?"

Brandon pulled up a mental calendar, wondering if he'd even still be around by then, but he realized he most likely would. They had until December to exercise the option, and while business was really picking up, he expected he'd need almost all of that time to get the money together he needed.

"Okay," she said. "Can I take a quick tour through the house and see what needs to be done? I'll need to report back to the board."

"Yeah. Sure. I've already thrown myself on your mercy. Why stop now?" He circled his gaze around the living room. "This place could use a complete renovation. Just how much do you think is necessary to bring it up to par for the tour?"

"I'm thinking just cosmetics. That's it."

They went through the entry hall and the living room in short order. Nothing but cleaning and rearranging in there. Then they went into the dining room. Ditto. And the whole time Alison kept telling him how wonderful the woodwork was, and the crown moldings, and the light fixtures. Brandon had always had plenty of vision for renovating houses and seeing profit in the most dilapidated properties, but he would never consider living in a house like this if he had a choice. Alison, on the other hand, talked about it as if she'd stepped into Buckingham Palace.

They went into the kitchen. "Okay, this room needs a paint job. But we can handle that." She looked down. "The floor shows lots of wear, but I know where I can get a rug to put over it. If we can't fix it, we'll hide it."

Then they went out to the back patio.

"The stone is cracked in a lot of places," Alison said. "But if we trim the grass coming up through the cracks, it'll hardly be noticeable. And I know I can get Simpson's Nursery to donate a few big clay pots and some flowers to put in them. It doesn't have to look perfect. Just pretty."

"Sounds fine."

"Otherwise everything looks—oh, boy."

"What?"

She pointed to the magnolia. "That tree. It doesn't look as if it's been trimmed in twenty years. One bad thunderstorm with enough wind and one of those big branches will pop off and go right through your roof."

"Hmm. Maybe I can rent a chain saw. Trim it up."

"Have you ever used a chain saw?"

"Uh . . . no."

"You cut your finger on the air-conditioning unit. I don't have a big enough Band-Aid if you lose a limb."

"Tree trimming is probably pretty expensive."

"You won't know until you get an estimate."

Then Brandon remembered the guy in his grandmother's files who did landscaping work. Yeah, he looked an ex-con, but he wouldn't be hiring him for his handsome face.

"There's a guy who was a client of my grandmother's who owns a landscaping business. I'll see if he can drop by the day everybody comes to work on the house. But I'm warning you. If it's going to be a lot of money, I'll just have to hope thunderstorm season is mild this year."

"It'll probably be cheaper than you think."

"You're a real optimist, aren't you?"

"I've tried pessimism. It just doesn't work for me. Let's take a look at the second floor."

They went back inside and up the stairs, and Alison gushed over the stained-glass window on the midfloor landing. She also loved the black-and-white tile and the claw-foot tubs in the bathrooms and the walls of windows in the bedrooms. Then they went into the room where the pool table was, and her eyes lit up again.

"Oh, my God," she said as she walked slowly toward it. "That is the most amazingly beautiful thing I've ever seen."

"It's a little rough around the edges," Brandon said. "It was in the house when my grandparents bought it, and it was already a little beat up. Age hasn't helped it much."

"Yeah, but it's still gorgeous. Look at the legs! Lions? I've never seen anything like it before."

Brandon smiled, pleased that somebody finally appreciated the old Brunswick Monarch. Tom still thought it looked like a piece of junk.

"Would you like to play?" he asked her.

"Really?" she said with a smile.

"Sure."

"I'd love to," she said, tossing her list and her purse to the chair behind her. "And you'd better look out. I'm pretty good at pool. Eight ball?"

Brandon smiled furtively. "Eight ball it is."

As he gathered the balls, Alison grabbed a cue from the rack on the wall, rubbing the tip of it with chalk. She was dressed in a pair of khaki shorts and a snug little T-top that drew his gaze right to her breasts, and he didn't stop looking as she leaned over the table. He really needed not to do that. Unless she wasn't looking. Then he intended to look all he wanted to.

As it turned out, her proclamation of pool prowess

turned out to be nothing but trash talk. Her stance was all wrong, and she lined up a shot with all the expertise of a five-year-old. She swung her arm back in a funny arc, then whacked the cue ball just a little too hard. Okay, a *lot* too hard. It leaped into the air, then clattered back to the felt. Then, unbelievably, it traveled the length of the table and actually collided with the balls. The seven headed for the corner pocket.

Slowly.

"Come on, come on, *come on*," Alison murmured as the ball crept toward the pocket. It teetered on the edge, then finally dropped. She threw both arms in the air. "*Woo hoo!* Did you *see* that?" She spun around to Brandon with a sly smile. "*Ha.* Told you I'm good."

He decided not to mention that it didn't count if she hadn't called the shot. "I had no idea. Let's see if you can do it again."

Alison turned back around to study the table. "Hmm. Maybe I'll sink that four, huh?"

"The four? You might want to think about the nine instead."

"Yeah, of course you'd suggest that. It's a harder shot. Do I *look* like a fool?"

"No, ma'am," he said. "You most certainly do not."

She lined up the cue ball with the four to knock it into a side pocket, only to stand up again with a quizzical expression. "Now, which one was I again? Stripes or solids?"

"I thought you were good at this."

"I can shoot. I just can't remember . . . you know. Which balls I am."

"Stripes."

"Oh," she said, looking back at the solid four ball she'd had her eye on. "Well, then. Forget the four. That would be silly. The nine it is."

Alison's gentle, self-deprecating humor was such a breath of fresh air after most of the women Brandon had known, ones who were either so insecure they couldn't admit to a fault if their lives depended on it, or so egotistical they couldn't admit to a fault if their lives depended on it.

He rested on his cue, watching her, and as she leaned over again, he had the perfect angle to admire her ass. Her positioning was all wrong, assuming her goal was to play pool. If her goal was to drive him just a little bit crazy, she was positioned exactly right. For just a moment, he entertained himself with the thought of easing up behind her—just to correct her position, of course. He'd lean over, slide his hand down her arm, close his hand over hers, and there he'd be, his lips only inches from her neck, so close he could turn his head and—

No. Off limits. Verboten. Get your mind back where it belongs.

She leaned over her cue, and the dainty silver chain she wore around her neck swayed back and forth, sparkling in the lamp light. She moved her arm back, then took her shot. She missed the ball she was aiming for by approximately a foot and missed scratching by millimeters. Brandon leaned in, intending to dispatch the eleven and the ten simultaneously with a bank shot off the rail, which would set him up perfectly to take out the seven after that. But then it occurred to him that if he did that, a few shots later, the game would be over, and so would his entertainment for the evening.

Instead, he made a half-ass shot that sent balls banking in ways that never were going to win the game for him. But then Alison got to shoot again.

And he got to watch.

Alison crunched up her eyebrows, her forehead crinkling, as she concentrated on the shot. It was an easy one, and the three disappeared into a side pocket. She got lucky and took out one more before missing the shot after that.

Brandon dropped the twelve ball just to keep up, then missed the nine on purpose. Several rounds later, only the eight ball remained. He missed it on his turn, but managed to set it up so she could take it out with no problem.

She moved around the table and took the final shot. The eight ball fell. She let out a whoop, then turned and gave him a smug smile. "Well. You just didn't know who you were up against, did you?"

"Oh, no. I knew exactly who I was up against."

"Which was why you let me win?"

Brandon drew back. "What makes you think I let you win?"

"Did you?"

"Well...yeah. But what made you *think* that?"

"Because you missed shots even I could have made. And you held the cue like somebody who actually knew what he was doing."

"Does that offend you?"

"Did you let me win because I'm a girl?"

Hell, yes. Would he have been watching a *guy's* ass as he shot? "Yes. That's it exactly. Men are genetically predisposed to win at pool, and I'm a big believer in affirmative action."

She actually laughed at that. "Good. That meant I actually got a chance to take a shot. How much fun is it when one person runs the table and the other one just stands there?"

He grinned. "Well, if you're the one running the table and there's money on the game, it can be one hell of a lot of fun."

"So that's what it takes to flush you out? Money?" She reached into her purse. "There," she said, slapping a dollar down on the table. "I've had my fun. Now let's see what *you've* got." She grabbed the rack. "I'll put the balls in the thingy."

"The thingy?"

"I don't know the technical term."

"That would be 'rack.'"

"Whatever." She deposited the balls inside the rack, then lifted it. Brandon took a position at the opposite rail and prepared to break.

"Hey!" Alison said.

"What?"

"Let's see your money first."

Brandon reached into his wallet and matched her dollar bet. "You're such a high roller."

"I'm feeling lucky."

Brandon leaned over. Broke. In fewer than five minutes, he'd run the table. He dropped the eight ball to finish things off, then stood up and leaned casually on his cue.

"Wow," Alison said. "You really are good."

"And a dollar richer."

"Too bad we weren't betting when you let me win."

"If we'd been betting, I wouldn't have let you win."

"If we're going to play again, you need some kind of handicap that'll give me a chance."

"Sweetheart, I could tie one hand behind my back and I'd still beat you."

"Well, then," she said, taking a step closer to him, "maybe you should teach me how to play better."

He smiled. "Maybe I should."

They looked at each other a long time. Gradually the moment shifted, and Brandon's vision grew a little blurry around the edges until the only thing in sharp focus was Alison's face. She blinked, and it seemed as if those golden lashes stroked her cheeks in slow motion before rising again to reveal those beautiful brown eyes. A strand of hair fell along her cheek, then curved beneath the junction of her jaw and throat. Then his thoughts went completely off the rails. He started to imagine pushing that strand of hair aside and touching his lips to the place it had been, and then—

"Hey, Brandon. Alison. What's going on?"

Brandon spun around to find Tom standing at the door. Brandon blinked his way back to reality, resenting the interruption even though he knew it was probably for the best. Tossing Alison down on the pool table and having his way with her probably wouldn't have been a good idea.

"Just playing a little pool," Brandon said.

"Well," Alison said. "I guess I'd better go. I'm late for movie night at my father's house."

"Movie night?"

"Yeah. We watch a movie together. If my father likes it, all is well. If he doesn't, I get to hear all about how Hollywood just doesn't make good movies anymore and everyone who lives there is going straight to hell."

"Sounds like fun."

"I think we've talked about everything that needs to be done before the home tour, haven't we?"

"Yeah," Brandon said, wincing. "But I'm still not totally thrilled with people I don't know being in my house on the day of the tour."

"I know. But I'll be acting as your tour guide. And we'll have people posted in most of the rooms to make sure nobody touches anything. How about Saturday after next for a workday to get the house shipshape?"

"Sure."

"You won't regret letting us use your house. Really. It'll be fun. And when we finish, it'll be all pretty. Won't that be nice?"

Great, he thought. *The First Baptist Church is going to love it.*

"You're opening this house up for a *home tour*?" Tom said. "Why the hell did you agree to that?"

Brandon shoved a pair of TV dinners into the microwave, set the timer, and turned it on. Then he sat down at the kitchen table with Tom. "I don't know. I wasn't going to, but then Alison was standing there looking up at me, and then..." He shrugged helplessly. "Then suddenly the words were coming out of my mouth."

"You're such a pushover." Tom went back to reading something on his phone. Then he stopped and looked up again. "Wait a minute. Since when are you a pushover?"

"I'm not."

"I didn't think so. I've never seen anybody negotiate the way you do—with a smile on your face and a knife behind your back. You don't give an inch of ground you don't intend to. So what's going on here?"

"Nothing's going on."

Tom stared at him a long time. Then a knowing look came over his face. "My God. You like her."

"Like who?"

"Uh...Alison?"

"Like her? *Alison?*" He shook his head wildly. "She's a client. That's all."

"No wonder you didn't like me staring at her when we saw her at McCaffrey's. *You're* hot for her. And you looked pretty cozy together when I showed up a minute ago."

Brandon frowned. "You are *so* off base."

"So you don't like her?"

"No! I mean, yeah. I *like* her. What's not to like? But I don't like her like *that.*"

Tom grinned. "Ha! You sound like a teenage kid. 'I *like* her, but I don't know if she likes *me*, but my *friend* said she did, but if I like her and she *doesn't* like me—'"

"Oh, for God's sake," Brandon snapped. "Will you shut *up*?"

Tom smiled, then poked at his phone again. Silence, except for the infernal ticking of the grandfather clock in the hall that Brandon was ready to smash with a baseball bat.

"So why *did* you agreed to let her use your house?" Tom asked.

Brandon frowned. "It's for a good cause."

"Since when do you put philanthropy at the top of your list?"

He didn't. Not usually, anyway. At the very least, he certainly hadn't developed a sudden interest in the preservation of the historic buildings of Plano, Texas. And yet here he was doing this when he knew for a fact that it was only going to irritate him. Good God, what was *wrong* with him?

He didn't know. There was just something about Alison's unrelenting good nature and cheerful persuasion that made it almost impossible for him to say no to her. Sometime in the past few weeks, her happiness had become his happiness, and he couldn't understand why.

"All kidding aside," Tom said. "Watch getting too tangled up in this stuff when you're going to be out of here soon."

"What do you mean?"

"I wasn't the only one staring at Alison the other night. You can't start messing around with your clients, or you'll jeopardize our plan."

"I have no intention of messing around with Alison. Our relationship is strictly business."

"Yeah? Every time I turn around, you're with her for one reason or another. You're letting her use your house for the tour. And you're really dragging your feet on finding her another match."

"I'm not dragging my feet," Brandon said. "I'm just being careful. After the two I've set her up on that went south, I can't afford to screw up again."

"Well, set her up with somebody so she becomes off limits."

Actually, that was a pretty good plan. If he made another match for her that stuck, she'd be taken, and anything happening between them would no longer be a possibility. That way, when it came time for him to leave, there would be no ties to sever.

*   *   *

"Now, that was a damned fine movie," Charlie said, sitting in his well-worn recliner, watching the closing credits roll. "Assuming you like zombies. Me, I love zombies. They just keep coming. They don't give up until you pop them right between the eyes."

Personally, Alison had always felt sorry for zombies. They had to die, but then they came back to life again looking like hell, only to get killed all over again. Didn't seem fair to have to go through it twice.

The truth was, though, that for the past couple of hours she hadn't been thinking about the zombies.

She'd been thinking about Brandon.

When they were playing pool, she'd challenged him to run the table just so she could step back and admire every move he made. He was clearly a man in his element, moving gracefully from one side of the table to another, taking shots with practiced perfection. She hadn't been able to take her eyes off him. Her imagination had run wild: *I wonder what it would be like to make love on a pool table?*

And then Tom had shown up and blown a hole right through that particular daydream.

All through the movie, Blondie had stretched out inch by inch beside Alison until she'd shoved her right up against the armrest. Now that the dog had her fair share of the sofa, she was snoozing soundly. It reminded Alison of the time she'd had a window seat on a commuter airplane next to a three-hundred-pound man.

"Hey, Blondie," Alison said, poking the dog on the shoulder. "Hope you're comfortable. I'd hate it if you weren't."

Without even bothering to open her eyes, Blondie took a deep breath, then released a sigh of doggy satisfaction.

"Shove her aside," Charlie said. "She's a sofa hog."

"I know. But she looks so comfy."

"And you say *I* spoil her." Charlie tossed the remote aside. "Let's eat. I'll order a pizza."

"You know you shouldn't be eating pizza."

"Chinese?"

"You'll only eat the fried stuff."

"So you want to tell me who delivers sacks of broccoli?"

"I'll fix us a salad."

Charlie frowned. "How about a compromise?"

"What?"

He made a face. "A vegetable pizza?"

From the tone of his voice, he might as well have said *and toss a little anthrax on top while you're at it.* Alison still thought there was entirely too much fat in the veggie variety, but she'd take what she could get.

A minute later she had a pizza on the way, and her father was searching the Zs on his cable channels to see if he could score another zombie classic.

"Damn," he said. "I don't see any other zombie movies scheduled."

"Try searching 'dead.'"

"Nah. All that vampire crap comes up. I hate vampires. But not your mom. She loved them. Said they were sexy. Wrong. Vampires are not sexy."

Alison's heart skipped a little, just as it did every time he mentioned her mother.

"Dad?"

"Yeah?"

"Have you thought any more lately about maybe dating a little?"

Charlie frowned. "You know how I feel about that."

"I think you need some companionship."

"That's what a dog's for. I have a dog. Case closed."

"What would be wrong with going out with a woman now and again?"

"Because most of the women out there have no balls."

"Anatomically speaking, they really can't help that."

"You know what I mean. If I was on a date with a woman and I said her perfume made her smell like a French whore, she'd probably cry or something."

"Yeah? You think?"

"But your mother wouldn't have. She'd have told me my cologne smelled like monkey sweat, so we were even. I'm too old to tiptoe around anyone." He turned to the dog. "Hey, Blondie!"

She lifted her head, coming to attention.

"You're having a bad hair day. And you run like a girl."

Blondie panted with excitement, her mouth turning up in a doggy smile.

"There. Do you see her crying over that? No. Which is why I'm good with a dog."

Alison sighed. If he compared every woman he met to her mother, not one of them would ever have a chance.

When she'd come into her father's den that evening, she'd glanced at the bookcase where their wedding album was. Her father wasn't exactly fastidious about dusting, so she could usually tell if it had been moved. About once a month, it had, which meant that even though he'd carried on with his life for the past fifteen years as if he'd put his wife's death behind him, Alison knew just how often he looked at that album and how much he missed her.

"I almost forgot," Alison said. "I need your help."

"Doing what?"

"Getting a house ready for the home tour."

"Which house?"

"A friend's. He's agreed to let us use it, but it needs a little work."

"Where's the house?"

Alison gave him the address.

"What day?"

"Saturday after next."

"What tools do I need to bring?"

"We need to do some painting, some cleaning, and a little general repair stuff."

"Okay. I'll bring the big toolbox just in case. Will I need to stop by the Home Depot for anything else?"

"No. I'll make sure we have any supplies we need."

"So what's wrong with this guy's house that it's such a mess he needs a repair crew?"

"He just inherited it from his grandmother and hasn't had time to renovate it. I told him we'd help get the house ready if he'll let us use it for the tour."

"Don't tell me he's one of those guys who doesn't know what the business end of a screwdriver looks like. I *hate* those guys."

"No. Actually, he's done a lot of real estate investing, so he knows home repair pretty well. He just needs some extra hands to get the place ready in time."

"Then it looks like we'll get along just fine."

Alison smiled. For some reason she couldn't figure out, she really liked the sound of that.

Chapter 15

The next day at work, Alison waited until most of her co-workers were on their lunch breaks. Then she grabbed the unmarked sack and moved stealthily to Lois's desk.

"Hey, Lois. I need a business card design."

"Yeah?" Lois said, still typing. "What's in it for me?"

Alison held up the bag. "The usual."

Lois's eyes flicked back and forth with interest. "Same client?"

"Yep."

"Standard size cards?"

"Yep."

"Two-sided?"

"One will do. I already e-mailed you the info."

"What kind of design are you looking for?"

"Incorporate the logo. Consistent branding. Other than that, it's up to you. Oh—I do want the owner's photo on the card."

"Photo? That's so hokey. I mean, this woman is a matchmaker, right? Photos on business cards are for cheesy insurance salesmen and real estate agents."

"The matchmaker isn't a woman. It's a man."

Lois screwed up her face. "Huh?"

Alison grabbed her phone and brought up Brandon's photo. Lois looked at it and froze.

"*He's* the matchmaker?"

"Yep."

"A guy?"

"That's right."

She leaned away, clearly struck by the force of Brandon's universal good looks. "Oh. Well, then. A photo it is."

Alison smiled to herself. A picture was indeed worth a thousand words.

"I'll run the final by you, then send it to the printer," Lois said. Then she turned around and opened her lower desk drawer, and Alison dropped the sack inside. As she walked away, Lois nonchalantly shut the drawer and kept on working. But five minutes later, history repeated itself. She took the sack and disappeared into the bathroom.

Alison didn't know when the Godiva people had started adding heroin to their product, but for that she thanked them.

"When you bought this monstrosity," Heather said, "did you think about having to get it up these stairs?"

Alison looked at the massive Victorian armchair she'd scored from a seller on craigslist, then looked up at the stairs leading to her second-floor condo. Okay, so it wasn't exactly going to be a piece of cake to haul it up there. She'd picked it up after work, and Heather had offered to help her move it upstairs. Of course, that was before she found out the sheer depth, breadth, and width of it.

Yeah, it was huge, but the moment Alison saw it, she had to have it. It had a carved rosewood crest with flowers, leaves, and nuts. Cabriole legs. Gold damask upholstery with diamond tufting. Just sitting in it made Alison feel as if she'd come home.

"We're powerful women," she told Heather. "We can do this."

"A powerful man could do it better. Tony will be home in a few hours. Why don't we wait until then?"

"So what am I supposed to do with it in the meantime? Have a seat in it out here and wait for him?"

"We could put it back in your car."

"We almost didn't get it out of my car," Alison said. "Now, come on. You pull from the top, and I'll hoist from the bottom."

With a roll of her eyes, Heather lifted her end, and Alison lifted hers. They started up the stairs. The trouble was that neither one of them could see where they were going—Alison because the chair was between her line of sight and the stairs, and Heather because she was walking backward. And that made for slow going.

"Okay, wait," Alison said when they were halfway up. "I have to rest a minute."

She set the chair down on one of the steps and took a deep breath.

"I suppose it is kind of pretty," Heather said. "If you're into old stuff."

"It's more than just pretty," Alison said. "It's all original and in almost perfect condition. You don't find them like this one every day."

"But don't you already have a chair like it?"

"I'm thinking ahead. One of these days I'm going to

have a house with lots of rooms to furnish. If I see something I like at a good price, I'm going to buy it."

"Ready to go again?" Heather said.

"Yep. Let's do it."

Alison started to lift her end of the chair, but Heather wasn't joining her in the effort. Instead she was looking over Alison's shoulder toward the parking lot.

"What?" Alison said.

"The Wicked Witch of the West just rode up on her broom."

Alison looked over her shoulder. "The Wicked Witch of the West?"

"Oh, did I say that? I meant Judith just drove up in her Volvo."

"Well, crap. Wonder what she wants?"

Judith got out of her car and walked to the bottom of the stairs. "Alison, I have to talk to you."

"We're kinda in the middle of something here," Alison said, "so it's going to be a minute. But if you'd like to help us get this chair up the stairs, we can talk that much sooner."

"No. I'm not in a big hurry. I'll wait."

Thanks a bunch, Judith.

Heather and Alison managed to maneuver the chair the rest of the way up the stairs and into Alison's living room. Judith climbed the stairs behind them.

"Okay, Judith," Alison said, brushing her hands together. "What do you need to talk to me about?"

"I got your e-mail that the owner of 614 State Street agreed to let us use his house. You said the owner's name was Brandon Scott. But it wasn't until I drove by that I realized you were talking about Rochelle Scott's house." She frowned. "He's her grandson."

"Yes, I know," Alison said.

"He's not a good person."

Alison came to attention. "What are you talking about?"

"Rochelle and I were acquainted through the First Baptist Church," Judith went on. "It's a big congregation, so I didn't know her well, but I do remember her grandson when he was a teenager." Judith leaned in, her mouth set in a grim line of disapproval. "He was a *juvenile delinquent.*"

Alison almost laughed out loud. Judith taught at a private Christian school, where chewing gum or being late to class was considered delinquent behavior.

"Exactly what are you calling delinquent?" Alison asked.

"Well, every time Rochelle brought him to church, he just sat there with an insolent look on his face. She tried to introduce him to people, but he barely spoke. And a few times I saw him in the parking lot smoking a *cigarette.*"

Heather gasped. "Oh, good heavens! Tell me it isn't so! A teenage boy with an attitude smoking a cigarette? That *never* happens!"

"It was more than that," Judith said. "He came to live with Rochelle when he was sixteen years old, and there was never a more angry or disrespectful boy. He used to sass his grandmother. And stay out late. She had such a hard time with him."

"Brandon?" Alison said. "No. I think you're mistaken. He and his grandmother got along very well."

"Not from what I saw."

Suddenly Alison had the funniest feeling inside. Even

if Brandon had changed, Judith's account of his teenage years didn't exactly fit in with the warm, loving relationship he'd led Alison to believe he'd had with his grandmother.

"I didn't know he actually lived with her," she said. "I just assumed his family lived near his grandmother's house and he visited her."

"I don't know where his family was, only that he stayed with Rochelle for a couple of years." Judith huffed with disgust. "And he wasn't a very nice boy."

"He was a kid back then," Heather said. "Cut him some slack."

"Rumor has it he once went to jail," Judith said.

"Jail?" Alison said, that sick feeling in her stomach intensifying. "What for?"

"They say he and another boy vandalized the school."

Alison drew a breath of relief. "Come on, Judith. Vandalism isn't exactly capital murder."

"It's still a crime. And there's something more."

"What's that, Judith?" Heather said on a sigh.

"He doesn't actually own the house."

"Don't be silly," Alison said. "His grandmother willed it to him. Of course he owns it."

"Wrong. I talked to some of the elders at the church. It seems Brandon can live there as long as he wants to, but if he chooses to leave, the house reverts to the First Baptist Church. They're the ones who actually hold title to it."

Alison had a funny feeling in her stomach, as if somebody wasn't telling the truth here, and it wasn't Judith. Then again, he'd never actually said he held title to the property, and if he never intended to leave, what was the difference whether he held title or not?

"From our point of view, that doesn't matter," Heather said. "Brandon has possession right now, so it's up to him if we use the house or not. And he's said we can."

"Did you know Brandon has taken over his grandmother's matchmaking business?" Alison said.

Judith froze. "Excuse me?"

"That's right. He's a matchmaker."

"A *male* matchmaker?"

"Yes. And he's doing everything he can to be a success at it. I don't care what he was back then. People change. He's a matchmaker now, Judith. Just like she was. Does that sound like a man who's hung on to his criminal tendencies from over ten years ago?"

Judith twisted her mouth with irritation, and Alison could tell she didn't want to give an inch. "I suppose not. I just think we should keep an eye on him where the tour is concerned."

"It's his house," Heather said. "What's he going to do? Steal something from himself?"

"I just thought you should know the kind of person we're dealing with," Judith said.

"Yes," Heather said, "A guy who's kind enough to offer us his house for the tour. If I were you, I'd thank him for that."

"It's just something to keep in mind," Judith said as she turned and walked away, clearly disappointed in the amount of chaos she'd been able to stir up.

Once she was gone, Heather turned to Alison. "He doesn't even own the place? Did he tell you that?"

"No," Alison said, a little worried. "But it's like you said. As long as he's living there, he gets to decide who comes and goes. And thanks for sticking up for Brandon."

"I only did it because I hate to see Judith going after anybody. If it were Judith versus Hitler, I'd stick up for Hitler. But Alison...doesn't it make you wonder a little?"

"Judith could have it wrong. She teaches at that pristine little private school. She doesn't know what a real juvenile delinquent is."

"Vandalism?"

"She said that was a rumor."

Heather nodded. "I'm inclined to think she's exaggerating about all of this, because Judith does that. But so much about Brandon just doesn't add up."

"In the end, does it really matter? It was more than ten years ago. Like you said. People change."

"That's true. But I thought he was taking over his grandmother's business because they were one big, happy family and he wanted to continue the tradition."

"Again," Alison said, "Judith could be exaggerating."

"Which is why I'm inclined to give him the benefit of the doubt."

Alison was happy to hear that from Heather. Alison wanted to give him the benefit of the doubt, too. But still she couldn't shake the feeling that there was more to him than met the eye, and when she found out what it was, she wasn't sure she was going to like it.

On Saturday morning, Brandon grabbed a cup of coffee and a stack of files, and by the time he'd gone through a couple dozen on Alison's behalf, he was seriously considering—for about the tenth time—hiring a temp to put all this information into a database. Then he thought about what that would cost and kept on flipping. There were about a hundred things he could do to make this business a success over time, but he didn't have the time or the money for any of them. He was just going to have to wing it and hope for the best.

Then, just as frustration started to set in, he ran on to Zach Tyler. Judging from the notes in the file, he'd been one of his grandmother's networking contacts two months before her death. He was the chief operating officer for a nonprofit agency that raised funds for cancer research, which probably meant the guy had a heart. Alison would like that.

Then he saw it. The deal breaker. He was a smoker. *Crap.*

But reading a little further, it said he was trying to quit. Brandon grabbed his phone and gave the guy a call. Fortunately, he was still unattached and looking for the right woman. And as it turned out, he'd been smoke free for a few months now, and he was optimistic he'd be able to continue that.

The next day, he came to Brandon's office so they could meet in person. Brandon talked to the man for a solid hour, trying to discern if there was anything about him that might blow up in Alison's face.

Nothing.

After Zach left his office, Brandon ran a background check him and it came up clean. Then he reached for his phone to let Alison know he had another match for her that he was highly recommending. She hesitated about the smoking thing, but when he told her that Zach was thirty years old, decent looking, had a good job, loved animals, and wanted a family, she decided maybe he was worth a shot.

He e-mailed each of them details about the other and

held his breath. Two hours later, he had a match. Zach called Alison and asked her if she wanted to go to an exhibit opening at a local art gallery on Friday night, and she accepted. Thank God.

Of course, there was still the smoking thing. A lot of people tried to quit. How many actually succeeded?

No. He had to think positive. This was going to be her perfect date, leading to her perfect man, leading to her perfect life. Alison would get what she wanted, so when he left town a few months from now, he could do it with a clear conscience.

Then he thought about Delilah.

He'd told her to be patient, that finding a quality man for her would take time. But sooner or later he was going to have to stop the procrastination and tackle the issue of finding her a match, too. How he was going to do that, he didn't have a clue.

When Alison arrived at the gallery on Friday evening, she spotted Zach right away. He stood talking to a couple of people, looking smartly casual in a pair of jeans, a blue cotton shirt, and a sports coat. He was a nice-looking guy, with wavy brown hair just touching his collar in the back, and eyes so blue she could make them out from halfway across the room. He wasn't Greg-handsome, but she certainly wasn't going to mind being seen with him. After all, what good did Greg's hotness do her when he was going to be spending the next umpteen years in prison?

Brandon had assured her that Zach was a regular altar boy where his background was concerned. There was the smoking thing, but if he truly was quitting, could she really hold that against him? No. Of course not. Still, she found herself glancing down at his coat pocket for a tell-tale bulge of a pack of cigarettes. Fortunately, she didn't see one.

No longer a smoker. Well dressed. Clean background. Good job. Those were good things. So why did she have such a bad feeling?

Fool me twice, shame on you. Fool me three times...

Or whatever.

She took an extra-deep yoga breath and walked over to him. "Hi," she said, holding out her hand. "You must be Zach. I'm Alison."

"Alison. Hello." He gave her a smile, took her hand, and pulled her into an air kiss.

An air kiss. God, she hated those. But what could she expect? He'd invited her to a gallery opening. Flamboyantly artsy people abounded, and he appeared to be acquainted with a few of them. The only other people she knew who air kissed all over the place were...

She froze, memories sweeping through her of Richard Bodecker, Gay Biker in Denial. What if Zach was gay? Gay and not facing up to it?

No. She had to cut this out. He was clearly heterosexual. Richard had never looked quite right on that Harley, but she could see Zach hopping aboard one and zooming off into the sunset.

"I was thinking of grabbing a drink," Zach said. "Would you like one?"

"Uh...yeah. Sure."

They walked to the cash bar, where a smiling bartender waited to take their order.

"What would you like?" Zach asked her.

She wanted a martini, but martini glasses were designed for maximum spillage.

Not good on a first date.

"Chardonnay," she said, then had the most terrible feeling he was going to order the same thing. *Please don't order white wine, please don't order white wine . . .*

"Vodka and tonic," he said.

She let out a silent sigh of relief. It wasn't Fat Tire ale, but on the heterosexuality scale, it was at least neutral. Not that there was anything wrong with gay men. She just couldn't see marrying one.

Zach paid for the drinks, leaving the bartender a nice tip, and then they strolled toward the exhibit.

"So you work for a nonprofit agency?" she said.

"Yeah. It's tough, though, with the economy and all. Charitable contributions are really down." He shook his head sadly. "But it's such a good cause. Our beneficiaries are saving lives every day. They could save more if only we could get more people to give."

That made Alison feel weirdly guilty, as if she should be cleaning the cash out of her wallet and handing it over.

"Brandon told me you're in marketing," Zach said. "That's very interesting."

Interesting? Did he mean truly interesting, as if he wanted to hear more? Or did he mean interesting in the way some people did when they were too polite to say it sounded boring or weird? She'd done that herself more than once, most recently on her first date with Randy when he told her he still had a closet full of Star Wars action figures.

Good Lord. Shouldn't she have pulled the plug on that relationship right then and there?

"Yes. I'm in marketing."

He smiled and nodded, but he probably hated that. After all, he worked for a nonprofit agency. He probably thought marketing was all about manipulating people into buying things they didn't need or even want, money that would be much better spent on philanthropic causes. Tweaking the packaging on a sugar-filled lump of empty calories was hardly in the same league as raising cash for cancer. Hell, Spangler's products probably *caused* cancer.

She waited for one of those judgmental eyebrow arches. She didn't see it, but that didn't mean he wasn't thinking it.

"A marketing company?" he asked. "Or the marketing department of a single company?"

"I work for Spangler Sweets," she said.

"Ah," he said with a big smile. "Mallorific bars. I love those."

"Yeah, me too. They're my favorite."

She wasn't sure, but when she glanced away for a moment, she thought she saw his gaze go toward her hips. Just for a split second. One of those eye flicks you don't want somebody else to see. What was he doing? Checking for a few Mallorific bars bulging her hips from the inside out?

Then she heard a man's voice behind them. "Excuse me."

Alison turned around to see a tough-looking guy in a uniform. *Oh, God. No, no, no!* Here it came. In the span of a nanosecond, she imagined him grabbing Zach, slamming him against the wall, handcuffing him, and then dragging him away in a police car because he was an art thief or a forger or something equally vile, leaving her with nothing to do but plot murder for hire. And guess who the target would be? Was his name *Brandon Scott*?

But the man simply held out a wallet to Zach, a man she could see now was a gallery security guard, not a cop. "I think you left this at the bar."

"Oh!" Zach said, taking it from him. "Thank you."

The guard smiled. "You folks have a nice evening."

Okay. So maybe a SWAT team wasn't gathering outside preparing for an assault, but after Greg, she decided she'd better keep her guard up.

Zach nodded at a painting with random red, white, and black blobs. "What do you think of that one?"

She thought it looked as if a zebra had fallen into a blender, and then somebody had dug out the contents and slapped them onto a canvas.

"I'm afraid I don't know much about modern art," she said.

"Just think about how it makes you feel."

That was easy. Nauseated.

It was probably a trick question. As if there was a right answer, but she didn't have a chance in hell of coming up with it. He was probably an art snob trying to flush out an art moron.

"How does it make *you* feel?" she asked, seeing if she could do a little flushing of her own. She waited for him to say something about how the painting was a commentary on the magnificence of nature, or how it represented mankind crying out in a figurative wilderness, or maybe go the other way and say how tedious and pedestrian and altogether *jejune* it was and therefore not worthy of his time.

"Actually, it kinda makes me feel depressed," Zach said.

Alison blinked with surprise. Depressed? That was second on her list, right after nauseated. After all, a zebra *had* died for the cause. Maybe they had something in common after all?

After their casual stroll through the exhibit, they sat down to dinner at a nearby café. It was cozy and candlelit, which contributed to Alison's growing feeling that maybe this date really was going well. She tried to keep her hopeful thoughts at bay. After all, she'd been so sure about Greg, too, until they were fitting him for an orange jumpsuit. And David had seemed absolutely normal, right up to the opening ceremonies of the Psycho Games he was playing with his ex.

Stay on your toes.

But then, as dessert arrived, Zach knocked her right off her toes.

"I've had a wonderful time tonight, Alison," he said.

"Yeah," she said. "I have, too."

"I feel like we have a real connection," he said.

Alison started to fall right into a swoon, but caught herself at the last second. "Yes. I think we do, too."

"I thought we'd go out and have a good time. A few laughs. What I didn't count on..."

"What?"

"I didn't count on lightning striking."

Lightning striking. Her heart *kathumped*. This was good. This was *big*.

"You're the girl next door, Alison. And I mean that as a real compliment. I just want to have a normal life with a nice home and kids." He paused. "And a wonderful partner to share all of it with."

More *kathumping*, followed by some weird little fluttering thing that made her feel as if she just might pass out.

"And because you weren't really into all that modern art," he said, "I kinda hoped..."

"Yes?"

"That it means you're more traditional. That maybe you like antiques. My aunt died a year ago and left me some midcentury furniture. I've started reading up about it. I'd like to collect more."

"Yes. Yes! Me, too. I love antiques. Right now I'm living in a condominium, but one day I'd love to live in an older house. Someplace historic."

"That sounds *great*," Zach said, his smile so broad and so genuine that Alison want to grab his face and kiss him senseless.

My God, this man really is wonderful. And Brandon is wonderful for introducing me to him.

It had finally happened. She'd finally paid her karmic dues, and now there was nothing ahead but smooth sailing. The glass of white zinfandel she'd had with dinner had traveled north to cloud her eyes with the most pleasant rosy glow, and every time she blinked, things felt even more fluffy and wonderful. And when Zach reached across the table and took her hand, she knew she'd finally made it over the mountain. Not a damned thing she saw made her think there was any reason at all that—

"*Aaargh!*" Zach yanked his hand away suddenly, clapping his hands to the side of his head as if he had the migraine of the century. Alison recoiled, her back slamming into the chair behind her.

"What's the *matter*?"

"I can't do this!"

"Do *what*?"

"Be with you one second longer without telling you!"

"Telling me *what*?"

Zach paused, gathering his thoughts, all of which Alison knew were going to cause this lovely date to go straight to hell. She tried really hard to tell herself he was only going to confess that he hadn't been able to quit smoking after all. But no. She could tell this was something more, and she did *not* want to hear it.

"See," he began, "back when I was a teenager..."

"No!" she said. "Here's the deal, Zach. Whatever you're getting ready to say, if you'll keep it to yourself, not just for now, but for eternity, I'll buy you a whole truckload of Marlboros. We can take up smoking together. Just you and me. Won't that be nice?"

He shook his head sadly. "Alison, Alison, Alison...that's what I like so much about you. You have such a wonderful sense of humor."

He thought she was being *funny*? Oh, *hell*, no. She'd risk lung cancer ten times over to avoid hearing what he was about to tell her.

But, damn it, he told her, anyway. And just like that, one more date had gone to hell.

And Brandon was going to hear all about it.

Chapter 16

Brandon took a sip of his beer and tried to concentrate on the game he and Tom were watching on the TV over the bar at McCaffrey's. It was a battle he was losing. All evening he'd been imagining Zach quivering through his date with Alison. His hands trembling. And finally he wouldn't be able to take it anymore. He'd pull out a Marlboro, light it, take a deep drag, and blow out the smoke in a long, satisfying exhalation. Then, months after quitting cold turkey, he'd start chain-smoking again like a prison inmate.

Prison? Good Lord, don't even think it.

No. He had to stop worrying. Instead, he closed his eyes and visualized Alison telling him how wonderful Zach was. *Ahh.* That was much better than her beating on his door to tell him what a disaster their date had been. This was going to be her perfect date, leading to her perfect man, leading to her perfect life.

All at once, Tom smacked him on the arm. Brandon's eyes shot open wide. "Hey! What are you—"

"Here comes trouble."

Brandon whipped around to see Alison walk through the door. For a split second he hoped for the best. Then he saw the look on her face. A woman with first date infatuation wouldn't be striding toward him with that crazed expression, as if she'd been to hell and back and had barely lived to tell the tale.

Brandon turned on his bar stool. She stopped in front of him. With a deep, angry breath, she smacked her purse down on the bar and skewered him with an angry glare. "You weren't home. I figured I'd find you here."

He braced himself. "Uh, yeah. Here I am."

"Brandon? Do you know what the definition of comedy is?"

He had no idea where she was going with this. He only knew he didn't want to go there with her. "What?"

"Comedy is pain. Plus time."

"Uh...I don't get it."

"What it means," she said, "is that maybe sometime in the far, far future, perhaps when I'm approximately ninety years old, I might look back on what happened tonight and laugh."

"So it was...funny?" he asked hopefully.

"Will you pay *attention*?" she snapped. "Have sixty years passed since I went out with Zach?"

"Uh...no."

"Then it's not funny yet, is it?"

"Hard to say," Tom said. "Comedy's like that. What's tragic to one person might be really funny to another. I read an article in *Scientific Mind* about the way people process—"

Both Alison and Brandon turned to glare at him.

"Uh...I think I'll go play pool now."

Tom grabbed his beer and slid off the stool. Alison climbed onto it. She looked over at Tony, who was working behind the bar. "Hey, Tony!"

Tony looked over his shoulder, and the moment he saw the look on Alison's face, his usual congenial smile vanished. "Yeah?"

"Bring me a vodka martini. And keep them coming until I tell you to stop or I lose consciousness, whichever comes first."

Tony flicked his gaze to Brandon. *I don't think I'd want to be you right now.* Brandon gave him a look in return. *I don't want to be me, either.*

"Okay, Alison," Brandon said, "why don't you tell me—"

She held up her index finger, stopping him. A minute later, Tony set her martini down in front of her. She picked it up. Started to drink. Kept drinking. Drained the glass. Smacked it down in front of her. Tony's eyes widened with surprise.

"Don't just stand there," she snapped. "Bring me another one."

Tony spun around and did as he was told. Alison slowly turned to face Brandon. "So, Brandon," she said with eerie sweetness. "Would you like me to tell you about the man you set me up with?"

No, ma'am, I most certainly would not. "Uh...sure. Go ahead."

"You set me up with a man," she said, "who decided tonight that he definitely wants to go through with his sex change operation."

For at least the count of five, those words refused to penetrate Brandon's skull. They just meandered around, looking for an entry point, but the door to his brain was locked solid.

"Come again?" he said.

"Sex change operation," Alison snapped. "What part of that do you not understand?"

"I understand what a sex change operation is," Brandon said. "But Zach? No way. The man plays *rugby*, for God's sake."

"Manly sport notwithstanding, he wants to be a woman, and he wants to be one *now*."

"No," Brandon said, shaking his head wildly. "No way. That's just weird."

"You think that's weird? That's not weird. That's the *normal* part. You haven't heard anything yet."

"There's *more*?"

"Oh, yeah. I'm just getting started."

Tony set another martini down in front of Alison. She drank half of it in one gulp.

"Wait a minute," Brandon said. "If he's going to have a sex change operation, then he's interested in men. So why did he agree to go out with you?"

"Ah," Alison said, holding up her index finger. "That's where the freak show begins."

Brandon braced himself. This was definitely going to be one for the record books.

"Wrap your brain around this," Alison said. "He wants to become a woman, and then he wants to *date* women."

For the span of several seconds, Brandon looked at her dumbly. When light finally dawned, his eyes shot open wide.

"Are you telling me the man is having a sex change operation so he can become a *lesbian*?"

"Wow. You catch on fast. It took me a full minute to get it."

"No. No way. You're making this up. You *have* to be making this up."

Alison held up her palm. "As God is my witness, the man wants nothing to do with penises, his or anyone else's, ever again. See, he told me he's always felt that penises were very threatening. Even his own. Every time he gets an erection—"

"Alison!" Brandon said. "You want to spare me here? Just a little?"

"Hey, all you have to do is hear about it. I had to live through it."

"I'm sorry. I had no idea. My grandmother met him at one of his agency's cancer research benefits and added him to her database. He looked perfect on paper, so I met with him face-to-face. I asked him every question I could possibly think of."

"Here's a question you forgot. How about, 'Hey, Zach. About your sexuality. Have you ever considered becoming a woman and then dating women?'"

Brandon sighed. "Guess I'd better add that to the questionnaire."

"At this rate, the damned thing is going to be twenty pages long."

"I still don't get what he hoped to accomplish by going out with a woman while he's still a man." Brandon winced. "Did I just say that?"

"He said he was still denying wanting the operation right up to the moment he went out with me. When he met me—get this—he said it made him realize how much he wants to become a lesbian. I think there's a compliment in there somewhere. I'll let you know when I find it."

"I can't believe you hung around long enough to hear all that."

"You don't understand. I was stunned into paralysis. Not that I have anything against lesbians, but I'd have to fall out of a closet if I were going to marry one."

"Speaking of that," Brandon said, "I really don't get it. What's your rush to get married? You're still young."

"Thirty-one is not young. Look at these crow's feet around my eyes," she said, pointing. "I'm getting gray hair. And I can practically feel my eggs drying up." She sighed. "Sorry. Inappropriate. Forgot you weren't a woman."

"No problem. After this evening, I think we're all a little gender confused."

Alison took another long sip of her martini and then set it down with a body-heaving sigh. "You realize if I were still paying you for the privilege of going on dates like this, this might be the time I'd ask for my money back. For real."

"I know you find this hard to believe," Brandon said, "but I'm actually pretty good at matchmaking. I've missed a few times, but it's been normal missing. They just didn't have the right chemistry. Nothing like this. I mean, *nothing*."

Alison let out a dejected sigh. "Then maybe it's me."

"You? How can it be you? I'm the one picking the men."

"You don't understand. I'm cursed. My love life has always been crazy like this. You just got caught in the vortex."

"So you've had dates before now that were a little strange, too?"

"A little strange? Get this. I thought my last boyfriend was going to propose, and instead he wanted to know if I'd arrange a threesome for us with a friend of mine."

Brandon just sat there, dumbstruck.

"I can't believe I just told you that." She looked down at her glass. "Thank you, vodka."

"What else?" Brandon asked. "Now that the vodka is talking."

"Well, let's see. There was the guy I dated for two years who owned a Harley dealership and decided he was gay." She paused. "Wow. Plain old gay sounds like no big deal after what happened tonight, huh?"

"He owns a Harley dealership and he's gay?"

"Zach plays Rugby and he wants a sex change operation?"

Good point.

"Lemme ask you something, Brandon," Alison said, her words starting to run together.

"Yeah?"

"You think a person oughta go to a restaurant and blow his nose on a cloth napkin? Just a big ol' *honk* right there at the table?"

"That's gross."

"You bet your life it was. See, before I even met you, my dating life was filled with a gazillion million potholes. And I've hit every stinkin' one of them."

She drained the rest of martini number two, and then called out to Tony to bring her number three. He walked over and eyed her carefully.

"I don't know," he said. "You might want to slow down on those."

"Oh, hell, no. I'm just getting started."

"You can't hold your alcohol." Tony turned to Brandon. "She does crazy things when she drinks too much."

"I do not."

"Yeah? Remember the state fair incident?"

"Hey!" Alison said. "I thought we agreed not to talk about that!"

"I'm just saying that sometimes when you drink—"

"Tony?"

He stopped short. "Yeah?"

She leaned in. "If you don't bring me another martini, I'm going to tell Heather what really happened to that god-awful shirt she bought you on your birthday, and it had nothing to do with spilled motor oil."

Tony's eyes widened. "Oh. Well, then. Martini number three coming right up."

As he walked away, Brandon said, "Wow. You play hardball."

"Damn right. Nothing's worse than a bartender who won't bring you a drink." She paused. "Well, unless it's a man who wants to be a lesbian." She tilted her head, thinking. "I tried really hard to picture Zach as a woman. Couldn't do it. Maybe after about fifty rounds of electrolysis. And if he sucked in a little helium before he talked. Because he was a pretty hot guy, you know? I'm not so sure he'll be a hot woman, though. I'd have to think about that one."

A minute later, Tony brought Alison's martini, but he didn't set it down. "You did walk here tonight, didn't you?"

"No, Tony. I drove my car, like, a block and a half. Of *course* I walked here."

"And I'm going to walk home with her," Brandon said.

Alison looked offended. "You don't have to do that, Brandon. I am *not* drunk."

"It has nothing to do with you being drunk. I just don't believe a lady should have to walk home alone after dark."

Alison frown rose into a rapturous smile. "Oh, that is so *sweet!*" She turned around and shook her finger at Tony. "I want you to go straight home tonight and tell Heather what a nice, *nice* man Brandon is. Emphasize the word *nice*." Alison leaned in and whispered loudly enough for half the bar to hear, "I'm afraid she doesn't like him very much."

Tony set her martini down in front of her. "Drink it *slowly*."

She made a face at him, picked up the glass, and took a long, gulping swallow. He rolled his eyes helplessly.

"You know what?" Alison said to Brandon. "Now that I think about it, it might not take sixty years. A man who wants to be a lesbian is pretty darned close to being funny already. What do you think?"

"Yeah. It's hilarious, all right."

"Wait a minute," Tony said. "A man who wants to be a *lesbian*?"

Brandon shook his head. "Don't ask."

"Yes, my date with Zach was indeed hilarious," Alison said. "I'm thinking it's the funniest thing that's ever happened to me. To anyone. *Ever.* And what a story, right? I bet not one woman in ten zillion has dated a male lesbian wannabe."

"And I'm so very proud to have set you up with him," Brandon said glumly.

"Nah," she said, waving her hand. "You just gave me

what I wanted, right? Greg without a felony warrant, and David without a crazy ex-wife." She paused, giggling. "Except he's Zach without a penis."

Tony looked at Brandon. "You set her up with a man with no penis?"

"No, no, no," Alison said, waving her hand. "He has one for now. But he's scared of it. A man should not be scared of his own penis." She looked at Brandon. "So I think he's doing the right thing by getting rid of it, don't you?"

"God, no," Brandon said, cringing. "That's a bad idea. A very, *very* bad idea."

"So how about you, Tony?" Alison said. "If you were scared of your penis, wouldn't you just whack that sucker off?"

"Uh...I think I'm with Brandon on that."

"Men. *God.* They're so sensitive about their manhood. You don't see women freaking out over their vaginas." Then she looked distressed. "Oh, poor Zach. What if he's scared of his new vagina, too?"

Tony gave Brandon a look that said, *Time for her to go.*

"I think I'd like to get some fresh air," Brandon said to Alison. "There's a lot of that on the walk home. How about it?"

"But I haven't finished my drink yet. Hold on."

Brandon winced as she grabbed her martini glass and drained it. Then she slid off her bar stool and started for the door.

"Oops," she said spinning back around. "My purse. I need to pay—"

"My treat," Brandon said, tossing some bills on the bar. He grabbed her purse, then grabbed her as she wobbled hard to one side.

She was going to be *so* sorry in the morning.

"Take it easy there," he told her.

"It's these shoes," she said, plopping down in a nearby booth and kicking them off. She scooped them up and stood up again. "There. That's better."

She walked to the door, those shoes dangling from her fingertips. Brandon caught up with her.

"Here," he said, handing her the purse and looping his hand around her upper arm. "Put that over your shoulder. You hold your stuff, and I'll hold you."

She looked up at him with a loopy grin. "You're a nice guy, Brandon. Did I ever tell you that?"

"Yes, I believe you did."

He opened the door for her, and they stepped out into the night. "Which way?" Brandon asked. Alison pointed, and they started down the sidewalk.

"So what exactly happened at the state fair?" he asked.

"Nothing happened," she said. "And I don't care what Tony says, *nobody* called the cops."

"Good thing, since nothing happened."

"Damn right."

As they strolled along, Brandon took a deep breath, inhaling the heavenly aromas coming from a nearby Italian café. They passed a beer and wine shop, a dry cleaners, and a clothing resale store, all of which had been totally updated, even as they held onto the historic feel of life a hundred years ago.

A few minutes later, they reached her condo complex. It had design elements that made it look like a turn-of-the-century apartment building even though it was clearly only a few years old. She pointed to a second floor unit. This was going to be a challenge.

Brandon wrapped his arm around her shoulders and headed for the stairs.

"Come on," he said. "Up we go."

She trudged up the stairs beside him, tripping a little on the third step. After that, she wrapped her arm around his waist, leveled out, and managed to make the rest of the climb. When they reached the top, she took a deep breath and blew it out.

"*Boy*, that was a lot of stairs," she said. "Like, twice as many as usual."

"Where are your keys?"

"Oh. Keys." She fished through her purse and pulled them out. He took them from her and opened her door. He led her inside, leaving the door ajar, and got a surprise.

Her condo may have been new, but her furnishings weren't. In the living room was a sofa the size of the Queen Mary upholstered in a heavy floral fabric flanked by a couple of side chairs in green velvet. He looked around for a TV. When he didn't see one, he assumed it was inside the cabinet on the wall across the room from the sofa. Big, ornate lamps lit the room with a warm glow. It looked as Victorian England had time traveled and landed squarely in the middle of Allson's living room.

"You have a new condo but old furniture," he said. "What's the deal?"

"I want to wait to buy a big old house until I'm married. But just because I have a modern condo, it doesn't mean I have to have furniture that's all...*ugh*. Contemporary."

All at once, three cats galloped into the living room, meowing all at once. Brandon thought Jasmine was bad.

This was worse. They were like a preschool choir. Cute and all, but, God, the *noise*.

"There are my darling kitties!" Alison said, petting one of them when she jumped onto the arm of the sofa. Alison stroked her down the length of her back. "Okay, this is Ethel, and that one over there with the white paws is Ricky, and that one is...uh..." She tilted her head questioningly as she stared at the third cat.

"Lucy?" Brandon said.

Alison looked at Brandon quizzically. "How did you know that?"

"I'm psychic, remember?"

"Oh, yeah." Alison sank to the sofa with a heavy sigh. "I think I should sit for a minute."

She sat down on the sofa, then fell to one side, her head on the sofa pillow but her feet still on the floor. Brandon lifted her legs by the ankles and put them on the sofa, those gorgeous legs he definitely needed to be ignoring right now.

He sat down beside her. "Alison? Are you all right?"

"Maybe that third martini wasn't such a good idea after all."

Just then, Lucy jumped up on the back of the sofa, walked the length of it, and stopped to stare down at Alison, letting out a plaintive meow. *Oh, no. Mom's tipping the bottle again.* At the same time, Ethel jumped onto the sofa behind Brandon and rubbed her head against his arm.

"Whoa!" Alison said.

"What?"

"Ethel likes you!" she said, her voice awestruck. "She doesn't like anybody. There was this guy I dated once. She threw up on him."

As long as *Alison* didn't throw up on him, all would be well. "So why did you drink so much tonight?"

She lifted one shoulder in a weak shrug. "I don't know. Frustration, I guess."

"Because of the men I've been setting you up with?"

"Not completely. It's like I told you. My bad experiences with men started way before you ever showed up."

"Don't worry. It's all going to work out."

"How can you be so sure?"

"Because I'll keep at it until I make it work out. Okay?"

The second the words were out of his mouth, he wanted to kick himself. Why had he said that? He might not even be around long enough to keep a promise like that, no matter how much he wished he could.

She tilted her head. "I've never met a man like you before."

"Yeah? What makes me so different?"

A dreamy smile crossed her lips. "A lot of men don't believe in love. But you do."

Brandon didn't know what to say to that, because anything that left his mouth now would be a lie.

"But not just for yourself," she went on. "You want as many people as you can to find it. I mean, God, Brandon. You've dedicated your whole *life* to it. Do you know how *amazing* that is?"

Now he officially felt like crap. She was looking at him as if he was some kind of saint, when really he was about as opportunistic as a man got. If he hadn't gotten to know her, he'd say she was a gullible fool. But as he looked at her now, all he saw was a trusting soul who deserved a far better man than the ones he'd set her up with.

"I know how you can find me the right man," Alison said.

"How's that?"

She smiled. "Make sure he's just like you."

Brandon shook his head. "No. You don't want a guy like me. Trust me on that."

"Oh, yes, I do," she said. "What's not to like?"

"Plenty."

"You're modest, too," she said. "Add that to the list. Course, if I found a guy like you, he'd have to want a girl like me."

"A girl like you? Of course he'd want you. What's not to like?"

He hadn't meant anything at all by that. He'd merely intended it as an offhand compliment that mirrored the one she'd given him, and he figured that was the way she'd take it.

Until he felt her hand on his leg.

When she flexed her fingers against him, he realized he might have started something he was going to have a hard time getting out of.

"Alison," he said warily. "I'm not the man you think I am."

"Oh, no. You are." Her voice fell to a grainy whisper. "You are."

No, he wasn't. Not even close. And no matter how many times he'd had borderline carnal thoughts about her, nothing was going to happen here. *Nothing.* He was a self-serving man in any number of ways, but he drew the line at taking advantage of helpless women. And right now, Alison was about as helpless as a woman got, which meant he needed to get up and get out of there *now*.

He eased away. "Uh, Alison, I don't think—"

But before he could get all of *I don't think we should do this* out of his mouth, she grabbed a double handful of his shirt, pulled him down to her, and kissed him.

Alison was kissing him.

Alison?

It happened so quickly he was stunned into submission. But it wasn't just the speed of her kiss that froze him where he sat. It was the quality of it. The sheer abandonment of it. The softness of her mouth. The way she wrapped her arms around his neck and pulled him closer with a sweet insistence that made him want to melt right into her.

And for several long, heavenly moments, that was exactly what he did.

Gradually the kiss that had started so abruptly dissolved into a slow, hot feast for the senses. She might not have much luck when it came to finding a husband, but it wasn't her talent for kissing that was holding her back. A little voice in the back of his mind was shouting at him to stop, but it was almost impossible to hear when blood was pounding through his ears with every heartbeat. Instead he listened to an even louder voice that was shouting *more, more, more*. He angled his mouth and dove deeper, until his nerves were raw with pleasure and stars exploded behind his eyelids.

Then the first voice got louder.

Brandon knew this didn't compute. The Alison he knew would never grab a man and kiss him like this, which meant that the vodka that had started talking earlier was now screaming at the top of its lungs. So he put his hand against her arm, intending to ease her away from him, but the moment his palm met her bare flesh, it turned into a caress instead.

No. Stop it right now. Don't touch what you can't have.

But the truth was that he *could* have her. He had no doubt he could seduce her any time he wanted to, because she thought he was a completely different man than the man he really was. But he knew *exactly* who she was. He'd kissed a lot of women in his life, but never one whose heart seemed to flow from her lips to his. And that was the problem. He could practically feel all that love bubbling up inside her now, dying to be released, and it wasn't fair to her if he took even the tiniest bit of it. She needed to save it for the man who could give her forever.

He took her by the shoulders and managed to ease her away from him. She lay back against the pillow and stared up at him with a heavy-lidded expression of total bliss. It was all he could do not to dive right in again.

"We really shouldn't do this," he said.

She blinked lazily. "No?"

"No." He tucked her hair behind her ear, soft, silky hair that seemed to glide along his fingers. "As nice as that kiss was, you're my client, so I don't think it would be right if you and I…"

He realized her eyes were drifting closed, so he let his voice trail off. Several seconds passed, and soon the steady rise and fall of her chest told him she'd fallen asleep.

Amazing.

He had no idea what she'd done at the state fair, but if it was anywhere nearly as impulsive as the kiss she'd just laid on him, it must have really been something. Fortunately, there was a chance she wouldn't even remember this in the morning, which meant they could proceed as if nothing had ever happened. Then tomorrow he'd redouble his efforts to find her the kind of man who didn't drive her straight into a twelve step program.

Just as he was getting ready to leave, though, he heard something behind him. When he turned around, he got a most unpleasant surprise.

Heather was coming through the front door.

Chapter 17

"What's going on here?" Heather asked, her face all scrunched up with suspicion.

Brandon sighed. Could this night get any worse? Was it even possible?

"Alison had a little too much to drink," he said, rising from the sofa. "So I walked her home."

"That's what Tony said. I came by to check on her."

"She's fine. Just sleeping."

"Come out here," she said, walking out to the porch. "I want to talk to you."

Shit. He'd done something nice for Alison, walked her home so she'd be safe, and this was what he got? With a surge of irritation, he followed Heather out the door and pulled it closed behind him.

"I saw you sitting on the sofa beside her," Heather said.

For a moment, he was afraid she'd seen that kiss, too, but if she had, she would have said so. Thank God for small favors.

"What's wrong with sitting with her? I was just making sure she was all right."

"And if I hadn't shown up what would have happened?"

Brandon narrowed his eyes. "I'd be doing what I'm doing right now. Leaving."

"Is that all?"

"What are you suggesting?"

"I'm suggesting that if Tony hadn't called me to come check on Alison, this night might be ending differently."

Brandon drew back with disbelief. "Are you telling me you think I would have taken advantage of Alison when she was *passed out*? What kind of guy do you think I am?"

For a moment, Heather didn't give an inch. Then she looked away with a heavy sigh. "Okay," she said. "I'm sorry. Of course you wouldn't do that. It's just that there's so much about you doesn't add up." She folded her arms, looking at him warily. "What's up with you, Brandon? Really?"

"I'm just a guy trying to run a business. And take care of his clients."

"I think there's something else going on. You've set Alison up with guys who were all wrong for her. It doesn't sound to me as if you're serious about your business. It sounds to me more like you build people up, take their money, and give them nothing in return."

"Wrong. I've had good success with other clients."

"So why not Alison? Tony told me the date you set her up on tonight was horrible, and that was why she was drinking so much."

"The guy wasn't right for her. That's true. But in the end, she was fine with just moving on to the next one. She even laughed about it."

"Damn it, are you *blind*? She's only laughing so she doesn't cry. Every time she goes out with a guy and it's nothing but a dead end, it hurts her. More so every time. She's lost so much in her life already. I don't know how many more times she can hit the wall before she just can't take it anymore."

"What are you talking about?"

"It's not my place to tell you about her personal life," Heather said. "What you need to concentrate on is finding her the right man. I don't think you can do it, but she does. Alison has a habit of putting her faith in people whether they deserve it or not because she believes the best about everybody. Please don't make her wrong about you."

Brandon was itching to come back at Heather, but it would get him nowhere. He told himself it was just as Alison had said—Heather was the overprotective, intrusive sister she'd never had, and her heart really was in the right place. But that didn't make her accusations any easier to take. And really, in the end, he had to face facts. Heather was more right about him than wrong.

"Why don't you just go?" Heather said. "I have a key to lock her door."

With a sigh of frustration, he turned and went down the stairs, growing more irritated with every step he took. He knew he'd screwed up with the matches he'd made for her. Big-time. But he didn't like the implication that he would do something to hurt Alison. He liked her way too much for that. And she'd helped him so much with his business that he'd never be able to repay her. Because of her, he was going to have plenty of money to invest in the deal of the century and get his real life back again.

But for the first time, that didn't sound so wonderful.

No. It *was* wonderful. It was exactly what he wanted.

Once he was back doing the thing he loved the most, all this would become a distant memory, just a small detour on the road back to the top. But as he strode along the deserted sidewalk, he wasn't thinking of ways to keep his distance from Alison.

He was thinking about that kiss.

Alison opened her eyes to late-morning sunlight stabbing its way through her living room blinds, penetrating her eyeballs to lodge directly in her skull. Groaning, she snapped her eyes shut, and several disorienting seconds passed before she dared ease them open again. She blinked against the sun, then looked around without lifting her head from the pillow. Wait a minute. She'd slept on the sofa? Why had she done that?

Then, slowly, she remembered.

Gritting her teeth against the headache of the century, she got up, stumbled to the bathroom, and looked at herself in the mirror. If she hadn't slapped both palms against her mouth, she'd have screamed so loudly her neighbors would have called the police.

The good news was that part of her hair still looked relatively smooth and untangled. The bad news was that the other side looked as if it had been hit by a tornado. And whatever mascara had once been on her lashes had congealed in dark circles beneath her eyes.

She dragged herself to the kitchen, started a pot of coffee, and by the time she got out of the shower, most of the rest of the evening was coming back to her. Zach and his lesbian dreams. Three martinis, *bam, bam, bam*. And then Brandon...

Brandon had walked her home?

Yes. And she'd bobbed and weaved the whole way. Once inside her apartment, she'd collapsed on the sofa. What else?

She sat down at her kitchen table and sipped her coffee, thinking about it. Now she remembered. She remembered Brandon sitting beside her, staring down at her with those beautiful dark eyes and that handsome face. He'd apologized for setting her up with another bad date. She'd told him...uh...what was it? Oh, yeah. How wonderful he was. And then...

OH MY GOD.

All at once what happened next came back to her in Technicolor splendor, practically knocking her off her chair with the sheer humiliation of it.

No. Please God. Tell me I didn't do what I think I did.

But she *had* done it. She'd kissed Brandon. And it hadn't been just any old kiss. It had been the kiss of a woman who gave new meaning to the words immodest, immoral, and shameful. She put her hand to her chest, feeling as if she was on the verge of hyperventilating. Why the *hell* had she done that?

She remembered thinking how wonderful he was, and how nice it was that he'd taken her home, and how he'd dedicated his life to finding love for other people, and then suddenly the matchmaker seemed way better than any match he could set her up with. Then she did something she'd thought about doing approximately a hundred times since she'd met him, but never, *ever* would have done without the benefit of three martinis.

It was a state fair moment all over again.

Up to now, that incident had singlehandedly ruled as her life's most humiliating experience. This beat that by a mile. *Note to self: you have a one-drink limit, now and forever.*

She had to apologize to Brandon and hope he didn't hate her forever. And she had to do it *now*.

She got dressed, put on enough makeup that she didn't look like a cadaver, and, when half a bottle of Visine didn't help her bloodshot eyes, slipped on a pair of sunglasses. She still looked like hell, but she didn't intend to hang around long. Just long enough to apologize, squirm with embarrassment, and leave.

Ten minutes later, she pulled up in front of his house. The Matchmaking by Rochelle sign was still in his front yard, and that bugged her. Yeah, he needed something to direct prospective clients around to the back of the house, but it was definitely going to cause some confusion for people who knew his business by its new name. He needed a new sign, and she made a mental note to bribe Lois to design one on Monday morning.

But first things first.

She climbed the porch steps, cringing as she knocked on the door. It took a long time, but he finally opened it, and she was treated to the Saturday morning version of Brandon. It nearly stopped her heart.

He had on a pair of jeans. Nothing else. Bare feet, bare chest—a big, broad expanse of bare chest that seemed to go on forever. His hair was sleep-mussed in a way that should have looked scruffy and unkempt but looked outrageously sexy instead. He rubbed his left eye with the heel of his hand and blew out a breath.

"Hey, Alison," he said. "Long time, no see."

"Can I come in? Just for a minute?"

"Why not? I'm up." He paused. "Now."

He stepped aside, and she walked into the house. He closed the door behind her.

"First of all," she said, "I want you to know that I hardly ever drink like I did last night. Like, almost never. So when I said on your questionnaire that I'm a light drinker, I didn't lie. It really is true."

"I know. If it wasn't, three martinis wouldn't have put you under the table."

"Secondly, I want to thank you for walking me home."

"You're welcome."

"And thirdly, I want to apologize for something."

She thought she saw a tiny smile of amusement curl the corner of his mouth, and she wasn't sure how she felt about that.

"Tony was right. I can't hold my alcohol. When I've had too much to drink, I do stupid things."

"Like what you did at the state fair?"

"You will *never* hear that story."

"I don't know. If I get Tony alone sometime, he might—"

"If he does, he's a dead man."

"Okay. Go on."

She exhaled. "I don't know why I did what I did. But I did, and I just wanted to say I'm sorry."

"For what?"

"You know what."

"No, I'm afraid I don't."

"Will you stop playing dumb? I got drunk and kissed you, Brandon. You were kind enough to walk me home, and I practically attacked you. I've never done anything like that in my life!"

"Well, there *was* the state fair incident."

"Will you *stop*?" She sighed miserably. "I just came here to say I was out of line, and I'm *so* sorry. And I know it wouldn't be right for me to say, 'Hey, I was drunk. It wasn't my fault.' Because it was my fault for getting drunk. So everything I did after that was my fault, too."

"Is there anything else you'd like to accept blame for? The state of the economy? The wars in the Middle East?"

"Can I trade this for one of those?"

"Will you stop worrying? I once got drunk and woke up on a commuter train in Atlanta."

"You lived in Atlanta?"

"Nope."

Alison blinked. "Oh, my."

"Feel better now?"

"I don't know. When you were on that commuter train, did you come on to a woman in a highly inappropriate manner?"

"Not that I know of."

"I didn't mean anything by it, Brandon. It wasn't personal."

"So I was just a placeholder guy? If any other guy had taken you home, he'd have gotten a kiss, too?"

"No! I mean, yes." She closed her eyes. "Oh, hell. I don't know what I mean."

And he was still smiling.

"That's the last thing I remember." She winced a little, hating to ask. "What happened after that?"

"You fell asleep."

"Nothing else?"

"That's about it." He paused. "Well, I guess Heather showed up."

"Oh, no. Heather was there? Did she see me kiss you?"

"Nope. She just gave me the evil eye and sent me on my way, then locked up your condo."

"Thank God." She rubbed her temples.

"Headache?"

"Nah. There's just this little man with a jackhammer inside my head."

"You're indoors. Any reason you're still wearing sunglasses?"

"My eyes. I look like an alcoholic bloodhound."

"Let me see," he said.

"No way."

"Come on," he said with a smile. "Take off the sunglasses."

With a sigh of resignation, she slowly slid them off her face, then turned to look at him.

"Wow. Alcoholic bloodhound? Not a bad analogy."

"You're teasing me," she said, shoving them back on her face. "I am *not* in the mood."

Brandon laughed. "Come on, Alison. You're making too much of this."

"No. It was awful. It was like I violated you, or something."

"Violated?" He barked out a laugh of disbelief. "Are you *kidding* me? Not one man in ten thousand would look it like that."

"Hey! People practically go to jail these days for just looking at somebody funny, much less invading their personal space. You wouldn't believe the sexual harassment training we have to go through where I work." She rolled her eyes. "See? I *know* better, so it makes it even worse!"

"I'm not your employee."

"But we do have a professional relationship, so for me to jeopardize that—"

"You didn't jeopardize anything."

"Yes, I did."

"It can't be sexual harassment unless the harassee sees it that way. I didn't see it that way."

"Then it's a good thing you don't work for a big company. They'd send you for remedial training."

"Alison—"

"You can downplay it all you want to, but it was still awful. I mean, I just *dove* right in there and—"

"Oh, for God's *sake*!" Brandon grabbed her arm and yanked her up next to him. He dropped his mouth against hers, pulling her right up against that big, expansive, *naked* chest and kissing her until she nearly fainted in his arms. It was a hot, reckless kiss that thoroughly invaded her personal space and would have sent any human resources director on the planet into a frenzy. Finally he released her, but every nerve in her body was still sizzling like raindrops on a summer sidewalk.

"There," he said. "We're even. We've violated each other. We're both practically criminals. Now, can we forget all about it?"

Alison just stood there, shell-shocked, barely able to catch a good, solid breath. It hadn't been remotely real. She knew that. He was just making a point. But...*wow*.

"Uh...yeah. Sure."

"Good." He opened the door. "I'll let you know when I have your next match for you. It may be a while—I intend to get it right this time. And I'll see you and your chain gang next weekend. Saturday morning, nine a.m.? Isn't that what we decided?"

Alison just stood there, gaping at him.

"Alison. Nine o'clock?"

"Oh, yeah. Nine on Saturday."

She walked out of the house, and he closed the door behind her, leaving her standing on his front porch wondering what the hell had just happened. Somehow he expected that kiss to cancel out what she'd done? No. All it had accomplished was to make her stop thinking about the kiss she'd given him and start obsessing about the one he'd given her.

She got into her car, but her heart wouldn't slow down. She sat there for a long time, her hands on the steering wheel, her skin hypersensitive and her breathing just a little out of control. The strangest sense of exhilaration was boiling up inside her, giving her the weirdest urge to run around the block, or drop and do fifty push-ups, or maybe get on a bicycle and ride fifty or sixty miles just to release some of her pent-up energy. Unfortunately, exercise was that thing she did by walking to McCaffrey's and having a burger and fries, so all those things were out. She'd just have to live with it until her heart decided to save itself and calm down, or she came to her senses and could truthfully say she wasn't falling for Brandon.

She waited a minute. Two minutes.

Nope. She was definitely falling for him. And not in a small way. She was falling for him like a skydiver fell to earth from twenty thousand feet. And she could no more stop it than the skydiver could reverse course and get back into the plane. But it wasn't only because of the kiss he'd just given her. This had been coming almost from the first moment she met him. But since he was her matchmaker, he was supposed to find her a man, and it wasn't until now that she actually started to let herself think about what it would be like if he *was* that man.

She touched her fingertips to her lips, telling herself he hadn't meant a thing by that kiss. He was merely trying to make a point. More to the point, trying to get her to shut up, which was embarrassing enough in its own right.

She took deep yoga breath and tried to put it out of her mind, even though she knew it was going to linger there for a long time to come. If a fake kiss could generate these kinds of feelings, what would it be like if he ever gave her the real thing?

Chapter 18

The next Saturday morning, as Alison stepped out of the shower, her phone rang. She threw on a robe and ran to answer it. She looked at the caller ID. Brandon? Just seeing his name brought back memories she'd been trying all week to forget. Her next thought, though, was considerably more panicked. *Oh, please don't be calling to back out of the home tour.*

She punched the talk button. "Brandon? What's up?"

"About everybody coming here this morning," he said. "Small problem with that."

She came to attention. "Oh, no. You're not backing out on me, are you? You can't do that. You promised we could use—"

"Will you take it easy? It's not that."

"Then what?"

"It's supposed to get to a hundred and three degrees today."

"That's a problem?"

"It is when my air conditioner is acting up again."

Alison slumped with dismay. "Oh, that's just great. Can you fix it?"

"I haven't had much luck up to now. I can call a repairman, but if the offer of your father's help is still open, that'd be great."

"Oh. Yeah. No problem. He was planning on coming to help today, anyway. I'll give him a call."

"Everybody else will be here in an hour and a half."

"We'll get there as fast as we can," Alison said. She started to hang up, only to have another thought. "Brandon. Wait."

"What?"

"I meant to tell you something before today."

"Tell me what?"

"Well, my father doesn't know you're a matchmaker. He especially doesn't know you're *my* matchmaker. Can we keep quiet about that?"

"He wouldn't approve?"

"There are only five truly manly occupations. Firefighter, policeman, mechanic, soldier, and truck driver.

"Cowboy? Astronaut?"

"Second tier, but acceptable."

"Which one was he?"

"Firefighter."

"Where does real estate investor fall on his list?"

"Probably neutral. But if you have tools and fix things, you get extra points. And he'd definitely turn his nose up at me paying a matchmaking man to find me a husband. As far as he's concerned, the only people licensed to matchmake are nosy friends and relatives."

"Gotcha. I'm a real estate investor, and we met at McCaffrey's. In case it comes up."

"Oh, it'll come up. Trust me. See you soon."

Alison hung up and called her father, who said he'd meet her at Brandon's house. She threw on a pair of shorts and a T-shirt and left her condo. Later, as she was pulling to the curb in front of Brandon's house, her father pulled up behind her. Thank God she'd beaten him there. It was always best for her to be around as a buffer the first time anybody met Charlie Carter.

Charlie grabbed his toolbox, and together they walked toward the side of the house. She wondered what the odds were of her father getting through this day without offending somebody. Just about everybody who got to know him eventually saw beyond the perpetual frowny face and tidal wave of unsolicited advice, but sometimes it took a while.

"Do me a favor, will you, Dad?" she said as they walked.

"What's that, sweetie?"

"Try not to be crabby today. And remember—your way is *not* the only way."

"That's true."

"Wow. I'm glad to hear you finally admit that."

"But it's always the *right* way."

Gee, maybe this wasn't going to be bad after all.

It was going to be terrible.

Brandon was already there, with the cover of the air conditioner off and more tools than he'd ever use scattered around. He wore a pair of wrinkled cargo shorts, a T-shirt, and a pair of sneakers. How in the world could he dress so shabby and still look so gorgeous?

He rose as they approached. Alison introduced the two men, and they shook hands.

"I was going to get a repairman out here," Brandon said, "but Alison said you're pretty good with air conditioners."

"I've piddled around with a few of them."

Charlie squatted down and peered into the unit. After a few minutes, he said, "There's your problem. You just need to get the fan blade seated right."

"I haven't had a lot of luck with that."

"It's not easy, but we'll get it done."

Charlie grabbed a wrench, and soon he had the fan blade off.

"What do you do for a living, Brandon?"

Alison shot him a furtive glance. *Told you so.*

"I'm a real estate investor," Brandon said.

"Yeah?" Charlie said. "Real estate? Fixing this one up to sell?"

"No. I'll be staying here for a while."

"What kind of real estate do you usually invest in?"

"Apartment buildings, strip centers, single family homes if the potential profit is good enough."

"So how's business? I hear the real estate market stinks."

"You're right about that," he said. "So I'm taking some time off to settle my grandmother's estate. She died several weeks ago. Hopefully the market will rebound soon and I'll be back at it."

Charlie turned his attention back to the air unit. "So where do you two know each other from?" he asked, and Alison shot Brandon another *I told you so.*

"McCaffrey's," Alison said. "Everybody who lives around here eventually ends up there."

"Well, don't eat the turkey burger," Charlie said. "Tastes like crap."

Brandon smiled. "That's because turkey doesn't belong on a bun."

Charlie turned to Alison. "I like this guy. Listen to him, will you? No more of the damned turkey."

For the next few minutes, Brandon and Charlie held this, twisted that, and threw a few tools around.

"Are you married?" Charlie asked Brandon as they worked.

"No, sir."

"Ever been married?"

"Dad, stop. You're being intrusive."

"No, I haven't," Brandon said.

"Seeing anyone?"

"No. Not right now."

"Dad!"

"I just thought maybe he'd like to date a nice girl. That's all."

Alison's face was so hot it could have set off a brush fire. "Could you embarrass me anymore, Dad? Could you? Is it even *possible*?"

"What makes you think I'm talking about you?" Charlie said with a wink, making Alison want to crawl into a hole and pull the dirt in after her. This was worse than the time she was at her father's house and the UPS guy showed up. Her father invited him in and tried to set them up with all the subtlety of a charging rhino. What made it even worse was that he was a really cute guy, and she was wearing sweatpants, a beat-up Hard Rock Café T-shirt, and no makeup, with her unwashed hair in a pink scrunchy. After that humiliating incident, Alison hadn't ordered anything online for three months on the outside chance that she'd open the door and it would be that same poor guy delivering the package.

Yeah, her father thought it was just fine to try to fix her

up and embarrass the crap out of her in the process. But did it go both ways? No, it did not. The one time Alison had tried to suggest that perhaps her father might want to consider meeting one of the woman she worked with, he'd tossed down his newspaper and left the room.

"Let me tell you something about Alison," Charlie said. "She has a college degree. A good job. If you're looking for a wife—"

"Dad!"

"What? You'd make a great wife." He turned to Brandon. "Don't you think she'd make a great wife?"

"Of course," Brandon said.

Alison sighed. Oh, what the hell. She was thirty-one years old. It was time to stop worrying about her father foisting his opinions on the entire human race. Even if those opinions were loud.

And numerous.

And made people wish they were anywhere else.

"Brandon couldn't go out with me even if he wanted to," Alison said.

"Why not?" Charlie asked.

"Professional ethics," she said.

"Professional ethics? What's professional ethics got to do with real estate? You live in the wrong neighborhood, or something?"

"Okay, Dad," Alison said on a sigh. "We lied. Brandon used to be a real estate investor. Now he's a matchmaker."

Brandon raised an eyebrow. *So we're going there after all?*

"Huh?" Charlie said.

"You know. He matches people up. His grandmother died, and he took over her business."

"So that's what that sign is out front? Matchmaking by Rochelle? And now he's the matchmaker?"

"That's right."

He turned to Brandon. "Might want to think about changing the name."

Brandon smiled. "I'm working on it."

"But what's the matchmaking thing got to do with him going out with you?" Charlie asked Alison.

"He can't date his clients," Alison said, trying to shelve the issue once and for all. "I'm his client."

Charlie blinked with surprise. "So he's *your* matchmaker?"

"Yeah."

"Oh. Why didn't you just tell me that?"

"Because I thought you'd think it was weird. First that I hired a matchmaker. And second that you'd think Brandon was weird because he was one. No offense, Dad, but sometimes you're a little judgmental."

"I'm not judgmental. I just tell the truth." He turned to Brandon. "So why do you want to be a matchmaker?"

"I want to continue my grandmother's business."

"Good money in matchmaking?"

"Yeah. Not bad."

"Do you like it?"

"Yeah. I do."

"My daughter's wrong, you know. I've never been one to give a damn what a man did for a living, as long as it was legal and he could support his family."

"Oh, come on, Dad," Alison said. "How about the guy I dated who was an interior decorator? He made eighty grand a year, and arranging furniture isn't illegal."

"That was different. He was gay."

"No, Dad. He was straight. The guy I dated who owned the Harley shop—*he* was gay."

"I still don't believe that."

Alison just shook her head.

"So does this mean you've been setting up Alison on dates?" Charlie said.

"A few," Brandon said.

"How's that going?"

"I haven't found quite the right match for her yet."

"But he's getting closer," Alison said, even though a guy with lesbian dreams wasn't exactly moving in quite the right direction.

"Good," Charlie said. "It's about time she started dating men who are good enough for her. She wants to get married, you know."

"Yeah, she's mentioned that a time or two."

Brandon gave her a furtive smile, and she decided to just quit being embarrassed by all this or it was going to be a very long day.

A few minutes later, Charlie gave a wrench one last twist. Brandon went into the house to flip the breaker, then try the unit. When it came on again, she heard was the low rumble of the ancient appliance chugging back to life.

Brandon came back outside. "Thanks for the help, Charlie. You saved me a bundle of money."

"No sense paying somebody through the nose to do something I can do for free. If you have any more trouble with it, you just give me a call." He looked back and forth between them. "So what's next on the agenda?"

"I have a list," Alison said. "We'll go over it when everybody gets here."

As Charlie gathered up his tools, Alison looked at Brandon and mouthed *I'm so sorry*, then gave a little eye roll in her father's direction. He just smiled.

Alison heard a car door slam. She looked to the curb and saw Tony and Heather.

"Oh, good," Brandon said. "Heather. She hates me."

"I wouldn't say she hates you. It's more like she's *wary* of you. Big difference."

"Gee. That makes me feel way better."

A minute or two later, Bea showed up, and everybody jumped in to get things done. Her father volunteered to paint, so he and Bea started spreading drop cloths in the kitchen. Tony and Brandon moved furniture so they could polish the floors and clean the rugs. Alison and Heather joined forces on the windows, starting with the ones in the kitchen and breakfast room. They hadn't been washed in years, and it was a heavy-duty job to scrub them clean. Once they were finished with those, it was time for Bea and Charlie to start the painting.

Bea pried open the first can of wall paint. "So. Girls. What do you think of the color?"

Alison and Heather glanced over. It was a rich, creamy gold. Perfect for a Victorian kitchen.

"It's just right," Alison said.

"It's going to be beautiful," Heather said.

Charlie crinkled his nose. "It sucks."

Alison sighed. "Dad—"

"It's a re-creation of a popular Victorian color," Bea said. "We had it expertly mixed."

"Waste of money," Charlie said. "What's wrong with beige?"

"Beige?" Bea said, making a face. "What do you think this is? A 1970s tract home?"

"Don't knock 1970s tract homes. At least they don't look like Shanghai whorehouses."

Alison was horrified. Her father had known Bea an entire five minutes, and already he was talking whorehouses? She glanced at Heather. *What am I going to do with him?*

But Bea seemed unfazed. "Which begs the question, of course—what were you doing in a Shanghai whorehouse to know what color the walls were?"

"You don't know what men do in whorehouses?"

Bea rolled her eyes and poured the paint into a pan. She picked up a roller. Then Charlie did the same, only to stop and watch as Bea swiped her roller down the wall.

"You're not doing it right," Charlie said.

"Yes, I am. I know how to paint."

"You're not getting the right coverage."

Bea slumped with frustration, then turned around. "I suppose you can do better?"

"In my sleep."

"Then why don't you show me?"

"Your problem is that you're not getting enough paint on the roller. Here. Watch and learn." Charlie collected paint on his roller and rolled it on the wall.

Bea frowned. "That's fine, as long as you go back over the places where you've gooped the paint up on the wall."

"There's no gooping," Charlie said as he rolled over one of the goopy places.

Bea turned to Alison. "Is he always this aggravating?"

"Yeah," Alison said. "I'm sorry."

"No apologizing for your old man," Charlie said. "I can apologize for myself."

All three women turned and waited.

"As soon as there's something to apologize for."

Bea just shook her head and kept painting.

Alison and Heather finished up the kitchen windows and moved to the dining room, then the living room, following Tony and Brandon as they moved furniture and rolled rugs so they could come back later and polish the floors. Alison was pleased to see that the two men always seemed to be chatting about something sports related or laughing or otherwise having a good time. When lunchtime rolled around, Alison ordered pizza for the whole crew, cringing when her father ate four pieces of pepperoni.

In the early afternoon, Alison and Heather cleaned the second-story windows, and Alison was happy her father had brought a telescopic pole so she didn't have to use a ladder. By early afternoon they'd finished all the windows, and the sun pouring through the just-washed glass made the rooms positively glow. Once Brandon and Tony were through with the floors, they made some minor repairs on kitchen cabinets and light fixtures and cussed their way through unsticking a sticky bedroom door. Alison and Heather cleaned up the patio area and put the planters that Simpson's Nursery had donated on either side of the old wooden glider, and the whole area looked positively charming.

Later that afternoon, Heather and Alison were inside the house again rolling the rug back out in the living room when Alison heard something out front. Glancing out the window, she saw a man get out of a truck parked at the curb. A very large man. A very large, very *intimidating* man.

"Oh, my," she said, feeling her own eyes grow wide.

Heather came up beside her and looked out the window, too. "Oh, my God. Who's he?"

"Judging by the name on his truck, he's Brandon's landscaping guy. He's here to give an estimate on trimming the magnolia tree in the backyard."

"Yeah? Well, judging by his face, he just escaped from prison."

"Brandon!" Alison called out.

A few second later, he ducked his head around the doorway. "Yeah?"

"I think your landscaping guy is here."

"Oh. Good."

Brandon went to the door and greeted him, then led him through the house to the backyard.

"That is one scary-looking man," Heather said as soon as they were out of earshot.

"Will you stop?" Alison said. "I'm sure he's very nice."

"Maybe. But if I had a choice between walking down two dark alleys and that guy was at the end of one of them, I'd definitely pick the other."

Marco Perrone gave Brandon a decent price to trim the old magnolia, then offered to cut that in half when he found out Brandon was getting his house ready for a charity event. Brandon thought about his grandmother's note in Marco's file: *He's a very sweet man. Remind him to smile a lot.*

It looked as if his grandmother was right. Marco

seemed like a really good guy. Unfortunately, he still didn't seem to have a handle on the smiling thing.

Marco checked his watch. "I have a few hours before my next job. If you'd like, I can do the work right now."

"Sounds like a deal to me," Brandon said.

Marco went to his truck for a ladder and a chain saw, and a few minutes later, he was sawing off low-hanging branches to raise the canopy of the tree. Then he actually climbed up into the tree to thin out the foliage. Branches dropped one by one, and soon the yard was littered with them.

During a moment when the chain saw was silent, Brandon heard a screen door slap shut. He looked over the fence to the house next door to see Delilah step onto her patio. She wore a pair of gardening gloves, and she had a pair of shears in one hand and a basket in the other. She knelt down by one of the rosebushes that lined the back of her house, feeling gingerly along the stem of one of the roses before clipping it.

Brandon glanced back up into the tree, and strangely, he saw Marco just sitting there on a branch. Not a single muscle so much as twitched.

He was staring at Delilah.

For the span of a solid minute, Marco never moved. He held the chain saw in one hand and a nearby branch in the other and continued to look down at her. Totally unaware, Delilah held one of the flowers up to her nose and drew a deep breath.

And Marco couldn't take his eyes off her.

Hmm, Brandon thought. *Isn't this interesting?*

Eventually Marco turned back to his work, and a few minutes later, he came down out of the tree and started gathering up the branches to toss out at the street for the city to pick up.

"You stopped working up there for a minute," Brandon said.

Marco grabbed another branch. "Just taking a breather."

"Nah. I think you were watching Delilah."

Marco froze for a couple of seconds, then reached for another branch. "Delilah?"

"That woman next door you couldn't keep your eyes off of."

Brandon wouldn't have thought it possible, but that rugged face actually blushed.

"Delilah is a client of mine," Brandon said. "I'm been looking for the right man for her. Would you be interested in going over there to meet her?"

Marco whipped around. "No! I mean, I'm...you know. Working right now."

"You're the boss. You can give yourself a break, can't you?"

"No. I'm not interested in dating anyone."

"Yeah? You sure seemed interested in Delilah."

Marco didn't respond. He just started toward the gate with an armload of branches. Brandon grabbed a few himself and walked alongside him.

"So you're not attracted to her?"

"Nope."

"Hmm. I could have sworn—"

"I told you I'm not interested."

"She's smart. Personable. Owns her own house. Has a good job. I can show you her questionnaire if you're interested."

"Nope."

"Why not?"

"Look at her," he said, still walking. "And then look at me. This isn't a face women flock to."

"I don't think she's going to get all that hung up on looks."

"Think again."

"But—"

"I know you've taken over your grandmother's business. But don't think you have to do anything for me. Your grandmother already tried. Once women saw my photo, she couldn't even get anyone to agree to a first date."

"Are you sure that's why?"

He heaved the branches into a pile at the curb. "Your grandmother was nice enough to say it wasn't. But I knew the truth, because it was nothing new. It's always been that way for me. Eventually I just told her to forget it. So that's what I want you to do. Forget it."

He started back toward the gate to gather more limbs, and Brandon followed. "Come on, Marco. Don't you *want* to meet someone?"

Marco spun around, then leaned in and spoke intensely. "Look, I know this is hard for a guy like you to understand. I'm sure women line up all over town just hoping you'll speak to them. So there's no way you could possibly understand how it feels to have every woman you meet look at you as if you're going to steal—"

"She's blind."

Marco stopped short. "What did you say?"

"Delilah. She was in an accident, and now she's totally blind."

Marco's brows drew together as if he couldn't quite reconcile that. "But just now...just now she was out on her patio. Clipping roses."

"She's not helpless."

"I-I didn't mean that. I just didn't think..." His voice faded away.

"When she lost her eyesight," Brandon went on, "she lost her fiancé, too. Once he found out she was blind, he was out of there. So she's kinda gun-shy now, Marco. Same as you."

Marco glanced back toward the house next door, swallowing hard.

"So I guess you just ran out of excuses," Brandon said.

The jaw muscles of that craggy face tightened, and Brandon could tell he was thinking about it. But just as it looked as if he was going to agree at least to meet Delilah, he suddenly turned away.

"I'll get the rest of these limbs cleaned up," Marco said, starting for his truck again. "Then I need to get on to my next job."

Before Brandon could say anything else, Marco turned and headed for the backyard again, leaving him standing there in frustration. He didn't know how his grandmother had done this for thirty years. How had she dealt with people whose hearts had been broken too many times to try again?

Then he had an idea.

He figured most couples liked going the traditional route. Boy calls girl. But this time...this time he had the feeling that it was time to turn tradition on its ear.

As soon as Marco was gone, Brandon grabbed his phone and dialed Delilah's number.

Chapter 19

As the workday wound down and Tony and Heather were leaving, they suggested everybody meet up at the bar that night for dinner, which was enthusiastically embraced by all. Alison saw them out the front door, then headed for the kitchen to see how her father and Bea were doing. As she approached it, she heard her father's voice.

"See? Now that's a damn fine paint job. I hope you've learned something today."

"Yep," Bea said. "I learned how easy it is to get a pompous know-it-all of a man to do my work for me."

"And I learned how much women need men no matter how much they say they don't."

Aaargh! He was at it again.

When Alison came into the room, Bea rolled her eyes. "Your father is hopeless. And you're such a nice girl. Who would have thought it?" She turned back to Charlie. "I suppose you'll be at McCaffrey's tonight just to annoy me?"

"It's the *only* reason I'm coming."

"Jesus," Bea muttered as she left the room. "The crap I have to put up with."

As soon as she was gone, Alison wheeled on her father. "Dad! You can't talk to Bea like that!"

"Why not?"

"Because it's rude! You told her she was painting wrong."

"That's because she was."

"But you can't *tell* her that!"

"I already did," Charlie said. "See you at the bar later, sweetie."

Alison dropped her head to her hands, hoping Bea wouldn't hold her father's behavior against her forever. He was like a time bomb. He sat there just ticking away softly until the moment he blew up right in your face.

As her father was leaving, Brandon came into the kitchen.

"One of these paint cans is still half full," Alison told him. "You can keep it for touch ups."

"Thanks."

She turned and looked at the newly painted walls. "The color is pretty, isn't it?"

"Yeah. It looks nice."

"I'm getting ready to go, but before I leave...can I ask another favor?"

"Do I want to hear this?"

"Don't worry. It's not a big one. I saw an old wardrobe in one of the bedrooms upstairs. It was so gorgeous that I just had to open it up to see inside." She held up her palm. "No, I wasn't trying to be nosy. I just love old furniture."

"Your point?"

"I found some of the most beautiful vintage clothes inside. And I was wondering..."

"What?"

"Come upstairs. I'll show you."

He followed her up the stairs and into the bedroom. She opened the wardrobe with a flourish. "Look at these dresses. They're from the early nineteen hundreds, which means they were probably your great-grandmother's." She pulled out a blue empire dress and held it up. "This is my favorite. Isn't it pretty?"

Brandon shrugged. "It just looks like an old dress to me."

"No. It's way more than that. It's your family *history*."

"Uh...okay."

"Anyway, would you mind if I wore it on the day of the home tour?"

"You want to *wear* that? It smells like mothballs."

"It would have to be cleaned, but I can do that."

Brandon shrugged. "Sure. I don't care."

"If you don't mind me taking the dress..." Alison opened a lower drawer and pulled out a matching hat. She rested it carefully on her head and struck a pose. "How about a hat, too?"

"What's a dress without a hat? And the feathers are definitely *you*."

Alison pulled it off again. "This is going to be so much fun. I can't wait."

Then she looked again at the clothes in the wardrobe. "Brandon?"

"Yeah?"

"There are men's clothes in here, too. I don't suppose..."

"What?"

"Maybe on the day of the tour, you'd like to—"

"No! No. Absolutely not. Are you kidding me? I'm not wearing those clothes. I'd look like a total idiot."

"No! You'd look *so* handsome. Come on. We'd look like the lord and lady of the manor."

"I said no."

She dropped her chin, then slowly peered up at him.

"No," he said, shaking his head. "No way. You're not conning me again with that look."

"What look?"

"That one," he said, pointing.

She tilted her head. "Are you sure?"

"Positive."

Heavy sigh. "Oh, well. It was worth a try."

"I draw the line at donating my house. I have no intention of donating my dignity, too."

"For now."

"For*ever*."

"Sure, Brandon. Whatever you say."

He looked at his phone. "It's getting late. I need a shower before we go to dinner."

"Okay. I'm out of here."

She carried the clothes back down the stairs. They went to the front door, where she grabbed her purse and tossed it over her shoulder.

"I'll see you at McCaffrey's," she said. "Thanks for the clothes."

"No problem."

"And thanks so much for agreeing to wear the suit on the day of the tour."

"And that would be another no."

"Can't blame a girl for trying," she said with a smile. "See you tonight."

* * *

Fifteen minutes later, Brandon had just stepped out of the shower when his phone rang. He swiped a towel over his dripping hair and grabbed it. He looked at the caller ID, then answered it.

"Hey, Marco. What's up?"

"Didn't I tell you I didn't want you to match me up with anyone?"

"Uh...yeah. I believe you did."

"But you had her call me, anyway."

"Yeah. I did."

"I was in the middle of planting a dozen holly bushes."

"Surely you had time for a short conversation."

"She asked me out, Brandon," Marco said, sounding a little panicked. "*She* asked *me* out."

"Is that a problem?"

"Yes!"

"Why?"

"Because I told you I didn't want a match!"

"So you don't like her?"

"Don't like her? What's not to like? Of *course* I like her!"

"Then what's the problem?"

"I haven't been out with a woman in five years!"

"Well, then I'd say you're due, wouldn't you?"

Long silence.

"So..." Brandon said. "Are you going out?"

"Yes, we're going out," Marco snapped. "We have a date Saturday night."

"You agreed to go? That's great!"

"What else was I supposed to say? Huh? She caught me by surprise."

Brandon smiled. That was exactly what he'd hoped

would happen. "Don't worry, Marco. You're going to have a good time."

"I wouldn't bank on that if I were you. If I make a fool of myself—"

"That's not going to happen."

"Listen to me, Brandon. I didn't want this. I *told* you I didn't want it. So if this date goes wrong, I'm going to be blaming *you*."

And then the line went dead.

Brandon sat there for a moment, the phone still pressed to his ear, his elation fading away. He'd thought it was just a matter of pulling any strings he had to in order to get them together, and then nature would take its course. But had it been a mistake after all? Marco might be so uptight that even if the date was going well, he'd never know it.

Brandon had never realized just how lonely some people were and how hard it was for them to slip out of their shells and take a chance that they wouldn't face rejection one more time. If Marco had one more bad experience, he might never put himself out there again. And whose fault would that be?

Brandon tossed his phone aside and slumped against the headboard, feeling a headache coming on. If he was wrong about this, it would be more than just a single date that didn't work out. It might be proof positive to two people who desperately needed someone that their someones might not be out there after all.

Well, it was in the works now, and there was nothing he could do to stop it. He'd just have to let what was going to happen...happen.

*   *   *

When Alison arrived at McCaffrey's at six o'clock, Heather was behind the bar, restocking the ice bins with beer.

"Martini?" she asked.

"Better make it a Coors."

"Still can't stand the sight of vodka?"

"I'll come back around to it eventually," Alison said. "Maybe sometime *next* century." She sat down on one of the bar stools. "I'm pooped. How about you?"

"Yeah. But Brandon's house looks great, doesn't it?"

"It does. It's amazing what a little bit of elbow grease can accomplish."

"It was nice of him to let us use it," Heather said.

Alison blinked with surprise. "Hold on. Did you say Brandon did something *nice*?"

"Yeah."

"But you don't like him."

Heather shrugged offhandedly. "I don't know. Maybe he's not such a bad guy after all."

Alison couldn't believe it. "So what changed your mind?"

"Tony, mostly. He won't get off my back about it. He says he spent a lot of time with Brandon today, and he thinks he's a great guy. Now, to be fair, my husband never met a man he didn't like. But in Brandon's case..." She shrugged. "I don't know. Maybe he has a point. Brandon is letting us use his house. And even though he can't find you a match, you say he's pretty successful with other people, which means he's the real deal as a matchmaker."

"That's right."

"And when he walked you home the other night, he acted as if he actually cared about you."

A warm little shiver shot between Alison's shoulders. "What do you mean?"

"It's just a feeling I had." She nodded over Alison's shoulder. "But now that the devil has shown up, maybe we'd better stop speaking of him."

Alison turned to see Brandon walking toward her, and her heart did that weird fluttering thing again that made her deliciously lightheaded. As he slid onto a bar stool next to her, Heather popped the top on a Blue Moon and set it in front of him.

"Don't forget," she said. "The first round is on us."

Brandon picked up the beer, tipped it in her direction, and took a long drink. He set it down, then turned to smile at Alison.

"After the heat today," he said, "that tastes really good." He looked at Alison's bottle of Coors.

"Still can't face vodka, huh?"

"You're the second person tonight to point that out."

"And Heather was the first?"

"She jumped on that right away."

Brandon nodded toward an empty pool table. "I promised you a few pointers. Want to play?"

"I'd love to."

They picked up their beers and went to the table. Brandon handed Alison a cue, then racked up the balls. He grabbed a cue and broke to scatter the balls, then turned to Alison.

"Okay," he said. "Let's see your form."

Without a clue what she was doing, she leaned across the table to take a shot.

"No," he said. "Don't lean on the table with your bridge hand. Your weight needs to be completely controlled by your stance."

She shifted her weight a little to her feet instead of her hand.

"That's right. Now, hold the cue with your forearm perpendicular to it. Picture a line right through your elbow, down your arm, and to your hand."

She shifted the cue around a little, but Brandon shook his head.

"Here," he said. "Let me show you."

She thought he was going to grab a cue and demonstrate. Instead, he came up behind her, putting his hand right behind hers on the cue. He stood so close she could feel the warmth of his body radiating to hers as he leaned across the table with her.

"Think of your forearm as a pendulum swinging from your elbow."

He tried to move her cue to demonstrate, but it was as if her muscles had seized up.

"Relax," he said, and she actually felt his breath against her ear. *Relax?* Was he out of his mind?

"Lean in," he said. "Your chin should be only about six or eight inches above your cue."

She bent over a little more, and Brandon bent right along with her, moving forward another scant inch until she felt the fronts of his thighs graze the backs of hers.

"Keep your eyes on the cue ball."

Her eyes *were* on the cue ball. It was her mind that was somewhere else. Specifically, on the gorgeous man behind her.

"Okay," he said. "Take the shot."

She swung the cue. Softly. Smoothly. The cue ball clacked against the four and sent it cleanly into the corner pocket.

"There you go," he said, standing up. "It wasn't so hard, was it?"

Was he kidding? It was the hardest thing she'd ever done. She'd sent that four into the pocket when every muscle in her body was taut as a bowstring and every nerve was on fire.

He had her take one shot after another, showing her the physics and the strategy of the game, occasionally moving in to correct her stance. It got to the point where she wanted to screw up just so he'd show her a particular technique up close and personal. When she finally put the last ball away, she stood up and turned around to find Brandon behind her, staring down at her appreciatively.

"Nice shot," he said.

"Thank you."

"With just a little coaching, you should get better fast."

She smiled. "You're a good teacher."

"There are more lessons where that one came from. I could show you all kinds of things."

Alison felt a quiver of awareness, as if he was suggesting that the things he wanted to show her had nothing to do with pool. If so, she'd make sure she was his star pupil.

"Hey, you guys. Charlie and Bea just showed up."

Alison spun around to find Heather behind her. *Damn.* Her timing *sucked.*

"The big round corner booth is all set up," Heather said. "Let's eat."

As Brandon returned the cues to the rack on the wall, Heather and Alison started toward the table.

"You two sure seemed to be having fun together," Heather said.

Alison shrugged. "Yeah. I guess we were."

"That game was getting pretty friendly."

"He was just giving me some pointers."

"It's one thing to tell somebody how to play. It's another thing to show them."

"What do you mean?"

"He's interested."

"In what?"

"Oh, for heaven's sake," Heather muttered. *"You."*

Alison stopped short. *"Me?"*

"Yep."

Alison felt a surge of hope, but she refused to allow herself to believe it.

"No," she said. "We've been around each other a lot lately. If he wanted to ask me out, he'd have done it before now."

"Maybe it's that you're a client, so he doesn't feel as if he can."

Which was exactly what Alison had told her father, but she hadn't actually believed it herself. If Brandon thought he was the best match for her, why wasn't he stepping up?

"So do you have feelings for him?" Heather asked.

Feelings? Oh, *hell*, yes. Her attraction to Brandon had taken a whole new turn since he'd given her the kiss that wasn't real, bubbling up inside her like a volcano ready to blow. Every minute she'd spent with him lately made her feel weak and breathless and mushy inside. She'd watched him off and on all day long as they worked on his house, and the more he sweated, the hotter *she* got.

But she wasn't about to tell anyone that. Not even Heather. And she sure didn't want to admit that he'd kissed her, because it had meant nothing. And she'd also have to admit why he'd done it, and she'd been humiliated enough already.

"Feelings?" Alison said. "You mean, like, romantic feelings?"

"No. Like feelings of seething hatred. Of *course* I mean romantic feelings."

"*Hmm.* Not exactly."

"Not exactly? What does that mean?"

"It means I haven't really thought about it."

"Haven't *thought* about it? Alison, I've known you a long time. I can tell when you're thinking about eating a Mallorific bar, much less thinking about a man. Do you like him, or not?"

"Of course I like him," she said carefully. "But I'm not sure I like him like *that*."

"Like what?"

"Like more than just, you know. Liking him."

"Oh, please! You sound like you did in junior high when you had a crush on Bobby Wentworth. I'm talking about big-girl feelings, Alison. Got any of those lying around?"

"Oh, all right!" She let out a breath of frustration, grabbing Heather and pulling her aside at the same time she kept one eye on Brandon. "I can't stop thinking about him. I count the minutes until I can see him again. Every time he smiles at me, I feel like I'm melting from the inside out. There. Are you happy?"

Heather smiled. "Are you?"

"No," Alison said. "I'm miserable. You try having a

conversation with a man when you can't stop looking at his lips. I feel like a deaf person."

"I'm glad you finally admitted it."

"But he doesn't feel the same way about me."

"I wouldn't be too sure about that."

"No. Don't do this. Don't you *dare* do this."

"Do what?"

"Get my hopes up. I don't like getting my hopes up. The fall from there isn't fun."

Heather sighed. "Okay. I hear you. Maybe I'm wrong."

"Well, don't tell me *that*, either. Give me…I don't know. About a twenty-five percent chance? That way I can still hope, but if nothing happens, I'll feel as if I haven't lost much."

Heather rolled her eyes. "Okay. You have a twenty-five percent chance that Brandon has the hots for you. Now, come on. Let's eat."

Chapter 20

Alison had eaten at McCaffrey's approximately a thousand times, but not one of those meals had tasted anywhere nearly as good as this one. But it wasn't really the food that was so wonderful.

It was the company.

With the six of them stuffed into the round booth, she was squashed right next to Brandon, the length of his thigh pressed against hers. It felt heavenly. He swore he didn't like having a lot of people around, but he sure seemed comfortable there tonight, talking and laughing and in general having a good time. Every time his arm brushed against hers or he turned to talk to her and their eyes met, a shiver of excitement rushed through her. He suggested a trade—two of his buffalo wings for one of her quesadillas. She detested buffalo wings, but she ate them anyway, smiling as if the spicy heat wasn't blowing the top of her head off. The music gradually grew louder as the place filled up, the rhythm of it pulsing through her body in a most pleasant way. And when she pretended to occasionally have a hard time hearing what Brandon was saying to her, which caused him to lean that much closer to her when he spoke—well, that was just icing on the cake.

"We've had a very productive day, everyone," Alison said, speaking up so everyone at the table could hear her. "Brandon's house looks great." She held up her drink. "Here's to us."

They all clinked glasses and then drank.

"And here's to Brandon," Heather said, "for letting us use his house. Without it, the home tour would have been a disaster."

More clinking and drinking.

Brandon leaned in and whispered to Alison. "Heather was just nice. Does this mean she doesn't hate me?"

Alison whispered back. "I think it means she doesn't hate you," and felt a tremor of delight when he seemed pleased by that.

Brandon picked up his glass. "And here's to Tony and Heather for a wonderful dinner."

Everybody clinked. Except Charlie.

"Hey, Dad," Alison said. "We're toasting."

"Not me," he said, staring down at the remnants of his turkey burger. "Dinner sucked."

Bea held up her glass. "Here's to the loving daughter of a hardheaded man, who cares enough about her father to make sure he eats right at dinner after consuming four pieces of pizza at lunch."

Clinking. Drinking.

"Oh!" Alison said to Bea and Heather. "I meant to tell you guys. After you left today, Brandon and I found some vintage clothes in one of his closets. There was a dress that was probably his great-grand-mother's. He said I could wear it on the day of the home tour."

"Oooh, that'll be good," Bea said.

"And Brandon is going to wear one of his great-grand-father's suits."

Brandon turned to Alison. "Correct me if I'm wrong, but didn't I already say no to that? Twice?"

"Did you?" Alison said, blinking innocently. "I must have heard you wrong."

"Well, maybe you'll hear me this time." He leaned toward her and enunciated carefully. *"No."* Then he turned to Tony. "Back me up on this later, will you? When she tries to bring it up again?"

"Will do," Tony said. "Guys gotta stick together." He drained his beer and set the bottle down.

"It's getting busy in here," Heather said. "Tony and I probably need to get back to work. You guys enjoy the rest of the evening, okay?"

As they slid out of the booth, Charlie turned to Bea, nodding toward the dartboard on the far wall. "So are you as bad at darts as you are at painting?"

"Bad? Try again, buster."

"So show me. Ladies first."

She slid out of the booth, and Charlie followed. Now that there was extra space in the booth, she waited for Brandon to scoot over, giving each of them more room. Instead he stayed right next to her, his thigh still pressed against hers, and for the first time she allowed herself to think that maybe Heather was right.

They watched as Bea and Charlie grabbed darts and headed to the throw line to start playing. But then her father said something to Bea, and she turned around and put her fist on her hip and said something back. When he responded, she rolled her eyes and shooed him away so she could start the game.

"*Aaargh*," Alison said, dropping her head to her hands.

"What?" Brandon asked.

She looked up again. "My father is being just awful."

"Awful?"

"Yes. I was hoping he would straighten up his act just a little bit today. But he's been saying rude things to Bea, and she's been forced to come right back at him. He's my father and I love him, but she must think he's just horrible."

Brandon stared at Alison dumbly, then started to laugh. "You're kidding, right?"

She blinked. "Kidding?"

"That's not what's going on."

"What do you mean?"

He made a scoffing noise. "And I thought women were supposed to be the intuitive ones."

"What are you talking about?"

"Alison. They're flirting."

Alison drew back. "That's *flirting*? My father being crabby, and then Bea snapping back at him?"

"Yep."

Alison turned to watch them again. Bea threw her third dart, and it hit the bull's-eye. But Charlie wasn't watching the dartboard. He was watching Bea.

And he was smiling.

In that moment, Alison had the most startling revelation. *He used to look at Mom like that.*

"I don't believe it," she said, her voice hushed with amazement. Tears welled up in her eyes. She blinked quickly, but not quickly enough. She turned away from Brandon and wiped them away with her fingertips.

"Alison?" Brandon said, sounding worried. "What's the matter?"

"Nothing," she said, turning back. "Nothing at all."

"You don't seem happy about your father and Bea."

"Oh, no. I am. Trust me. This is good. He's barely talked to another woman since my mother died."

"When was that?"

"About fifteen years ago."

"That's a long time. So this is a big thing for him?"

"Very big. I want so much for him to be happy, and he hasn't been. Not completely. Maybe this will change things. I don't want him to be alone for the rest of his life."

She'd told the truth. She could see her father heading down the path of solitude, and she wanted so much more for him than that. But she wanted more for herself, too. What if she were the one who ended up alone from now on?

"I'm sorry I haven't found you another match yet," Brandon said.

It was as if he was reading her thoughts. He'd done that from the first day she'd walked into his office—read her as clearly as the average man reads a newspaper. It had unnerved her at first. It was strangely comforting now.

She forced a smile. "Hey, when you take away the drug dealers and the ex-wife addicts and the sexually conflicted, who's left?"

"Nobody who's good enough for you."

His voice was strangely serious, and his eyes never left hers as he spoke. The strangest tremor of awareness shot right up her spine.

"I don't know whom to fix you up with anymore," he told her. "I go through the files, and I seem to find something wrong with every one of them."

"You're just afraid of making a mistake again."

"What if none of those guys are right for you? What do I do then?"

"I don't know. I guess I'm back to square one. But, hey. Nothing ventured, nothing gained, right?"

"You deserve better than that."

Yes, I do. How about the matchmaker himself?

"It's okay," she said. "I've been so busy. I don't know if I would have had time to go on another date, anyway."

"No time? You're here with me now."

"Yeah, but this isn't a date."

"Maybe not. But is it what a date with you is like?"

Her heart stuttered, not so much because of his words, but because of the sound of his voice—soft and low and suggestive. Or was she hearing things that weren't there?

"Yeah," she said. "You get to watch me play a lousy game of pool and listen to my father flirt with women. How exciting is that?"

"Sounds like good times to me."

Oddly enough, he seemed to mean that, and Alison decided she could move that twenty-five percent up a little. Say, to twenty-six.

As Brandon sat at that table with Alison, listening to the music and watching Bea and Charlie play darts and argue, he ticked off in his mind the dumb things he'd done recently, one by one.

He shouldn't have kissed Alison that day she came to his house to apologize.

He shouldn't have come here tonight, where there was too damned much temptation in the form of the woman sitting next to him.

He shouldn't have had that second beer, which made him all the more willing to give in to that temptation.

And he shouldn't be sitting so close to Alison that he could feel her warmth and see her smile and think about that kiss all over again.

It was an endless cycle that he really needed to find a way out of. But there was something about this night, this place, and this woman that gave him a sense of well-being he'd never felt before. For once in his life, he was more than just a face in the crowd. He felt as if he belonged there, and he wanted to enjoy it as long as he could. And as long as he kept things on friendly terms, a little casual flirting with Alison wouldn't do any harm, would it?

No. It wouldn't. Then next week he'd get serious and double down on finding her another match, and everybody would be happy.

"Funny thing," Alison said. "Did I tell you that one of the Preservation League board members knew your grandmother?"

Brandon was startled by the question. "No. You didn't tell me that."

"She went to the First Baptist Church with her. And she remembers you when you were a teenager."

Brandon had no idea where this was going, and he was pretty sure he didn't want to know. "Oh, yeah?"

"Yeah. And she said you didn't just visit your grandmother. You actually lived with her for a couple of years."

All at once, Brandon's mind was spinning, trying to remember what he'd told Alison. Had he ever said he just visited? He wasn't sure.

"Yeah," he said finally. "I did live with her. Didn't I tell you that?"

"No, I don't think so. So where were your parents?"

"It was just my father. My mother was dead."

"Oh. I'm so sorry! How old were you when she died?"

"I was only four. I don't remember much about her."

"Do you have brothers and sisters?"

"No. It was just me."

"So why did you go to live with your grandmother?"

"My father traveled a lot with his job."

"What did he do?"

Damn it. The last thing he wanted to do was talk about his father, or anything else about his past. He wasn't proud of the fact that his old man was a pool hustler who'd dragged him all over the country with zero regard for his own son's well being. So Brandon ended up stretching the truth so hard it almost snapped.

"He was a professional pool player."

Alison sat back with a smile. "Ah, so that's why you're such a good player. You learned from your father."

"Oh, yeah. He taught me everything he knew."

Yep. When it came to hustling, his father was the best teacher on the planet.

"Judith told me you gave your grandmother a pretty hard time," Alison said. "Now, understand that she's a bit of a stick-in-the-mud. To her, a hard time could mean that you didn't say 'Yes, ma'am' at the appropriate time."

It had been more than a lack of polite behavior. Way more. By the time he went to live with his grandmother, he'd had a chip on his shoulder so big that nobody could knock it off, even the one person on earth who tried so desperately to give him his first taste of the normal life his father had always denied him.

"I was a teenage boy," he said with an offhand shrug,

even as the memory of those days still ate away at him. "They can be real pains in the ass, and I was no exception. Sometimes my mouth got the better of me."

"But I thought you had a good relationship with your grandmother. You told me you used to sit on the stairs and listen to her with her clients, and—"

"I listened to a lot of things. But admit I listened? Hell, no. Again. Teenage boy." He forced a smile. "It's all about the attitude."

"Let's see…" Alison went on. "What else did Judith say? Oh, yeah. You were once…arrested."

He didn't know who the hell this woman was, but he sincerely wished she didn't have quite so good a memory. *Just downplay it. It's all you can do.*

"A friend and I were arrested for vandalism," he said. "Which only proves exactly how stupid teenage boys can be. It was kid stuff, Alison. I wasn't a saint." He paused. "I'm still not."

Given the lies he'd told her, that was the understatement of the year.

"But at least you don't vandalize things anymore, do you?" she said with a smile.

"No," he said. "I did outgrow that."

"Oh," she said. "One more Judith thing. She said you don't actually own your grandmother's house. That if you move out, it goes to her church?"

Good God. Was there anything this woman didn't know?

"That's true," he said. "It was the only asset my grandmother had of any real value, and she wanted the church to have it. But she also made the provision that I can live there as long as I want to before that happens. So if I never move out, I guess I have a house forever, don't I?"

Alison smiled. "Yeah. I guess you do."

He smiled back, but it was the last thing he felt like doing. He'd told her the truth—if he stayed there forever, he had a house forever.

But he wasn't staying forever. Not even close.

Suddenly every bit of the euphoria he'd felt earlier had seeped right out of him, leaving him feeling like crap. He'd done nothing but lie to Alison since the day he'd met her, making her believe he was somebody he wasn't. And she believed every word of it.

That was the hardest part for him. That she believed every word.

If he'd never gotten to know her, it wouldn't have mattered. If he'd just kept things professional, he wouldn't be sitting there trying to put a spin on his past that wouldn't have her questioning the things he'd already told her. This conversation was proof positive that he was in too deep with Alison and he needed to get out *now*.

Then all at once he heard a commotion across the room. Bea's voice rose above the crowd. "Alison! Something's wrong! Get over here! *Now!*"

They both spun around to see Bea hovering over her father, who was lying on his back on the floor.

And he wasn't getting up.

Chapter 21

The next half hour was a sickening blur for Alison. By the time the paramedics got her father to the hospital, he was fully conscious and talking to them, but until a doctor saw him and said he was going to be okay, Alison was going to keep worrying.

Brandon insisted on driving her to the hospital, and he was there now, sitting in one of those uncomfortable plastic waiting room chairs beside her as they waited for the doctor to come out and tell them her father's condition. Heather and Bea were there, too, assuring her things were going to be just fine.

"But what if he had a heart attack?" Alison said. "Just because he was conscious doesn't mean there wasn't heart damage."

"The paramedics didn't think it was a heart attack," Brandon said.

"But they won't know for sure until they do tests."

"That's true," Heather said. "But I don't think he's in any immediate danger."

Alison just nodded and stared down at her hands. They didn't understand. Bea or Brandon, or even Heather, who'd known her forever. They didn't understand the gut-wrenching feeling she'd had when she saw her father passed out on the floor, that horrible fear that something terrible had happened and he was gone. From one instant to the next, he could have been gone from her life forever.

Sometimes in the middle of the night, she lay awake in bed, huddled under the blankets, waiting for the phone to ring, waiting for the bad news she was sure was coming. Then daylight would come, and it would all be shoved to the back of her mind and she'd forget about it for a while, but it was always there.

"I hate hospitals," Alison said.

"I know," Heather said.

"It makes me sick just to get near one. It's hard even sitting here."

Heather patted her arm. "Your dad will be out of here soon."

They sat in near silence for another fifteen minutes. Alison tried to focus on the *Good Housekeeping* magazine on the waiting room table and the smiling woman on the cover who looked as if she didn't have a care in the world.

Finally a man wearing blue scrubs stepped out into the waiting room. "I'm looking for the family of Charlie Carter?"

Alison looked up. "Here." She rose as the doctor approached, sliding her hand to her throat, fearing the worst. "I'm his daughter. How is he?"

"He's going to be fine."

"It wasn't a heart attack?"

"No. There's no evidence of that."

Alison let out the breath she'd been holding, but the fear still hung on. "So what happened?"

"He just got a little dehydrated and his electrolytes were out of balance. He passed out and fell. We're giving him some fluids now and he's feeling better. But he took a pretty solid bump on the head, which means he could have a concussion. So we need to watch him overnight."

"That's all? Really?"

"Yes. We've moved him to a regular room. You can see him now if you want to."

The doctor gave them the room number and left. Alison turned to the others and told them it might be best if she visited him alone. She knew her father. Being seen in any kind of compromised position wasn't something he felt comfortable with.

"I hate for you guys to have to hang around," Alison said. "Heather, I know you need to get back to the bar."

Heather nodded. "I'll take Bea home on my way." She turned to Brandon. "Assuming you don't mind sticking around to take Alison home."

"No. Of course I'll stay."

Heather gave Alison a quick hug, and when she pulled away, a furtive wink. Alison didn't know exactly when she'd changed her mind about Brandon. She was only glad she had.

"I'll wait for you right here," Brandon said, as Heather and Bea walked away. "Take all the time you want to with your father."

"Thank you for staying."

"No problem."

She nodded and went to the elevator, feeling a myriad of emotions pulling at her. Relief that her father was okay. Fear that it was only a matter of time before he wasn't. Helplessness to control any of it.

A few minutes later, she peered into room 416. Her father was hooked up to a couple of monitors, and there was an IV in his arm. He wore a hospital gown, and his ashen skin against the white sheets made him look every bit of his sixty-four years.

She came into the room. "Hey, Dad."

He looked over. "Hey, sweetie."

"How are you doing?"

"I feel fine. A little headache is all. I tried to talk them into turning me loose, but they wouldn't do it."

"You hit your head when you fell. You may have a concussion. Those can be dangerous."

"A concussion? Dangerous?" He made a scoffing noise. "Try putting out a four-alarm fire on a hundred-degree day with a twenty-mile-an-hour wind. *That's* dangerous."

She sat down in the chair beside his bed. "You look pale."

"It was the turkey burger. You want me to have rosy cheeks? Feed me some red meat. Which I bet I'm not going to get in this place."

"Don't give these people a hard time. They're trying to help you. Can you just eat whatever they put in front of you?"

"If it tastes like crap, they're going to hear about it."

"Dad—"

"Okay. Fine. As long as I get to go home tomorrow."

"The doctor is just being careful. And you need to be, too. You can't work as hard as you did today and not drink plenty of water. And then when you put beer on top of that—"

"I know. You think I don't know? I just got busy, that's all."

"That's all? Well, you can't get so busy that you forget. That's what lands you in the emergency room. Not taking care of yourself. You *have* to take care of yourself."

"Lighten up, kid. It's not like I had a heart attack, or something."

Alison's stomach knotted just hearing the words "heart attack." Ever since they'd found out six months ago that his cholesterol was high, she'd envisioned the worst happening. Most of the time she could just put it out of her mind, but right now, seeing him in this hospital bed, listening to the mechanical sounds of the monitors and breathing in the antiseptic smell of the hospital, it was hard to shake those thoughts. She remembered a time years ago when she'd sat beside a hospital bed like this. When that vigil ended, she no longer had a mother.

"Who came to the hospital with you?" Charlie asked.

"Heather and Brandon." She paused. "And Bea."

"Bea came?"

"Yeah. She's worried about you. Now that we know you're fine, Heather's taking her home."

"Did you know she carries a gun?"

"Yeah. I know."

"She threatened me with it."

"I don't doubt that."

"She's a crazy old broad."

"No crazier than you are, Dad."

A tiny smile curled his lip. "I want all of you to go home so I can get some sleep."

"Are you sure? I can hang around for a while longer."

"I said *go*."

"Okay. Good night, Dad." She gave him a kiss on the cheek, then headed for the door. "I'll be back in the morning."

                         *   *   *

When Alison came back downstairs, Brandon hoped she'd look at least a little relieved, but her face was still pinched with worry. He was happy to be here to take her home, but expressing sympathy wasn't his strong suit. It always felt awkward to him, and he never knew what to say.

"Ready to go?" Brandon asked, standing up.

"Yeah."

"How is he doing?"

"He's okay. For now."

They went through the automatic doors into the parking lot. "What do you mean, for now?"

"It's going to happen someday," she said. "He's going to have a heart attack."

"How can you be so sure?"

"He has high cholesterol. He doesn't eat right, and he doesn't exercise. But he tells me the devil doesn't want him because he's too mean, so he's going to live forever. That's his rationale to get me off his back."

They got into Brandon's car. As he pulled out of the parking lot, Alison dropped her head against the headrest.

"You look tired," he said.

She took a long, deep breath and let it out. "Yeah." And she didn't say another word until he pulled into a parking space in front of her condo. Being around Alison for a full ten minutes without her talking was something he'd never experienced before, and it worried him.

"Thank you for taking me home," she said, and started to get out of the car. He caught her arm.

"Hey, are you okay?"

"I'm fine."

"Don't take this wrong, but you don't look fine."

She took another long, deep breath. "I'm just worried."

"You don't need to be. It was just a fluke. It had nothing to do with his heart. It could have happened to anyone."

"But what if it *had* been a heart attack?"

"It wasn't. Don't borrow trouble."

"But he has high cholesterol. It isn't inconceivable that he could have one."

"That's true. But there was nothing about this tonight that makes that any more likely."

"And hospitals. God. They're full of disease. I've heard of people going into hospitals with ingrown toenails and then getting horrible bacterial infections and dying."

"Aren't you getting a little carried away?"

"No, I'm not. I've read about it. It happens all the time."

"Yes, but it's not going to happen to your father."

"Are you one of those 'glass half full' people? Because I am *not* in the mood for that right now."

"Just relax," Brandon said. "He's fine."

"But he might not have been!"

"Alison. Calm down."

Her eyes narrowed. "Who are you to tell me to calm down?"

Her sudden anger surprised him. "This just isn't worth getting worked up about. Your father fainted and got a bump on the head, and you're acting as if he's at death's door."

"You know nothing about this," she said fiercely. "Less than nothing. So if I were you, I'd keep my mouth shut."

This was it. This was exactly why he didn't get too involved with women. Sooner or later all their emotions came roaring out, emotions he had no idea how to deal with. He needed to get out of Alison's world and back to his own, back to a place where things made sense to him and he didn't get tangled up in stuff he knew nothing about.

"You're right," Brandon said. "I'm sorry. It's none of my business."

Alison closed her eyes, her anger fading away.

"I'm sorry," she said quietly. "I didn't mean to bite your head off." She folded her arms protectively and looked away. "It's just that I can't lose him, Brandon. I can't."

"I understand that. You're very close."

She nodded, but suddenly her eyes were glistening with tears. He hated that. *Hated* it.

"You were so right about me," she said.

"What do you mean?"

"My childhood was wonderful. The kind every kid ought to have. My father seems crabby and everything, but that's just his way. He was such a good father."

Brandon didn't know what to say, so he just let her talk.

"And my mother was one of those who was born to the job," she went on. "And the two of them together..." Her mouth turned up in a brief smile. "Fireworks. The good kind. They loved each other more than anything. Sometimes I think I must remember it wrong, that my life growing up couldn't have been all that wonderful. But then I look back at pictures, and sometimes my dad and I talk, and I realize that it really was. It really was perfect." She paused. "But when I was sixteen, everything changed."

"What happened?"

"My mother got cancer. She died three weeks before Christmas."

Oh, God. This was way out of his league. *Way* out. "I bet that was hard."

"Yeah," Alison said. "After her funeral, it was about the time of year when she would have started decorating and baking. But the house was silent. My father hid himself away in his bedroom most of the time. I couldn't stand it. I'd just gotten my driver's license, so I grabbed my brother, took my father's truck, and I bought a Christmas tree. And I got out her mixer and baked. And when Christmas day came, I fixed dinner and played Christmas carols. It helped my brother get through it, I think. But my father..." Her voice quivered at the memory. "He sat through Christmas dinner. Barely ate anything. Then he went to his bedroom for the rest of the night. I cried myself to sleep, thinking I'd never have a real family again."

Brandon didn't know what to say. Christmas had never meant much to him, because it had been just he and his father from the time he was four years old, and his old man sure hadn't given a damn about the glow of the holiday season. Hell, until he'd lived with his grandmother, he'd never even had a Christmas tree. But he could imagine what it must be like for somebody like Alison.

"What about your brother?" Brandon said.

She was silent for a long time. "He enlisted in the military when he turned eighteen," she said finally. "He was deployed to Iraq. By the time he was twenty-one, he was engaged. I was so excited. Finally our family was going to grow. I loved his fiancée." She paused, her voice quivering. "We planned a wonderful wedding that was going to take place two weeks after his discharge."

When her eyes filled with tears, Brandon's throat tightened with dread. "God, Alison. Please don't tell me—"

"Roadside bomb," she said, her voice choked. "He came home in a coffin."

Brandon felt as if he'd been hit with a sledgehammer. He wanted to say something warm and soothing and helpful. "I'm sorry" was all he managed, and it sounded so weak and worthless that he wished he hadn't said anything at all.

"His fiancée was devastated," Alison said. "But time passed, and she moved on. She was married last summer." Her lips tightened as if she were going to cry. "She invited me to the wedding, but I just couldn't bring myself to go. I couldn't bear to see her so happy when my brother was dead. Isn't that awful?"

"No," Brandon said. "It's not awful. You just do what you can do."

"When I was younger, I assumed I'd eventually get married and have a family of my own. But as the years went by, it was one bad relationship after another, and my father was getting older, and I had nobody else. And then several weeks ago, after the marriage proposal that wasn't, I got to thinking, my God. It's possible. I could go through my entire life alone."

"So you hired me."

"Yes."

Brandon closed his eyes, wishing he'd never gone through with this crazy scheme. How could he ever have thought this business would be something he could just toss off, take people's money no matter what the outcome was, and disappear? Not once had he stopped to think how important he might be to the people who came to him, and how horribly ill-equipped he was to help them. Christ, he didn't know the first thing about marriage, family, any of it. And in his own arrogance, he thought he was going to help people find the true love they were looking for?

No. That wasn't what he'd thought at all. His thought process had stopped at matching them up. That was what they were paying him to do. What came after that, he hadn't given a single thought to.

How dumb could he have possibly been?

"Don't you have other relatives?" he asked her.

"An aunt and uncle on my mother's side in Phoenix, but after my mother died, we drifted away from each other. My father has a brother, but he's divorced and works overseas. None of my grandparents are still living. So really, my father is just about it."

Her teary eyes told him how much she loved her father. How much love she had to give, period. He'd felt it when she'd kissed him that night, and he was feeling it ten times that now.

"I need a family," she said quietly. "Like I need air to breathe. I want a husband and children and summer vacations and Christmas mornings. I can't bear the idea of going through my life alone, with nothing but a houseful of cats to keep me company." Tears rolled down her cheeks now, and she swept them away with the back of her hand. "My cats. God, I'm even pitiful about them."

"Come on, Alison," he said with a tentative smile. "You're still one away from being a crazy cat lady, right?"

A smile briefly touched her lips, only to disappear into misery again. "Do you know the real reason I took them in? Because they lost their mother. I knew how that felt. But they had each other. Brothers and sisters. And when the time came, I just didn't want to split them up. So I kept them all. I know they're just cats, but...oh, God. See? Pitiful."

Suddenly what Heather had told him that night came back to him, and he knew now what she was talking about. *She's lost so much in her life already. I don't know how many more times she can hit the wall before she just can't take it anymore.*

"And then tonight," she said, her voice harsh with emotion, "when I saw my father lying on the floor, I was sure the worst had happened. Do you know how horrible it feels to be only one person away from having no family at all?"

She bowed her head, her hand over her mouth, trying to stem the tide of tears that was coming. But she couldn't. And in that moment, her grief made the heart Brandon swore he didn't have come very close to breaking.

He wrapped his arm around her and pulled her close, and she fell against him, sobbing. Any pain he'd ever felt in his life he'd just shoved aside, pushing it to the depth of his subconscious so he'd never have to face it. But Alison was different. Her pain was so raw and real and so near the surface that all it took was a whisper of a breeze to bare it to the world. Maybe for another person the things that had happened wouldn't have been so traumatic. But for Alison, who had been cherished as a child, tangled blissfully in the heartstrings of a warm and loving family, it had been excruciating.

She splayed her hand against his chest and then drew up his shirt in her fist, holding on tightly. "I'm sorry," she said as she cried, but he didn't care about apologies, didn't want them, didn't need them. He just let her curl up in the comfort of his arms as he stroked her hair, remembering now how silky soft it had felt beneath his hand the night she'd kissed him. He murmured nothing words to her until finally her sobs wound down and she lay motionless in his arms. Her hair was mussed, her long, golden lashes wet with tears. She looked like an angel who'd tumbled out of heaven into a world where bad things happened, things she was helpless to face by herself.

He rested his palm against her cheek and brushed away a tear with his thumb. She turned slowly and looked up at him, her head still resting against his shoulder, her soft, full lips parted slightly. Brandon felt the air between them quivering with unrealized possibilities, and every one of them was flashing through his mind right now.

He felt things for Alison he'd never felt with another woman before. As if his emotions were getting tangled up with hers and he couldn't disengage. His thoughts turned blurry and incoherent, and suddenly all the dangers of being so close to her right now seemed to fade into the background. Without another thought, he slid his arm around her shoulders, pulled her to him, and kissed her.

The moment his lips fell against hers, she slid her hand to his shoulder and leaned into him, wanting it every bit as much as he did. He knew he shouldn't be doing it, but the longer he kissed her, the longer he wanted to kiss her. Just as he'd think about maybe pulling away, she'd thread her fingers through his hair and pull him closer, or she'd drop her hand to his thigh and grasp it gently, asking him to continue, or he'd hear the faintest whimper in the back of her throat, begging him for more. He mentally cursed the console between them, even though he should have been grateful for it. If they'd been anywhere else but this car, he could only imagine what this might already have led to.

Finally he slid back to his senses enough to pull away, but when he looked and saw her heavy-lidded expression of total satisfaction, he damned near kissed her all over again.

"I should go," he said.

"No," she whispered. "Stay with me tonight."

His heart slammed against his chest. Everything he wanted and everything he couldn't have were wrapped up in those four little words. And when he looked down and saw the gentle, pleading expression on her face, he realized just how badly he'd screwed up. Why the hell hadn't he kept his lips to himself?

"I can't," he said.

"Why not?"

"Tonight has been crazy. I think you just need to sleep."

"Fine," she said. "We'll sleep."

"Alison—"

"This isn't like the other night. I wasn't thinking straight then. But now...now I know exactly what I'm doing."

She slid her hand to his neck and stroked it with her thumb, sending hot shivers up and down his spine. Then she leaned in and kissed him, taking his face in her hands and angling her mouth to engulf his, answering his kiss with one of her own, making it clear what she wanted and that she wanted it *now*. It took every bit of willpower he had to take her by the shoulders and ease her away.

"Alison," he said, breathing hard. "Stop. Please stop."

She blinked, edging back to reality.

"I can't do this," he said. "I know I started it, but I can't do this."

She looked at him warily. "I don't understand."

"This was a mistake. You're a client. If we got involved with each other, it would be bad for business."

She leaned away. "Oh, that is *so* much crap, and you know it."

"Alison—"

"Am I really that unappealing?"

"No!"

"Did you kiss me because you were feeling sorry for me?"

"Will you *stop*?" He blew out a breath of frustration. "I'm just not looking for any relationship right now."

"I don't believe that. Look at what you're doing. You run a business dedicated to helping other people find true love. How can you not want that for yourself?"

He hated this. *Hated* it. Every question she asked made another lie come out of his mouth.

"Someday I will," he said. "But you want it now, and I can't be the one to give it to you."

"God, Brandon. Why don't you just tell me the truth? You're not attracted to me."

"Not attracted to you? I kissed you, didn't I?"

"Then what the *hell* is going on here?"

He turned away. "This has nothing to do with you. I'm the one with the problem."

"Oh, please! Will you spare me the old 'It's not you,

it's me' thing? As if I haven't heard that a thousand times before?" She turned away. "You had it right the first time. Maybe you should just go."

She grabbed her purse off the floor by her feet and opened the car door. He grabbed her arm. "I'm sorry, Alison. I didn't mean for this to happen."

"But you didn't do much to stop it either, did you?"

"I'll find the right man for you," he said. "No matter what it takes."

She looked at him with disbelief. "You're telling me that *now*? After this? You turn me down, but, hey, no problem, my next date is just around the corner?" She made a scoffing noise. "I was right in the first place. You *are* clueless about women."

She was right. His timing was just impeccable.

"All I meant was that you deserve a better man than me."

"And you still think you can find him for me? Sorry, Brandon. I'll have to see that to believe it."

With that, she turned and got out of the car, slamming the door behind her. She trotted up the stairs and disappeared into her condo, leaving him sitting in frustrated silence, wondering how he could have been stupid enough to get himself into this mess.

He glanced up at her living room window. The curtains were pushed aside, and Alison was standing there, staring down at him. Even at this distance, he could see the look on her face and knew that the anger and sarcasm she'd left him with were nothing but a mask to hide what she was really feeling.

He'd told her the truth, whether she believed it or not. He didn't have much time left, but one way or the other, he was going to do it. He was going to find her the man she was so desperate for so she could have the family she'd always wanted. Soon her memory of the kiss they'd just shared would fade away into oblivion, and maybe she wouldn't hate him forever.

Chapter 22

"D ad, you just got out of the hospital. Would you please take it easy?"

Charlie twist-tied the trash bag and started for the back door. "It's trash day. That means I gotta take out the trash."

"Why don't you let me do that?"

"Do I look like an invalid to you?"

No, he didn't. At least not now. But Alison still couldn't get that picture out of her mind of her father in a hospital bed and the inevitability that someday it was going to happen again.

She watched out the kitchen window as Charlie headed across the backyard to the alley, Blondie bouncing at his heels. Late afternoon sunlight slanted through the trees, dappling his perfectly manicured lawn. He dumped the trash, then turned around, grabbed a stray ball from the grass, and heaved it across the yard. Blondie took out after it as if her bushy gold tail was on fire.

Alison heard the doorbell. She went to the front door and looked out the peephole.

Bea?

She opened the door. "Bea! What a surprise!"

But thinking about it, was it really?

"Hi, Alison. I just came by with something for your father." She nodded down at the casserole pan she held. "Is he here?"

"Sure. Come on in."

By the time they got to the kitchen, Charlie and Blondie were coming through the backdoor. He stopped short when he saw Bea.

"You have food," he said. "What is it?"

"Lasagna," she said, then turned to Alison and whispered, "*Vegetable* lasagna."

Charlie frowned. "I heard that."

"I figured you wouldn't be up for cooking," Bea told him as she shoved the lasagna into the fridge. "So there. You have dinner." She knelt down and ruffled Blondie's ears. "And if I'd known you had such a gorgeous puppy, I'd have brought a soup bone instead. What's your name, sweetie?"

"Blondie," Charlie said. "As in *dumb* Blondie."

"Watch it, buster. Before the gray took over, I used to be a blonde." She scratched Blondie's ears. "You poor, precious puppy dog. How do you put up with that man?"

"I feed her, brush her, and scoop her poop. What more does she want?" Charlie went to the sink to wash his hands. "So do you want to stay for dinner?"

"Why, Charlie," Bea said. "How sweet of you to ask."

"I just want somebody to eat the lasagna first so I'll know it's okay."

Bea turned to Alison. "So what does he think? I'm poisoning him?"

"You stay too, sweetie," Charlie said to Alison.

Under normal circumstances, she would have. But

then the strangest thought crossed her mind: *two's company; three's a crowd.*

"Nah," she said. "I have a lot of stuff to do tonight. I think I'll head on home."

"You're leaving me alone with her?" Charlie said. "I told you she's packing, didn't I?"

"Yeah, Dad. You did." She turned to Bea. "If he gets out of line, shoot him."

She gave her father a quick kiss on the cheek and left the kitchen. When she reached the front door, she heard him say, "So do you like zombie movies?" and Bea said, "What's not to like?"

Alison stopped for a moment, feeling the strangest push-pull of emotions she didn't know what to do with. She loved seeing her father happy. But at the same time it magnified her own feelings of despair.

Stop being selfish. Your father deserves happiness, too. Your day's coming. You just have to stay positive.

But that was becoming harder and harder to do. She didn't know why Brandon had rejected her after giving her the kiss of the century, but it had chipped away at her hope for the future and made her feel lonely all over again.

The next afternoon, Brandon went to the living room, where Tom was taking a nap on the sofa. He tossed a file onto Tom's chest. "Tell me what you think of this guy."

Tom opened one eye. "I think he's perfect," he said, then closed his eye again. "She's going to love him."

"Come on, Tom. I need your opinion."

"You're the matchmaker. So make a match."

"This is Alison we're talking about. I think I have the right guy for her."

Tom's eyes slowly came open again. With a stretch and a yawn, he sat up and opened the file.

"Okay. Let's see. Hmm. He owns a uniform-manufacturing business? That's exciting."

"Not exciting. Just lucrative. He's pretty well off."

"Background check?"

"Clean as a whistle."

"Nonsmoker…never been married…where's his photo?"

Tom flipped a page over, revealing the photo, and made a face of disgust. "What's that he's wearing?"

"A sweater vest."

"That's really dorky."

"It's not permanently stuck to him. If Alison doesn't like it, she can dress him herself."

"Good point. Otherwise I suppose he's okay looking."

Tom flipped back to the questionnaire. "Says here he's from a big family and wants a big family. Alison should like that."

She would. Justin Moore had two brothers, and both of them were married with kids. Brandon pictured those Christmas mornings Alison wanted so badly, the ones filled with warmth and family. She'd be right in the middle of things, decorating and cooking and playing with the kids.

So why hadn't he already set him up with her? Justin had first come to him last week. He'd had plenty of time to do it.

Oh, hell. Who was he kidding? He knew why. In the last week, he hadn't considered anyone for Alison, with the possible exception of himself.

"What was your feel for the guy when you interviewed him?" Tom asked.

"He was smart. Motivated. Successful. Average looking, but Alison doesn't care about that. A little dry, but that may have just been a first impression. Sharp businessman, but socially awkward. He has a lot going for him, but he needs help getting things kicked off with a woman."

"So set them up. What have you got to lose?"

Alison. That's what I have to lose.

But the truth was that she wasn't his to lose. She never had been, and she never would be. *Set them up, and do it now.*

He took the file to his office, where he sat down at his desk and dialed Justin's number.

"Just three quick questions," he said when Justin came on the line. "Have you ever had anything to do with drugs?"

"Of course not."

"Do you have an ex you're dying to get back with?"

"Uh...no. Why would I go to a matchmaker if I wanted to get back with an ex?"

"Are you sexually conflicted in any way?"

"What do you mean?"

"Have you ever had a desire to be anything but a man with the equipment God gave you?"

"Hell, no!"

"Then I have a match for you," he said, forcing himself to say the words. "And there's no doubt about it. You're going to love her."

*   *   *

On Tuesday morning, Alison checked for any co-workers who might be loitering near her cubicle. When she saw none, she headed over to Lois's desk. No matter what had happened between her and Brandon, she'd promised him a yard sign, so she needed to put Lois to work.

"Hey, Lois."

Lois turned around, and Alison discreetly held up the unmarked bag. Lois whipped back around to stare at her computer, denying, of course, that she'd seen anything at all.

"What's the job?"

"I need a design for a yard sign."

"Same branding as the business card?"

"Yep."

"What do you want on it? "

"Logo. Business name. Phone number. I'll send you the dimensions. You give me the design, I'll order the sign."

"Time frame?"

"ASAP."

"I'll have the design for you tomorrow. But it'll take the sign itself a while to come in."

"I understand."

Lois turned her back to Alison and opened her lower desk drawer. Alison dropped the unmarked bag into it and walked away.

Just then she heard her phone ring. She hurried back to her desk and looked at the caller ID.

Brandon.

She closed her eyes and took a deep breath, hoping deep in her heart that no matter how final he'd made things between them on Saturday night, no matter how much he'd professed that nothing would ever happen between them again, he was calling to tell her how wrong he'd been and that he wanted her every bit as much as she wanted him.

With a trembling hand, she hit the talk button. "Hello."

"Hi," he said. "It's Brandon. I just called to tell you I have another match for you."

Alison felt as if the floor beneath her feet had opened up and the ground had swallowed her. *Please tell me he didn't say that.*

But he had said it. And it was her fault for thinking it was possible he was going to say anything else. He'd made it pretty clear he didn't want her, and not because of matchmaker ethics. That was just something she'd made up, and he'd used it so he could let her down easy. She'd been an emotional wreck. What else had she expected him to say?

"I think you're going to like him," Brandon said, sounding friendly and upbeat and very professional. And she hated it.

She swallowed hard. "So tell me about him."

"He's nice looking. Has a good job. A big family. And he wants to get married."

"That sounds...wonderful."

"I'll e-mail you some more information. Then you can get back to me to tell me if you'd like to go out with him."

"Have you told him about me?"

"Yes. And he's really excited about meeting you." There was a long pause. Then Brandon said the one thing she should have been thrilled to hear, but instead it sounded empty and hollow.

"Alison, I really think this man may be the one you've been waiting for."

*   *   *

The next Saturday evening, Alison met Justin Moore at a coffeehouse in the high-rent district of West Plano. It had mismatched chairs and tables, oddball art on the walls, and offbeat employees behind the counter. Strange, then, that every patron in the place had laptops flipped open and iPhones beside them, dressed as if they'd stepped out of a boardroom. They were the kind of people who prided themselves on embracing cutting-edge weirdness, then went home to half-million-dollar houses with Lexuses in every garage.

Justin spotted her first and tapped her on the shoulder. When she turned around, she couldn't say it was exactly love at first sight. He was slightly geeky, with glasses perched on his nose and his hair falling down over his forehead, but if she squinted a little, he looked kinda cute. And because he wasn't drop-dead gorgeous, he probably didn't spend his entire day looking in the mirror and marveling at how irresistible he was. And it also probably meant that he wasn't expecting a woman who looked like a supermodel. In other words, he was a man who had substance over style. She repeated that to herself a few times and decided she liked the sound of it.

"Cute place," she said after they got their coffee and sat down at a cozy table for two.

"I come here sometimes on the way to work," he said. "I thought it would be a nice place to get to know each other."

As they sipped their coffee and talked, she started a mental list of pros and cons. There was the matter of the way he dressed that went along with the geek thing—

polyester slacks, a plain white dress shirt, and wingtip shoes with everything tied down and buttoned up tightly. *Con.*

He had a nice haircut and smelled good. *Pro.*

She told the candy pusher joke. He didn't seem to get it. *Con.*

He was intelligent. *Pro.*

Which he demonstrated by telling her about the intricacies of the machinery his employees used to create a janitor's uniform. *Con.*

Unfortunately, the pro-con thing didn't seem get her anywhere. By the time their date was nearly over, the pros and the cons had pretty much balanced each other out.

Then he started talking about his family, and things took a turn for the better. He had two brothers who lived within a few hours of Dallas, and they were both married with kids.

"I've spent the past fifteen years building my business," Justin told her. "I guess I've pretty much ignored anything else. But I'm getting older, and it's time for me to take that next step. I want what my brothers have."

I want it, too, she thought. She actually felt a tiny surge of excitement as she imagined the possibilities that might lie ahead. He seemed a little shy, but first dates were hard under any circumstances. She decided he just might be exactly what she'd asked for. A nice, reasonably attractive man who was financially responsible and wanted a family, who had the ability to eventually utter the words "I do."

Later, he walked her to the parking lot. They reached her car and stood there with classic end-of-first-date awkwardness.

"You like antiques, right?" Justin said.

"Yes. How did you know?"

"Brandon told me."

Brandon. Of course he would know that since she loved his house so much. And he'd seen her furniture. And she'd gushed over the period clothes in his grandmother's wardrobe. And—

Forget Brandon. It's Justin you're interested in.

"I can get tickets to the Dallas Antique Show at Market Hall," Justin said. "Would you like to go to the opening night preview party?"

Alison just about had an orgasm on the spot. That was a big ol' charity event where posh antique galleries displayed zillion-dollar pieces and charged through the nose for rich folks to come look at them.

"Those tickets have to be really expensive," she said.

"They are. Five hundred apiece."

Well, don't tell me, she thought, even though she was impressed that he had the money and didn't mind spending it when it was something he knew she'd be interested in. It beat the hell out of the date she'd once had with a guy who took her to dinner at Golden Corral because he had a coupon for two dollars off the all-you-can-eat buffet, and it was crab legs night.

"Yeah, I'd love to go."

"Good. I'll get the tickets."

They said good night, and Alison got into her car to go home. She played the date over in her mind, and one word kept coming to mind. *Nice.* It distressed her a little that she couldn't come up with a better adjective than that. Then again, when some of her first dates could have been described in terms far *worse* than that, she decided to count her lucky stars.

Later at home, just as she was turning out the light to go to sleep, her phone rang. She looked at the caller ID.

Brandon?

She fingered the button without pushing it, her heart suddenly beating faster and her mouth going dry.

Oh, will you stop freaking out? Just answer the damned call.

She rolled to her back, her head on her pillow, and hit the button. "Brandon. Hi."

"Hi, Alison. I'm just calling to see how your date with Justin went."

She squeezed her eyes closed. "Good. It was good."

"I didn't get a knock on my door, so I figured it must have been okay."

She wasn't sure if he was going for an inside joke and she was supposed to laugh. In the end, he didn't, so she didn't either.

"I talked to Justin," Brandon said. "He really liked you, Alison. And he says you're going on a second date."

"Yes. He's taking me to the Dallas Antique Show next week."

"That's perfect. You should like that, right?"

You should know. You put him up to it. "Yeah."

A long silence stretched between them.

"If things don't work out between you and Justin—"

"I think they will."

"Good. Maybe he's the one, huh?"

"Maybe he is."

Another long silence.

"Well," Brandon said. "Keep me posted. And let me know if there's anything else I can do for you."

"I will."

That damned silence again.

"Well, good-bye," he said finally.

"Good-bye."

Alison clicked her phone off and tossed it to the bed beside her. She stared at the ceiling, telling herself that if she'd never met Brandon, she'd think she hit the jackpot with Justin, so it was time to put thoughts of him behind her. He wasn't her future, but Justin might be. And from this moment forward, *he* was the one she was going to be thinking about.

So there it was. Brandon had done it. He'd finally sent Alison on a first date that had been a success. And that meant he was a success for matching them up. He knew that should make him happy.

So why didn't it?

Get over it. You gave her exactly what she wanted.

He tried to focus on the TV show he'd been watching before he called her, but his mind wandered all over the place. Pretty soon he was thinking about Marco and Delilah, whose first date was tonight, too. With luck, he'd be as successful with them as he'd been with Alison.

Assuming you could call what he'd done with Alison a success.

She hadn't really sounded like a woman who was enamored with the new man she'd just met. But hadn't she told Brandon that she didn't expect fireworks? That if she wanted a family man, she'd have to settle for a little bit of ordinary? Yeah. That was exactly what she'd said.

And he'd told her that was bullshit.

But if really was bullshit, why had he matched her up with Mr. Ordinary?

Because that was what she said she wanted.

Damn it. His mind was going in so many circles it was making his head hurt.

Finally he gave up on the TV show he was watching, grabbed a beer, and went out to the front porch, where he sat down on the swing. He'd turned off the porch light, telling himself that lately it had drawn too many bugs, but the truth was that he wouldn't mind catching a furtive glimpse at Marco and Delilah when they returned to her house after their date.

He didn't have to wait long.

He heard the low hum of an engine, and a few seconds later, Marco's truck pulled up in front of Delilah's house. He got out and opened her door for her. He took her hand, a little awkwardly, and helped her out. Then she took his arm and he led her toward her front porch.

Marco was being a gentleman. Brandon had expected nothing less. But was there more going on between them than just that? What had their date been like? As they climbed the steps and stopped at Delilah's door, both of them looked so uncomfortable that he started to think things hadn't gone well at all.

Then Marco turned around to walk away.

No, no, no! Talk, smile, laugh, do something. I have to know. Don't leave me wondering!

And then Delilah opened her door and was going inside, and Marco was walking down the porch steps. *Damn it.* It was over, and Brandon still didn't know how things had gone between them.

Suddenly he imagined the phone call he was going to get from Marco, the one where he berated him for setting him up on a date that had been excruciating for him. And

Delilah. How was she going to feel about the evening? As if one more man was rejecting her?

Then suddenly, halfway down the steps, Marco stopped. Apparently Delilah heard his footsteps stop and wondered why, because she turned back around and tilted her head to listen. Marco looked over his shoulder at her. His indecision hung in the air between them, and it seemed as if an eternity passed before he finally turned around and went back up the steps. He came to a halt in front of Delilah, and she tilted her head up at him expectantly. He leaned in and said something to her. She smiled and looked away. After a moment, he put his fingertips beneath her chin and tilted her face up again.

And then he kissed her.

Just a soft, gentle kiss. The barest brush of his lips against hers that lasted only a few seconds. Delilah put her hand against his arm, resting it there as lightly as a butterfly landing. When Marco pulled away, she put her hand against her chest as if to calm her beating heart.

Marco backed away, but before he could leave the porch, Delilah reached out and caught his arm. Brandon watched, holding his breath. Slowly she coaxed Marco back again, sliding her hand down his arm to take hold of his hand. Then she turned around and led him inside, and the man who had to be reminded to smile was smiling ear to ear.

As the door closed behind them, Brandon felt a rush of pure joy. He pumped his fist in the air. *Yes, yes, yes!*

Marco and Delilah desperately needed somebody, and he'd helped them find each other. He didn't know if it would lead to anything permanent, but at least for one night, maybe the pieces of their hearts that had been iced over for so long would finally begin to thaw.

God, that felt good.

A three-quarter moon cast a soft glow around the neighborhood, surrounded by a clear, star-filled sky. Brandon drained his beer and set the bottle down on the porch, then started to swing again—back and forth, back and forth—as he listened to the night wind rustling through the trees. And in that moment, the most surprising thought crossed his mind.

Life is good.

Then he thought about Alison, and his heart twisted with regret. He only hoped she and Justin were as happy as Delilah and Marco were right now, no matter how miserable he felt about that himself.

It's for the best, he thought. *For both of us.*

The next weekend, Justin took Alison to the antique show. It was spectacular in every way, just as she'd expected it would be. Then they went on a third date to dinner and a play at the Eisemann, and when he took her home from that, he actually got up the nerve to kiss her good night. It wasn't half bad, really. Way better than Randy, who had a tongue like a piece of raw liver.

But not one tenth as good as Brandon.

Over the next few weeks, they occasionally spent time at Justin's house, a soulless McMansion in West Plano that was very pretty to look at but no different from the twenty other houses on the block. At her condo, the cast of *I Love Lucy* was having a hard time warming up to him, mainly because he had never had cats and was mildly afraid of them. She gave him points for trying, but when Lucy took up residence on the sofa behind his head one evening and started batting at his hair, it was all he could do not to run screaming.

But she was confident he'd learn to love them. Eventually.

They went to Heather and Tony's one night for dinner, and they had a good time. Heather said he was nice, even though she offered only a halfhearted smile when she said it. Tony said he was nice, too, but Alison got the distinct impression that maybe he'd found that one man he didn't like. Not that he said that. She was probably just being overly sensitive.

Because Justin *was* nice. And nice was good. Expecting fireworks and arrow-shooting cupids and starry-eyed infatuation was only going to keep her alone for the rest of her life. It was as she'd always said. Adult relationships were all about modest expectations, and she intended never to forget that again.

As the weeks passed, Brandon had more business than he ever could have anticipated. Most of his days were taken up with appointments, background checks, and phone calls. When he wasn't busy in the office, he got out and about around town, talking to people wherever he could and passing out his business cards. Pretty soon he had more clients than he knew what to do with. He'd learned which questions to ask and what body language to watch for, so he was having good success with his matches.

Maybe it really was true. Maybe there really was somebody for everybody.

"Do you think people have soul mates?" Brandon asked Tom one evening as they were in the kitchen eating takeout Chinese. "That one person they're destined to be with?"

"Absolutely," Tom said, grabbing a crab wonton. "Tracy and I are destined to be together in a big ol' king-size bed with a six-pack of beer and a stack of condoms on the nightstand. But for some reason, I can't get her to see that."

"Seriously."

"Well, I did read in *Paranormal* magazine that soul mates are people who knew each other in a former life. Then they're reincarnated and end up together in this life. But that means in order to believe in soul mates, you also have to believe in reincarnation."

"Hmm. I don't know about the reincarnation thing, but I've made matches for three clients who told me they thought I'd found them their soul mates. I used to think that was a crock, but..." He shrugged.

"Oh, come on. You're not actually believing your own press, are you? Love is a crapshoot. You said so yourself. Matchmaking is just the power of suggestion. You tell a client that somebody is their soul mate, and because they trust you, they believe it."

"Yeah. Maybe so."

"And the more you can get them to believe it, the more money you make. So how's it going? Your office needs a revolving door to keep up with the traffic. Does that mean you're on track moneywise?"

"I need to take stock this weekend. Do some projections for the next few weeks. But things are looking good. In fact, I'm sure I'm ahead of schedule."

"Hey, the quicker you can get the money and shut things down here, the better. Just let me know when to set up the closing. I'm itching to get this project under way."

"Me, too," Brandon said, and then wondered why he didn't really feel the words he was saying.

No. That wasn't true. Of course he did. The profit potential of the project was huge, and more than once he'd sat back and imagined what it was going to be like to finally have money again, and he'd reveled in the feeling.

So why wasn't he reveling in it now?

No. That wasn't true. He was doing plenty of reveling. Who wouldn't, with that kind of money on the horizon?

But he was also imagining the day he'd have to shut down this business. He'd have to tell his clients he hadn't matched up yet that he couldn't work with them anymore, and then send them back out into the world to figure it out for themselves. But if they'd had a chance at finding somebody that way, they never would have hired him in the first place.

Then he thought about Alison. Had she ever looked into Justin's eyes with that soul-deep twinge of recognition? Did she say to herself, *This is the man. He's the one I'm destined to be with forever?*

Maybe soul mates did exist. And maybe Justin was hers.

Brandon still went to McCaffrey's once or twice a week, but these days he made it a point to show up only on weekday afternoons when he knew Alison would be at work. He was happy she was happy with Justin. He just didn't want to see all that happiness in person.

"Here's what I think we should do once you have the money in place," Tom said. "We should go to Houston. Sign the papers. Then we can get a couple of rooms at some ridiculously expensive hotel, dump our luggage, and hit the town. With luck, we can round up a few lovely ladies and make an evening of it. It'll be like that night in Vegas all over again."

When this whole thing began, Brandon would have looked forward to that right along with Tom. Now it seemed like something he'd done in another lifetime and barely remembered.

Then he heard a knock. He went to the door and looked out the peephole.

Justin?

Chapter 23

Brandon opened the door. "Hey, Justin. What can I do for you?"

"I know it's not your office hours, but I was hoping you'd have a minute."

There was usually only one reason a client came back for a return visit, and that was because his current match wasn't working out and he was looking for a new one. What if he'd split with Alison? What if she was free? What if . . .

"Is something wrong between you and Alison?" he asked.

"No. Of course not." He paused. "Well, maybe a little. I need your advice about something."

"Sure. Come in."

They sat down in the living room, and Justin said, "I know Alison wants to get married someday, and so do I. I have a profitable business. A nice house. Nice car. Money in the bank. So a wife is next."

Brandon wondered how Alison felt about being number four on Justin's to-do list.

"We've been dating a while now, and I want to move things to the next level with her, but I'm not sure how to do it."

"The next level?"

"You're the kind of guy who's probably slept with a lot of women, right?"

Good Lord, where was this *going?* "A few."

"Right. So I thought maybe you could help me. It's the next step, you know. Dating for a while, and then sex. But she doesn't seem all that interested."

Brandon tried to quell the part of him that was irrationally happy to hear that. "She's doesn't?"

"No. And I don't know why."

I'll tell you why. You're a screaming bore. "No idea at all?"

"No. I cooked dinner for her the other night. I lit candles. Played music. But...nothing. She said she needed to get up early to do some work from the office, and she left right after dinner."

Brandon felt a surge of pleasure over that, only to slap it away. *This is what she wants, so help the guy get it right. You want her to be happy, don't you?*

Yes. He did. So he said the words that almost made him choke. "Maybe you should take her away for the weekend."

"A weekend getaway? I've heard women like those. *Hmm.* I have a certificate for a free night's stay at the Holiday Inn in Waco. My TV wasn't working the last time I was there, so they gave me a voucher for a free night."

Was this guy as clueless as he sounded? Yeah, it was the ultimate seduction scenario, all right. A crappy double bed with kids screaming next door and a free buffet breakfast.

"No," Brandon said. "Someplace nice. Go to Austin or San Antonio. And think five stars."

"Hmm. They have that river in San Antonio. And the Alamo."

"Justin. No Alamo."

"But she likes old stuff."

"This isn't a sightseeing weekend. You're there for romance. Two hundred people died at the Alamo. Death is not romantic. *No Alamo.*"

"Yeah. Okay. I hear you."

"Take her to the Hotel Contessa on the River Walk. Dinner at Le Rêve."

"Sounds expensive."

"Is she worth it?"

The man hesitated. He actually *hesitated.* Brandon had the urge to smack him one to get him really clear about the woman he was hesitating about.

"Yes. Of course she is."

Damned right she is.

"And I do want to take things to the next level."

"Then pull out all the stops," Brandon said. "Romance her like you've never romanced a woman before."

"Thanks," Justin said. "I really do want to do this right. I like Alison. I like her a lot. I think we could...you know. Eventually get serious. But sex is the next step, right?"

"Yep. That's the next step." A step he didn't really want to talk about anymore since he wasn't the one taking that step with her.

"Thanks for the advice," Justin said. "I'm going to try to set something up for a week from Friday."

Then he shook Brandon's hand. For the first time. Brandon noticed what a weak grip Justin had. He'd always believed that men with weak handshakes were weak in other ways, as well. Why hadn't he noticed that before?

It didn't matter. He was the right guy. Just what Alison was looking for.

Weak handshake and all.

A few days later, Brandon slid onto a bar stool at McCaffrey's, intending to relax for a while and catch a Rangers game. The place was rarely busy on weekday afternoons, so he usually found himself sitting on the same stool and ordering the same beer. Heather was behind the bar when he came in, and before he even sat down, she had that usual beer in front of him.

He'd come to realize that, in general, Heather ran the business end of the place with a firm hand, while Tony's job was to make sure anyone who walked through the door felt comfortable enough to sit down and stay a while. Their marriage was clearly a case of opposites attracting, but anyone who stopped long enough to watch them saw just how much they loved each other.

Until now, Brandon had been the kind of guy who wouldn't have noticed that in a million years. But in the past few months, he saw love and romance wherever he turned. A young couple pushing a baby in a stroller down State Street. An elderly couple sitting in lawn chairs beneath their magnolia tree. Twenty-somethings in this very bar executing every imaginable kind of mating ritual. And the people who came to him looking for that one special person to make their lives complete. He'd become so immersed in getting new clients and making one match after another sometimes he almost forgot what his life had been like before.

Heather rested her forearms on the bar. "So did you see who's sitting in the corner booth?"

Brandon turned around to look, and he immediately wished he hadn't.

Alison was there with Justin.

Just then she turned and saw him staring. She froze for a moment, then looked away, turning her attention back to Justin. No wave, no smile, no nothing. So she wasn't even going to speak to him. She was going to act as if he wasn't there. But did he really want to talk to her? Especially when she was sitting with the guy who was going to be spending a romantic weekend with her?

By what seemed like mutual consent, he and Heather hadn't discussed Alison at all these past few weeks. It was as if the moment he set her up with Justin, the topic became off limits.

"I thought Alison worked until five," he said.

"She took the day off to take her cats for their annual checkup," Heather said. "Evidently that's quite an ordeal."

"Justin skipped out of work, too?"

"He's the boss. He can do anything he wants to."

Yeah. He was a highly successful businessman who could put a diamond ring on Alison's finger and promise her forever.

"So I guess they're getting along pretty well," he said.

"You haven't talked to her lately?"

"Not since right after her first date with him. Once I know things are going well, I usually just step aside. So what's he doing here with her today?"

"He had a meeting in East Plano, so they met for a late lunch." Heather wiped some water drops from the bar with a dishrag. "Do you know why they're sitting in a booth?"

"Uh...no. Why?"

"Because Justin says the bar stools are bad for his back. He has slight curvature of the spine, you know."

Actually, Brandon didn't know that. And really, he could have lived from now on without ever knowing it.

Heather wiped some more, even though the water drops had long since disappeared. "He doesn't like her hot pink pumps."

"What?"

"You know the ones."

He did. He'd go to his grave with those shoes indelibly imprinted on his brain. "Why doesn't he like them?"

"Because he's only three inches taller than she is, and when she wears them, she can look down at the top of his head. I think he's self-conscious about his bald spot."

Brandon wanted to ask why Justin was concerned with his bald spot when he could be looking at Alison's legs in those incredible shoes, but who was he to judge?

"When he eats, he doesn't like one food on his plate to touch another one," Heather said.

What did she want him to say to that? The truth? That it was just a little bit weird?

"He has three humidifiers in his house," Heather said, just about wiping a hole through the bar. "He says he needs to keep his nasal mucosa moist."

"So?"

Heather threw the dishrag down and leaned in, her voice an irate whisper. "So why did you set her *up* with him?"

Brandon drew back with surprise. "What?"

"Okay, I know I shouldn't say anything, but Justin is *such* a drag." She pointed to the dishrag. "Alison turns about as animated as *that* every time he walks into the room."

"He's everything she said she wanted in a man."

"Then maybe you need to read between the lines."

Brandon turned away. "Not my job."

"Beg to differ. It's your job to set her up with the right man."

"There's nothing wrong with Justin."

"But there's not much right about him, either."

"Yeah, there is. He's smart, decent looking, successful—"

"He's a *bore*."

"Alison is my client. She's the one I answer to."

"Okay," Heather said. "Better question. What's going on between you two?"

Brandon's heart skipped. "What do you mean?"

"Something was happening between you that night at the bar when her father was taken to the emergency room, and it looked like a good thing to me. And then you set her up with that guy."

And that was just about to kill him, no matter how much he wanted to say it didn't.

"And when you turned around just now and saw her with Justin...well, let's just say you weren't a happy man."

"Hey, you wanted me as far away from Alison as possible, remember? So I'm giving you what you wanted."

"Yeah. About that." She exhaled. "I was wrong about you, Brandon. You're not the kind of guy I thought you were. I treated you like crap, and I'm sorry."

No, damn it, she hadn't been wrong. She'd been so right it was scary.

"I appreciate that," he said. "I never wanted any hard feelings."

"I can't get anything out of Alison. She just keeps saying she thinks Justin is the one, and that she's very happy."

"Then I think you need to take her at her word." Brandon rose from his bar stool.

"She hasn't slept with him yet," Heather said.

Brandon kept his face impassive, as if it didn't matter at all. But for some reason, it mattered very much.

"But that won't last for long," Heather went on. "He's taking her to San Antonio this weekend. They're staying in a nice hotel on the River Walk." She paused. "One room."

He wished Heather hadn't brought that up. Not that he intended to tell her he was the one who had suggested the trip in the first place. He just could have done without somebody else saying it out loud when he was already having such a hard time pretending it wasn't happening.

"How do you feel about that?" Heather asked.

Brandon tossed a few bills on the bar. "I think San Antonio is fun. The weather should be nice. If they get there before sunset—"

"It's you she wants."

Don't tell me that. I already know, and it's killing me.

He knew it in the way she'd looked at him that night, the way she'd kissed him, the way her eyes had been filled with disappointment when he'd turned her down. But he could never be the kind of man she needed. Justin could.

"No," he said. "It's Justin she wants. And that's the end of it."

With that, he left the bar, telling himself it was the last time he was going to risk stepping foot in McCaffrey's again.

On Monday afternoon, Alison was sitting at her desk reading her e-mail and eating her third Mallorific bar of the day, when Lois sidled up next to her.

"So... you got any jobs for me?"

"No," Alison said. "Not right now."

"It's been a while. Sure you don't need some letter-head?"

"Nope."

"Brochures?"

"Nope."

"Door hangers?"

"Nope."

"Surely that matchmaker guy needs something else."

"No," Alison said through gritted teeth. *"Nothing."*

Lois's eyes shifted back and forth. "You can't just *do* that, Alison."

"Do what?"

"Give me work, then take it away. It's like you laid me off, or something."

"It's contract work. That's the way it goes."

"You don't have to be so mean about it."

Alison spun around. "Lois. That's not the only way you can get Godiva. You want Godiva? Go buy it."

Lois gasped. "Will you keep your voice *down*?" She leaned in, berating Alison with a furious whisper. "I don't buy competitor's products!"

But you sure do eat them.

"Wait a minute," Lois whispered angrily. "I know what you're doing. You're giving the jobs to Sherri. You've always liked her better than me."

Alison liked just about anybody better than Lois, but that wasn't the point. The point was that nobody else in this place would do hundreds of dollars of work on the side for a box of chocolates, so really, Sherri wasn't even an option. Assuming there were going to be more jobs, which there weren't.

"No, Lois. I'm not giving work to Sherri, either."

"Fine." Lois started for her cubicle, only to turn back with a hopeful expression. "Have you thought about postcards? Maybe those oversized ones—"

"Don't need them."

"His website could use some work."

"Maybe later."

"Magnets. People keep those. I could design you a—"

"Lois," Alison snapped. "There will be no more Godiva. There will be no more jobs. None. Never again. Do you hear me?"

Lois drew back. "Well, okay. You don't have to bite the head right off my shoulders." She started toward her desk, then looked back. "It's like I've always said. You're not a nice person, Alison. No matter what people say."

No. She *was* a nice person. Brandon had told her so. Many times. He might even have said so again if she'd been nice enough to speak to him yesterday afternoon at McCaffrey's. Then again, he hadn't exactly jumped up off his bar stool to greet her, either. She'd thought about casually asking Heather if he'd said anything about her, but that would be an admission that she cared either way, which she didn't.

She had Justin now. And she was sure he was going to be everything she'd ever wanted.

The next Tuesday afternoon, Brandon sat at his desk, staring at his laptop screen, almost unable to believe what he was looking at. Just to be sure, he double-checked the numbers, but there was no mistake. His revenue minus expenses, including refunds he'd be giving to clients for matches never made, plus the eight thousand that his grandmother had in the business account when she died, equaled thirty-two thousand six hundred dollars and change.

He'd done it.

Tom came into his office and sat down in the chair in front of his desk. "So what's the verdict?"

"The money's there. Two months ahead of schedule."

"Are you kidding me? You already have it?"

"Yep."

"Your crazy plan *worked*?"

"Looks that way."

Tom grinned. "I swear to God I'll never question you again." He rubbed his hands together. "Hot damn. We're back in the game again."

"Uh-huh."

"And don't forget. There's still the possibility that the rezoning request will be approved for the property next door."

"That may not come through."

"But if it does, we're gonna be filthy freakin' *rich*."

"When's the hearing on that?" Brandon asked.

"We should know something in a few days. Hey! How about we hit McCaffrey's tonight and celebrate?"

Nope. No way was he ever going there again. "Nah. I think I'll just hang out here tonight."

"Hey, why are you being such a party pooper? This is what you've been working toward for the past four months."

"I know."

"So smile, will you? This is gonna be *great*."

"Justin is taking Alison on a trip to San Antonio this weekend."

Tom flicked his eyes left and right. "Uh...so?"

"I'm the one who suggested he do that."

"I know. And now your work there is done. Another successful match. Which we can also celebrate at McCaffrey's."

"No. It was a mistake. Justin is the wrong man for Alison."

"What do you mean? He looked right to me."

"She's going to be miserable with him."

"She's also a big girl who can take care of herself."

"She shouldn't be settling for a man like him."

"That's up to her."

"But I'm the one who set her up. If he's the wrong man, it's my fault."

Tom sat back, eyeing Brandon carefully. "This isn't about your responsibilities as a fake matchmaker, is it? This is about the fact that you have an incurable case of the hots for Alison that you just can't seem to shake."

Brandon closed his eyes, feeling miserable.

Tom leaned forward. "Listen to me, Brandon. I get it. I like Alison, too. But we're on the verge of something big here. If you get distracted, we're going to have problems. And you and I both know that in the end, you'd make her way more miserable than Justin ever could."

"What do you mean?"

"You're just like me. We don't stay put. We go where there's money to be made. But what does Alison want? A guy who'll do the eight to five, mow the lawn, raise three or four kids with her, and be at the dinner table at exactly six o'clock every evening. Now, is that the kind of life you want?"

Tom was right. Brandon used to say he'd shoot himself in the head if he ever found himself tied down like that. And nothing had really changed. He'd used the matchmaking business as a means to an end, and the end had come.

It was time for him to go.

"I'm heading to McCaffrey's," Tom said. "Tracy's working tonight. I think I'm starting to wear her down. Come on over if you change your mind."

"Yeah. I will."

"I'll call down to the title company and get the closing set up. If I can get an appointment for next week, is that okay with you?"

"Yeah. That's fine."

After Tom left, Brandon looked again at the figures on the screen, then closed the file. The *tick, tick, tick* of the grandfather clock in the hall seemed to grow louder with every minute that passed, counting off the seconds until he left this house, and this town, for good.

Tom was right. He'd known for a long time he could never be the kind of man Alison wanted, so that was off the table. But he still couldn't shake the feeling that he'd made a terrible mistake when he'd matched her up with Justin, and if she eventually married him, she'd be miserable for the rest of her life.

Stay out of it. What's done is done.

Over the next few days, he genuinely thought he'd convinced himself to do that. But by the time Friday came and he knew Alison was leaving town with Justin, he was in a dilemma all over again.

He decided he just needed to talk to her. That was all. He just needed to express his professional concern. If she agreed with him, she'd break up with Justin and find another man. If she disagreed with him, she'd stay with Justin and that would be the end of it. Then he could leave town with a clear conscience and get on with his life.

And she could get on with hers.

Chapter 24

Alison decided the unseasonably warm October weekend the weatherman had predicted meant she'd better bring a few sleeveless shirts along, particularly if they were going to be spending a lot of time on the River Walk. She grabbed a couple from her closet, folded them, and stuck them in her suitcase. Beside them were the sexy nightgowns she'd bought for the occasion, scraps of satin and lace that left little to the imagination. She'd suffered a minor body image crisis when she tried them on, then decided what the hell. She'd also bought some sexy bras and panties, too. In the event that Justin suddenly went wild and dragged her into a hotel linen closet, ripped off her clothes, and ravished her, she wanted to look the part of a wanton woman.

If only.

I'd like to book one room instead of two, he'd said when he told her he wanted to take her away for the weekend. And if only he'd stopped there, given her a smoldering look, raised an eyebrow, or otherwise offered any reason at all for her to feel the fantasy, everything would have been fine. Instead, he'd instantly backtracked. *It's not that I'm being cheap. That's not why I want only*

*one room. We can get two if you'd rather. I just thought
that the two of us could, you know, if we were in the same
room together, we might be able to . . .*

And she'd had to jump in to tell him one room would
be fine, because it really was time. She'd put it off long
enough. And then he'd gone on to tell her not to worry,
that he wasn't taking her to the Alamo because dead people weren't romantic. Whatever the hell that meant.

For some reason, she still felt as if she needed one
more date, one more opportunity for her to feel that close-
ness she craved. Justin was twice the man Randy was,
and she'd been ready to *marry* him. So why couldn't she
warm up to Justin?

Because she didn't want nice. She wanted hot and exciting. She wanted her heart to beat so fast it was painful.
She wanted to feel a man's eyes boring into her with an
I want you look that made her bones melt. She wanted to
feel her blood heat up and race through her veins, telling
her this man was *the one*.

But that was unrealistic. It was time to put those
thoughts behind her.

Modest expectations.

She was zipping up her suitcase and setting it on the
floor by her sofa about the time her doorbell rang. She
checked her watch. Justin was early. She opened the door
without checking the peephole and got a shock.

Brandon was standing there.

For a moment she couldn't speak. Even standing upright was a bit of a challenge, and she felt her face heat
up as if she was standing in front of an open furnace.

"Hi, Alison," he said. "Mind if I come in?"

"Uh . . . no. Of course not."

She stepped aside and he walked into her living room, and as he passed by she caught a whiff of that wonderful soap or shampoo or whatever it was he used that made him smell all earthy and woodsy and brought back all kinds of nice memories.

What are you doing here? And why do you have to smell so damned good?

He glanced at her suitcase. "Heather told me you and Justin are going away for the weekend."

"Yeah. San Antonio. We're staying at a hotel on the River Walk."

"How are you two getting along?"

"Good," she said. "Good."

"Are you sure?"

"Uh... yeah. Why wouldn't we be?"

He shoved his hands into his pockets, then blew out a breath. "I'll admit it, Alison. I think I've made another mistake. I'm not sure you and Justin are right for each other."

She just stood there, stunned. "What are you talking about? Justin and I are perfect for each other."

"Are you really?"

"Yes. He has everything I've ever wanted in a man. He's responsible and hardworking, and he wants to get married and have a family."

"What else?"

"What else is there?"

"How do you feel when you're around him?"

"What do you mean?"

"You told me once that people want to be wrapped up in soft, fuzzy little strings from their heart to their soul mate's heart. Is that what it feels like?"

Alison turned away and zipped up her suitcase. "Yeah. That's what it feels like."

"You're lying."

She whipped back around. "What?"

"I'm a pretty good matchmaker when it comes to other people. But when it comes to you? I can't get it right. I've never gotten it right. What makes you think I got it right with Justin?"

"Don't sell yourself short. You *did* get it right. Justin and I are meant for each other."

Brandon took a couple of steps forward. "Okay, then. Imagine this. Imagine Christmas morning. Imagine opening your gift from Justin. It's a vacuum cleaner. Every attachment there is. Top of the line. And Justin has the documentation to prove it, which he'll be happy to recite to you."

"What's wrong with that?" she said. "It's practical. I like practical."

"And then it'll be a washing machine on your birthday, and a DustBuster on Valentine's day."

"At least he'll buy me gifts. That's more than some women can say about their husbands."

"How does he feel about your cats?"

She paused, suddenly feeling a little shaky. "He's okay with them."

"Okay?"

"He'll learn to love them."

"Hmm. Let's recap here. You're getting serious about a man who wears sweater vests, hates your cats, and gives you appliances on special occasions."

"If he's so awful, why did you set me up with him?"

"Because he's what you said you wanted. The trouble is, what you want isn't good for you."

"But he *is* good for me," Alison said, even shakier now.

"Are you in love with him?"

She turned away, hoping he didn't see the answer on her face. She wanted to get all huffy and tell him it was none of his business, but since she'd been asking herself that same question, huffiness was hard to come by.

"I think I need a little more time for that," she said. "But it's coming. I know it is. We're going away this weekend. I'm sure after that—"

"How about a little excitement? A little passion? Don't you want those things?"

"I did when I was twenty and ignorant. I know better now. Love isn't going to strike me like a thunderbolt out of the blue. That's unrealistic."

"So you're giving up?"

"Giving *up*? I'm not giving up anything. For once in my life, I'm finally *getting* something."

"Yeah. Maybe. But not half as much as you deserve."

Alison narrowed her eyes. "Why are you doing this? Justin and I have been dating for weeks. Why are you suddenly showing up and telling me all this now?"

"Because Heather told me you're going away for the weekend with him. That ups the ante. And the more I thought about it, the more I realized what a mistake I'd made. What a mistake *you're* making. You're just not right for each other."

Just then the doorbell rang. Alison turned around to look at the door. Her future was on the other side of it. Or, at least, she was pretty sure it was.

Wasn't it?

Yes, damn it, it was. And Brandon had no right to characterize it any other way.

"That's Justin," she said. "He's here to pick me up."

"Don't do it, Alison," Brandon said. "If you stay with him, you'll be miserable for the rest of your life, and it'll be my fault for setting you up with him."

She lowered her voice. "You know what? You're right. Justin isn't the most exciting man in the world. But I'm tired, you know? Tired of searching. Tired of hoping. Tired of life passing me by. Tired of watching good things happen to everyone else while nothing good ever happens to me. Justin is giving me ninety percent of what I'm looking for. If I wait for the other ten, I'll be alone for the rest of my life. So *don't* screw this up for me!"

With that, she went to the door and opened it. Justin stepped inside, and Alison gave him a kiss. She didn't get carried away with it, but it was more than just a peck on the lips. Then Justin turned and spotted Brandon.

"Brandon! Hey, how are you?"

"Good. I'm good. So . . . you two are heading down to San Antonio, I hear."

"Yeah. Making a weekend of it."

Silence.

"Uh . . . Brandon just dropped by to give me a key to his house for the home tour," Alison said.

"Yeah," Brandon said. "And I need to be going now. You two have a good time."

As Justin went over to grab Alison's suitcase, Brandon looked at her one last time before walking out the door. His expression said it all: *he's not the man for you, and he never will be.*

Alison closed the door behind him and stood there a moment, wishing Brandon had never shown up, never said all those things that only added to her own uncertainty.

"Alison?" Justin said. "Is something wrong?"

She turned around and managed a smile. "No. Of course not."

"You look a little sick. There's flu going around, you know. Did you get your flu shot?"

Preventive health measures. One of Justin's favorite topics. "Yeah, I got my flu shot."

"At least two weeks ago? It takes that long for the vaccine to take effect."

"To tell you the truth, Justin, I really don't remember. Does it change our plans for the weekend?"

He paused. Actually *paused*. "Well, no. I guess not. Unless you really are sick."

"I never said anything about being sick. You did."

Justin blinked. "Okay, then. Let's get on the road. I'd like to get there as soon after sunset as possible. These glasses don't have antireflective coating, and the glare of headlights gives me a headache."

As he grabbed her suitcase, Alison pictured five hours in the car with him. If that was painful, what would a lifetime be like?

It's Brandon's fault. He's put all this crap in your head. Ignore it and go.

Just go.

Two hours later, Brandon sat alone in his living room with Jasmine purring on his lap, watching dumb things on TV he couldn't have cared less about and picturing Justin with Alison. And it made him feel as if he wanted to hit something.

He'd really blown it this afternoon.

He shouldn't have done it. He should have just left well enough alone instead of barging into Alison's condo and telling her what she was supposed to think and how she was supposed to feel. It wasn't his business. It wasn't Heather's either. The only thing that mattered was what Alison thought and felt, and she was fine with Justin.

But now...what if she dumped the guy because of what he'd said? Because truthfully, it was a dating jungle out there, and her luck up to now had been terrible. What if she broke up with Justin, and then she never met a man who was even half as good?

He'd be responsible for *that*.

Good Lord. He couldn't win.

He hated that Tom was gone tonight. He'd finally talked Tracy into going out with him, so he definitely wouldn't be home until dawn. On this night, when Brandon really could have used some kind of distraction, he was sitting there in that big old house by himself with nothing but bad TV, an intrusive Siamese cat, and his own irritating thoughts for company.

Then heard a knock. A very loud, very insistent knock.

He scooted Jasmine from his lap and went to the door. He looked out the peephole, and suddenly he felt a little breathless.

Alison? She was *here*?

Yeah, she was. But, boy, did she look pissed.

He opened the door, and she blew into the house like the Hurricane Alison of old. She spun around. "Well, Brandon. It looks as if you've blown it again."

"Huh?"

"I know, I know," she said, rolling her eyes. "You're

sick and tired of me telling you that you screwed up. But to be fair, this time you admitted it first."

"What are you talking about?"

"You were right. Justin's a bore. What were you thinking when you set me up with him? At this rate, I'm going to be a hundred and twelve before I finally get married!"

"Wait a minute. I don't get this."

"What's not to get? I broke up with him."

"You did?"

"Yes. What else could I do?"

"Hold on. Didn't you tell me—"

"We were about an hour down the road, and he started talking about how the beds at the hotel had Posturepedic mattresses and hypoallergenic linens. And I thought, hot damn, I'll wake up with a spine in perfect alignment and not a sneeze in sight. But will he throw me on that Posturepedic bed and ravish me? Not likely."

Brandon just stood there in disbelief. Was this the woman who had defended Justin not two hours ago?

"And he made sure I knew the hotel has no bedbugs," she went on. "And how did he know that? Because he went to bedbugregistry dot com and checked it out."

Brandon winced. "There's an actual bedbug registry?"

"Yes, but only incredibly anal people know about it. And is it romantic to talk about it? No, it is *not*. And get this. We pulled into a truck stop for gas. There was a rack with bumper stickers. I pointed at one and laughed. *Keep honking. I'm reloading.* He didn't get it. He lives in Texas, where guns outnumber people, and he didn't get it. You set me up with a man with zero sense of humor. Why did you *do* that?"

"But I *tried* to tell you—"

"So I guess you'd better find me another match. And this time, could you at least try to get it right?"

"I have been trying! But for some reason—"

"You call that *trying*? I mean, it's not as if Justin is a felon like Greg, but—oh, wait. Yes, he is. He committed third-degree *boredom*."

"Alison—"

She held up her palm. "Is it really that hard?" she said, her voice softer now. "Really?"

Brandon lifted his shoulders helplessly.

"After all, I think I've shown you quite clearly what I want."

"I know, but—"

"Sometimes I think the right man could be standing right in front of me," she said, her voice strangely quiet now, "and you'd never even know it."

"Come on, now. That's not fair. I've been really good at this with other clients. Just because I can't seem to get it right with you doesn't mean—"

Oh.

From one second to the next, it was as if the whole thing with Justin fell into the background, and the world tunneled down to just the two of them staring at each other. Alison swallowed hard, and the anger he thought he'd seen in her eyes gave way to what was really beneath it. Hope. Vulnerability.

Desire.

The grandfather clock ticked rhythmically in the hall, which was the only sound Brandon heard except for the blood pulsing through his ears. He took another step toward her, feeling every beat of his heart like a jackhammer pounding his chest. When he drew closer still, she turned away, resting her hand on the back of the sofa, refusing to meet his eyes. She was probably afraid of what she'd see there if she looked. And could he really blame her for that?

"This is your last chance to find me the right man, Brandon," she said softly, her eyes drifting closed. "Please get it right this time. *Please*."

He inched up behind her and slid his arm around her, splaying his hand beneath her breasts, and pulled her gently to him. He heard her soft intake of breath, and when he pushed her hair aside with his other hand and touched his lips to her neck, the tiny gasp became a sigh. Then he turned his head and whispered in her ear.

"I found him, sweetheart. He's standing right behind you."

Chapter 25

Alison's first thought was, *He doesn't mean what you think he means*, but there was really no other way to take it. And when he turned her around and took her in his arms, she caught a flash of his dark, demanding eyes right before he kissed her, and she knew. He wasn't stopping this time. Instead he slid his fingers through her hair and pulled her close, crushing her against him, and he felt so warm and solid and strong that she could have stayed in his arms forever.

This was it. This—*this*—was what she'd wanted all her life, what she'd dreamed of night after night but swore she'd never have. A man like Brandon. A kiss like this. A night to remember. And then another night...and another...

"Are you sure it's not Justin you want?" he said, dragging his lips along her cheek, then kissing her neck.

"Justin's very nice. But I don't want *nice*."

"What's the opposite of nice?"

"*This*," she said, and he smiled at her, a hot, wicked smile that sent a warm, melty feeling right down her spine. Then his hands were under her shirt, lifting it, tugging it off over her head, and she was thankful for the wanton woman underwear, even if it had ended up in the hands of the wrong man. Who was really the right one. And then she was unbuttoning his shirt, which was nearly impossible to do when her hands were quivering with anticipation. She fumbled so much with the third button that he finally just ripped it off over his head, and she heard one of those buttons tear loose and *plink* against the hardwood floor. He grabbed her and kissed her again, backing her up at the same time. When her legs met the edge of the sofa, he lowered her to it.

"Here?" Alison said.

"Yes, here," he said, breathing hard. "You need some excitement. The sofa barely qualifies, but it beats a bed. I'd rent a hot air balloon, but I'm a little desperate here."

Oh, *God*, she was, too. Desperate to touch him, to kiss him endlessly, to make love until they couldn't stand up so she'd have to stay in bed with him forever. She'd spent weeks trying to decide if she wanted to sleep with Justin, and all it took was a single touch from Brandon and she would have gotten naked in Times Square if that was what he wanted.

"What about Tom?" she said.

"Out for the evening. It's just you and me, sweetheart."

Just you and me. Those words made her feel singular and special, and she realized now that she'd wanted it to be *just you and me* almost from the first moment she'd met him.

"Too fast?" he asked, his hands hovering over the button of her jeans.

"God, no." She ripped the button open herself and jerked the zipper down. He grinned and grabbed the legs of her jeans, yanking them off and slinging them aside. He turned back and stopped short.

"Wait a minute," he said, looking at her bra and panties. "Red underwear? I would have sworn you wore blue."

"It usually is blue. Red's a little out there for me." She paused. "I was hoping to be ravished tonight, and I wanted to look the part."

"I hope you're not disappointed at who's doing the ravishing."

"God, no."

She sat up quickly, unhooked the bra, and tossed it to the floor. Seconds later he had her completely naked, tossing those skimpy red panties aside with a flick of his wrist. She had a fleeting thought that maybe she should be self-conscious. After all, she was with a man who gave women whiplash just by walking past them, but things were moving entirely too fast for that. And when he looked down at her with an expression of pure lust, she forgot all about her body image issues. She merely dropped her arm lazily over her head and watched him rip off the rest of his clothes, thoroughly enjoying the show.

There was a tense moment when Brandon wasn't sure he had a condom, but Alison produced one from her magic purse. He praised her organizational skills and tore it open. A moment later he rose above her and sank into her, and the feeling was so intense that for several seconds she couldn't find her breath. And then he was moving inside her, hard and fast. She wrapped her legs around him and gripped his shoulders as he drove her toward a climax so quickly it astonished her. Finally, *finally* she was one of those heaven-blessed women who knew what it felt like to be with a man who could make her nerves hum and her stomach turn upside down and her brain spin around inside her head in a blur of wild, crazy, gotta-have-it sex.

She felt a spark deep inside. *Yes.* This was good, so good, *so good*, and in a few moments it was going to be even better. *More, more, more* . . .

Then all at once, Brandon froze, his breath coming in sharp spurts.

"Brandon?"

"Hold still," he said, squeezing his eyes closed. "No—absolutely *still*."

"What's the matter?"

"It's okay. Wait for just one second—"

"No! Don't stop. More, Brandon. *Please* . . ." She arched her hips against him, squeezing her muscles tightly around him.

"No! Sweetheart, no! Don't do that! Don't—oh, *God*."

Then all at once he was moving again, as if he couldn't *not* move, and after three or four strokes, he let out a guttural groan and buried himself deep inside her. She felt a shudder pulse through his body, his back muscles bunching and releasing. She tightened her arms around him, and after a moment he collapsed against her, his breath harsh and raspy.

"*Damn* it," he muttered.

She turned her head and placed a warm kiss against the side of his neck. "What's wrong?"

"I'm sorry. I couldn't stop. I know it was too soon, but I couldn't . . . there was no way . . ."

He sounded so distressed that Alison couldn't help smiling. "It's all right."

He rose to sit beside her on the sofa, still breathing

hard. "For future reference, when I say don't move, I mean *don't move*, or else."

"Or else what?"

"Or else it's over before you want it to be. Before *I* want it to be. But I'll make it up to you."

He looked so serious that she almost laughed out loud. "Brandon. It doesn't matter. Nobody's keeping score."

"When it's one to nothing and I'm the one, *I'm* keeping score." He huffed with irritation. "I haven't lost control like that since I was eighteen years old."

"Yeah, that is kinda weird," she said with a sly smile. "I thought men were supposed to outgrow that. Now that you're an old man, I thought it went the other way."

"Hey! This is *not* funny. And it wasn't even my fault!"

"Uh...then whose was it?"

"Yours."

"Mine?"

"Yes!"

"Why was it my fault?"

"You *moved*."

"Oh, okay. I understand. No movement." She paused. "Do I have to hold my breath, too? Because I'm telling you...that's going to be damned near impossible."

Brandon looked down at her, a subtle smile playing across his lips. "Have you always been a smart ass, or do I bring out the worst in you?"

"The best," she said, trailing her fingertip across his thigh, thinking she could lie here and look at him forever. "The very best."

"I didn't lie," he said, serious now. "It was your fault. Your fault just for being here. And being you."

But how could that possibly be? She'd always been

the average girl, the one most men passed by without even noticing, the one who had a hard time standing out in a crowd of two. But here she was with this gorgeous man who was staring down at her as if she was the most beautiful woman on earth. It was an amazing feeling of feminine power she'd never experienced before.

He lost control because of you.

Brandon dipped his head and kissed her neck. "The score may be one to nothing. But I have all night to even things up."

She loved the way his words tumbled off his tongue, low and sexy, and landed gently on her ears. He gave her another kiss, then rose from the sofa and went to the bathroom, and when he came back, he picked up his jeans.

"Tell you what. Let's sit out on the patio for a while."

She didn't know how that was supposed to even up the score, but she didn't really care. Anywhere Brandon wanted to go was the place she wanted to be.

He pulled on his jeans, and she reached for her clothes.

"No," he said, tossing her his shirt. "Wear this."

She looked down at it. "Uh...okay."

She put it on. Buttoned it down the front. It very nearly swallowed her, but still it felt soft and warm and smelled like Brandon. She rolled up the sleeves and reached for her panties.

"Nope. That's enough clothes."

"You want me to sit outside wearing nothing but this?"

"You're covered. And there's no light. Not even a moon tonight. Just you and me, sitting on that glider in the dark."

There it was again. *Just you and me.*

The modest woman inside her wanted to object further.

After all, she wasn't completely covered—there was the matter of a ripped-off button. But he looked so incredibly hot standing there barefooted, bare-chested, wearing nothing but a pair of jeans, that she decided she'd follow him anywhere, no questions asked.

A few minutes later, they left the house through the back door and walked across the patio to the glider. Brandon sat down and stretched one leg out, then pulled Alison down to sit between his legs, her back to his chest. She lifted her feet up into the seat of the glider and relaxed against him. He leaned against the arm of the glider and wrapped his arms around her, enclosing her in a cocoon of warmth.

"Nice night," Alison said. "Especially for October."

"But still a little cool. You have goose bumps."

"I like the way it feels."

It was just the two of them, a soft night breeze, and darkness. In the far distance, Brandon heard a siren. Then a dog barking. Then silence. He rocked the glider back and forth, just a little, back and forth. His gaze drifted to Alison's legs stretching out from beneath his shirt, those gorgeous legs he'd been dying to touch since that night in the bar when she'd been wearing those hot pink shoes. She had flawless skin. Narrow feet with a high arch. Toenails painted cherry red.

Beautiful.

"How did Justin take it when you broke up with him?" he asked, finally breaking the silence.

"Really well, actually. I don't think he was any more in love with me than I was with him. I wanted a family. He wanted to check one more life goal off his list. To make those things happen, both of us were willing to overlook the fact that we were totally incompatible."

"For a while, anyway."

"Yes."

"So I failed again."

She smiled. "Miserably."

Thank God.

"Have I ever told you I love this old house?" Alison said.

"A time or two."

"Which bedroom was yours when you stayed here?"

"The one on the front of the house that looks out on the driveway."

"So what were you like as a teenager? I bet you had a lot of girlfriends."

"A few. Did you have a lot of boyfriends?"

"Nope. I was a really ugly teenager."

"Oh, come on."

"No, seriously. Ugly ducklings didn't come any uglier than me. I was really gawky, with a nose I hadn't quite grown into and your standard teenage complexion problems. The boys weren't exactly interested."

"So how old were you before you turned into a swan?"

She laughed a little. "Are you kidding? I'm still waiting."

"No," he said. "It happened. You just must not have been paying attention."

She smiled when he said that, and he wondered how many times in her life a man had told her she was beautiful. If they were as blind as he'd been in the beginning, it hadn't happened nearly enough.

"It was so good of your grandmother to take you in

when you were a teenager," Alison said. "That way you got to stay in one place for a while. That's important for kids."

Please don't talk about that. Not now.

But he knew she was only continuing on with the picture he'd painted of a father who wanted stability for his son and a grandmother who had so kindly offered to provide it. But he was tired of trying to keep up the façade that he'd had a the life of an average teenager with a little bit of attitude and a touch of vandalism thrown in. Because it hadn't been like that. Not even close.

He just didn't want to lie anymore.

"I didn't have a choice about living with my grandmother," he told her. "And my grandmother didn't have a choice when it came to taking me in."

"What do you mean?"

"What I told you that night at McCaffrey's about my father wasn't quite right." He paused. "He wasn't a professional pool player. He was more like a pool hustler."

"Hustler?" She paused. "Isn't that illegal?"

"No, not illegal. Immoral, maybe. But my father didn't care about that. And when I told you he taught me everything he knew about pool, that included hustling."

"He taught you that?"

"We did it together. I would play the part of a cocky, obnoxious kid who'd had too much to drink, wanted to bet on pool, and didn't know when to quit. My father would play the part of a levelheaded guy who would beat the crap out of me three or four times, then tell me he just couldn't take my money anymore. After that, there was always some greedy guy who would step up to take me on. Then I'd squeak out a win and walk away with the money."

"Wait a minute. You said you were a teenager then."

"I was fifteen."

"Your father had you doing *that* when you were fifteen?"

"Oh, yeah. He was good at it alone. Together, we almost never missed."

"But most pool tables are in bars. How did you get in?"

"I looked eighteen. They didn't card at the crappy places we went."

"How did you feel about that?"

He shrugged. "I didn't really know anything else."

"Did you go to school?"

When he thought back to those days, they seemed like nothing more than a blur of interchangeable schools in interchangeable towns.

"Most of the time," he said. "But if my father felt like picking up and taking off, we did. He said the worst thing in life was to be tied down. He said a man always needed to be free to go where he wanted to and make a buck any way he could. Then one night, I blew a big hustle, and it all came to an end."

"What do you mean?"

"I screwed up. My old man lost a thousand bucks. I'd never seen him that angry. He said he gave me the opportunity to win a big stake, but I couldn't handle it. Then he told me I was a worthless little bastard who'd never amount to anything."

"That's terrible," Alison said, her voice hushed.

"Two days later, he brought me here to visit my grandmother. He stayed one night. The next morning he was gone."

"What do you mean, gone?"

"He left town."

Alison looked stunned. "He left you there? Just because you lost a game of pool?"

"My father held a grudge like no one else on the planet. I'd made him thousands, but suddenly because I lost one game, I was worthless to him. It wasn't rational, but he wasn't a rational man."

"But he came back to see you, didn't he? While you were living with your grandmother?"

Brandon thought about how he'd looked out his bedroom window, day after day, hating his old man and wishing him dead at the same time he prayed he'd see that old Ford F-150 pulling into the driveway.

"No," Brandon said. "Not once."

Alison turned in his arms to look up at him. Tears filled her eyes, and they shimmered in the near darkness.

"Alison. Sweetheart. Don't cry. It was a long time ago."

"I can't help it. I just…I…" Her voice choked up. "How could your own father *do* that to you?" She put her palm on his cheek and kissed him. "I am *so* sorry."

He swallowed hard, remembering just how betrayed he'd felt, and how the anger had built up inside him until nobody, including his grandmother, could take it away. But there was something about Alison lying in his arms right now, so warm and tender and empathetic, that lessened the power the memory had over him.

"So really, your friend was right about me," Brandon said. "I was a pretty angry kid. I had a chip on my shoulder my grandmother couldn't knock off to save her life. She did her level best to do right by me, but I didn't give an inch. I left this house when I turned eighteen, and I never came back."

"Where is your father now?"

"The last time I talked to him, he was heading for a pool tournament in Atlanta. That was right after he neglected to come to his own mother's funeral."

Alison closed her eyes. "My God. That's awful."

"He called me only because he found out I inherited and he didn't. Now that he knows he can't get any money out of me, I wouldn't be surprised if I never saw him again."

All at once, Brandon felt the most profound sense of loss he hadn't anticipated. His father didn't give a damn, and his grandmother, the only real family member he had, was gone. He thought about what Alison had said that night her father went to the hospital. *Do you know how horrible it feels to know I'm only one person away from having no family at all?*

Now that his grandmother was dead, and that was exactly what he had. No family at all.

"I should have come back," he said. "After all my grandmother did for me. I should have come back and thanked her."

"You have thanked her," Alison said.

"What do you mean?"

"I told you once how amazing you are," she said with quiet intensity. "And I still mean it. You're not the boy you were. None of that matters anymore. I know your grandmother is looking down on you right now. Imagine how proud she must be that you've taken over her business and dedicated yourself to helping other people find happiness. That's how you've thanked her, Brandon. It says more than words ever could."

Brandon closed his eyes, feeling more like a fraud than

he ever had before. In spite of what he'd told her, she still believed his motives were pure. And the more she talked, the more the truth was going to hurt her. But he just couldn't make the words come out to tell her how wrong she was about him. That adoring look would instantly vanish, and he just couldn't bear to lose it.

The air grew cooler, but he didn't want to move, and he could tell she didn't, either. He just continued to rock the glider gently back and forth as they listened to the autumn leaves rustling in the trees, imprinting this moment with this woman on his brain so he could remember it forever. Then slowly he pushed the tail of the shirt aside and closed his hand over her inner thigh. She jumped at little at his touch.

"Sorry," he said. "Is my hand cold?"

"Uh...yeah."

At the same time his hand grew warmer against her thigh, he dropped his other hand to one of the buttons of the shirt she wore and flicked it open.

"What are you doing?" she asked.

He whispered in her ear. "Evening up the score."

He slid his hand inside her shirt, cupped her breast and gave it a gentle squeeze.

"Kids are next door," she said, her voice a little hoarse.

"It's late. They're in bed. Shrubs block the windows. And we have no lights on out here. They can't see a thing."

He eased his hand between her legs and began to stroke her there. He thought she might object, but instead she let one leg fall over the edge of the glider and the other rest against the back of it, opening herself to him. With his other hand, he circled her nipple, then dragged his fingertip across it, finding it hard and tight in the cool night air.

"You're not cold, are you?" he whispered.

"I'm warming up fast," she whispered back.

The longer he touched her, the harder he got. Again. Good Lord. He'd be able to take her again right here and now, just as he'd done not twenty minutes ago. And he probably wouldn't have any more control now than he'd had then.

He held her breast, squeezing, releasing, letting his thumb trip back and forth across her nipple as he continued his rhythmic stroking between her legs. Her breath came faster. He kissed her neck and whispered encouragement, telling her how hot she felt and how beautiful she was and how much he loved being with her like this. Soon her breathing became shallow and irregular and she pressed up against his hand, her body tight with anticipation as he gently but relentlessly drove her right to the edge.

And then she fell.

She clamped her hand on his leg, her entire body going rigid. He could practically feel her pleasure pulsing through his own body.

"Oh, *God*," she said, her voice a hoarse whisper. "Brandon..."

He continued to caress her until her breathing slowed and she gradually fell against him, every muscle becoming lax, a soft sigh slipping through her lips. He wrapped his arms around her and kissed her neck.

"Relax, sweetheart. I've got you."

"I know," she murmured, relaxing in his arms, making him want to hold her forever. "I know."

Alison put her knees together and rested them against the back of the glider as she lay against Brandon's chest. They stayed there for a long time like that, just rocking back and forth.

"It's wonderful that you've made other people happy," Alison said, breaking the cool silence of the evening. "But it's time you found some happiness of your own." She turned to look up at him, her expression so sweet and tender that his heart nearly melted. "It's time both of us did."

No. I'm not a matchmaker. I never wanted to be a matchmaker. That gig has come to an end. So that guy you think you're crazy about? The one who has love and romance in his blood? He doesn't exist.

But then her hands were on him again, and her lips, and he let the truth dissolve to the back of his mind. After a while, they went back inside and up to his bedroom. He made love to her again, sinking into blissful oblivion. Afterward, he pulled her into his arms and she fell asleep against his chest, and he couldn't remember a time in his life when he'd felt more content.

He didn't know how he was going to tell her the truth. To fix the mess he'd made of this. He only knew that he didn't want to lose Alison, and he didn't want to lose the deal in Houston. Somehow, tomorrow, he was going to find a way to pull it all together.

When Alison woke the next morning, she turned and peered at the clock. Nine fifteen. She looked the other way.

Brandon was asleep next to her.

Feeling warm and drowsy, she turned to her side and

just stared at him. One arm was thrown back over his head in sleepy abandon, and the other lay across his chest, his palm resting over his heart. His chest rose and fell rhythmically, his breath making a whisper of a noise as it exited through his slightly parted lips. His hair was mussed and there was a pillow crease in his cheek, but somehow it only made him look that much sexier. And Jasmine was sprawled out beside him, her head against his knee, projecting the kind of warm, homey scene that filled her with contentment.

She wondered if he was dreaming. She hoped *she* wasn't. It was a distinct possibility, though. After all, she was in bed with a man whose body was filled with testosterone and whose mind was filled with love and romance. What better combination could there possibly be?

She remembered last night on the patio, how his hands and his lips had seemed to be everywhere at once. She liked the way he'd evened up the score, leaving her feeling as if her bones had liquefied and her body had melted into his. And when he'd told her the truth about his past, she'd only felt that much more drawn to him.

Unfortunately, the instant replay going through her mind was interrupted by thoughts of what her hair must look like this morning and what remnants of her makeup had moved to random parts of her face. She decided she'd try to get up, get a shower, and crawl back into bed before Brandon woke up.

She pushed the covers back gently and started to get out of bed, when she felt a hand grab her wrist.

"Where do you think you're going?" a beautiful male voice behind her said.

"Uh . . . I need a shower."

"First things first," Brandon said, pulling her back down until she was lying in his arms. Jasmine looked up, her expression a little huffy at the interruption, then laid her head down again.

"A shower *should* be first," Alison said.

He ran his hand up and down her thigh. "I have other ideas."

"Okay, as long as you implement those ideas with your eyes closed."

"Why in the world would I do that?"

"Because I'm quite certain I look like I got caught in a wind tunnel in a Maybelline plant."

He laughed.

"You're laughing. Why are you laughing?"

"Because you're funny."

"Funny *looking*."

He smoothed her hair away from her face. "No. *Beautiful*."

Well, she knew *that* was a crock right about then, but still it gave her little tingles of delight to hear him say it. Pretty soon he was kissing her, implementing those ideas he'd talked about in ways that rendered her speechless. Half an hour later, the poor man looked so wiped out that she told him to go back to sleep while she took that shower she desperately needed.

"Back in a little while," she said, and slipped out of bed.

Brandon had just dozed off again when he heard a frenzy of knocks on his bedroom door. He woke with a start and rose on one elbow just in time to see Tom come barreling into the room.

"Hey, Brandon!" Tom said. "Get up. I've got news."

"Good *God*. You scared the hell out of me!" He flopped to his back again. "The house had better be on fire."

"Nope. The house isn't on fire, but we are. As I was leaving Tracy's place, I got a call from Bennett. You're not going to believe this, but it came through."

"What came through?"

"The zoning change. The property next door is now mixed-use, and they're going full speed ahead with their project. Do you have any idea what this does to the value of *our* property?"

Brandon sat up again. "I thought there was no way they were going to pull that off. How did it happen?"

"Bribery? Witchcraft? Divine intervention? Hell, I don't know. I only know we're damned lucky it did."

Brandon couldn't believe this. It was going to happen. They were going to make a freakin' fortune.

"How soon before they're moving ahead with the urban living center?"

"They've been champing at the bit already. Now that they've got the go-ahead, I bet they break ground within a few months."

"So by the time we finish the lofts, it'll be well underway?"

"Yep. Buyers will be able to visualize the whole area. We were going to do okay before, partner. Now we're going to make a *killing*."

This was it. This was what Brandon had been waiting for. That one deal that would put him on the road to the top again. No more pinching pennies, no more feeling broke, no more hanging his head because his life had fallen apart.

"Wait a minute," Tom said, glancing at the purse on the nightstand. "That's Alison's. What's it doing in your bedr—" He stopped short, his eyes widening. "Tell me you didn't sleep with her."

He was silent.

"Oh, God. You did." Tom blew out a breath. "I knew it. I knew sooner or later you'd end up in bed with her."

"Will you keep your voice down?"

"Where is she?"

"Taking a shower in the hall bath. This is my business, Tom. Not yours."

"No. It's not just your business. It's my business, too. Tell me you're not flaking on me. Tell me you're still planning on being in Houston at that closing table on Wednesday morning."

"Hell, yes, I'll be there. I'd be out of my mind to pass up a deal like that."

"So what about Alison?"

He paused, his head starting to hurt. "I don't know."

"I thought she was dating that Justin guy."

"She broke up with him."

"So you moved in on her?"

It hadn't been like that. Not that he wasn't an opportunistic man. He jumped on a good deal every time one popped up. But last night with Alison hadn't been a spur of the moment thing. His feelings for her had been a long time coming, growing bit by bit, seeping into his consciousness, until it had taken only the tiniest tip of the scales for them to come together.

"What's she going to do when she finds out you're leaving?" Tom said. "Hell, forget that. What's she going to do when she finds out you never intended to stay?

That you've been playing matchmaker all this time just to scrape thirty grand together to do the deal? That'll be pretty."

"I'll handle it," Brandon said. "Don't worry."

"Don't you think maybe you should have had an exit strategy before you slept with her?"

No. There was going to be no exit. Somehow he was going to make this work. He wasn't giving Alison up. But he wasn't staying here and giving up the deal of the century, either. Somehow there had to be a way to work this out.

"Break it off with her," Tom said. "And do it now."

"It's my problem, and I'll deal with it."

"You'd damn well better, or—"

Tom froze, staring over Brandon's shoulder. Brandon whipped around to see Alison at his bedroom door, her hair wet, wearing nothing but a towel. He prayed to God she'd missed all that, but judging by the look on her face, she'd heard every word.

Chapter 26

"Tom," Brandon snapped. "Out."

This time Tom didn't hesitate. He was out of the room in seconds. Alison hurried in to grab her clothes she'd laid on a chair last night, a look of anger and betrayal on her face. She tossed the towel aside and put on her underwear, then her bra.

"Alison, please," Brandon said, coming to his feet and yanking on his jeans. "Stop. We need to talk about this."

She reached for her shirt, but he came around the bed and caught her arm. She shook loose and spun around to face him.

"Is it true? Are you leaving for Houston?"

Brandon lowered his eyes.

"And not coming back?"

"Alison—"

"Oh, my God. Everything Tom said is true. You never intended to stay here. The moment you conned enough people out of fifteen hundred dollars, you were out the door."

"I didn't con anyone!"

"Then what do you call it?"

"I delivered the services people paid for. If I didn't, I'm returning their money before I shut things down. Where's the con in that?"

"You lied," she said, putting on her shirt. "You lied about who you are and what you were doing here."

"Come on, Alison. That was just business. I had to convince prospective clients I was the real deal. If I'd told people I was going to be around for only a few months, how much business would have come my way then?"

"Business came your way because I helped you!"

"And I appreciate everything you did, believe me."

"I'm sure you do." She reached for her jeans.

"Alison. Listen to me. You have to understand what we have going in Houston. It's the deal of the century. There's a development going in next door to our property that's going to make its value go sky-high."

She yanked on her jeans. She ran her fingers through her wet hair, then picked up her purse.

"Even with renovation costs, we could walk away with at least half a million apiece," he went on. "*That* was why I did it."

"I defended you to Heather," she said, as if she hadn't even heard him. "*Defended* you. I told her you weren't what she thought you were, that you didn't have an ulterior motive, that all you wanted was to carry on your grandmother's business. I should have listened to her. I mean, it wasn't as if every red flag in the book wasn't there where you were concerned. But I ignored every one of them."

She started for the door.

"Alison!"

She spun around and glared at him. "You coerced me into breaking up with Justin. Then you made love to me last night, making me think you cared about me. How could you *do* that?"

"I do care about you! Just because I'm leaving Plano, it doesn't mean we're never going to see each other again. People have long-distance relationships all the time."

"That's not what I want."

"Come on, Alison! Do I really have to be at the dinner table at six every night? Is that the only kind of relationship you'll accept?"

"You know what I'm looking for," she said hotly. "You've always known. An absentee man isn't it. And a man who lies to me *certainly* isn't it." She turned and strode out of the bedroom.

"You know what?" he said, following her, "I've been listening to you for months now, telling me what you want. Well, how about what *I* want?"

They reached the stairs, and she turned back. "Okay, Brandon. Why don't you tell me what you want?"

"When I was a teenager slogging around in those crappy bars with my father, at least I was making him happy. As much as I hated it, I was doing what he expected me to do. Then he dumped me like yesterday's garbage. I felt like the biggest failure alive. I told myself I was going to do something with my life. Something big. I happened into real estate, and suddenly I was raking in the money. Finally I was getting somewhere. Then the market fell apart."

He inched closer to her, wanting to reach out, wanting to touch her, but he knew he didn't dare.

"When I came here in June," he went on, "I was dead, flat broke. I had notes coming due I couldn't pay. My credit was shot. When Tom contacted me about the Houston deal, I knew it was the opportunity I'd been looking for, but I didn't have my part of the down payment. That was when I decided to use the matchmaking business to get the money to buy in."

She turned away as if she was dismissing every word, and his frustration mounted.

"I want to be back on top again," he said, desperation lacing his voice. "I want money in the bank. I want to be able to look at myself in the mirror again and not feel like a failure. What's so wrong with that?"

"What's wrong is that you lied in order to do it," she said. "All those things you said on the radio, in interviews, in articles...you don't believe in any of that, do you?"

"I gave people what they wanted."

"But *you* don't believe it."

"I didn't have to believe it. I just had to give them what they were paying me for. And that was exactly what I did."

"All this time I put my heart and soul into helping you, and it wasn't even a real business for you." Her eyes filled with tears. "Heartstrings. My God. How stupid does that sound now?"

"It wasn't stupid. Just because the business wasn't forever, it doesn't mean any of it was stupid."

But he knew the humiliation she felt was just too much to bear. She'd gone on and on that day about soul mates and why he needed a name like that, thinking he understood, thinking he felt it, too, only to find out that all he'd ever been interested in was the bottom line. How had he let it come to this?

"Are you sorry you broke up with Justin?" he asked.

She shook her head. "No. It wasn't right." Then she looked up at him plaintively. "But if not him, then who?"

Brandon opened his mouth to answer, only to close it again. He didn't know what the hell to tell her anymore. He only knew he didn't want her leaving like this.

"I don't know," he told her. "I just..." He shook his head helplessly. "I don't know."

"I have to go."

She walked down the stairs. Brandon followed her, desperate to keep her from walking out the door. But he just didn't know how to do it. When they reached the entry hall, she slowed down. Turned around.

And tears were streaming down her face.

The sight of Alison crying was just about more than he could bear. If only he'd backed away last night, shut things down, sent her home, she wouldn't be standing there looking at him like this today. But he'd wanted her so much that he'd lost his head, and now he was paying the price for it.

And so was she.

"Alison," he said. "Please believe me. I never wanted to hurt you. I don't want you to leave here thinking anything else."

"I know." She looked away. "I know you wouldn't do that. Not on purpose."

He could hear it in her voice that she'd already begun to forgive him, just as she'd forgiven him for every lousy date he'd ever set her up on. He couldn't believe it. After everything he'd done, her anger was already slipping away.

But the misery was still there.

"Do you know I've never been in love before?" she said, her voice hushed. "All these years... all the men I've dated... not once."

He just stood there, no clue what to say to that.

"I thought I was a couple of times," she went on. "But looking back now, I know I wasn't." She paused. "And then I met you. That's how I knew. Because it had never felt like this."

Her words hit him like a thunderbolt. She was telling him she was in *love* with him?

No. He couldn't let this go on. He couldn't let her have any of those feelings, because if she thought he'd let her down today, it was nothing compared to how he'd let her down in the future. He'd want her so much that he'd promise her anything, and then the next deal would come along and he wouldn't be able to turn it down. It was what he did. It was who he was. It was the only thing in his life he'd ever been a success at. He couldn't give that up, so he needed to end this now.

"You didn't fall in love with me," he said gently. "You fell in love with the man you thought I was. But he was never real."

"Are you sure?" she said, her voice a plaintive whisper. "Isn't that man in there somewhere?"

Let her go, and do it now.

"You deserve a much better man than me, Alison. And I hope one day you find him."

She wiped her fingertips beneath her eyes. "Yeah. I kinda hope so, too."

God, what an understatement.

He hated himself for this. All of it. After what he'd

done, she'd be so wary and so guarded that she might never open herself up again, and every dream she had of a husband and a family might never come true.

She started to leave, then turned back. "The home tour—"

"You can still use the house. We'll work it out."

She nodded. "Maybe I don't know who you really are," she said quietly. "But I'm still going to miss you."

Brandon swallowed hard. "I'm going to miss you, too."

She turned and left his house, and as he stood at the doorway and watched her walk down the steps to her car. He gripped the door frame tightly, tormenting himself by watching her drive away. As her car disappeared from sight, he realized it might be the last time he'd ever see her.

What had Tom said? *In the end, you'd make her way more miserable than Justin ever could.*

And that was exactly what had happened.

Ten minutes later, Alison knocked on Heather's door. When Heather answered, her eyes flew open wide with concern.

"Oh, sweetie," she said. "What *happened*?"

Alison opened her mouth to answer, but tears overcame her for the umpteenth time since she'd left Brandon's house, and she couldn't speak. Heather led her inside, sat her down, and brought her Kleenex, and Alison told her the latest sob story in her quest for a husband and family. Heather hugged her and told her everything was going to be all right, even though Alison was pretty sure nothing was ever going to be right for her again.

"I should have listened to you," she told Heather. "You had it right. Brandon was just what you said he was." She balled her hands into fists. "God, Heather, I'm such an idiot! I keep making mistakes, over and over. I just want a man to love me. Is that really so much to ask when the world is full of them? What's wrong with me that I can't find at least *one*?"

"I don't know," Heather said quietly.

"You managed to do it," Alison said, wiping her nose for the twentieth time. "And I don't know how. I don't know how one day you could have been groveling around with me in the dating muck pile, and then suddenly you looked up, and there was Tony. The perfect man for you. And he carried you off on his white horse like you were some kind of princess, and I was still sitting there with nothing. I *still* have nothing."

Heather didn't say anything. But really, what could she say?

Alison wiped tears from beneath her eyes with her fingertips. "I don't want to be alone. I don't want to be that awful woman who's forty or fifty years old who has nothing to talk about except her health problems and her cats. I can't bear the thought of that. I just can't."

Alison felt as if there was a hole in her heart that grew bigger with every beat, and judging from the look Heather was giving her, every bit of the despair she felt was showing on her face.

"Alison?" Heather said gently. "Are you going to be okay?"

Alison took a deep yoga breath. Let it out slowly. Then she wiped her eyes for what she was determined was going to be the *last* time.

"Oh, come on, Heather." she said, smiling through the last of those tears. "I'm always okay eventually." She paused. "This one may just take a little longer than usual."

And then, damn it, she was pulling out another Kleenex and crying all over again, because this time it was different. This time she hadn't felt as if she was settling for an average man and hoping she would eventually learn to love him. She felt as if she'd found that one wonderful man the universe had been holding for her, just waiting for the right time to hand him over. And there would have been no learning to love him, because she already did.

The trouble was that she didn't know how to stop.

On Wednesday morning, Brandon drove to Houston and met Tom, who had driven down the day before. At two o'clock, they sat down at a conference room table at United Title, and over the next forty-five minutes, it seemed to Brandon as if he signed his name fifty times on that pile of closing papers. And every time he did, he felt as if he was betraying Alison one more time.

Good God. Would he ever get her out of his mind?

"So what do you think, buddy?" Tom said as they left the title company, a big grin on his face. "We pulled it off. We actually pulled it off. It's going to be smooth sailing on this one, don't you think?"

"Yeah. It is."

"Listen, I've already checked into the hotel. I reserved a room for you, too. What say you check in, and then we go have a drink or two, and then have dinner at some ridiculously expensive restaurant? And then, who knows? One way or the other, we are *celebrating.*"

Brandon stopped at his car. "You know, I'm not so sure I'm up for that. I think I'll just head back to Plano. I have a lot to do there."

"Oh, come *on*, Brandon! Don't flake on me! Tell you what. I'll spring for champagne. The good stuff this time. Not like that stuff in Kansas City that tasted like old sweat socks."

"No. Really. I'm going to head back." He pointed the remote and flicked open the driver's door.

Tom grabbed his arm. "Hold on a minute."

"What?"

"We just pulled off the deal of the decade. You don't sound properly excited about that."

"Come on, Tom. You know I am."

"I'm not so sure," He eyed Brandon carefully. "Are you good with this deal? I need a partner who's one hundred percent on board."

"I am," Brandon said. "I just have a lot on my mind."

Tom let out a sigh of resignation. "Yeah. And her name is Alison Carter."

Just hearing her name made Brandon feel depressed all over again. "There's nothing between us. Not anymore."

"That's right. There's not. So there's no need for you to sound so miserable, is there?"

Brandon kept telling himself he just needed to get back in the swing of things. Once he put a crew together and renovations were under way, his old life would come roaring back, and he'd be in the groove again.

"No," he said. "There isn't. I just need to get back to Plano and shut things down. Then it's full steam ahead."

"Hell, yeah," Tom said, clapping him on the shoulder. "Just wait until we get the warehouse roughed in. Once the framing and Sheetrock are up, that's when you'll start to see it come together. And that, my friend, is when all those dollars signs will start dancing in your head."

Tom was right. There was always that one moment during every project that he felt it shift from what it had been to what it was going to become. From that moment forward it was a race to the end, the excitement building, until finally it was ready to be put on the market. And then came the money.

In this case, it was going to be one hell of a lot of money.

Brandon got into his car and drove back to Plano, ticking off in his mind the things he needed to do once he got there. Tomorrow he'd spend the day getting his business documents and tax information in order and deciding how he was going to break the news to his clients that he was shutting down the business. Then he had to get the home tour out of the way. Alison's plan was to put the finishing touches on the house on Friday before the tour on Saturday, but he decided he'd call in a professional cleaning service to do the last minute cleaning so they didn't have to. He'd say it was his contribution to the cause. The least he could do.

The very least.

But no matter what, he didn't want to see Alison. He just couldn't. So he decided he'd drop a house key off with Heather, then make himself scarce on Friday and Saturday. Once the tour was over, he'd spend the next week making calls to his clients and issue refunds for matches unmade. After that, he'd contact his grandmother's attorney, let him know that he was leaving, and turn over possession of the house to the First Baptist

Church. Then he'd hit the road for Houston, where he was going to turn an old warehouse into luxury loft apartments and watch the money roll in.

It was nearly nine o'clock when he reached Plano and pulled into his driveway. He grabbed the mail and went into the house, where Jasmine greeted him with that screeching meow, winding her way around his ankles. He hadn't yet figured out what he was going to do with her when he left. Maybe the neighbor across the street who'd kept her when his grandmother died would be willing to take her again. He had no intention of abandoning her, but the answer hadn't come to him yet.

He started to toss the stack of mail onto his kitchen table when he noticed an oversized square envelope hand-addressed to him. He opened it up, and he couldn't believe what he saw.

A wedding invitation?

Mr. Jack Warren and Ms. Melanie Davis request the honor of your presence as they join each other in holy matrimony…

Jack and Melanie? Brandon had to think for a moment, but then he remembered. They were the first couple he'd successfully matched up.

Then Brandon saw a handwritten note included in the envelope. *It never would have happened without you, Brandon. We hope you can be with us on our special day. Love, Jack and Melanie.*

Brandon picked up the invitation again and stared at it, thinking back to the beginning when he'd been so cynical. He'd matched up these two with very little thought. The fact that they actually liked each other meant he could collect his money with no further work, and he'd considered that a good thing. But not for one moment had his thought process gone beyond that. Not once had he ever envisioned this.

Brandon had never been to a wedding in his life. He'd always imagined lace and bows and men in uncomfortable suits and cake and punch and old ladies pulling out tissues to dab their eyes because it was all *so beautiful*.

Then all at once, he was transported back fifteen years, to the times he'd watched his grandmother put on her best Sunday dress and leave the house to go to her umpteenth wedding. She said nothing made her happier than to watch the people she'd matched up commit to each other forever and know she'd had a part in it. *That's how I know I'm doing what the good Lord wants me to*, she'd told him. *Someday you'll find your calling, too.*

And all he could think back then was *My calling is to travel the country, make millions, and live it up for the rest of my life.*

When he'd jumped into his grandmother's business; it had been almost like a joke to him. Pair people up almost at random, and if something stuck, okay. If it didn't, that was okay, too. He'd take whatever money he'd earned and move on.

But this...this proved it had meant so much more.

His first wedding. He hadn't had a clue it would feel like this.

At nine o'clock on Thursday night, Alison sat with Heather on her sofa, leaning against the sofa pillow, sipping the martini Heather had made for her. She'd pulled her feet up beside her, which she'd tucked into a pair of fuzzy purple socks that had been hideous even before

Lucy had clawed them half to shreds. Ricky had plopped his fat butt on the sofa beside her, his head against her thigh, purring so loudly she was surprised the neighbors hadn't complained. She petted him absentmindedly, and he turned and looked up at her adoringly.

Well. At least one male on the planet was crazy about her.

She looked down at her martini. "I think I'm going to stop drinking."

"Please don't," Heather said. "Tony and I own a bar. You're half our revenue."

Alison dropped her head to the sofa cushion behind her. "But it's not working. I can't get him out of my head. I dated Randy for eight months and thought he was going to ask me to marry him, and I banished him from my brain in about two hours."

"That's because Randy was slime."

"And Brandon? What was he?"

Heather shrugged. "I know what he did. The lies he told. But I still think he cared about you. He was just the wrong man at the wrong time."

"Please don't tell me that. I need to find a way to hate him. Tell me he's slime like Randy, and maybe I'll forget all about him."

"He's slime like Randy." She paused. "Except that he offered to bring in a professional cleaning service so the house would really sparkle for the tour and we didn't have to mess with it at the last minute. That was nice."

"Will you stop with the redeeming qualities? He's a terrible person who hurt me and I hate him." Alison sighed, her shoulders drooping. "Or not."

Heather tilted her head. "Do you need some ice cream to go with the vodka?"

"No. Right now I'm just a lush. That'll make me an overweight lush."

"You have a right to drown your sorrows for a while."

"Do you know I spend half my life having sorrows, and then I have to spend the other half drowning them? But I guess that's good news for you and Tony, economically speaking."

She looked at her half-empty martini glass, thought about taking another sip, then simply set it down on the coffee table with a heavy sigh.

"You're not doing too well with this, are you?" Heather asked.

Alison took a breath. "No. Not really. And I'm *so* not looking forward to going to Brandon's house on Saturday."

"Would it help if I took over as tour guide?"

Alison forced a smile. "You? Please. I don't think you could work up much enthusiasm for a hundred-year-old house. You'd be telling people how ugly the furniture was and swearing there were rats and spiders in the basement."

"Hey, I could keep my thoughts to myself. Just give me your notes on the history of the house, and I swear I'll play nice." She shrugged. "To tell you the truth, the place kind of grew on me."

Alison's smile faded. "I know. Me, too."

Heather sighed. "I'm sorry, sweetie. That was the wrong thing to say."

"No. You don't have to tiptoe around me. And you don't have to take over for me, either, okay? I'll be just fine."

She hoped so, anyway. But until the tour was over and she left Brandon's house for the last time, she couldn't even begin to put it all behind her.

Just then, Ethel jumped up on the sofa beside Ricky. She reached out a paw and tapped Alison on the leg. Alison scratched her behind the ears, and she practically turned herself inside out to take full advantage of all five fingernails.

Then Alison remembered. Jasmine had done the same thing.

She felt a shiver of worry. Jasmine. Brandon was leaving town. What was he going to do with her?

The next morning, Brandon slept late, only to be awakened at nine-thirty by the musical trill of an incoming text message. He rolled over and fumbled for his phone on the nightstand.

The text was from Alison.

His heart beating rapid fire, he opened it. *What about Jasmine?* she asked.

If only he knew. He still hadn't come up with a solution.

I'll find her a home, he typed, and sent the message. A moment later, Alison responded. *She's too old. Nobody will want her.*

Sadly, Alison was right. He wouldn't mind keeping her, but since he rarely stayed in one place for long, taking her with him would be next to impossible. But how was he going to find a home for a fifteen-year-old cat?

Then he heard his text tone again. He looked at the screen. *I'll take her.*

That instantly brought back memories of the day he'd

been working on his air unit and she brought him her questionnaire. *I know what you're thinking*, she'd said. *Don't even go there. Three is absolutely normal. Four means you're a crazy cat lady.*

That seemed like a hundred years ago.

Since he didn't know what else to say, he texted back. *Thank you.*

A minute passed, then another message came in. *Of course, I'll need to change her name to Fred.*

For some reason he couldn't fathom, Brandon felt tears burn behind his eyes. It was a *joke*, but...

But it was so Alison.

He'd realized there was something special about her from the first time he met her. But it had taken him until now to realize just how special, and just how much he was giving up by leaving her behind.

He texted back. *She'll need a sex change operation.* And a minute later, Alison responded. *I'll call Zach. He'll advise.* And she followed that with a smiley face.

Even now, even with how much he'd hurt her, her gentle sense of humor was still there. He would have thought she'd carry the betrayal with her for a long time to come, but now he knew that wasn't going to happen. Once he was gone, hope would blossom inside her all over again that true love might be just around the corner, because there wasn't a pessimistic bone in her body. She was the most trusting soul he'd ever known, a person who wanted to be cynical and wary, but in the end it was a weight she just couldn't carry. And when it fell away, all that was left was a woman who trusted that strangers wouldn't hurt her irreparably and the people she loved would always look out for her.

He'd told her he was going to miss her. He just hadn't known how much.

He lay back against his pillow, a memory flashing through his mind of that day his father had left him, something he thought he'd long forgotten. Not the gut-wrenching abandonment he'd felt. He'd take that to his grave. He was just now remembering what his grandmother had said to him that morning when he got up to find his old man gone.

You can call this place home, Brandon. I don't care where you go or what you do, now or twenty years from now. You can always call this place home.

And that was exactly what it felt like now.

His grandmother had been the one person on this earth who had tried to give him some semblance of family, but he had already been so screwed up that he never would let her. It wasn't until now, looking at his adolescence through the eyes of an adult, that he realized just how much she'd tried to be the family he desperately needed. How might his life have been different if he'd taken the love his grandmother had wanted to give him?

Better question. How would his life be different in the future if he took the love Alison wanted to give him?

When Alison's alarm clock went off on Saturday morning, she slapped it silent and collapsed against the pillow again, wishing she could sleep straight through this day rather than go to Brandon's house.

Brandon's house? It really wasn't his house after all. Technically it belonged to the First Baptist Church.

Finally she shoved the covers back as best she could with three cats draped over them and rose from the bed.

She was thankful, at least, that he didn't intended to be around for the tour. She didn't know if she could handle seeing him without losing it all over again. Since she'd left him that morning, she'd tried to get angry. Had every right to get angry. But any anger she managed to summon would last for only a second or two, and then she'd remember the night they spent together and start wishing one more time for something that could never be.

An hour later, she and Heather loaded tour programs and raffle baskets into her car and headed for Brandon's house.

"You're not wearing the blue dress," Heather said.

Alison shrugged weakly. "Yeah, I know. I just... couldn't."

Heather just nodded. "It's just as well. You said it was uncomfortable."

Yeah, but it wasn't the discomfort of the dress itself that kept her from wearing it. It was the discomfort of knowing it had belonged to Brandon's great-grand-mother. After what had happened between them, she just couldn't face putting it on.

A few minutes later, Alison pulled up to the curb. She and Heather got out, and as they were grabbing boxes from the trunk, Karen pulled up behind them. She got out of her car with a tray of hors d'oeuvres from Maggie's Café.

"I have this one and two more for this house," she said.

"We'll come back for them," Alison said.

Heather unlocked the front door and the three of them went into the house. Alison went into the dining room to set down the box of programs she was carrying. Then she went back to the entry hall, intending to go back outside to grab another hors d'oeuvre tray from Karen's car. On the way there, she happened to glance up the stairs, and she was shocked at what she saw.

Brandon was standing on the midfloor landing, looking as handsome as ever.

And he was wearing his great-grandfather's suit.

Chapter 27

Karen came back into the entry hall, and when she saw Alison looking up, she looked up, too.

"Holy moly," she whispered, her jaw practically dragging the ground. "Is that the guy who owns the place?"

"Yes," Alison said, her voice hushed. Just as she'd imagined, the suit made him look taller, broader, and ten times sexier, and she felt a stab of longing so powerful it nearly knocked her to her knees.

"I thought he wasn't going to be here."

"I thought so, too," Alison said.

"All this house stuff is too much trouble," Karen said, still dazed. "We should just sell tickets to look at *him*."

Heather came up beside Alison. "What's he doing here?" she whispered.

"I don't know."

"Do you want me to hang around?"

"No. I'm okay. Just...just give us a minute."

"Come on, Karen," Heather said. "We're out of here."

"But we have to set up for the—"

"*Now.*"

Karen shook herself out of her trance and followed Heather out the front door.

Brandon started down the stairs, and every nerve in Alison's body tightened with anticipation. He wasn't supposed to be here. And the suit. Why was he wearing the suit?

She was dying to go to him. To run straight back into his arms again. But maybe this wasn't what she thought it was. *Don't do it. Don't be a gullible fool.*

Again.

"What are you doing here?" she asked.

"Isn't this the day of the tour?"

"Yes."

"That's why I'm here."

"But you said you wouldn't be."

"I changed my mind."

"No," she said as he hit the bottom step. "Don't do this. Don't you *dare* do this."

He stopped in front of her. "Don't do what?"

"This roller coaster ride is making me sick."

"What roller coaster ride?"

"The one where first you're here, then you're not. The one where you want me, and then you don't. I can't do that anymore." She turned and walked toward the dining room. "I have to get ready for the tour."

Brandon followed her, and when she stopped at the table, he put his hand on her shoulder. She spun around. "Don't *do* that!"

"Why not?"

"Whenever you touch me, I lose my head. Right about now, I need to hang on to it."

"We need to talk."

"Fine." She pointed to the other end of the dining room table. "But you'll have to stand over there."

"Huh?"

"*Way* over there."

He stepped back a little.

"More."

He moved a little more.

"Brandon—"

With a roll of his eyes, he walked all the way to the other end of the table. "There. If I walk any farther away, I'll be in the neighbor's dining room."

"That's fine."

"Can you hear me clear down there?"

"Perfectly."

"This is weird."

"You're lucky I'm not making you text me from the other room." She nonchalantly grabbed a stack of programs from the box. "Okay. You can talk now."

"I gave up the Houston deal. Another investor bought out my position."

She dropped the programs as if they were on fire. "What?"

"I'm keeping this house."

"What?"

"And I'm keeping the matchmaking business."

"Stop!" She held up her palm, suddenly feeling breathless. "I told you. No more roller coasters, or I swear to God I'm going to throw up."

Brandon frowned. "Gee, Alison. I imagined you having a lot of reactions, but that wasn't one of them."

All at once, she felt exposed and vulnerable and helpless, as if her emotions were being laid bare all over again and she couldn't do a damned thing to stop it from happening. But she *was* going to stop it. This time she wasn't going to act like she had in the past, just handing over her heart so a man could stomp all over it.

"So let me get this straight," Alison said, her formerly helpless heart racing out of control. "You decided to give up real estate investing, and you're starting by backing out of a deal that was going to make you hundreds of thousands of dollars?"

"That's right."

"And you're going to live in a house you said was nothing more than a money pit?"

"The thirty thousand dollars I was going to put into the Houston deal will go a long way toward making this money pit a home."

"And you're going to continue being a matchmaker?"

"As long as there are people out there looking for true love, I'm going to be finding it for them."

That sounded so wonderful. Every last bit of it. But for Brandon to show up here and now and say those things sounded like a product of her own wishful thinking. And if there was one thing she'd learned in this life, it was that her own wishful thinking led absolutely nowhere.

"I don't understand," she said. "A few days ago, you were planning to leave. You didn't want any of this. Why the sudden change?"

He put his hands on the back of a dining room chair and looked away, seemingly lost in though for a moment. "It wasn't a sudden change," he said finally. "It didn't happen in a day. Or a week. Or even a month. It's been happening since the day I met you. I was just too dumb to see it." He bowed his head, and when he lifted it again, he fixed his gaze on her, and his dark eyes were filled with longing. "What I finally realized is that the man you want is the man I've become. And I was hoping you'd give that man a chance."

Alison's throat felt so tight she could barely breathe. Oh, God, how she wanted to. But did he mean it? Did he know what he was saying? Would he give up his old life because of her, and then resent it later?

"What would you do if I said no?" she asked.

He paused a long time, swallowing hard. "I'd still stay here."

Alison was stunned. "You would?"

"I love matchmaking. I love this town. I love this old house. I love going to McCaffrey's. All those things have made me happier than I've ever been in my life." He paused, his voice hushed. "But they won't mean half as much to me without you."

She lifted her hand to her mouth, clenching her teeth, trying to hold back the tears.

"But if you decide I'm not the one," he said, "I'll move heaven and earth to find the man who is."

"No! Please, Brandon. Stop. After the first four you set me up with, I couldn't even fathom what number five would look like."

"I was hoping he looked like me." His fingers tightened on the back of the chair, his knuckles whitening, as if he was afraid of what she might say. "Alison? Am I the man you're looking for?"

She wanted so badly to cross the room, throw her arms around his neck, and beg him to kiss her until she passed out. But she'd been there before. Feeling as if a wonderful future was dangling right in front of her, only to have it ripped away from her at the last minute.

Brandon sighed softly. "Look, I know you don't trust me,

and I don't blame you. But if you don't believe everything I've just told you, then at least believe this. There's only one reason on earth I'd put on this horrible, itchy, uncomfortable suit and walk around looking like a total idiot."

"Why is that?"

"Because I love you."

She opened her mouth to say something, but nothing came out. She was afraid if she spoke, all the wonderful emotions bottled up inside her right then would come tumbling out, setting off Richter scales across the globe. Did she really want to be responsible for that? She took an extra deep yoga breath to try to stay calm, but yoga breaths only went so far.

"My life changed the day I met you," Brandon said. "With you, I found out I could be a better man than I ever imagined. You showed me that family means everything when I barely knew what one was. You made me believe in love. And if you'll let me," he said, his voice deep with emotion, "I'll move heaven and earth to make your world a better place, too."

In that moment, Alison was absolutely sure she felt fuzzy little heartstrings reach out from Brandon's heart to wrap around hers.

"Just one more question," she finally managed to say.

"What's that?"

"What the *hell* are you doing clear over there?"

He came around the table and she met him in the middle. He swept her into his arms and spun her around, then set her down and kissed her, a long, slow, scorching kiss that promised a whole lot more to come. Later. After about five hundred people traipsed through his house. Alison seriously considered locking the door and telling everybody to go home so they could be alone for the rest of the day.

"Are you going to regret giving up all that profit on the Houston deal?" Alison asked. "Maybe you should have stuck around with Tom and made a few hundred thousand dollars before coming back."

"If I had, would you have ever believed that I intended to stay here for good? Or would you figure I'd stick around only until the next deal came along?"

"I don't know." She paused. "Maybe."

"I didn't want to lose you. If I hadn't given up that deal, I might have. It just wasn't worth it to me."

His words sent warm shivers along every nerve in her body, making them hum with pure joy.

"Wait a minute," Brandon said. "Why aren't you wearing the blue dress? The tour starts in an hour."

She shrugged. "After everything that happened, I just didn't think it would be right."

"Is the dress ready?"

"Yeah."

"Well, go put it on. How else are we supposed to be lord and lady of the manor?"

Right about then, Alison didn't even need the stairs. She could have floated up to the second floor.

"Tell the truth," she said. "You just don't want to be the only one dressed funny."

"Exactly."

"I know you don't like the suit, but it's hot."

"Damn right it's hot. I'm suffocating."

"Wrong kind of hot," she said with a smile, trailing her fingertip down his lapel. "You know how old stuff turns me on."

"Good. At least I know when I start losing my hair and need a prescription for Viagra, you'll only love me more." He gave her a soft smile, then brushed a strand of hair away from her cheek and kissed her. "Time's wasting, sweetheart. Better get dressed."

But she just couldn't make her feet do their job. She stood there a moment longer, and her chin started to quiver. Then tears filled her eyes. She took a step forward and wound her arms around his neck again, and he circled his arms around her.

"This is going to be the best day of my life," she whispered in his ear.

He stroked his hand up and down her back. "It's already the best day of mine."

Karen's reaction to Brandon definitely set the tone for the rest of the day. All the female tour patrons seemed far more interested in viewing Brandon than in viewing his house. Maybe that really was a viable fund-raising opportunity. And if he didn't want to wear the suit again next year, he could just go naked. Charitable giving to the East Plano Preservation League would go through the roof.

Or maybe Alison would just keep Brandon—naked—to herself.

"Well, we did it," Heather said as they closed the door behind the last visitor. "I can definitely say that the East Plano Preservation League is far better off financially today than it was yesterday." She smiled at Alison and Brandon. "And you guys deserve gold stars for getting into the spirit of things and dressing the part. I'm thinking we need to make period costumes part of the home tour every year."

"No!" they said in unison, then looked at each other and laughed.

"What's wrong?" Heather asked.

"I already knew I didn't want to wear an itchy, uncomfortable suit all day," Brandon said. "But guess who got a taste of her own medicine?"

"God, it was awful," Alison said. "I couldn't breathe. I could barely walk in the damned thing. How did women wear dresses like this every day of their lives?"

"But you both *look* fabulous," Heather said.

"And next year I'm going to look fabulous in a pair of fat pants with an elastic waistband," Alison said.

"And I'm going to look fabulous in a pair of sweatpants and a Dallas Cowboys T-shirt," Brandon said.

Alison smiled at him. "People will demand their money back."

"But won't we be comfortable?" He leaned in and gave her a kiss.

"Hey, what did he just do?"

Alison spun around to see her father and Bea coming down the hall. Bea was smiling. Charlie looked confused.

Bea poked him. "So I need to explain the birds and bees to you?"

"I know all about the birds and bees. What do you think? A stork dropped Alison through the chimney?" He turned to Brandon. "I thought you couldn't date my daughter because you're her matchmaker. So what's the deal with that?"

"She's no longer a client," Brandon said, still staring at Alison.

"Huh?"

"His job was to match her up," Bea said. "And it looks as if he did a damned fine job of it."

Charlie turned to Alison. "Well, I guess he beats that gay interior designer you used to date."

Alison sighed. "Dad. I told you. He wasn't gay. The Harley guy...*he* was gay."

"I still don't believe that."

"Well, Brandon isn't gay," Bea said, "so it's a moot point. Come on, Charlie. Let's head to McCaffrey's. I could use a drink."

But on their way to the front door, her father proved that he wasn't nearly as clueless as he acted. He looked back at Alison and gave her a furtive wink and an approving smile, and she read the gesture loud and clear. *Good choice, kid. Hang on to him.*

As Bea and Charlie left the house, Alison went to the window and watched them walk side by side toward the street where her father's truck was parked. Halfway there, he eased closer to Bea. After a few more steps, his hand rose to the small of her back. A small, wispy memory drifted through Alison's mind, slowly coming into focus: her mother strolling down a sidewalk with her father, and that same warm, protective hand was guiding her.

Brandon came up beside Alison and slipped his arm around her. "Your father seems happy."

"He is."

"I think Bea is, too."

"I think you're right."

"And so am I." He kissed her hair and pulled her closer. "What do you think, Alison? Do we have a family in the making?"

In light of everything that had happened that day, just

the word "family" was enough to make tears come to her eyes.

"Stop it," she said. "You're going to make me cry, and I look like hell with runny mascara."

"Would it help if I told you I love you, runny mascara and all?"

Alison smiled. This day just got better and better.

Heather came up behind them. "Hey, are you guys coming to the bar? Tony's already there. The first drink's on us."

"I never turn down free drinks," Alison said. "But one's my limit."

"Hey, Heather," Brandon said. "I'll give you twenty bucks to tell me the state fair story."

Alison looked at Heather, raising a warning eyebrow.

"Sorry," Heather said. "What happens at the state fair stays at the state fair." She gave Alison a hug and whispered, "I'm just so glad things worked out."

"Yeah," Alison whispered back. "Me, too."

Heather left the house, only to poke her head back in the door. "Hey, you guys have a package on the porch. UPS delivery."

Brandon stepped out onto the porch and brought a big, flat box inside.

"Wonder what it is?" Brandon said.

Alison glanced at the return address and smiled. "Let's find out."

They took the box to the living room and sat down on the sofa. Brandon opened it. And when he saw what was inside, a smile of contentment spread across his face.

It was a yard sign. Heartstrings. Tying Two Hearts Together Forever.

Alison thought about how she'd felt when all this began, back during that time when she'd been so eager to help him. She couldn't have imagined what would happen between then and now to give this sign ten times more meaning than it could ever have had before.

"I ordered it weeks ago," she said. "It was supposed to be here long before now. Do you like it?"

"I love it," he said, holding it up. "It looks as if my grandmother's business is mine now, doesn't it?"

"Yeah, it does. Shall we put it up?"

They took the sign out to the front yard. Brandon pulled up the Matchmaking by Rochelle sign and set it aside. He pushed the stakes of the new sign into the ground, and they backed away to look at it.

"It's perfect," he said.

They admired it a little while longer, and then he walked back over and picked up the old sign. He held it a moment, his expression growing solemn. A look of remorse filled his eyes.

"As I got older, I knew I needed to go back to see my grandmother. To make amends. To show her I wasn't the kid she remembered. And I think I would have eventually. But then one day passed, and another, and another. And then..." He swallowed hard. "And then she was gone."

Alison put her hand around his waist and lay her head against his shoulder, standing with him in the late afternoon sunlight as he continued to stare at the sign.

"You said my grandmother would be proud of me for taking over her business," Brandon said. "Do you still think so?"

"Yes. I do."

He was silent for several more seconds, a hint of sorrow crossing his face. "I never told her I loved her."

"Did you?" Alison said.

"I barely knew what love was back then."

"Do you now?"

He turned and looked down at her. "Yeah," he said, his lips edging into a gentle smile. "I think I do."

"I have an idea," Alison said.

"What?"

"Let's put the old sign in the backyard. For just the two of us to see."

They walked around to the backyard, where Brandon planted the sign near the patio in the shade of the old magnolia tree. Then they sat down on the glider together. As Alison curled up in Brandon's arms and he rocked them gently back and forth, she decided relationships weren't about modest expectations, and that soul mate thing wasn't a crock after all. Brandon had told her once to forget ordinary, that she should be looking for somebody extraordinary.

And she'd finally found him.

A good girl can be bad
for one night…

but can a bad boy be good
for a lifetime?

Please turn this page
for an excerpt from

*Black Ties
and Lullabies*

Available now

Chapter 1

Bernadette Hogan wished that when this night was over, she could tell Jeremy Bridges to go to hell. She was about ten times more emotionally stable than the average person, but if she had to spend one more evening watching him pick up vacuous blond women for fun and recreation, she was going to go insane. Yeah, he attended all these charity events as the philanthropic CEO of Sybersense Systems, but in the end it wasn't about generosity. It was about putting one more notch in his hand-carved Louis XIV bedpost.

But it wasn't Bernie's job to plan a principal's itinerary. Her job was to protect him wherever he decided to go. And, of course, there was the small matter of the outrageous amount of money he paid her to put up with this nonsense, money she was going to need desperately in the coming years. So she kept that resignation letter only in her head, staring at it longingly with her mind's eye every time he aggravated her to the breaking point.

Tonight would be one of those times.

Carlos pulled the limo into the driveway of the San Moritz Hotel behind a string of unusually small and sedate vehicles. Tonight, it seemed, the filthy rich of Dallas society had left their Mercedeses and Beemers and gas-guzzling Hummers in their five-car garages, opting instead for their hybrids and electric cars.

Bernie sighed. "So which environmental cause are we championing this evening?"

Jeremy's brows drew together thoughtfully. "Hmm. Good question." He reached into his breast pocket and pulled out an invitation. "Ah. Global warming. Emphasis on diminishing polar bear habitats."

"And here you are in your limo. Last I checked, it gets about nine miles to the gallon. People are staring."

"People are hypocrites."

"True, but it's all about appearances."

"It's all about comfort," Jeremy said. "I didn't make all this money to cram myself into a car the size of a shoebox."

"You don't seem to mind cramming yourself inside your Ferrari."

"The Ferrari doesn't count. It's the only vehicle on earth that makes it worth giving up my wet bar and HDTV."

With that, he drained his Glenlivet and set the empty glass down with a contented sigh. There wasn't much that Jeremy denied himself in the way of creature comforts. He drank the best Scotch, lived in a gazillion-dollar house, traveled the world, and dated women who were knockout gorgeous with brains the size of golf balls. *Nice to look at,* Jeremy had told Bernie more than once, *without all that pesky intelligence to get in the way of a good time.*

Bernie sighed. With that one statement, he singlehandedly set feminism back fifty years.

There had been a time when total professionalism had dictated the way she dealt with Bridges. *Yes, sir. No, sir. Very good, sir.* But the longer she worked for him, the more she spoke her mind. Her attitude didn't mean she didn't take her job seriously. It just meant she had an outlet for the irritation she felt around him just about every minute of every day. Fortunately, because Jeremy was a bored rich guy who refused to play by the rules, a smart-ass bodyguard seemed to suit him just fine. Good thing, because if she had to hold her tongue around him, she'd probably end up killing him herself.

"Are you planning on tying that tie?" she asked him.

Jeremy looked down at the tie dangling around his neck. "The invitation said I had to wear a black tie. It didn't say how I had to wear it."

"Did it also say you had to wear athletic shoes?"

"No," he said with a smile. "That's my fashion statement."

Truth be told, Jeremy could show up in what he usually wore in his spare time—crappy cargo shorts, a Rangers' T-shirt, and flip-flops—and they'd still let him in. If he wrote a big enough check, he could show up stark naked. But it wasn't like him to be in their faces about it. He always dressed well enough that they would admit him without question, but just shabby enough that they wished they didn't have to. Now that he was thirty-seven years old, Bernie thought maybe he ought to knock off the eccentricities and play it straight, but hell would probably freeze over first.

Over the years, the press had tried to dig up any dirt that might explain his quirkiness, but except for the basics, his background remained something of a mystery.

He had grown up in Houston with his father. Mother unknown. Graduated from Texas Southwestern University. Short stint as a software engineer before starting his own company, which eventually became Sybersense. Except for more current professional and civic activities, that was about it.

Bernie looked at the rich folks strolling into the hotel and sighed. "Must we do this?"

"Now, Bernie. This is a very special occasion. After all, how many times in this city does somebody have a benefit for such an outstanding cause and invite all the rich, pretty people?"

"About once a week."

"Exactly! Not nearly often enough. It's time for us to party."

"Us?"

"Okay. So it's time for me to party and you to watch for bad guys. Everyone should stick with what they do best."

Bernie glared at him. "It's a credible threat this time, you know."

"That also happens about once a week."

He was right. When a man had Jeremy's money and influence, somebody was always out to get him. She was reasonably certain the recent death threat had something to do with Sybersense's new medical management software that was due to launch early next year. Word on the street was that it was so revolutionary that it would forever change the way the medical industry conducted its business and bring untold riches right to Bridges's doorstep. But in order to accomplish that, he'd executed hostile takeovers of two of his hottest rivals, which allowed him, among other things, to cherry-pick the best and brightest programmers and other employees who could help him develop and market his new product. Then he kicked the rest to the curb. Unfortunately, that had removed a lot of formerly wealthy, high-powered executives from the gravy train at their respective companies and given them a reason to want to see Sybersense fail or Jeremy dead. Or both.

But in Bernie's experience, the threat could also be coming from somebody who drove a taxi or washed windows who decided he didn't like rich guys, which was why she had to stay vigilant.

Bernie felt pretty certain this event would be the harmless experience it seemed to be on the surface, but there was no way for her *or* Jeremy to know that for sure. All Bernie knew was that every time she tried to figure out why he behaved the way he did, she realized how pointless that was and merely concentrated on keeping his body and soul together.

"Don't you ever get bored doing this?" she asked him.

"What? Going to charity events?"

"No. Going to charity events, picking up Paris Hilton wannabes, and having your way with them."

"Oh. Well, when you put it like that..." His mouth turned up in a cocky smile. "Nope. Doesn't bore me at all."

"Good *God*, I hope you practice safe sex."

"Of course. You never know when some dread disease will rear its ugly head. Your concern is heartwarming."

"Concern, my ass. I just want you to do the world a favor and keep your genetic material to yourself."

"Not to worry," he said, patting his pants pocket. "I'm nothing if not prepared."

She shook her head. The man singlehandedly kept the latex industry afloat.

"Why go to all the trouble of attending these events?" she asked. "Why not just stay home and order out?"

"Order out?"

"Haul out your little black book and take your pick. Send Carlos to pick her up."

"But if I did that, I wouldn't have the opportunity to . . . what is it we're doing again?"

"Saving the polar bears."

"Oh, yeah. We have to think of the wildlife."

"Come on, Bridges. The only species you're interested in preserving is the Perpetual Bachelor. Unfortunately, the world's never going to run out of those."

"Now that's where you're wrong, Bernie. Polar bears are at the forefront of my consciousness nearly every minute of every day."

"And I'll believe that the moment polar bears grow blond hair and big breasts."

"If you object so much to this event, stay in the limo. I restocked the DVD collection. *Terminator, Alien, Die Hard*—all your old favorites."

"I'm paid to stick close to you."

"Not too close. You have a tendency to cramp my style."

"I have a tendency to keep you alive."

"Do you have to be so dramatic?"

Bernie narrowed her eyes. "Are you forgetting the London incident?"

"That was an accident."

"That was an out-of-control car that may not really have been out of control."

"We'll never know for sure, will we?"

"Fine. Die. See if I care."

"Of course you care. Would you be able to abuse another client the way you abuse me?"

"*Abuse* you?"

Jeremy leaned forward and tapped the Plexiglas window. "Carlos?"

The window came down. "Yes, sir?"

"Would you categorize Bernie's attitude toward me as abusive?"

"Oh, yes, sir. Absolutely."

"Thank you, Carlos."

As the window went back up, Jeremy turned to Bernie. "Now, there's a man who knows who signs his paychecks."

Bernie glared at Carlos. "Ass kisser."

"Tell me something, Bernie," Jeremy said.

"Yeah?"

"Exactly where do you hide your weapon when you're wearing a skirt?"

She met his gaze evenly. "That's none of your business."

Jeremy's gaze slid away from her eyes, slithered down to her breasts, fell to her thighs, then lazily made its way back up again. "So you're leaving it to my imagination?"

For a moment she felt the oddest twinge of awareness, as if she was one of those glowy, showy, magazine-perfect women he was so fond of. Just the sound of his voice made her heart beat a little faster. And those gorgeous green eyes. Good God, it was no wonder women fell in his wake.

It wasn't as if she didn't know he was pushing her buttons. Jeremy thrived on knocking people off guard, and he wasn't above using every weapon in his arsenal to do it, including sex. But that didn't mean she was immune to him as a man, and when he looked at her with that unrelenting stare, she couldn't help the hot, sexy thoughts that entered her mind.

In a few minutes, though, he'd be zeroing in on some dazzling daddy's girl or elegant divorcee, at which time he'd suddenly go Bernie-blind. In the end, she was just one more employee at his beck and call, like his housekeeper or his pool boy. And that was fine by her.

"Knock it off, Bridges. All you need to know is that I'm armed, I'm dangerous, and whether it's good for the world or not, I'll get you home in one piece."

"Actually, I doubt you'd even need a weapon," Bridges said. "Didn't I hear that you once killed a man with a Popsicle stick?"

"A Popsicle stick?" She made a scoffing noise. "That's ridiculous."

"So the rumor isn't true?"

"Of course not." She paused. "It was a Q-Tip."

Jeremy just smiled, then turned his attention to a glittering Barbie doll standing near the front door of the hotel beside a planter full of periwinkles. Her mile-long legs protruded from beneath the hem of a sheath of silvery fabric that clung to her body like Glad Wrap, and her headful of stunning blond hair glinted in the evening light.

The car ahead of them drove away, and Carlos pulled to the curb directly in front of the hotel. A uniformed man opened the door of the limo and gave Jeremy a deferential smile. "Good evening, sir." Then he turned to Bernie, and his smile faltered. She could read it in his eyes as clearly as if he'd shouted it: *What's a woman like you doing with a man like him?*

He cleared his throat. "Uh... good evening, miss."

Miss? Bernie cringed. Nobody had referred to her as "Miss" since... well, *ever.* And it was none of his damned business what she was doing with Jeremy, anyway.

The man dutifully held out his hand to her, as if she needed help getting out of a car. She ignored him and climbed out, quickly scanning the area for anything out of place. She and Jeremy headed for the front door of the hotel, and she got a good look at the blond for the first time.

Even though the woman wore enough mascara to sink a freighter, Bernie thought she recognized her. Two days ago, outside the gates of Jeremy's house, a woman had been standing at the curb, watching as they pulled through the gates. Bernie also remembered a woman loitering outside a restaurant yesterday where Bridges had met his chief financial officer for lunch. Bernie couldn't say with absolute certainty that it was the same woman, but her instincts rarely failed her. Two sightings was a coincidence. Three was a pattern. And even though the woman was dressed to the nines, she didn't mesh with the sophisticated crowd here tonight. Bar hopping in the West Village seemed more appropriate. Her makeup was too extreme, her dress too flashy, her heels too high. When somebody didn't fit the profile of the occasion, it was always a reason for a heads-up.

As they passed her on their way into the hotel, the woman turned slowly and gave Bridges a suggestive smile. Not surprisingly, he matched her smile with one of his own. But Bernie sensed something about the woman's demeanor that went beyond the usual high-society mating ritual she'd witnessed a hundred times before.

Then the woman shifted her gaze to Bernie.

Her smile vanished, replaced with an oddly irritated expression that made a chill snake between Bernie's shoulders. In spite of the fact that Bernie had arrived with Jeremy, there was no way on earth this woman considered her a romantic rival. Something else was going on, which meant Bernie needed to keep a close eye on her for the remainder of the evening.

As Jeremy stepped into the ballroom, the same feeling of déjà vu passed over him that he always felt on nights like this. Interchangeable hotels. Interchangeable causes. Interchangeable, ingratiating people who wanted his money.

Mile-long buffet—*check*. Silent auction—*check*. Bar in every corner stocked to the hilt—*check*. Young, sexy society women looking for husbands—*check*. Just once he'd like to see something different at one of these events. Maybe a margarita machine or a beer bong. A rock band instead of the symphony strings. Karaoke. A wet T-shirt contest.

Anything to keep him from being bored out of his mind.

But if he showed up at these things, Sybersense held on to its reputation as a philanthropic leader in the community, and he held on to his reputation as a wealthy, eccentric bachelor. Then, at the end of the evening, he invariably had several incredibly gorgeous women to pick from to entertain himself with later. As for the events themselves, he got his laughs by watching the looks on the faces of the old biddies as they tried to ignore whatever fashion faux pas he'd decided to perpetrate for the evening. They were all about propriety—almost all about it, anyway. In this crowd, money trumped taste, but just barely.

"Mr. Bridges! Good evening!"

He turned to see one of those old biddies waddling toward him. Genevieve Caldwell was a chunky senior citizen with silver hair, a brassy voice, and a gold-plated portfolio of oil fields all over the world.

"I'm just so delighted you could make it here this—"

He knew the exact moment she caught sight of his slack tie and scuffed Nikes. Her voice faltered, and for a split second, he saw it. That look of disapproval. That expression that said, *You're not one of us.* That vibe of superiority that the socially blessed radiated to those less fortunate. But, as always, he consoled himself with the fact that for all her riches, he could buy and sell her ten times over.

In spite of her momentary gaffe, she recovered like a pro, pasting on a smile and holding out her hand.

"—this evening," she finished.

Jeremy took her hand and kissed it, then flashed her a dazzling smile. "Mrs. Caldwell. What a joy it is to see you again."

The old lady practically quaked with delight, her disapproval momentarily vanishing in a wave of pure ecstasy.

Jeremy nodded toward Bernie. "Mrs. Caldwell, I'd like you to meet Bernadette. She's a family friend visiting from Arkansas. *Rural* Arkansas. It was a slow time at the chicken farm, so she put on her best dress, hopped a Greyhound, and here she is."

At the same time he got a furtive eye roll from Bernie, Mrs. Caldwell's nose crinkled as if she'd smelled something rotten. Hearing *rural, chicken farm,* and *Greyhound* all in one sentence made her disgust meter shoot through the roof.

"It's a pleasure to meet you," Mrs. Caldwell said, even though it clearly wasn't a pleasure for her in the least. Then she tilted her head questioningly. "But I'm certain I've met you before." Her eyes narrowed. "Do you know you look remarkably like Mr. Bridges's astrologer?"

"My astrologer?" Jeremy said.

"Yes. Three months ago at the Sunshine Gala for Solar Energy, you had your astrologer with you. You said she told you that your moon in Pisces simply demanded you give an extra thousand dollars." She looked back at Bernie. "There *is* a resemblance."

"Ah, that's because she *is* my astrologer," Jeremy said. "Did I not mention the connection before?"

"Why, no, I don't believe you did." Mrs. Caldwell turned to Bernie. "Do you do readings for others?" She smiled. "I can only hope for more moons in Pisces tonight."

"It's more of a hobby of hers," Jeremy said. "She wouldn't want the responsibility of suggesting another person's path in life."

"But you'll be happy to know," Bernie said, "that Jeremy's moon is in Gemini today. The Twins. Which means he's going to give twice as much money as he did at the Sunshine Gala."

"That's wonderful!" Mrs. Caldwell said, beaming.

"You're such a generous man, Mr. Bridges. With patronage such as yours, the polar bears will live on for generations to come." She glanced over Jeremy's shoulder. "Please excuse me. I have other guests to greet. I hope you and your friend have a lovely time tonight!"

Mrs. Caldwell moved toward her next victim, and Jeremy turned to Bernie. "You just set me up for twelve grand," he muttered. "Thanks a bunch."

"Consider it penance. Now maybe you won't go to hell for lying."

"That might cover *this* lie. But what about all the others?"

"You have no respect at all for these people, do you?"

"Their games aren't my games."

"So you make up games of your own."

"Exactly."

"Just don't make me your financial planner again. I don't know a damned thing about the stock market."

With that, she turned and fanned her gaze over the crowd with the same intensity she always did, never relaxing for a moment, never cracking a smile. Bernie was nothing if not predictable. She wore the same plain black dress she always did whenever she shadowed him at events like these, one that hit her legs midcalf. It was so shapeless that it was impossible to get a mental picture of what her body beneath it looked like. Dark hair that grazed her shoulders in no particular style. Not a speck of makeup. Flat, sensible shoes. No stockings, of course. He couldn't imagine Bernie wiggling into a pair of pantyhose. Jewelry? Perish the thought. In this room full of peacocks, she looked like a plain brown starling, so bland she faded right into the wall and so unmemorable that he was surprised Mrs. Caldwell had recognized her at all.

Sometimes he cocked his head and narrowed his eyes and looked at Bernie when she wasn't aware he was doing it, just to see if there was an actual woman in there somewhere. Occasionally he got a glimpse of one, but it was like seeing something fleeting on the periphery of his vision that was there one second and gone the next.

He wondered what she did with all the money she made working for him, because it sure didn't go toward nice clothes or a decent apartment. She wore discount-store clothes and lived in a mediocre complex in east Plano full of questionable people. Not that it wasn't safe for Bernie. Somebody would have to have a death wish to mess with her. Aside from paying somebody to hack into her bank account or personal e-mail, Jeremy didn't have any way of finding out much more, and hell would freeze over before she offered any personal information of her own accord.

Her professional history, though, was a different story. He might show the world a cavalier attitude, but he never hired anyone without vetting that person from top to bottom. As bodyguards went, Bernie was the best of the best. Ex-military, she was a top-notch marksman and a martial arts expert. She had observational skills out the wazoo. And Jeremy had no doubt she could be lethal if the situation ever warranted it.

Still, she *was* a woman, and every once in a while he imagined what would happen if he sent her for a day at one of those stupidly expensive spas, then took her to Neiman's and sprang for the works. Just for fun. Just to see the result. Of course, if he ever actually suggested such a thing, he'd probably end up as one more notch on her Q-Tip.

"I'm heading for the bar," Jeremy said. "Can I interest you in a glass of outrageously expensive champagne? I have to recoup my twelve thousand somehow."

"You know I don't drink on the job."

"Do you drink *ever*? Or smoke, or park illegally, or spit gum on the sidewalk? What do you do for fun, anyway?"

"I am having fun," she deadpanned. "Can't you tell?"

"Lighten up, Bernie. This is friendly territory. Not much chance of a kidnapping attempt around here."

Bernie's laserlike eyes zeroed in on something across the room. "I'm not so sure about that."

"What are you talking about?"

"Do you know that woman?" Bernie asked. "The one by the buffet table in the silver sequined skirt up to her ass?"

Jeremy turned to look at the woman in question, who turned out to be the same women he'd seen as he was coming into the hotel. She was indeed showing a few more inches of thigh than the average woman here tonight. Bernie didn't seem to approve, but—funny thing—he didn't object in the least.

Did he know her? No. Was he going to get to know her? Absolutely. Before this evening was out, he intended to get to know her very, *very* well.

"Never seen her before tonight," he said.

"I have. A couple of times in the past few days. She may be following you. She was outside the gates to your house two days ago, and on the street in front of Rodolpho's yesterday when you were having lunch with

Phil Brandenburg. And she's barely taken her eyes off you tonight."

Jeremy smiled. "Ah, women...they just can't seem to control themselves around me, can they?"

"There *is* a chance she's just a groupie. She probably saw the article they did on you in *Dallas After Dark* and she's hoping to snag a handsome millionaire."

"So you think I'm handsome, do you?"

"I'm just quoting the article."

"Well, if it's in print, it must be true."

"Right. *Dallas After Dark.* Journalism at its finest." Bernie continued to eye the girl, then shook her head grimly. "There's something fishy about her. She doesn't belong here. She's dressed too slutty. And she's standing alone."

"Maybe you're right," Jeremy said. "Maybe I should check her out. Get closer to her. Infiltrate her evil plot."

"You're not taking this seriously."

"Now, that's where you're wrong. I'm very, *very* serious about taking her home with me." He glanced back at the woman. "And look at that. I don't even have to go on the hunt. The prey is coming to me."

THE DISH

Where authors give you the inside scoop!

♥ ♥

From the desk of Bella Riley

Dear Reader,

The first time I ever saw an Adirondack lake I was twenty-three years old and madly in love. My boyfriend's grandparents had built their "camp" in the 1940s, and he'd often told me that it was his favorite place in the world. ("Camp" is Adirondack lingo for a house on a lake. If it's really big, like the Vanderbilts' summer home on Raquette Lake, people sometimes throw the word "great" in front of it.)

I can still remember my first glimpse of the blue lake, the sandy beach, the wooden docks jutting into it, the colorful sails of the boats that floated by. It was love at first sight. My mind was blown by the beauty all around me.

Of course, since I'm a writer, my brain immediately began spinning off into storyland. What if two kids grew up together in this small lake town and were high-school sweethearts? What if one of them left the other behind for bright lights/big city? And what would their reunion look like ten years later?

Fast-forward fifteen years from that first sight of an Adirondack lake, and I couldn't be more thrilled to introduce my Emerald Lake series to you! After thinking she had left the small town—and the girl she had once been—behind forever, Andi Powell must return to help run Lake Yarns, her family's knitting store on Main Street. Of course everyone in town gets involved in a love story that she's convinced herself is better left forgotten. But with the help of the Monday Night Knitting Group, Nate's sister, Andi's mother and grandmother, and an old circus carousel in the middle of the town green, Andi just might find the love she's always deserved in the arms of the one man who has waited his entire life for her.

I hope you fall as much in love with the beauty and people of Emerald Lake as I did.

Happy reading,

Bella Riley

www.BellaRiley.com

P.S. That boyfriend is now my husband (Guess where we honeymooned? Yes, the lake!), and four years ago we bit the bullet and became the proud owners of our very own Adirondack camp. Now, just in case you're tempted to throw the word "great" around, you should know that our log cabin is a hundred years old...and pretty much original. Except for the plumbing. Thankfully, we have that!

♥ ♥

From the desk of Jane Graves

Dear Reader,

In HEARTSTRINGS AND DIAMOND RINGS (on sale now), Alison Carter has been stuck in the dating world for years, and she's getting a little disillusioned. In personal ads, she's discovered that "athletic" means the guy has a highly developed right bicep from opening and closing the refrigerator door; and that a man is "tall, dark, and handsome" only in a room full of ugly albino dwarves. But what about those other descriptions in personal ads? What do they *really* mean?

"Aspiring actor": Uses Aussie accent to pick up chicks

"Educated": Watches *Jeopardy!*

"Emotionally sound": Or so his latest psychiatrist says

"Enjoys fine dining": Goes inside instead of using the drive-through

"Friendship first": As long as "friendship" includes sex

"Good listener": Has nothing intelligent to say

"Likes to cuddle": Mommy issues

"Looking for soulmate": Or just someone to have sex with

"Loyal": Stalker

"Old fashioned": Wants you barefoot and pregnant

"Passionate": About beer, football, and Hooters waitresses

"Romantic": Isn't nearly as ugly by candlelight

"Spiritual": Drives by a church on his way to happy
   hour
"Stable": Heavily medicated
"Young at heart": And one foot in the grave
"Witty": Quotes dialogue from *Animal House*

Alison finally decides enough is enough. She's going to
hire a matchmaker, who will find out the truth about a
man *before* she goes out with him. What she doesn't expect to find is a matchmaking *man*—one who really *is* tall,
dark, and handsome! And suddenly Mr. Right just might
be right under her nose...

   I hope you'll enjoy HEARTSTRINGS AND
DIAMOND RINGS!

Happy reading!

Jane Graves

www.janegraves.com

♥ ♥

From the desk of Eileen Dreyer

Dear Reader,

I love to write the love story of two people who have
known each other a long time. I love it even more when
they're now enemies. First of all, I don't have to spend
time introducing them to each other. They already have a

history, and common experiences. They speak in a kind of shorthand that sets them apart from the people around them. Emotions are already more complex. And then I get to mix in the added spice that comes from two people who spit and claw each time they see each other. Well, if you've read the first two books in my Drake's Rakes series, you know that Lady Kate Seaton and Major Sir Harry Lidge are definitely spitting and clawing. In ALWAYS A TEMPTRESS, we finally find out why. And we get to see if they will ever resolve their differences and finally admit that they still passionately love each other.

Happy Reading!

Eileen Dreyer

www.eileendreyer.com

♥ ♥

From the desk of Amanda Scott

Dear Reader,

St. Andrews University, alma mater of Prince William and Princess Kate, was Scotland's first university, and it figures significantly in HIGHLAND HERO, the second book in my Scottish Knights trilogy, as well as in its predecessor, HIGHLAND MASTER (Forever, February 2011). The heroes of all three books in the trilogy met as students of Walter Traill, Bishop of St. Andrews, in the late fourteenth century. All three are skilled warriors and knights of the realm.

Sir Ivor Mackintosh of HIGHLAND HERO—besides being handsome, daring, and a man of legendary temper—is Scotland's finest archer, just as Fin Cameron of HIGHLAND MASTER is one of the country's finest swordsmen. Both men are also survivors of the Great Clan Battle of Perth, in which the Mackintoshes of Clan Chattan fought champions of Clan Cameron. In other words, these two heroes fought on opposing sides of that great trial by combat.

Nevertheless, thanks to Bishop Traill, they are closer than most brothers.

Because Traill's students came from noble families all over Scotland, any number of whom might be feuding or actively engaged in clan warfare, the peace-loving Traill insisted that his students keep their identities secret and use simple names within the St. Andrews community. They were on their honor to not probe into each other's antecedents, so they knew little if anything about their friends' backgrounds while studying academics and knightly skills together. Despite that constraint, Traill also taught them the value of trust and close friendships.

The St. Andrews Brotherhood in my Scottish Knights series is fictional but plausible, in that the historic Bishop Traill strongly supported King Robert III and Queen Annabella Drummond while the King's younger brother, the Duke of Albany, was actively trying to seize control of the country. Traill also provided protection at St. Andrews for the King's younger son, James (later James I of Scotland), conveyed him there in secrecy, and wielded sufficient power to curb Albany when necessary.

We don't know how Traill and the King arranged for the prince, age seven in 1402, to travel across Scotland from the west coast to St. Andrews Castle. But that sort of mystery stimulates any author's gray cells.

So, in HIGHLAND HERO, when the villainous Albany makes clear his determination to rule Scotland no matter what, Traill sends for Sir Ivor to transport young Jamie to St. Andrews. Sir Ivor's able if sometimes trying assistant in this endeavor is the Queen's niece, Lady Marsaili Drummond-Cargill, who has reasons of her own to elude Albany's clutches but does not approve of temperamental men or men who assume she will do their bidding without at least *some* discussion.

Traill's successor, Bishop Henry Wardlaw (also in HIGHLAND HERO), founded William and Kate's university in 1410, expanding on Traill's long tradition of education, believing as Traill had that education was one of the Church's primary duties. Besides being Scotland's first university, St. Andrews was also the first university in Scotland to admit women (1892)—and it admitted them on exactly the same terms as men. Lady Marsaili would have approved of that!

Suas Alba!

Amanda Scott

www.amandascottauthor.com

Find out more about Forever Romance!

Visit us at
www.hachettebookgroup.com/publishing_forever.aspx

Find us on Facebook
http://www.facebook.com/ForeverRomance

Follow us on Twitter
http://twitter.com/ForeverRomance

NEW AND UPCOMING TITLES

Each month we feature our new titles
and reader favorites.

CONTESTS AND GIVEAWAYS

We give away galleys, autographed copies,
and all kinds of exclusive items.

AUTHOR INFO

You'll find bios, articles, and links to personal websites
for all your favorite authors and so much more.

GET SOCIAL

Connect with your favorite authors, editors, and
other Forever fans, and share what's important to you.

THE BUZZ

Sign up for our monthly romance newsletter,
and be the first to read all about it.